Widowmaker

Clan Wars Book Two

BY THE SAME AUTHOR

The Horse Lord
The Demon Lord
The Dragon Lord
The Warlord's Domain
Prince Ivan
Firebird
The Golden Horde
Greylady: Clan Wars Book One

WIDOWMAKER

Clan Wars Book Two

Peter Morwood

LEGEND

Published by Legend Books in 1994

1 3 5 7 9 10 8 6 4 2

First published in the United Kingdom in 1994 by
Legend Books Limited
20 Vauxhall Bridge Road, London, SW1V 2SA

Random House Australia (Pty) Ltd
20 Alfred Street, Milsons Point, Sydney, NSW 2061
Australia

Random House New Zealand Ltd
18 Poland Road, Glenfield, Auckland 10,
New Zealand

Random House South Africa (Pty) Ltd
PO Box 337, Bergvlei 2012, South Africa

Random House UK Limited Reg. No. 954009

Typeset by Deltatype Ltd, Ellesmere Port, Cheshire
Printed and bound in Great Britain by Clays Ltd, St Ives plc

ISBN 0 09 931241 7

The Words of the Wise One

'THUS BAYRD AR'TALVLYN became Clan-Lord Talvalin, the first of that name and the first of his line. After much fair-speaking he prevailed at last upon the Lady Eskra, so that she consented to become his wife, and his consort, and the mother of his children.

'He built the fortress of Dunrath, the fortress in which we sit tonight, and made it his dwelling-place. But though he built it to be a stronghold against his enemies and a defence in time of war, no foemen came against it. For by his marriage he made alliance between the people of Now and the people of the time Before, and if there were many such in after times, yet his was the first of them.

'It brought long years of peace to the north country, so that the Land and all its people prospered, and all was well in Alba . . .'

The old man struck once upon the strings of his harp; not a discordant twang to attract the attention of a rowdy audience and bring them to silence, but a sweep of barely-touching fingertips that drew a fading shimmer of music from the instrument. He palmed the sound to silence and doffed his black slouch hat, bowing his head – and the last notes were swallowed in a thunder of applause. There were shouts of approval, the hammering of fists and cups against the tables, the hollow pounding of heels against the Great Hall's wooden floor.

There would be more tangible rewards later: food and drink, a warm bed for tonight and perhaps other nights to follow, and at his departure, gold. The well-wishing of Lord Halmar Talvalin would go with him and enhance his reputation, so that on later nights those same rewards would be more easily earned. But there would not be a night like this one. This was *Gorefan-tlai'cuith, dé*

I

Delestrau, the fifteenth day of the last month of summer, the holyday of Landing, and three hundred years since the keels struck shore.

The holyday would end tomorrow, at the rising of the sun, and the fourth century would begin. But for the rest of tonight, the celebrations would continue.

As he slipped the harp into its case of worked leather, the old man wondered how much applause he would have received, how many rewards, if he had mixed more truth with his story, or if he had continued it down the years and generations from Bayrd ar'Talvlyn's time. Not much of either, if any at all. He had made that mistake before, just once, early in his career. Never again. He had spent a cold night in the stables after a certain clan-lord's men had flung him bodily from the High Hall, for saying a deal too much about the man's ancestry and how he came to his high estate. There was every suggestion that even the straw and the company of horses was too good for him, that a storymaker who could not control the tongue with which he sang or the fingers with which he played might not have need of either. Now . . .

Now he left truth to the Keepers of Years.

The tales were what his listeners wanted to hear; tales where men were brave and women virtuous, where only villains set aside their honour in pursuit of gain, and where wicked sorcerers were inevitably brought to nothing by clean steel in the hands of heroes.

As the old man put out *his* hand, to accept the first of the many cups of wine he would be offered that holyday night, he smiled at the thought. And if those offering the wine thought he was merely smiling at the prospect of wetting a throat made dry by the long hours of his story, that was just as well. There had been a time, not so long ago as forever nor so far away as tomorrow, not far at all as such things are reckoned, when the Talent of sorcery, and the power of the Art Magic, were as worthy of respect as skill with a blade or a horse or a bow. That time had passed; perhaps it would return, or perhaps not.

But even in a Clan and House and line as noble as Talvalin, the Talent could emerge all unbidden. It had done so with Bayrd the Linefather himself – though the old man smiled again as he recalled how prudently he had made no mention of it in his tale. And as for the Lady Eskra . . . When a warrior with the Talent

2

married a trained wizard, their children were hardly born of common stock, let their descendants deny it how they would.

'Now that would be a tale indeed,' the old man murmured to himself, and despite the background noise in the Hall, the words were not spoken softly enough.

'What tale, *arr'eth-an?*' asked someone, a lord's-man or a high retainer by the fine material of his crest-coat. 'Why not tell us . . .?' He fell silent then, transfixed by a regard cold and hard as jewels, the empty opal stare of the harper's blind eye and the sapphire blaze of the live one.

'A tale—' the old man began, then hesitated. The blaze became a twinkle, and the chilly immobility of his bearded face flowed into yet another of those easy smiles. 'A tale for another night,' he said at last. 'Not a tale for this one.' He drank the wine and took silent refuge for a moment in the complex shadows of his own mind, remembering what he had heard, what he had read, and even – when he still had two good eyes – what those eyes had seen. An errant thought spoke to him from the darkness, and it said:

This is how it really *was . . .*

I

Troubles

THE LIGHT WAS bronze-green, an underwater light, cold and remote. Bayrd Talvalin stared drowsily at it, toying with the image, visualising himself deep beneath the surface of some still lake, far removed from the cares and concerns of an Alban clan-lord. It was an idle notion, and he knew it. Those cares and concerns hung around his neck like so many of the proverbial millstones, as impossible to set aside as any of the lesser responsibilities that came with marriage and parenthood.

And with the ever-present menace of Gerin ar'Diskan.

It was of no account that Gerin had not called feud or clan-war, and that so far his loudly-voiced threats had been proven nothing but noise and bluster. That *so far* was the problem. Until the man was dead and burned and his ashes scattered on the evening wind, Bayrd knew that he could never relax, not truly.

Patience was a Clan Talvalin virtue – or vice, there were enough who claimed it as such. But it was by no means the sole prerogative of the Talvalins, or the ar'Talvlyns before them, and the more Bayrd might have to lose, the more grim satisfaction ar'Diskan would have in engineering that loss. There was only one advantage about such a depth of personal animosity: it was no more than personal, a matter between Gerin and himself that had not involved family, retainers or vassals on either side. To the best of Bayrd's knowledge, the rest of the ar'Diskan'r regarded their Lord's resentful attitude towards the Clan-Lord Talvalin as a waste of time that could be better spent increasing the prosperity of his own line.

Bayrd hoped the rumours were true. There was more than enough trouble abroad in the Land to keep the most aggressive *kailinin* fully occupied.

As awareness replaced sleep, he gazed at the pale, cool green light, abandoning imaginings, knowing what it was: the dawn of another day, filtered through the small panes of his bedroom window. He could hear the wind blowing, even through the fortress wall, as it flung a spatter of raindrops against the thumb-thick glass. They beaded for a moment, then streamed down like so many tears.

That glass had been an unnecessary indulgence. Or maybe not so unnecessary. It had been a demonstration of wealth – and yes, of pride. Maybe it even smacked a little of arrogance, that any man – and especially the Lord of a newly-founded blood-clan – should put something so fragile into a fortress that even after six years was no more than halfway completed.

And that was why Bayrd had done it.

The glass was hardly a weakness in Dunrath-hold's massive walls, the windows in which it was set were far too small for that; but it was as much a show of unconcern as gilding on a battle-helm, or gemstones set into the hilt of a *taiken* longsword. Neither was necessary; both were done; and all three said the same thing:

I am confident enough of my own strength that I can make use of more than stark utility.

So this was the dawn of another day. Another tomorrow, tomorrow no longer. The day that, some day, might have Gerin ar'Diskan waiting in it, to take his revenge for an insult that was pure accident. That insult, and the incident leading to it, had been the founding of Bayrd's fortunes. It had been a means for the Overlord Albanak to put one unruly vassal in his place, and issue a warning to all the others.

And it had hung a sword on a fraying thread above Bayrd's neck ever since.

He had been Bannerman and Companion to Gerin before that, and had acted honourably as a Companion should, offering his hand – literally – in place of Gerin's so that his lord might win a race and the enfeoffed land that was its prize. It was a story both simple and elaborate, and painful in both respects.

Even though the severed hand had been restored by Bayrd's own Talent of sorcery, there was a thin, pale line like a bracelet around his wrist that still ached in damp weather. And even though Bayrd had given up his hand on his lord's behalf, for honour's sake alone and not through any hope of gain, Albanak had treated the result of the race in the most literal manner possible. Since Bayrd's was the first hand to shore, Bayrd had won the race: and so the Overlord granted him the land.

Gerin had at once suspected a trick, some conspiracy against him that this result had been Bayrd's intention all along, and no protestation of innocence would persuade him otherwise. From honourable Companion, and as close a friend as any low-clan warrior could be with a high-clan lord, Bayrd had become an enemy with Gerin's threats of vengeance ringing in his ears.

All for a land like this.

He had not known then that Dunrath and its domain lay in the Debatable Marches, a strip of territory that had lain along the borders of Elthan and Prytenon for time out of mind. It had changed hands as the seasons change, and blood had been spilled freely every time.

It was a hard land with hard names that echoed hard times; each of its tors and dales and rigs, its fells and laws, could tell their tale of generations of ravaging to and fro, and those who dwelt in it were perforce a hard people. It was a land that endured the heat of its short, hot summer with all the panting impatience of a thick-furred dog, because its true climate was the iron fist of winter – or, still more appropriate, a grim windblown greyness like today.

Bayrd had desired this land and this fortress when he saw them, first in winter with their outlines softened by a layer of snow, and then again on a warm summer day when the sun gave a glow to the jagged stones that they did not deserve. But had it not been gifted to him, a part of his new-found honour as Lord of his own clan, Bayrd Talvalin would not have held this place any longer than the first winter.

Little more than obstinate pride had kept him there – though now that the citadel had begun to take shape, his pride had increased in due proportion and its flavouring of stubbornness was almost gone. That change of mind had taken place slowly, over more than six years, and in all that time Gerin ar'Diskan's threats had come to nothing.

Yet.

But Gerin had as much awareness as any other Alban, that feeding full on vengeance for a slight made an infinitely more satisfying meal when taken coldly and at the proper time than anything done in the heat of rage. All the old tales said so; all the maxims and wise sayings concurred.

While an enemy lived, there was always a risk.

It had been six years of . . . not fear, Bayrd didn't rate Gerin ar'Diskan so highly, but certainly wariness. The nagging need for caution was as much a nuisance as a menace, and Bayrd had long since grown tired of the game. He had decided his response, if one was needed, would be as brutal as it had to be. It was as if Clan ar'Diskan knew it: there had been no provocations, no intrusions, no probings at the borders of the Talvalin domains. Nothing that might give Bayrd or his retainers any excuse to put an end to this nonsense once and for all.

Gerin was bad enough, but he was only a risk to Bayrd. Gelert, the last Lord of Prytenon, had also not yet been accounted for, and *he* was a risk for everyone. His escape had all the flawed dissatisfaction of a story badly told, a tale more concerned with truth than with entertainment. In a perfect world, the Alban's first foe would either have bowed to his conquerors, sworn his oaths of allegiance, and become their foremost and most trusted supporter in this Land – or he would have been destroyed in a satisfactory battle, and maybe even a single combat between notable per-sonages. Something, at least, worthy of record in the Books of Years.

Instead of which, he and his entire household had disappeared. Not fled, because there would have been some trace of it, but . . . vanished. As if they had somehow stepped sideways out of the world and closed the door behind them.

If his son Kalarr cu Ruruc was as skilled a sorcerer as Eskra claimed, that was more than likely. Gelert might still be alive somewhere out in the wilderness, or in some stranger and more distant place; and if he was, he would surely be laughing now.

Because the country was at war again.

Bayrd snorted soft disgust and groped for a robe before swinging his legs from the warmth of the bed into the chilly room. He was wide awake by now – the thought of this war, and particularly its causes, would have woken a stone statue – and moved carefully so as not to disturb his wife, still fast asleep beside him.

It was one of those stupid, pointless wars, the bloody-minded adult equivalent of two small boys kicking each other's shins because neither will allow that he might have been wrong. Bayrd had read of others like it in the Book of Years, what the chroniclers with their fondness for neatly naming things called *tsedakh*. The name meant 'small-war', a skirmish rather than a battle, something petty rather than important. Some of the small wars in the Archives were petty indeed.

Twenty years ago, the War of the Nose had started because the town guild of Morval had slit the nostrils of a Kalitzak merchant when he was caught giving short measure. It emerged only later, once King Daykin of Kalitz had added Morval to his domain and the bodies had been burned or buried, that the noseless merchant had been acting under instruction. Daykin had long had his eye on Morval and its rich agricultural lands, but had needed a better excuse than mere greed if he wanted to keep other lords and princes from interfering where they weren't wanted. The engineered insult offered to his merchant had been more than good enough.

That conflict had at least involved a twisted sort of sense. The War of the Standard, half a hundred years ago, did not. That was its formal title; the Alban mercenaries who had been involved in it called it the War of the Prick.

Two Vlakhan city-states had declared war on one another for no better reason than because both carried bulls on their banners. One bull was black, the other red; the black bull had its horns, hoofs, tongue, eyes and grossly masculine genitals picked out in a contrasting colour, in accordance with the Vlekh rules of blazon. The red bull – in accordance with those same rules – did not. And of course, someone on the wrong side had to open his big mouth and suggest that this lack of any obvious pizzle said something not merely about the bull on that banner, but the men who marched underneath it . . .

Bayrd Talvalin had always thought and hoped that his own people would have too much honour – or too much sense – to involve themselves in such an idiotic conflict. He was wrong. This present unpleasantness deserved to be commemorated in the histories as, of all things, the War of the Fine Point of Grammar.

The least foolish thing about it, indeed the only sensible thing about the whole affair, was that it was about a woman. Many truly epic confrontations had been started by just such an excuse. But after that, matters went rapidly downhill. Like all the other petty-wars, it would have been funny if lives had not already been lost; and for a man with a sense of honour as crooked as Bayrd Talvalin's sometimes seemed, it was *still* funny.

Her name was Yraine, she was the Overlord's daughter, and at twenty-six she was the eldest of his children by some several years.

And Albanak the Overlord was dead.

That would have mattered little enough had any of his sons achieved *eskorrethen*, the legal age of majority, and little too if the passing on of power had been formally observed before witnesses in the old way, from father to senior child of whatever gender. The ancient law was why some youths, not necessarily always the senior by age, had the title of Chosen: to avoid unnecessary confusion when their linefather went into the dark.

Albanak, perhaps because he was kept too busy pacifying his unruly country and controlling his unruly subjects, had omitted to Choose one of his sons, or the daughter who was already showing herself as much a man as any of them – though some wags were claiming the reverse, that the sons were more women than their sister.

Perhaps, said some cynical voices, it was no accident, but a part of some devious scheme simmering gently at the back of his subtle mind. And now the fire of life which warmed it had gone out. Albanak had passed with shocking speed from a rainstorm drenching during a hunt, to a shivering fever and at last to an inflammation which flooded his lungs. He had drowned in his bed, just as surely if he had been sunk in the waters of the deepest ocean.

The first and most natural suspicion was of sorcery. The elusive Lord Gelert had lost both lands and title to the Albans, and in his time he had been a notorious user of the uglier forms of the Art Magic.

However, Eskra Talvalin insisted that neither he nor sorcery was involved. She was the one who would know such things, and so at last she was believed, even though the belief came grudgingly. Clan Talvalin had already gained much from the dead Overlord – its land, its fortress, and even its right to exist – but not even Gerin ar'Diskan could prove that they stood to make profit from defending an enemy with proof of his innocence. And there was an air about the Lady Eskra, beyond even her known abilities as wizard and sorcerer, that made calling her a liar something no wise man would dare to do.

Albanak had died of a disease. It was as simple as that. But he had picked a damned awkward time to do it.

Yraine his daughter was as tall as most men, lean, fair-haired, and even though her angular features formed a handsome enough configuration, she was no delicate beauty. Nor was she the sort of fragile blossom to be picked to ornament another man's home; not unless Yraine approved the match herself, and by the number of discarded lovers she left in her wake, that approval was hard to gain.

Worst of all, she was claiming the full rank of Overlord of the Albans, and she was doing so in the old way; by name and by fame, by birth, by blood and by acclaim. Lying behind that was the last clause, the one she had not chosen to invoke. If worst came to worst, she had enough supporters to attempt a claim by conquest, as her father had taken the Land itself.

Yraine and her followers had reason enough to assume the rank would fall to her by default. Albanak, *Landmaster*, was not just the name of the Overlord, but the title as well. It had been handed down through the generations, its bearers giving up their own names, their own individuality, in favour of the power and prestige conferred by the word. But like so many other words in the language that were also a title of sorts – words like *warrior* and *lord*, *wizard* and *priest* – it was not gender-specific.

That was the fine point of grammar on which a turbulent people had impaled themselves.

The Albans had never, in living memory or in the written memories of the Books of Years – though for one reason or another, the study of those had been cursory indeed – had a female Landmaster. It was of no account to the younger, more progressive Albans. This Land, theirs for only eight years, was a new Land, *their* Land, and it could not be harmed by new customs and a certain breaking-away from the old, hidebound ways of the past.

So they said.

The older traditionalists claimed that they acted solely in hope of profiting from the inexperienced rule of a new Overlord. Those harsh, inflexible old men displayed an astonishing lack of diplomatic skill by stating out loud what they truly thought, when any sensible person would have kept such opinions to themselves.

They said, loudly and often, that a mere woman would be led in her decisions by the powerful, arrogant lords and warriors who surrounded her. Since her brother and rival Erhal was only seventeen, three years short of *eskorrethen* and thus incapable of legal decisions for those three years, it was not an argument with much weight.

Next they said that, never having endured war, she would not know how to properly conduct one, and would thus be forced to fall back on the self-serving advice of those same supporters. Erhal was no better fitted in that respect either.

Finally, with a breathless air of slight desperation, they pointed out that each month she would become, as they knew only too well from living with their own wives and consorts at such times, moody, irritable, unreasonable and impossible to deal with.

'Which simply means, dear lords and gentlemen,' Eskra Talvalin had said loudly during that last acrimonious council meeting, 'that such an Overlord will be a great improvement on a man.'

She had given them that thin half-smile which always managed to convey much more than words. 'Because I've heard nothing to prove that any of you need the excuse of a bloody weekend to be unreasonable for the whole bloody month . . . !'

Some were amused by what she said; some agreed; some disagreed; and some took such violent exception to being instructed by a woman who was not just a wizard but a foreign one besides that they went stamping out of the council chamber with their minds already set. Not so much about who they would support, as who they would *not*.

Anyone favoured by the Talvalins . . .

It was an odd situation. For all their protests one way or the other, none of the old-established high clans became involved in the actual fighting. They were, Bayrd suspected, keeping their noses clean so that however events might turn out, they could claim to have been in the right all along. It was the little people who were doing the dying.

As usual.

Bayrd had remained at a distance from all the verbal wrangling for as long as he was able. Since Clan Talvalin owed its very existence to the late Overlord Albanak, it seemed improper, almost dishonourable, to take sides with one of his children against the other.

He had advised the High Council in Cerdor that he would abide by whatever final decision they achieved, and warned his retainers that if their Houses and line-families became involved, they would do so without the Talvalin banner. And it had worked.

For not quite two months.

He sighed. It was a soft sound, but for all that it was loud enough to produce an echo behind him. Bayrd half-turned, then smiled slightly as a pair of cool blue eyes regarded him thoughtfully from the bed. 'The war?' said Eskra. 'Or is it something else entirely?'

'Both. Neither . . .' He shrugged, dismissing the question. 'I was thinking.'

'You—' she began to say, teasing, then shut her teeth on the rest at the expression which flicked across her husband's face.

'Think too much. Yes. Thank you.'

Addressed to anyone else it would have been a snarl of anger, and even to Eskra there was an irritable edge which Bayrd couldn't completely suppress. Everybody said that about him, and had been saying it so many times for so long that it had become a private joke – a very, *very* private joke – between himself and friends and family. But it could still strike a raw edge.

Especially since thinking was all he had done since the news came down from Cerdor five weeks ago. He, and the whole of Clan Talvalin, would have to jump one way or the other, and soon. The old maxims said so. Things like *The enemy of my enemy is my friend*, or more significantly, *Those not with me are against me*.

The trick was in judging which way to jump, and so far as Clan Talvalin was concerned, either way could be a leap into the dark.

Gerin ar'Diskan was not the only enemy Bayrd had made on his way up; marriage to a wizard had alienated many who might have supported him, and marriage to an *Elthanek* wizard had only served to deepen the rift. But if he – they – came out on the right side when all this was over, then his 'mistakes' would be forgotten, or at least set in the balance against his new advantages and found to have lost their value.

While if they chose the wrong side . . .

Eskra sat up in the big bed, pulling the sheets and the fur coverlet high around her shoulders against the chill seeping steadily from the mass of worked stone that was Dunrath-hold. With her free hand she ruffled her feather-cropped dark red hair into some kind of order and gave him the same sort of kestrel's stare that had clenched his guts seven years ago. It did the same today; part invitation, part speculation, all consideration. A gaze that would drill through rock and read the secrets written at its heart.

'And you,' she said. 'Which way will *you* jump?'

Wizard or not, sorcerer or not, Eskra had never claimed to have the power of reading thoughts. She had spoken truth in so much else that Bayrd had never pressed her on the matter. But every now and then she would ask a question or expect a reply that was so close to what had been in his mind that he couldn't help but wonder.

'Jump?'

'You're stalling, loved. Who will you support? The Old Order or the New? Are you going to back Yraine ar'Albanak? Or side with . . . with the others.' For decency's sake she didn't say 'Gerin ar'Diskan', even though he and his clan were most stringently against the prospect of a woman Overlord – and among those most likely to benefit from the manipulations of young Erhal. 'It's a decision that has to be made. One way or the other. Unless you think the clan can survive enemies on both sides of the rift?'

'Which way would you . . .' His words trailed off into a thin smile and he made the little gesture of 'avert' with his right hand, as though turning aside some thoughtless ill-speaking. '*Na. An-tleir'n na.* A hundred times no. The choice is mine. The weight of lordship, eh?'

'It's a heavy burden. Her father laid it on you – and turned a friend against you with the gift.'

Bayrd sat down heavily on the bed and took Eskra's hand between both of his own. 'You help, and don't help, all with the same words.'

'I am still *an-hlensyarl* to your people.' She spoke the Droselan word without any of the venom that an Alban might have used, but Bayrd could still hear the hurt behind it. 'That makes me outlander. Outclan. Unblood. So my views count for little. But it means I can look at matters from all sides. There are no old loyalties to colour the way I see them. And Bayrd . . .'

''Skra-*ain?*'

'You're hurting me.'

Bayrd stared at his two clenched fists, white-knuckled with their own pressure, as if seeing them for the first time; and then at Eskra's fingertips squeezed between them, wine-red with compressed blood. His face flushed equally dark with shame and he let go at once.

Eskra shook her hand to restore the feeling, and there was something about the casual flutter of fingers that suggested she was shaking aside any blame he might have borne. 'We might have had five children by now. I could bring no more than three of them to birth. Only two still live.' *And neither of them sons to bear your name*, he heard her think as clear as words, and winced at it. 'Give them a chance to grow in a land where there is something close to peace. Make your choice.'

'And if it should be the wrong choice?'

'Then they die. We all die. Bayrd-*ain*, my loved . . . Your people will not leave any to grow up and ride as landless *eijin* warriors until they can take their revenge. But at least they will have had the chance. Decide. Then hold to that decision as if it was your last breath.'

'It might well be.'

'But it will be *yours*.'

Bayrd Talvalin stared at his wife for a long time, then turned his face away and gazed instead at the calm green submarine light that filtered through the windows of the fortress. It was shot with gold now, the glow of the newly-risen sun breaking through the rainclouds. Bayrd, who had never thought of himself as a religious man, said a brief prayer to the Father of Fires and the Light of Heaven as that gold warmed the chilly bronze of deep water and turned it instead to the shade of leaves on a midsummer day. And he made his choice.

This was Alba; not the old Land, but the new. And for better or for worse, nothing would be the same again.

*

The man he had just killed had barely slithered to the ground when the crescent blade of a battleaxe whipped past Bayrd Talvalin's face. It came close enough that he heard the heavy whoosh as it clove the air, and the wind of its passage was clammy on his cheek.

He blocked the back-swing with a clanging parry that sent the thump of impact clear up his arm to the shoulder. Even though most of the blow's power was lost in a screech of metal and a shower of sparks, it still left Isileth's long blade vibrating like a tuning-fork.

Bayrd's return cut sent him leaning far out of the saddle, but its force was wasted. Like the axe, Isileth's blade cut nothing but air and the echo of a war-cry. The other man was already far out of reach, riding hard – like all the others – more in an attempt to evade the lawful pursuit that had caught up with them, than risk closing for combat.

Bayrd swore, swayed, regained his balance with a muscle-wrenching effort, then slammed the *taiken* back into its scabbard and wrenched Yarak's head around. As his grey Ferhana mare accelerated in pursuit he tugged his shortbow from its case, nocked, drew and loosed an arrow at the retreating back. It struck home with a smack that Bayrd could hear plainly, driving under the heavy curved shoulder-plate of the other *kailin*'s armour.

Even though the man reeled forward in his saddle, he straightened up an instant later, glanced back, and then ducked lower and plied his quirt and the tails of his reins with all the frantic energy of terror. He was still within bowshot but pulling clear when another arrow came whirring after him. This time the shaft struck against the crown of the man's helmet and went wavering away at an angle, no more damage in its wake than ringing ears. And a minute later he had topped the low hill to the north and vanished from sight.

At the crest of the ridge, Bayrd leaned back in his saddle and tried to get his breath back even while he wasted it on cursing the stupidities of warriors who insisted on fighting in the heat of high summer. Warriors like himself, who had ridden out without the heavy Greatbow that would have skewered his quarry like a roasting-joint . . .

And most of all, warriors who insisted on fighting at all, instead of sitting down with as many jugs of wine as it required and talking out their differences.

No matter that such behaviour was unAlban and not the action of *kailinin-eir* at all. It would at least silence the laughter of the Elthaneks and Pryteneks and Cernuans, who sniggered behind their hands to see their conquerors slaughtering each other over what they saw as no more than a trivial difference of opinion.

His heart was pounding, there was a taste of blood in his mouth, and underneath the scales and mail and leather of his battle harness he was soaked with sweat, soaked to the point of squelching. No amount of wishful thinking would leave him as comfortable as a long bath and an even longer drink of something that didn't taste of the leather canteen hanging from his saddle.

'Firecursed small chance of that,' he muttered venomously, and found himself suddenly grinning at the way Yarak raised her sagging head and twitched her ears at him. Those were the first words he had spoken in half-an-hour of frantic and bloody activity that hadn't been either war-shouts, oaths or simple incoherent yelling. For all he knew, the grey mare disapproved of blasphemous language — but it was far more likely that she was anticipating some sort of treat.

Light of Heaven witness that she deserved it, because she was panting as hard as he was, and under the lamellar barding of her own armour the mare was streaked and lathered. She was the second of his mounts to carry the name, and for all that this one was somewhat bigger, half-bred Andarran and Ferhana, there was still enough of her dam's blood that the original Yarak's line seemed undiluted. Certainly this Yarak was just as intelligent, just as nimble, just as wilful when she could get away with it — and when she had to be, just as vicious.

'Stupid day for a fight anyway,' Bayrd grumbled, trying to remember if there was an apple or a lump of sap-sugar tucked into his saddlebags. He kicked both feet free of the stirrup-irons and let them dangle, leaned forward to slide from his saddle, then winced, clapped one hand to his ribs and thought better of it.

Not just yet. Get your breath back properly *before you try anything.*

He hoped that the sudden jab of pain was nothing more than a bruise or a stitch in his side, rather than something more serious.

Though Bayrd's armour had taken several hits during the quick, swirling exchange, none of them had penetrated the mail or lamellar scales and, until now, he had thought the padding and the combat leathers beneath had muted their impact.

But there had been that *kailin* in a green-and-white painted helmet, the one who had been using a mace instead of a *taiken* longsword. Isileth's sweeping stroke had sheared off the man's skull just above the eyebrows, helmet and all, but the hard-swung mace in his dead hand had kept on coming – and maces didn't need to penetrate armour to do damage. That was their whole purpose.

He knew that well enough from painfully personal experience. His collarbone had been cracked by one half a year ago, right through the harness, and though it had healed fast enough – with only a little help from the sorcery he was growing wary of using too much, for fear of relying on it for his life on the day his Talent failed – it still ached occasionally.

He continued to breathe shallowly, carefully, as he unbuckled his helmet and pushed it to the back of his head. The metal war-mask dangled clanking against his chest as he unpicked the laces of his mail coif, leather thongs that no matter how carefully he tied them always contracted into tiny, impossible knots within minutes of his breaking a sweat. And he had certainly broken a sweat today. Knowing better than to wipe his face with mailed gauntlets, he could only snuffle dismally as freed moisture ran down the bridge of his nose and dripped from its tip.

Stupid day? Stupid battle? No.

It was a stupid war, and the sooner they realised it, the sooner they could set about putting an end to it. Whoever *They* were this month. And not that the *hanen-vlethanek'n* were calling it a war anyway. Oh no. That would be sure to offend someone, and there had been enough offence already.

As if by common consent – or maybe even by Guild instructions, assuming they had bothered to re-establish that old structure – the Keepers of Years had employed every euphemism in their extensive vocabulary to describe what had been happening in Alba this past two years. Troubles; incidents; conflicting principles . . .

Principles? Bayrd considered the word in disbelief.

No matter the real reason behind it, when they came to write down what had just happened today, the Archives would be calling it nothing more disagreeable than 'a frank and free exchange of opinions'.

From what Bayrd could see, a couple of dozen members of the conversation hadn't survived the experience of having their minds changed. His mouth quirked sourly at the sight of one corpse. Make that, having their minds smashed out and trampled into the landscape.

'Light of Heaven, how the Pryteneks must be laughing,' said the Clan-Lord Talvalin savagely. It was probably just as well that Yarak-the-Second couldn't report his sentiments back to the many ears who could have made use of them.

This war had gone beyond support for or resistance against a female Overlord. It had become an excuse to vent all the spleen of the past score of years; all the spite, all the lost opportunities, all the jealousy against those who Had, nurtured like a sickly favourite child by those who Had Not.

Even assassination had become a popular sideline to the main event. It indicated without question that there were those among the lower clans and line-families who found the killing of their enemies more satisfying than maintaining their own honour. When the lesser Families and Houses, those who held little of value except their generations of unblemished honour, were willing to throw all that away for a moment's satisfaction, it said nothing good about the rest.

Bayrd hissed an indrawn breath through his clenched teeth at the sound of approaching hoofbeats – noting warily that the ache under his ribs had already faded to a familiar crawl of heat as his Talent dealt with the injury whether he willed it or not – and dropped one armoured hand to his sword-hilt. The *taiken*'s long blade scraped as his fingers closed in the grip-and-twist of a partial draw that had become almost reflex in these past months. Isileth had ridden at his hip for more than a year now, without once being pulled up to the peaceful carrying position aslant his back. There was too little peace abroad in the land.

Then he let the caught breath out again, slowly, trying to relax his tensed muscles and his twanging nerves at one and the same time. The snap as Isileth's locking-collar was jammed back into its black scabbard was as loud as a breaking twig.

'Father of Fires, man, but you're jumpy today!' said Marc

ar'Dru, reining his own horse to a standstill at more than the usual safe distance. As Companion and Bannerman to the Clan-Lord he knew Bayrd well enough, and in the recent troubled times he had come to know Bayrd's sword a deal too well for comfort. The weapon was gaining itself a reputation, and not a wholesome one. Isileth was becoming known as *an-gortaik'n*, one of the swords with 'hungry blades' like those in the old stories, and for his own safety and continued good health Marc preferred to give it a respectfully wide berth.

'I've good reason,' Bayrd snapped. He knew that there would be weeks of dreams when he would feel the cold draught of that axe-blade going by. 'And you should know better than to come up behind me.'

The broad, flared neck-guard of a *kailin*'s helmet meant that except when it was being worn normally, his blind side extended from forward of one shoulder to forward of the other. Pushed back, as Bayrd had done, the area of clear view to the front was as narrow as that of a draught-horse in blinkers. After the past skirmish, when neither side knew for certain whether the battle was properly over or if it had simply paused to adopt a new formation, Bayrd and Marc were both in the right, and equally both in the wrong.

House ar'Dru, and especially Marc and his sister Mevn, had been Bayrd's friends this long time past. It went beyond politics, beyond alliance, beyond even romantic attachment. After the death of his second wife Bayrd and Mevn had been lovers for a while, in a casual, mutually-comforting way, but it had never gone further. Bayrd ar'Talvlyn, as he had been then, had made representations and proposals to both Mevn and her father the Head of House, but neither had taken them as seriously as his long-winded speeches might have suggested.

Bayrd and Marc's friendship had begun as just two young men with a habit of getting repeatedly and amiably drunk in one another's company. They had been brought together by the circumstances of military service – Bayrd a Captain-of-Ten, recently, suddenly widowed at the age of twenty-four; Marc one of that Ten, twenty-one and comfortably unfamiliar with any hurt more severe than a hangover.

As time passed they had become not exactly the lovers that

cheerfully scabrous bivouac gossip suggested, but as near to brothers as two unblood *kailinin* could be. They were also confidants, of career, of family, of what passed for private life in a mercenary barracks. What Bayrd knew of Marc was never known; and what Marc knew of Bayrd was told only to Mevn.

The matter of his Talent for sorcery was something that remained a secret between the three of them until Eskra became a fourth, and it was supposed among the three that Eskra – though she appreciated the gesture – had not needed telling anyway. There was no fifth. No other social, and very few military secrets, could lay claim to being still secret after almost eight years.

Even though his ripped, stained crest-coat still bore the light and dark blues of the ar'Dru House colours, there was a new, broad stripe of white edging the pigments. It gave indication, to all who could read the blazoning, that Marc ar'Dru was the honoured Bannerman of Clan Talvalin nowadays, Companion to its lord and entitled to this version of a high clan's colours. He was the holder of many more confidences, gleaned from the high-clan lords who visited Dunrath, and none of those was kept any safer by the requirements of honour than those guarded by friendship.

They watched another group of *kailinin* as the men dismounted and hobbled their horses near the ring of stones. There was nothing unusual about it. There were many such stones in the lands of the Debatable Marches, single standing stones, or avenues, or great circles of grey sarsens such as this, surrounding the collapsed remnants of a burial mound.

In ancient times the Albans had raised such mounds themselves, over the graves of dead chieftans, and that was all they were, gravestones. Nothing more ominous than that. All the same, it was plain that none of the warriors even thought of using one of the taller stones as a hitching-post, or of letting any of the animals graze on the lush green grass that covered the low mound within the circle. There was no indication of fear, or wariness, or even of respect.

They just didn't.

All were low-clan, or merely House or Family, but all had one thing in common: they moved with the awkwardness that comes of weariness and stiff muscles, and they pulled off their helmets in search of air just as eagerly as their clan-lord had done.

'It's over,' said Marc.

'For now.'

'Very pragmatic.' Marc glowered at him from within the shadow cast by his own helmet's peak. 'What now, lord?' There was very little respect evident in the honorific. 'Some sort of wise saying like, "after a victory, look to your armour?" '

'This wasn't a victory.'

'It wasn't a defeat either.'

'Exactly.'

'*Argh!*' Ar'Dru threw up his arms in despair, knowing only too well that he wasn't going to get any more sense out of his clan-lord when Bayrd was in this sort of mood. And the biggest annoyance was that neither he nor anyone else – with the possible exception of Eskra and Mevn – could tell when Bayrd was being serious or not.

This time he wasn't. At least, not *as* serious. Though Bayrd was serious enough, it was for a reason other than the usual.

There had been too many men cut down in this encounter for anyone to treat it lightly, but at the same time it hadn't been anything to do with the conflict between the two would-be Overlords and their supporters. This had been plain, simple armed robbery, a beast-reaving in the good old-fashioned Prytenek style. Before the Albans came, it had been both sport and profit along the Elthan-Prytenon border marches, a pastime as common as a fall of rain. It had taken only a few years, and the recent breakdown in what passed for law and order, before the Albans had adopted it themselves.

This one had followed the usual pattern. A couple of score mounted *kailinin* had been on their way from one place to another, and in broad daylight had decided to take advantage of the troubled times to help themselves to some of the famed Talvalin horses. Had they been satisfied with the horses they might have got clean away. They were not.

By the the time a hot trod – a lawful armed pursuit led by the lord and his household retainers – caught up with them, they had also pillaged several of the domain's outlying steadings and run off thirty head of cattle. That sacking of the farms was their undoing.

If the raid was a traditional border means of increasing one's possessions at the expense of someone else's, then this was an equally accepted means of getting those possessions back. The proper Alban for it was *yrel-gol'wan*, 'riding with fire', recalling the old Elthanek tradition that the riders carried torches to announce their presence, rather than entering another lord's lands in secret. But typically, the Albans living in Elthan had taken to the pungent Elthanek vernacular with the same unseemly enthusiasm as they had embraced cattle-raiding.

Organising a hot trod into a neighbouring domain was recognised as not being a counter-raid, since that was governed by entirely different protocols. Furthermore, it allowed only an attempt to recover the original stolen property.

But it permitted the use of whatever force was deemed necessary to achieve that recovery and an appropriate punishment.

Since following a trod also legalised the injured party's right to deal with the guilty as he or she saw fit – and the thieves all knew it – that force was often excessive. Today, and even though the fighting was done, it would have to be excessive indeed. There was a new and unpleasant twist to the raid that Bayrd had not encountered before.

The beasts and plunder were safely enough recovered, but nothing would restore the lives of the families of five yeomen farmers, killed in the course of the looting. They had been burned alive when the thatched roof of their farmhouse was set alight because they were slow in coming out. And then, because they hadn't come out willingly, the raiders had prevented them from coming out at all . . .

The deliberation of that killing had been ruthless, and yet not ruthless enough, otherwise no one would have known that the fire was anything other than an accident. But they had left one of the farm labourers alive to bear witness against them. It might still have been accidental, but Bayrd was inclined to doubt it. Because although the man who survived was Alban, all those who had been roasted in the flaming ruins had been Elthanek tenant farmers.

And that, more than any other reason, was why they had died.

As Bayrd walked his mare slowly towards where the prisoners were being rounded up, he suspected that some among them wouldn't even regard what they had done as murder. The dead were of the Old People. Old maybe, but otherwise *turlekh'n*, unblood, and not real people at all.

He knew for certain that there were honourable men among his followers who thought the same. Warriors who would cut their own tongues with a knife sooner than speak insult to a lady were still men who, while they wouldn't see much to be proud of in the killing of conquered peasants, couldn't see anything especially monstrous about it either.

He could hear the responses in his head already. Call them what you will: arguments, justifications, reasons, but not really excuses. Excuses were only an attempt to explain guilt, and if guilt wasn't felt . . .

So the thatch caught fire. No, lord, not by accident. Yes, lord, all right, so it was *deliberate. Yes, someone* did *set a torch to it. What difference does that make, lord? It would have burned either way. What of it . . . ?*

If they didn't know the answer to that question by now, it was time they learned. If they *could* learn. And if it was his task to teach them that lesson, then it would have to be hard to forget.

'What are you thinking about?' asked Marc ar'Dru. Bayrd blinked, and stared at his Bannerman. From the look of him Marc didn't much like the expression that had settled over Bayrd's face, and he could guess why. It would have gone shuttered, cold, secretive.

Even after hours of practice in front of the best mirror money could buy, that was the best Bayrd had ever managed in his attempt to match the control of old Lord Gyras. The Clan-Lord ar'Dakkur could become as unreadable as a blank sheet of paper, without indications of thought, or emotion, or anything else. It was a consummate skill for a politician.

Though he had long envied ar'Dakkur's ability, Bayrd had conceded at last that he was no politician. The best he could do was make it difficult for anyone trying to second-guess the trend of his thoughts; and today he had not been doing very well. What he had been thinking was grim enough that even Lord Gyras might have trouble hiding it.

'Making An Example,' he answered finally, giving the three words their full capital-lettered value, but still managing to pronounce them as if they left a sourness on his tongue. He closed his eyes for a moment, then opened them again and surveyed the gaggle of captives as they were herded alongside the ring of stones.

It was odd; they should have looked more disreputable somehow. Less neat, less decently clad and armed and armoured. More like bandits and less like . . .

Like his own men.

'Find out a few things for me,' he said, his voice quite calm, its tone suggesting nothing more than curiosity. 'How many were in the original party, how many did we kill, and how many got away.'

Marc didn't move off at once. He looked from Bayrd to the prisoners and then back again; and his gaze dropped to the ominous black steel hilt of the *taiken* Isileth. 'What happens to the rest?' The question rang flat, because he knew the answer already and it was confirmed in silence by a movement of Bayrd's mouth. It wasn't so much a smile, even a small, bleak, humourless one, just a bloodless compression of the lips. Marc swallowed. This was a mood he had never seen before. 'All of them?'

'I told you. I have to Make An Example.' Bayrd's voice was quiet, grim, edged with the forced severity of a man trying to convince himself that what he was about to do was right. And unfortunately, with warriors like these – and that included his own – it *was* right. That knowledge didn't make it taste any better in his mouth the second time around. 'Now go find out what I asked.'

Marc looked him slowly up and down, then saluted without another word and rode away, heeling his own horse from a walk to a canter as if eager to be gone.

2

Widowmaker

A S BAYRD CAME closer, it was very obvious that even though
Marc had said nothing, word of his intentions had flown
around the gathered *kailinin* of his household. He reined in,
leaning on the pommel of his saddle, and watched them for a
moment.

Some were watching him in turn, with a near-insolent directness
unusual when an Alban retainer met the gaze of his own clan-lord.
A few eyed their normally-affable lord with a surprise that
bordered on shock, but others seemed quietly approving that he
should have decided at long last to make his presence felt along the
border country.

There was just so much a man could stand before he weighed his
lord's dignified restraint in the balance against his personal
reputation as a warrior – and found that reputation wanting.

This past season had seen too many anonymous incursions
across the frontiers of the Talvalin domain. Not one of them until
now had been successfully followed by trod either hot or cold,
never mind brought to battle and captives taken. It was the bad
fortune of these prisoners that they would bear the weight of
justice for all the others before them who had got clean away.

And then too, there was the matter of the burned farmers.

Bayrd cynically diluted a grim smile. Those farmers were a
legitimate reason for what he was going to do; but for a good half
of his men, any other reason would have been equally acceptable.

It was as he had suspected. A few were sympathetic to the men
and women who had been killed, but none of them felt anything
deeper than insulted honour against those who had done the
murders. None of them ruled these people – and that rule was

responsible not merely for their taxes but for their welfare, dammit! – and so none of them felt any real anger.

Bayrd Talvalin *was* angry; and that was after hours of hard riding had passed, and a good deal of rage had been washed away in the fright and sweat and fury of a vicious little combat. But when he had slipped from Yarak's back outside the smouldering ruins of that cottage, and gone inside to where the charred, shrivelled bodies lay smouldering in the ruins of their home, he had been willing to set loose not merely feud but a full scale clan-war on the men responsible.

That dangerous passion had cooled somewhat; the risks of revenge in the guise of justice running out of control were all too obvious with the present mood in Alba. There was an old saying – there was always an old saying – *it is so easy to set the grass ablaze, and so hard to put it out*. He had no desire to be scorched without good reason, and this reason, though good, was not good enough.

It had been as if he had never seen a corpse before. But maybe he had not; not in this sense, anyway. Bayrd had been Clan-Lord Talvalin for almost seven years now. He had seen men die, and he had killed a number of them himself. But this had been the first time that he had failed people who looked to him for their protection. The failure hurt. It shamed him. And it took away his honour.

And that, once all the high-sounding reasons were set aside, was why he had decided to see all the surviving prisoners as dead as their victims.

No. Not just see them dead. For the sake of his men and their honour, to keep a feud from being needlessly called against them; and for the sake of his *own* honour, no matter what might come of it afterwards – he had to do this himself.

But he would do it cleanly; none of the impalements or guttings or elaborate knife-work favoured by other lords on the grounds that a lengthy, painful death made for a better example. Whether the road into the darkness was a long or a short one, dead was dead, and the meaning of that death would be unmistakable.

If his eye was good and his arms steady, Bayrd knew that there would only be as many sweeps of the blade as there were men to receive them. Isileth would do the rest. Since the day he drew the weapon out of a crevice in the rock far under where Dunrath's rebuilt walls now stood, it had never been touched by a whetstone, and even after all those years it did not need it now. The *taiken* was no heading-sword – its balance was wrong, for a start – but the grey steel's bitter edges, keen enough to shave hair from an arm, would be more than enough for however many cuts were needed.

'Ten of them,' said Marc ar'Dru at his elbow, so perfectly answering the question taking shape in Bayrd's mind that he stared in shock for a moment.

'What?'

'I said ten prisoners. Nineteen were killed during the fight, eleven got away.' He eyed his lord, Companion and friend with something that might have been poorly-concealed disapproval. 'That was what you wanted to know, wasn't it?'

'I . . .' Bayrd gathered himself together as he might have brought an unruly horse under control between knee and heel and bit. 'Yes. Yes, it was.'

'The men know. And, Bayrd . . . *they* know too.' Marc's disapproval was no longer concealed at all. He didn't like what was about to happen. 'All of them know what you have in mind.'

'They should have thought of that earlier.' The words came out in a disciplinary snap from the old days, when Bayrd was a Captain-of-Ten and Marc ar'Dru nothing more than one more subordinate. *Keep your opinions to yourself*, was the caution riding under the words. *At least in public. It's nothing to do with you, but this is something I have to do. Don't make it any more difficult . . .*

Marc picked up on the warning at once, because his voice lowered to a private murmur. 'You don't like this any more than I do,' he said quietly from the side of his mouth. 'So why go through with it at all?'

'Because if I don't, they'll be back.'

'Will they?'

'If not these, then others.' Bayrd glanced at them, looking for shame, remorse, some mitigating emotion besides the condescending defiance stamped on every face like a seal into wax. 'I know men like these. Men like ar'Diskan, like . . . dammit, Marc, like far too many we both know! If I don't do something severe, they'll

28

ride off full of false penitence, and then they'll say, "Talvalin has a soft heart. He's too honourable for his own good. He'll cut you down without a second thought so long as it's in a fair fight, but if you're taken prisoner, you're safe." Do you want that?'

'They won't—'

'They *will*!'

'Bayrd, you sound like a man trying to convince himself.'

That stung, perhaps because Bayrd had reached the same conclusion without help from anyone else. 'Maybe so. Because you're right; I don't like it. But I don't like seeing my peasants slaughtered either. If they want to try killing someone, then let them try it with armed men of their own rank. Or can you live with the thought of . . . of old Youenn Kloatr from Redmer, hung up by the heels as if he was a dead rabbit on someone's tally-sheet?'

Bayrd's left hand slapped against Isileth's pommel, and the sword seemed to shift uneasily in its scabbard like an excitable hawk under its hood. There was a faint creaking of leather, a faint ringing of metal, as if the hawk had strained briefly against the restraining jesses and stamped one belled, taloned foot. All of it might only have been from the pressure of Bayrd's hand; and then again, it might not.

If the tales were to be believed, a *gortaik'n* blade had what sometimes seemed a will of its own. Its owner would carry it in situations where it might easily be drawn; it would be drawn in situations where it might easily be used; and it would be used in situations where it could best fulfil the purpose for which it had been made.

The killing of men.

'Some of the men have given that thing another name,' said Marc softly. 'They're calling it the Widow Maker.'

'Are they so?' Bayrd drummed his ironclad fingers against the longsword's curved crossguard, making a tiny clinking sound that at least had an honest source. 'Then Widowmaker let it be. I must be growing older, Marc. It's not as easy to insult me as once it was.'

A wash of translucent azure flame splashed from the metal of the long hilt, to lick and gutter over the armour that backed his gauntlet. Both men stared at the fat sparks that crawled like incandescent bumble-bees over the black-lacquered plates, until Bayrd closed his fingers and squeezed out a drizzle of blue fire from between them as though he held a fistful of grapes. It crackled briefly on the air and faded from sight, leaving only the hot purple after-track of its passage glowing within their eyes.

Marc ar'Dru flinched and wiped dazzle-born moisture from the corner of one eye. 'I thought,' he said, blinking, 'you were able to control yourself better than that.'

'Mostly, yes.' Bayrd raised his hand and held it in front of his face as if studying something strange – and in a way, he was. Had it not been for the Talent of sorcery, that hand had no business being on his wrist any more.

Then his gaze shifted to Marc, and his eyebrows drew together in a frown directed less at his Bannerman than at something only he could see. 'But sometimes no. Be as righteous as you like, but don't fling that righteousness at me. Not while you don't need to worry about its consequences. If you want to wait until Mevn's been forced to straddle all forty of a gang like this before you think to do something about them, then do it. Just hope they cut her throat afterwards.'

Marc went red, then white, and his hand began a twitch toward the hilt of his own sword before he stifled the movement. 'That was hardly—'

'Hardly something you like to think about, Marc-*ain*, my old friend.' Still glowering, Bayrd leaned forward in Yarak's saddle. Only a consideration for their honour, their rank – and for more than ten years of comradeship – stopped him from seizing Marc ar'Dru's war-mask by the laces to either side of its iron chin, the old army way of a half amiable, half irritable superior driving home a point. They were no longer in anyone else's army, he reminded himself abruptly. They were *kailinin-eir*, men of respect, both of them past thirty and with their dignity to consider.

'I suggest,' he finished, sitting back hard in his saddle before the way his mind was tending made him say or do anything worse, 'that you start giving some thought to such things. Maybe that way you'll never have to face the reality. I have. It smells like burnt pork. I *knew* the people who smelled like that. I knew them by name, to take beer with, to . . .

'Marc, you know all this. I was their lord; they thought I could protect them. They might have thought I would come galloping up to save them. They might have thought it right up to the moment when the roof fell in and they started to burn. The Keepers of Years can call this mess what they will. A border incident. . . ?' His mouth curled downwards as though the words tasted foul.

'No. It's a war. And if it goes on, I might have to smell that stink again. But,' he turned his head to study the prisoners again, 'at least I won't smell it because of *them*.'

Paying Marc ar'Dru no further heed, Bayrd dismounted and flung Yarak's loose reins towards the first of his retainers within reach, not troubling to see if they were caught or not. 'Which clans?' he asked one of them, and again, his tone of voice suggested that he had little interest in the answer. The man to whom he had spoken rattled out a list of names, most just House or Family titles.

Bayrd nodded, recognising some of those names. It was much as he had expected. Further probing might have revealed what allegiances those Houses had formed to give their actions some semblance of legality, but that didn't matter any more.

There was only one that caused him a moment's hesitation. Ar'Kelayr was a clan from his own past – or at least at one remove from it. Lord Vanek ar'Kelayr had been Gerin ar'Diskan's rival in that race to claim the domain of Dunrath, and because of that had been, in a twisted way, responsible for Bayrd's present situation. He found the coincidence an odd one, slightly uncomfortable in the echoes it stirred. But nothing more than that.

He had neither the time nor the inclination to find out who else might be responsible for what had happened; not when there were ten murderers before him, all of them taken red-hand and guilt-proven. The frenzy of their defence when the trod caught up with them had indicated well enough that they had better reason to avoid capture than just the horses and the thirty head of cattle running with them. They had enough identifiable plundered goods in their possession – foolishly already divided up into shares – to confirm it.

Bayrd knew there were enough ears – and loose mouths – around that some sort of speech was probably required. Some explanation for what was about to happen. But he found himself strangely unwilling to waste breath on swine like these, any more than Master Dwayl, the headsman of Durforen, bothered clarifying why he was about his lawful business. That would all have been dealt with days before.

In this case, it was hours rather than days, but the condemned men should still know why they were to die. *And if they didn't*, thought Bayrd somberly, *then it was far too late to learn.* Even so . . . He bowed his head slightly, acknowledging them as *kailinin*; they deserved that much respect at least, not for what they were so much as for what they had been.

'I am the Clan-Lord Bayrd Talvalin,' he announced in a voice clear enough to carry to where the unseen ears of a spy might be listening. There were always spies nowadays, even if they were not always in human form . . .

'I administer the rights of high, middle and low justice in this domain, to grant mercy or withhold it as I see fit. You are all miscreant thieves and murderers, condemned by witness, by proof and by your own actions. What can you say in your defence?'

That confirmed his intention as much as anything short of a summary killing – though this was going to be summary enough to raise eyebrows from Datherga all the way to Cerdor. The words were not quite the usual formal phrases, but their meaning was clear enough. Nothing the prisoners might say could alter their fate unless he willed it so, but they had a chance to justify their actions for posterity – if there was any justification possible.

For a long time none of them spoke, but now that he was close enough Bayrd could see the ice of arrogance start to freeze each face. Young faces, all of them. The faces of men who had not been warriors, not even passed *eskorrethen*, when the keels struck the shore eight years ago. And now look at them. Little lords of Creation, one and all, proving how much power they possessed by killing their unarmed inferiors.

Or those someone had told them were inferior.

The ten *kailinin* didn't understand what he meant by asking them to explain themselves. For men like this and a killing like that, there was no explanation necessary. They stared at him, and as Bayrd returned the stares he realised that he was looking at total incomprehension, mingled with a sneering hate so intense that the reason for it was beyond him. It was not just the hatred of men who knew they had been beaten, or men who knew they were about to die. There was something deeper, something uglier, something he had never encountered before even when facing the most fanatical Prytenek lord's-man.

'I am the *kailin-eir* Dyrek ar'Kelayr, and we all know you, ar'Talvlyn,' said one of the young men at last. Bayrd gazed at him, his face expressionless. Yes. He might have expected something from this one. The father was notoriously difficult to get along with, even among his allies. Why should the son be any different?

'If you know me—' he began, and was cut off short.

'We do not recognise you, *turlekh*,' snapped young ar'Kelayr. 'We do not recognise your right to judge us. You have forfeited all rights, even to respect.' Instead of a bow of respect, or the deep Third Obeisance merited by clan-lord's rank, he spat expressively on the ground at Bayrd's feet, defying him to do anything worse than the death already hanging over them all.

Neither the spitting nor the deliberate use of the old form of his name insulted Bayrd at all. What fuelled a slow burning of anger in his brain and behind his eyes were the implications of that one word, 'unblood'. They knew who *he* was, but that didn't matter.

It was who and what his *wife* was that concerned them. That was where the hate came from. She was an Elthanek, like those they had burned. Worse, she was an Elthanek sorcerer, whose presence in an Alban high clan was a canker corrupting the purity of its blood.

Bayrd set his teeth to keep back a pointless response that would be no more than a waste of breath. He had seen and heard all this before, in Drosul. Daykin of Kalitz had been behind some of it, a part of his complex plotting to gain support for himself and strip it from his rivals. Allegiances had fluctuated like the wind crossing a field of standing grain as one faction strove against the next, and Daykin reaped the benefit of the harvest. It had set him on the road to empire, and even without the Albans at his back – the only people he could really trust, although he never knew it – he might still get there. If he lived long enough.

There had been much talk about purity of blood, about whether the people of one of the little city-states was superior or inferior to the people of the next, and that superiority was never reckoned in a sense that counted swords or wealth or knowledge. It was more like the desire of children to be members of this gang rather than that, for no other reason than that one faction claimed to be better and some of the others believed it. And now the children were learning the old tricks again. Bayrd wondered who was teaching them.

For these ten savage children, it was an attitude that was too well ingrained for them to unlearn.

At least they wouldn't plead mercy. They would more likely try to spit in his eye when their turn came. But it would not be honest courage prompting the defiance: just their contemptuous awareness that he had once been almost as good as them, and that he had chosen to throw it all away.

'Marc-*an* ar'Dru?' he said, deliberately turning his back on the prisoners.

'Lord?' said Marc, saluting much more formally than usual. He was still smarting from the earlier rebuke, and making no secret about what he thought.

'You're my Companion and my Bannerman,' said Bayrd. 'My advisor. Then advise me.'

'Advise . . . ?'

'As I see it, there are four options. One, that I execute all of them. Two, that I execute five, taking a life for a life, but being sure to do nothing against the son of a high-clan lord. Three, that I find out the murderers and execute *them*, without fear or favour and regardless of who ar'Kelayr might be, then let the rest go free. Four, that I release them all. I am a lord known to be even-handed in my judgements. So. What should I do?'

Marc was eyeing him as though he had taken leave of his senses; as if the topic had never come under discussion before, rather than prompting a near-fight less than ten minutes ago. And he was unsure that there wasn't some crooked reasoning behind Bayrd's question that wasn't immediately apparent.

There was.

A high-clan lord, even one who had only attained the rank as recently as he had, didn't need advice on matters like this. Or second opinions. Or support, either tacit or verbal. A high-clan lord did as he pleased in his own domain, just so long as it didn't interfere with other high-clan lords – which was the problem here. But a lord who wanted his judgements and the reasons for them to be understood as clearly as possible might, just once in a while, explain them.

'You've beaten them,' said Marc after a moment's thought. 'We know it. They know it. You've won. But if you kill them all, they'll just be dead.'

'So I should let all of them go? Or just the ones protected by their fathers' rank. What about the guilty ones?'

'They deserve to die.'

'All of the guilty ones, then. The high and the low together. So. And which ones are they?'

Bayrd saw a muscle twitch in Marc ar'Dru's cheek, and knew he was bringing home to his Bannerman all the complications which Marc had so blithely dismissed when they weren't his official problem. Which of them indeed? The ones who fired the thatch? The ones who barred the doors? The ones who would talk for wearisome hours about the value of their warrior's honour, even though they stood by and didn't stop what was happening?

Of the ten men on their knees before him, which of them had done what? And what amount of torture would be needed to find out?

'How would you measure guilt, Marc?' asked Bayrd quietly. 'Tell me. I need to know.'

Bayrd had sincerely considered releasing every one of them. For all his righteous anger, the prospect of a multiple killing in cold blood turned his stomach even when he had the law on his side.

And Marc was right. To be defeated, and to know they had been defeated by so despised a creature as they considered him, would probably be a worse punishment than death. Adding clemency to that would pour salt in the wounds of their pride far more than any physical pain he could inflict. And *not* hurting them would enhance his own reputation much more than killing ten children, even though they had proven themselves as cruel as children could be.

But that was all before he caught something he had not been meant to see.

It was a shift of expression, nothing more. Because he happened to be looking in the right direction, Bayrd had caught a certain spiteful satisfaction mingled with the hatred in the eyes of Dyrek ar'Kelayr, the only one among all of them who had spoken.

He was a slim youngster, no older than twenty, handsome in his red and blue crest-coat with the scarlet enamel of its eagle-heads sparkling bravely in the sun. He was the sort who should have been guilty of nothing more than breaking half-a-dozen lovers' hearts. Not of torching a building and listening unmoved to the sounds as the five people inside it burned alive.

It was a look frightening in its intensity and in its implications. Any notions of forbearance abruptly withered. These men were beaten; that was true enough. All they had left to them was their contempt for Bayrd Talvalin and everything he represented, and the cold comfort that he thought them dangerous enough to deserve death.

But because of that contempt, they would be laden with such a weight of insult as needed revenge if he dared to let them go. High clan or low, backed by powerful allies or not, they would hunt him. Until these ten men were dead, neither he nor his family nor his friends would ever be safe again.

As if a chill wind had stroked across his cheek, Bayrd Talvalin shivered. He remembered the axe that had almost planed his face off his skull-bones. These . . . these children were just as much of a threat.

And with that shiver came a stab of suspicion as sharp as an unseen thorn in a bunch of roses. His words had not just been empty boasting: he did indeed hold the rights of justice in his own domain, and never more so than in the matter of prisoners taken under hot trod. But the man who held those rights had to know something of the law. In this Land, he needed to be not merely justiciary for both prosecution and defence, he also needed to be something of a policeman.

Whatever *that* might be in Alban terms.

There had been policemen in Drosul – or at least the constabulary of the city of Kalitzim – whose function was the solving of crime and the apprehension of criminals. Their activities had been a source of sarcastic amusement to the mercenary cadre in their barracks. So much of their success seemed to be luck, and so much of their failure apparently involved rank and privilege or the greasing of palms. Yet some of their methods had been sensible, and some had rubbed off on at least one Captain-of-Ten with nothing better to do that day.

Those methods were nothing complex, thank the Fires; young Bayrd ar'Talvlyn had been paid to be a soldier, not a thief-taker. But there was a certain elegance about the way in which logical questions applied to evidence could lead down a crooked path towards the truth.

It was one of those questions that a still, small voice had uttered in the back of Bayrd's mind. *Who stands to profit most?*

That profit had not involved horses, or cattle, or any of the other booty that had been recovered. Nothing so blatant. But when the question became *Who would be most likely to gain from ten fanatics swearing vengeance on Clan Talvalin?* then only one name came to mind.

Lord Gerin ar'Diskan.

His hands would be clean, whatever happened. Bayrd would have done nothing against him, nor he against Bayrd. The Talvalin Clan-Lord would have shown himself – as always – humane enough to gain the approval of everyone. Everyone, that is, who had heard only of the extreme youth of the ten raiders, but had not seen what they had done, or the way they looked, or how they wore hatred like a well-cut cloak.

It was easier to believe than the alternative. Bayrd's first marriage had taken place when he was nineteen, for complicated dynastic reasons that seemed very unimportant now. It meant that any one of these ten young men were of an age to have been his own son. Even though he had no son to call his own, no son to take the lordship of the clan from between his hands as the last night drew darkness over his eyes. He put that thought from his mind. It hurt him; and worse, it hurt Eskra. But what they had done hurt more.

No matter what he might or might not do as punishment, he didn't want to believe that they had done what they did from sheer wanton cruelty. No one ever wanted to believe that about children and the young. There had always to be some outside influence, something to preserve a vestige of innocence. Otherwise the whole fabric of society threatened to fall apart.

What angered Bayrd as much as anything was the simplicity of the plot. A convoluted stratagem with half-a-dozen strands as tightly meshed as the rings in a coat of mail would have been a compliment of sorts, a nod in his direction that implied he was worth so much trouble. This . . .

This was just insolent.

Like the constables of Kalitzim, discovering the probable

identity of a malefactor was not enough. They and he both needed proof; and in this instance, proof was impossible. Bayrd was certain that not one of the ten knew they had been manipulated, and would ridicule the suggestion if he made it. But somehow they had been induced to ride and raid through Talvalin territory rather than that of some other lord. His was the one domain in a hundred miles to either side of its borders where they would find Elthaneks being treated as – they would have said, daring to behave like – every other ordinary human being who worked their clan-lord's land.

And after that, the whole scheme hinged on his past reputation in the matter of such raids. Granted, no one had been killed before, much less murdered so brutally as those peasant farmers, but still . . .

He was Bayrd-*arluth* Talvalin, magnanimous and forgiving, the man who treated those who preyed on his land as no more than naughty children, to be smacked on the wrist and sent home. Until he was confronted with real children, and killed them.

He was being manipulated, just as much as they had been, and he could prove none of it. This was a plot that had taken all the things which made him a good man and a good lord, and had turned them into a dagger for his own throat. And the most disturbing part was that it felt wrong.

For one thing, it was far too subtle for ar'Diskan. Gerin and his late father Serej were two of a kind. The ar'Diskan Clan-Lord's crest was a black bear on the clan colours of red and white, and both men behaved as though they too were bears. Rough, direct, noisy and violent. Their idea of subtlety – and Bayrd knew it well enough, having almost lost an eye to it – was to swing a blade without the preface of a war-cry.

He had fought a duel with old Serej, for some reason or other that he had forgotten and no one else troubled to remember. After that, he had been Bannerman and Companion to Gerin for more than half a year. Dainty refinement was not part of that clan's character, either in good humour or in bad. Even a paid assassin would be too much; killing an enemy at one remove would lack satisfaction.

There was someone involved besides Gerin, and right now there was no way of learning who it was.

'No answers yet?' Bayrd gave Marc a quick look that was laden with dour, sardonic amusement. His Bannerman had still not ventured a reply, much less an opinion. 'Not as easy as you made it sound before, is it?'

He closed armoured fingers on the *taiken*'s long hilt once more and Isileth Widowmaker's edges whispered softly, a faint scrape of metal against metal, as he drew the longsword from its scabbard. It was a sound to chill the blood, shockingly close to the final faint breath exhaled from the windpipe of a cleanly-severed neck, a gasp of protest uttered even though the head might already be rolling on the ground. Both men were already far too familiar with it. Marc glanced sidelong at the blade.

'You had already made your mind up?' he said.

Bayrd nodded. 'I'll tell you later.'

Ar'Dru hadn't seen that hopeful, hateful expression flit across young Dyrek's face. Without the evidence of his eyes, explanations would be long, tiresome and, with Marc in his present mood, ultimately unconvincing. This was neither the time nor the place for such a discussion, but Bayrd was grimly certain that it would be the last time he would hear any retainers question their lord's decisions.

Even so, it should have been someone other than Marc. They had been friends for a long time, but – and the realisation was unsettling – there were some occasions when friendship had to be set aside. When all was said and done, a clan-lord's decisions were his own, not to be helped, and certainly not to be hindered or changed, by anyone else.

He hefted the *taiken* in both hands, shifting his fingers on the braided leather of the grip, and saw again the sluggish flutter of blue-white flames over the black-armoured gauntlets. This wasn't anger, or even the lack of control that Marc had accused. It was simply focused determination to be done with the ugly consequences of an ugly decision, and any lingering resentment there might have been was directed entirely at Gerin ar'Diskan.

Bayrd lifted his gaze from the grey gleam of the sword-blade and the barely-seen azure haze that hung about it, turned towards the prisoners – and his eyebrows came together in a frown at what he saw.

The ten had been disarmed directly they were captured, all but their *tsepan* daggers. Those weapons were no threat; the battle harness worn by the fully-armoured men surrounding them was proof against all but the luckiest stab with the fragile little blades, and anyway, not even the most honour-lost outcast would use one as a fighting knife.

Each *tsepan* carried more than the personal crest engraved on the pommel; it carried the hope, never voiced but always present, of a quick, clean end to pain after suffering wounds that no other healer could cure. The presence of that crest was to avoid feud or clan-war, for each man's dagger, at the last, was carried for himself.

But now three of the youngsters had drawn their *tsepanin*, and Dyrek ar'Kelayr was one of them.

Though it had looked at first like an attempt to avoid Talvalin justice, Bayrd could see that there was more to it than that. None of the three had risen from where they knelt; none had made any aggressive gesture other than the futile one of drawing weapons as useless in their present situation as so many icicles. But Bayrd Talvalin felt his hackles rising all the same. There was a tension in the air that had not been there before, an anticipation of violence more intimate than just execution.

Dyrek looked from side to side, a cool, haughty glance that took in his companions and dismissed everyone else as unworthy of his notice. 'We deny your rights, ar'Talvlyn. We deny your justice. We deny your lordship, and we give you our defiance.'

'Are you offering to fight me for your life?' Bayrd was not overly taken aback. He had been half-expecting something like this for a long while, and the only surprise was that the supercilious whelp had taken so long to get around to a challenge.

Except that this was not a challenge.

Dyrek ar'Kelayr put his head back and half-hooded his eyes behind their lids before subjecting Bayrd to a disdainful scrutiny. Bayrd was hard pressed to decide what he felt more: offence, or sombre amusement. The haughty expression would have done credit to the late Overlord Albanak himself, but on the face of a twenty-year-old *kailin* it looked ridiculous.

'We would not pollute our swords by letting that wizard-forged blade touch them,' the boy said. 'And we will not pollute our

40

blood by letting that blade spill it. We do not fear you, ar'Talvlyn.' For the first time his voice was growing unsteady. 'But you should fear the Red Serpent. We will be avenged.' He nodded once, and watched the other two young prisoners as they exchanged their daggers. Then he nodded again, and watched without a flicker of visible emotion as each gave the other his *tsepan* back again.

Point first, and under the ear, where the big blood-vessels ran.

In the instant of shocked silence that followed, and even as the corpses began to fall, ar'Kelayr turned his own *tsepan* over in his hand. There was no one to exchange it with, and thus an instant's deadly hesitation among the men surrounding the prisoners before any of them moved to stop him. It was all the time he needed.

In that instant he stabbed the *tsepan* upward under his raised chin. The dagger's needle point went through the taut skin almost without resistance, pierced the roof of his mouth and drove into his brain. His lips moved, but whether he was attempting some dramatic parting words or just another cold smile, he completed neither. Bayrd could see a thin glitter of steel behind the boy's teeth as blood seeped between them, and he saw the life go out of those scornful eyes like the flame fading from an empty lamp.

Dyrek ar'Kelayr sagged sideways to the ground, but he was dead before his upright body even lost its balance.

Bayrd-*arluth* Talvalin wiped the Widow Maker clean and ran the long blade back into its scabbard. A single ribbon of blue fire ran snakelike along the steel as though burning brandy had been mixed with the sheen of blood. It swirled briefly and vanished as though it had never been there. Bayrd closed his eyes and stared at the glowing after-image with new respect, but right now he felt drained, and weary, and just a little sick.

Marc ar'Dru looked very sick indeed, and very shocked. 'I thought you would have let the others go,' he said. 'After that.' There was no reply. 'I mean, Bayrd-*ain*, three of them . . .'

'. . . saved me some effort. That was all.' Bayrd swung up into Yarak's saddle and turned the little mare's head towards Dunrath and home. 'Marc, you talk to me as though I was the hero of some storymaker's tale. But what I've just done would make me the villain. Don't you think?'

Now it was Marc's turn to say nothing. He mounted his own black Andarran gelding and fell into step beside his lord and friend. There were times when all a friend needed to do was listen, and he suspected that this was just such a time.

'I'm neither hero nor villain,' said Bayrd. 'But I'm lord of a turbulent domain, trying to keep it as safe as I can in turbulent times. And sometimes that means . . .'

He glanced back to the row of lances sunk half their length into the ground, between the standing stones, and at the head spiked on each one, and he shrugged. There was little else he could do. 'Maybe I *should* have killed all ten of them. It sounds as though I'm being blamed for it. But I think I can trust the five who are left. For a while. At least until they get clear of Talvalin territory.'

Marc looked at the heads, and his mouth twisted slightly. 'And you *know* that you can trust those others. Wasn't that what you were going to say?'

'No. Otherwise I'd have said it. But I've been fair, yes? They killed five of my people, I killed five of theirs. Even if three of them saved me the trouble. But if there's a next time, I'll take two for one. Or five. Or ten. Or as many as it takes. And anyway, *your* reputation is still clean enough.'

Ar'Dru coloured slightly. 'That wasn't my concern,' he said, and if the denial came out a little too quickly, Bayrd had the good grace to ignore it. 'At least Gerin knows you can't be taken lightly any more.'

'If it was Gerin after all.'

'Still harping on that string? Who else could it be? How many enemies have you?'

'Enough. More now than before. And even so . . .' His voice trailed off, and though his eyes stared at the horizon for a few seconds, Marc guessed that he wasn't looking at the landscape. Or at least, any landscape *he* could see. Then Bayrd came back abruptly from the brief daydream and shook himself as though awakening from sleep. 'I need to talk to Eskra about this. The more I think about it, the more it doesn't even have an Alban feel to it.'

Marc looked quizzically at him, then forced a laugh. 'I know all that. Because it's too devious for simple sword-swingers like you and me. Think again!'

Bayrd returned the meagre laugh with a smile, and though it still lacked form a little, it was evidence that the bleak mood was

42

leaving both of them at last. Those killings would stay with him for a long time, but privately, not in public. How he felt about them was his own affair.

'A pleasant change from being told I think too much,' he said. 'But remember what I told you. Gerin wants . . .' Bayrd glanced backward again. 'He wants my head, not my good name. And he wants to take it himself.'

'Then why do you worry about Eskra and the children?'

'Because, old friend, I suspect that Gerin ar'Diskan has found himself retainers and Companions far less squeamish than you. Ten years ago we were just mercenaries in the pay of Kalitz. There wasn't land and title and the inheritance of both to get in the way of a straightforward feud. Times have changed, and not for the better. You heard that arrogant little swine.'

'I heard. I didn't like it.'

'Pride is one thing, but it's being warped. And who's doing it. Remember: who stands to benefit?'

'Ar'Diskan, obviously.'

'Not obviously. I told you why. At least, none of them named him.' Bayrd shifted uncomfortably in the saddle. 'And even though both clans wanted the Dunrath lands, I can't see any son of ar'Kelayr supporting his father's rival, even to bring me down.'

'The boy didn't name Lord Vanek either,' Marc pointed out. 'Not even at the end, as a threat. Just the Red Serpent – whoever he might be.'

'No Alban I've ever heard of. So . . . *not* an Alban.'

Marc ar'Dru smiled sourly. 'Name the old High Lord of your choice, then. Even the ones we call our allies. Gelert of Prytenon, Yakez of Elthan, Torhan of Cerenau. All of their children. All of their lord's-men. Everyone who has lost something because of us.'

'And how would someone not an Alban persuade people like young Dyrek and the others like him to have anything to do with them? You saw. You heard.' Bayrd opened his water-canteen and took a swig, making a face at the brackish, leathery taste. 'We'll save this problem for Eskra. She's Elthanek. She knows more about the way they think than I do.'

'And might have some answers.'

Bayrd grinned crookedly and shook his head. 'Knowing her, just more convoluted questions. We'll see.'

3
Serpent

For the sixth summer in succession Dunrath-hold echoed to the sound of building. Saws rasped their way through wood and stone, hammers thudded against timber or clinked on masons' chisels, pulleys squealed, and always in the background was the rumble of the ponderous fifty-man treadmills that powered the largest cranes.

Though Bayrd had found the place a ruin, it had been destroyed not so much by enemies in war as by the local people working peacefully for many years. Abandoned and defenceless, the villagers and lords alike had mined the fortress for its well-cut ashlar stone, and for the wrought-iron clamps that held the largest blocks in place.

That mining had been so enthusiastic, according to Youenn Kloatr – the old headman of Redmer – that the donjon, the great central citadel, had alone provided material for two whole villages and part of their lord Benart's manor-house. After they were done, little remained even of the outer walls, except for their cores of mortared rubble. Anything else that could be taken away, had been.

But there was nothing their burrowing, or even a real siege-mine, could do to the foundations. Those were solid rock, the very bones of the mountains, and their survival left the bones of the fortress in better condition than after all the centuries of time and neglect seemed possible.

And now the phoenix fortress was rising again, from a bed of its own ashes. Fresh blocks had been squared and shaped, fresh mortar mixed, fresh iron clamps forged to hold those stones too massive even for mortar.

It was Bayrd's eventual intention that the walls and the towers of his fortress be coated with a white or coloured plaster, as was done in Drosul, to offset the brutal starkness of raw grey rock; but the events of the past few days had made the strength of the fortifications suddenly far more important than their appearance.

Within ten minutes of his riding through the gates, any work not concerned with strengthening Dunrath had ceased. The gardens lay half-planted; most of the newly arrived trees that were to be the fortress orchard remained not merely in their wooden tubs, but still in the carts that had brought them here; and any man, woman or well-grown child without something definite to do was helping the masons and their principal architect.

Bayrd watched the flurry of industry for a few minutes before turning towards the stables. There was no risk of it slackening once the workers were no longer under his eye. He had told them what had happened – more or less – and what the likely consequences might be. Whether it was counter-raid, feud, or maybe even a clan-war, with Talvalin and its allies ranged against five other Houses and *their* supporters, being on the proper side of tall towers and thick walls had become very appealing to everyone labouring to strengthen their circuit . . .

Eskra sat quietly and listened to everything her husband and his Bannerman had to say. She did not, either then or at any other time, pass judgement on what had been done. But then, that was one of the reasons why Bayrd had married her in the first place.

She sat quietly and digested all the information, all the involved opinions, all the doubts and wondering; then she accepted a refill of her cup of wine and sat quietly again, mulling matters over in a mind that all of them knew was as crooked as a corkscrew. Like a corkscrew, it had to be crooked if it was going to do its job properly. A straight, unswerving line gave access neither to wine nor to useful conclusions. This time the wine was bitter indeed, vinegar to the last drop.

'You were right,' she said at last. 'It was not Gerin's plot.'

'Then who . . . ?'

'I told you seven years ago. The boy told you as well. He talked of a Red Serpent; I spoke only of a red snake that deserved to die.

Both are the same. The same badge, the same man. Kalarr cu Ruruc.'

Bayrd's eyebrows went up. 'Cu Ruruc?' he echoed. 'He's been in the hottest of the seven hells this past five years!' Eskra gave him a coolly sceptical look, and the vehemence of his words faltered to silence.

'Whose authority makes you so certain of that?' she said.

'I . . . ' Bayrd began, then grinned an annoyed, rueful grin. 'People,' he said. 'The *They* of "They say". But all right. You win. Nothing I could ever confirm. So change that to a question, loved, and tell me this. Which hell of the seven did he appear from?'

'It's a better question than you think,' said Eskra, and felt her mouth crook in a sour little smile. 'I'd like to have the answer myself.'

'Never mind "which",' said Marc ar'Dru. '*Who* the hell is he?'

'You don't know?' said Bayrd, grinning, and Eskra hid a more honest chuckle when he got a sharp look that indicated Marc wouldn't have asked the question otherwise. 'He would be one of those potential, er, beneficiaries of misfortune. The ones that *you* suggested. Not an Alban. He's High Lord Gelert's son, and a wizard.'

'Both wizard and sorcerer,' corrected Eskra. 'He was born with the Talent. The rest . . .' She shrugged elaborately and took a sip of her wine. 'He taught himself the rest. A grounding in the Art Magic before he was ten years old. And the little viper would be twenty now.'

'Not so little, then,' said Marc, as he and Bayrd exchanged the significant glances she had expected. The right age to be part of an intolerant little clique of bigots, prejudiced against everyone older, everyone different . . . everyone else. Except that he was different too. The next question was an obvious one.

'A sorcerer and the son of a Prytenek lord would hardly have endeared himself to someone like Dyrek ar'Kelayr,' said Bayrd. 'I told you what he said about *us*.'

'Unless you know your friend is an enemy, why treat him so?' said Eskra simply. 'Marc has been your Bannerman for—?'

'Five years—'

'And he never heard the name before. But I warned you of Kalarr a long time ago. He was never mentioned since?'

'I've had better things to talk about.'

'Just so.'

'Anyway, he vanished. Disappeared. Gelert, his family, his entire household and retinue. Gone. Just – ' Bayrd snapped his fingers in the air, ' – just like that.'

'Because people said so. Your so-knowledgeable *They* said so. And now he's back.'

'Lady, what makes you so certain?'

Eskra favoured Marc with a small smile and a salute of fingertips to heart and mouth. 'Marc-*an* ar'Dru,' she said. 'You are a good man. An Alban *kailin-eir*. And far too courteous to state the obvious reason. That I am a wizard too. But you would be right. We of the Art, we . . . know about each other. And I listen to more than rumour.'

'For how long?' Bayrd wasn't smiling. His mind's eye could still see boys young enough to have been the sons he never had, staring at him, despising him, killing themselves and each other because they hated him and everything he stood for. The muscles of his forearms still held the jolting memory of a blade cleaving flesh, his eyes the sight of heads tumbling to the ground, his ears the spattering of blood and that final bubbling sigh from the gullet of each stump. And at last there was a name, a target, somewhere he could channel all that backed-up rage. 'When did you know?'

'Two days. Maybe three. It was just after you rode out with the hot trod. I recognised him.'

'How?'

Eskra's eyes narrowed at the sudden harshness of Bayrd's voice, and she winced inwardly. She had known Bayrd Talvalin for six years now, as lover, as husband, and most important of all, as a friend – because no matter what the songmakers might believe, the three were not always facets of the one. And what she had learned in that time was that when he used the word *honour*, he meant more than just the ritualised Codes that were being set down as an approximate basis for how a *kailin* should conduct his life. It was more than just the pride that came with his rank and his power, more than being a gentleman.

For all his skill with a sword, for all his ferocity on the battlefield, Bayrd Talvalin was a gentleman in the oldest sense of the word, a gentle man, giving respect and expecting it in return, who behaved as best he could in a way that seemed right and decent to him, down inside where it mattered to no one else. What he had done – what Kalarr had forced his hands to do – would stain his hands and his honour for a long time to come.

And when she chose her words, she knew that it would seem once more as though she had heard his very thoughts. She had always insisted that was not part of the Art she studied, but there had been times when Bayrd was none too sure.

Eskra spoke the truth; but the tenor of those thoughts had come through clearly to anyone with the wit to see his eyes and listen to his voice. Anyone who could hear how many times, he, familiar enough with the terrible glistening mess that was the result of killing close up with a blade, had spoken of trying to wash the blood of children from his hands.

No; not just children. Sons, though he had never used the word. The sons she had never given him and, after the last child, for all her power in the Art Magic she never would. The sons a man needed if his clan was to last more than his own generation. The sons from whom he would choose his heir, who would take the crest-collar from his neck, the ring from his finger.

The sons who would put their hands between his and swear in the silence of fading life to keep faith, with the Overlord and with memory and with honour.

The hands Bayrd would never feel.

'Hold your hands in a fire and tell me how you know it's hot,' she said. He winced and glanced at those hands, pink and raw from much scrubbing. Eskra swallowed down the rising catch in her voice before anyone could hear it. 'I recognised him because I know him. Remember? Just after your people invaded us.' There was no condemnation in that, just a simple statement. 'During *an-Dakh Gwaf'n*, the winter war, when Gelert was using sorcery to kill from a distance.'

'I remember. He was using up his wizards.'

Eskra nodded. 'Forcing them to overreach the limits of their power. That killed them fast enough. And if they were useless he killed them himself. Kalarr and I were the only ones left.'

She grimaced at an unpleasant memory. 'Recognising him is easy. I became familiar enough with the flavour of his mind. He was advanced in more matters than just the Art Magic. And Light of Heaven knows he was gifted in that. Oh, yes. Far beyond his years . . .'

Then she hesitated and her eyes went distant, looking beyond Bayrd, beyond the walls of the fortress, beyond the years that had gone by. What she had just said gave a possible answer to how Kalarr had gained the support of such people as ar'Kelayr. He was precocious indeed, enough so when she knew him at the age of twelve that now, fully grown, he might be familiar with that side of the Art which she would never even dare to read about.

And there were the other spells, not so horrific but dangerous enough in their way. Spells that simply because of their demands on one or another form of strength or stamina, placed a strain on the mind, or on the body, or even on the spellmaker's presence in this world. That was the sort of spell she was guessing at now. Spells that could take the structure of reality and wrench it ninety degrees out of true, so that the world within a mirror could become no more than a careless step away.

However he had managed the trick, she was sure that he would have an Alban name, and an Alban set to his features. and he would speak with an Alban accent. It couldn't be shape-shifting; that wouldn't have affected his voice.

But it might be what was called a glamour, a charm to twist the perceptions of those under its influence. They saw, and heard, and thought, not what surrounded them, but only what the wizard casting the spell wanted them to see. For as long as the spell lasted.

No. There was always that problem. When such a spell of deception ended unexpectedly, so frequently did the life of the wizard using it, and usually at the hands or blades of those deceived.

Unless he had an almost suicidal confidence in the extent of his powers, it would have to be a far more impenetrable disguise. And the most likely one would be the body of another man. Some one of Dyrek's companions might look, and sound, and act the same as he had always done, but the mind controlling the body would not be the same one he was born with. Somewhere, at some time, he would have met a young man of his own age, and died of the encounter.

Whatever he had done, its results were the same. Kalarr cu Ruruc was free to walk among the invaders and make mischief.

The *how* of what he had done might be difficult to find out, but the *why* was obvious. Certainly it was as much an Alban reason as anyone could understand . . .

'Revenge,' said Eskra flatly. 'And a more satisfying revenge than any mere Elthan or Prytenek could bring down on you.' She uttered the disparagement of her people without emotion; it was no more than fact to most of the Albans. 'To provoke a war and see his enemies kill each other would be agreeable indeed. Especially since the reason for the war would be no more than an error.'

'The reasons for most wars are an error of some sort or another,' said Marc.

'So the Book of Years would have you believe.' Bayrd glanced at him and uttered a short, not very amused laugh. 'It doesn't stop them being fought.'

He had read enough of the clan archives in his youth to know that History – the formal title given by Tomorrow to what Today usually calls Problems – was like Eskra's attempt to explain the difference between his Talent for sorcery and the Art Magic. Some of it was to do with reactions and responses, an action here producing not only an equal and opposite response there, but also possibly an amplified reaction somewhere else.

But mostly it was about not being careless, otherwise it was all too easy to go through life not knowing what was happening. At least until all the things that had gone unnoticed were already happening far too fast to stop.

In magic, just as in war, that could get you killed.

At least this time, thanks to Eskra, they knew what was happening before the event. Knowing what to do about it was another matter entirely.

'The lady is right,' said Marc ar'Dru. 'She has been right all along. He ought to be dead. And everyone in the Land of Alba would be safer if he was.'

Heads turned. Bayrd and Eskra stared at him, then at each other, and finally back at Marc. This was not the sort of statement that might usually be expected from him. He was good enough with axe or *taiken* on the battlefield, as Bayrd knew; but he was equally aware, most recently from Marc's resistance to his execution of the raiders, that killing was not his Bannerman's first response to a crisis. Besides, who would do the killing?

'I would even be ready,' Marc said carefully, 'to do it myself, if the means and method didn't touch on my honour.'

'That would be the snag,' said Bayrd – and was slightly shocked to find that he wasn't even questioning the offer. They weren't talking a duel here, or a feud with an exchange of challenges and a meeting in open combat. Whether the weapon used was dagger, arrow, poison, or some mind-shrivelling spell that Eskra might create, the method would still have to be secret and without any warning. That would make it murder. He dignified it slightly to assassination, and found the flavour of the word no better.

It was still murder.

There would be no way in which Marc's honour could come unscathed out of such a venture, and thus no way in which his Clan-Lord could honourably have the deed performed, either as the result of a direct command or simply as a favour. And never mind honour: there would be few enough ways for the Bannerman to bring himself away unscathed. Bayrd was still sufficiently disturbed by the offhand way his three prisoners had committed suicide as to be in no frame of mind to ask a friend to run that same risk.

Because if only half of what Eskra was suggesting about Kalarr cu Ruruc was true, then any attempt to go against him openly would indeed be suicide.

'On my Word and on my Honour, it was suicide.'

That, from one clan-lord to another, should have been more than enough. In this instance, as one eyebrow arched in faintly sneering disbelief, it evidently was not. Bayrd Talvalin drew in a deep breath and let it out slowly, lifted his wine-cup and set it down gently. Keeping his voice low and steady, and his fist from pounding the table in front of him, took more effort of will than he would have believed he possessed.

The man who sat at the far end had that effect, and it had grown immeasurably since the moment of his arrival.

He and a small party of retainers – enough to be an honour

guard, not enough to form a threat – had clattered up to the gates of Dunrath with green leaves around their spears as a sign of peaceful intent. There had been no bawling for vengeance; no demand for reparation in gold or in land; not even a request for explanation and excuse. None of the things that Bayrd was primed to deal with.

Just the annoyed disinterest of a man performing a distasteful task because his supporters expected it of him.

Bayrd had done that after the hot trod, and to be on the receiving end of the same situation caught him off his guard.

The Clan-Lord Vanek ar'Kelayr was known to be infamously quarrelsome, and the attitude he presented did not correspond to what Bayrd had heard of him. At least, not at first. But as time went by, Bayrd discovered that there were many ways to pick a quarrel, and the blustering ar'Diskan style he knew only too well was crude in the extreme.

Ar'Kelayr preferred to let his opponent do the work. He wore a studied air of cantankerous irritation with everyone and everything, as other men might wear their clothes, and his ability to find fault seemed to come almost as second nature. As a result, even the most patient man was raised to seething, to the point of erupting in violence – and Vanek ar'Kelayr would have witnesses from both sides to prove that *he* was not to blame.

He was separated from Bayrd Talvalin by many things. Most obvious was the sturdy oak of the table itself, an ocean of polished wood set here and there with bowls of fruit, wine-flagons filled with Jouvain, vintages purchased at no small expense from the Ship-Clans, cups of wood and glass and metal, all the trappings of civilised conversation.

It also filled the mandatory two sword-lengths of clear space between them with something more solid than mere good intentions.

That was just as well, for in Bayrd's case those good intentions were wearing very thin indeed. Without the table, without the armed and armoured Talvalin retainers that flanked it – for Bayrd's honour and Vanek's protection – that traditional distance separating men of differing opinions would have given him no more than a second's delay.

Least visible of all, but most apparent to Marc ar'Dru and Eskra

Talvalin sitting ignored in their advisory places to either side of the
long table, was a total opposition of mind. For the past hour Bayrd
had tried to be reasonable to his guest. The man was, after all, a
lord of equal rank, and a bereaved father with a justified grievance
and the right to an explanation.

The strain was showing more with every minute that went by,
because in all that time Vanek ar'Kelayr had contrived to be just as
*un*reasonable. With no effort at all.

At the back of Bayrd's anger was a small cool wondering as to
what it would be like to live with this creature year in and year out,
to never do anything right, never give satisfaction, never hear a
word of praise or approval.

A week ago the very thought would have been impossible, but
today . . . Today he felt a touch of sympathy with dead Dyrek, and
even the start of something close to understanding.

'You hacked my son's head from his shoulders, ar'Talvlyn,' said
Vanek in the same dry tone as before, 'and you still call it suicide?'

If there had been any passion in that rasping voice, any sense of
loss or outrage, then Bayrd might have found it tolerable. Instead
he heard only what had been there at the beginning, and had not
changed since. Impatience at this waste of his valuable time –
though with a son dead and the presumed slayer face to face, what
else he might devote that time to was not made clear; irritation
that anyone at all should do anything at all without taking his
convenience into consideration; but no hurt, no anguish, no sense
of loss at all.

Bayrd had felt it more.

'He killed himself,' he repeated for what felt like the hundredth
time. 'He took his *tsepan* and he . . .'

Bayrd hesitated, then shrugged inwardly. Delicacy be damned.
It hadn't worked on the other ninety-nine occasions.

'Your son stabbed himself through the brain, Vanek-*eir*.
Without persuasion. Without assistance. Under the chin and up.
And he died of it. That, my lord, looks very much like suicide to
me.'

'And then you cut his head off,' accused Vanek.

'*But I didn't kill him . . . !*'

Wood scraped as Bayrd kicked himself and his chair from the
table, and half-rose, barely managing to rein his temper in. It was

not as if this was news to ar'Kelayr, not after so long. Then he caught the other man's disapproving gaze and followed it, to where his own right hand had whipped across his body in an attempt to close on the sword-hilt that fortunately wasn't there.

Both men had *taipan* and *tsepan* at their belts, shortsword and dagger, but neither of those weapons was designed, or even worn in the proper position, for the slashing cut straight from the scabbard that was the most lethal demonstration of a warrior's displeasure. As Bayrd settled back into his chair and flexed those betraying fingers, he realised that was just as well.

Isileth was present, as was Vanek's *taiken*, the named-blade Katen, two hundred years old and of good repute. As the ultimate element in any negotiation, it would have dishonoured both the weapons and the men who bore them to have left them outside the room. Both longswords were leaning almost upright on simple cedar-wood racks; but those racks were mounted against the wall and therefore safely out of reach.

There were various traditions surrounding the reason why Alban warriors gave up their *taikenin* when guesting under another's roof. Courtesy was one, extended to the great swords as much as to their host; good manners was another, a recognition that there was no proper place for a battle blade except the field of battle; and simple caution was a third.

Especially, thought Bayrd soberly, when one of those swords is *an-gortaik'n*. Isileth Widowmaker would have been stirring hungrily in her black scabbard for hours now, making that eerie metallic whispering. He had always dismissed the sound before as a result of the blade, encased in a sheath of resonant lacquered wood, merely shifting slightly under its own weight. After the events of the past few days, his certainty had gone. It was becoming increasingly difficult to give the sword its formal title rather than the brutal nickname, or even keep the reference neutral, calling a weapon of cold iron 'it'. Instead of '*she*'.

Widowmaker was no ordinary sword.

Bayrd had known for almost seven years that because of the Talent, he was no ordinary warrior.

And he realised with a jolt that there was glowing, smoking evidence of that Talent scorching its way into the table.

Ar'Kelayr, lost in his portrayal of scorn, was beyond noticing anything, but both Marc ar'Dru and Eskra saw the sapphire-flaring signature of Bayrd's rage charring a hair-fine track into the wood. Bayrd felt a nervous inward spasm at losing control of himself so completely, and slapped his hand down on the blue sparks as though swatting a fly. They stung briefly, but when he lifted the hand again they had gone. All that remained were the burn-marks on the table, a faint scent of singeing, and a tiny constellation of blisters rising on his palm. The small pain helped to clear his mind.

'I did not kill your son,' he said again, forcing himelf to speak quietly, calmly, all the ways he didn't feel. 'There were witnesses who can prove it.'

'Your clan retainers and lord's-men, of course. Fair witnesses indeed.'

'And the five young men I did *not* kill. When you heard of this matter, my lord, which one of them was it who told you his version of events? Did he know how loosely his head was resting on his neck?'

Bayrd stared at Vanek ar'Kelayr, a cool, calculating appraisal from eyes that were as grey and hard as fresh-split flint. He knew the effect of that stare and used it deliberately, a calm consideration that Mevn ar'Dru claimed could see through a rock, given time.

Ar'Kelayr did not give him the time. The other man met his gaze for a few seconds, forced it for a few seconds longer, then looked away.

'What you did or did not do to anyone else does not concern me, ar'Talvlyn,' he said. 'We are discussing my son.'

'Your son and his companions may have saved that messenger's life, Vanek-*eir*.' Bayrd had his voice under control again. 'I had decided that I would take five heads as a warning, and let the remainder go. Three die by their own hand. I take two heads and the matter is concluded. *So.*'

He snapped his fingers for demonstration, the sound abrupt and sharp enough for Vanek to start slightly, then try to conceal that he had done so.

'But consider this, my lord ar'Kelayr. A more barbarous man would have considered that they had cheated him. Cheated his justice. A more barbarous man would have taken his five heads from living bodies. For all that your son did, only two men would have survived to ride away in safety and spread lies about me. Remember that, when next you see those five alive and breathing. I am not a barbarous man.'

His clenched fist came down on the table with such a crash that one of the flagons on it rebounded and fell over, spilling to the ground, splashing wine across the wooden floor. They all looked at the puddles, twenty crowns'-worth of Seurandec soaking into the boards, blood-red in the sunlight from the high windows of the council hall, and then they looked at him. Bayrd smiled, if a mere skinning of lips from teeth deserved the name.

'But if I must,' he said, soft but clear in the deafening silence, 'I *can* be.'

The jarring shock of the blow had awakened echoes in the bones of Bayrd's arm. Echoes of other impacts, echoes of other reasons. Some of those had been less than good, had left him feeling ill at ease or at the worst bereft of sleep, puzzling over whether what he had done was right. But this premeditated display of rage – no more than an act this time, so that there was no risk of the hot blue-white flare of sorcery becoming visible . . .

It had felt *wonderful*.

There were times when sitting still and silent, letting the other side take the initiative and do all the talking, was the best way to learn what another person thought. But on other occasions, attack was the best defence. Short of drawing a blade on him, he had gone for ar'Kelayr's throat in the best way that conventions allowed.

And it had worked.

As he massaged the bruised heel of his hand, he could see that though the man was doing his best to restore it, that maddening veneer of contrived disinterest across Vanek ar'Kelayr's expression and emotions had been shattered beyond repair. Try as he might, the cracks would always show. At least to Bayrd, and to the others here who now knew what to see.

And for the first time he saw the man's true face.

Without his self-constructed mask, Vanek looked human at last. He looked hurt, and sad, and most of all confused. Then between one breath and the next, the mask of manners was back in place, restored more by habit than from any need. Their eyes met, and in Vanek's Bayrd could read a plea that his weakness not be betrayed. There was fright in those eyes, the fright of a man whose most trusted weapon has been wrenched from his grasp, whose enemy has seen the weakness and is poised to take advantage of it.

Bayrd gestured for the guards to leave. 'Thank you, sirs,' he said, the courtesy not overdone since in token of Clan-Lord ar'Kelayr's presence they were all of *kailin* rank and not mere soldiers. 'Your presence is no longer required. But,' and he glanced at Vanek and nodded briefly, 'your silence is.'

Their officer, a Captain-of-One-Hundred, drew himself to attention as his men filed out, and made salute with a sharp click of metal against metal. That was all. No words of warning, no promises of secrecy. None were needed. The Talvalin lord's-men were all troopers that Bayrd or Marc had commanded in the past, and their loyalty was beyond question.

Iskar ar'Joren had been one of Bayrd's first Ten, back in Kalitzim a lifetime ago when they had all been no more than the hired swords of a small king – who was now a Great King, Bayrd reminded himself, and set fair to be an Emperor before he died. Unless he died before it . . .

Ar'Joren had been an artilleryman until he lost his hand in a stupid gambling accident, and it was only thanks to the insistence of young Captain ar'Talvlyn that he had kept his place. Bayrd had seen no reason why a trained brain and a skilled eye should be wasted when there were many other hands to do the work of the one that was gone.

That missing hand was an elaborate steel pincer now, linked by pulleys and fine cables to the stump of Iskar's forearm so that it was still surprisingly capable of even the most delicate tasks. And at the same time, Bayrd had seen it punched through a pine plank, just to prove that it would. For all its mechanical delicacy, it was a startling thing to see for the first time – it had momentarily unsettled even Vanek ar'Kelayr's composure – and as menacingly efficient in its way as the battlefield catapult which had crushed and severed the original.

Iskar ar'Joren was *kailin tleir'ek* in command of Dunrath's counter-siege artillery now. Somehow it seemed only appropriate.

Even after the guards were gone, they sat in silence as servants came in to clean up the spilled wine and replace it with fresh. After that they waited a little longer until the servants too had left the room. Only then did Bayrd lean forward with his elbows on the table and, despite all the hostile ways he had felt about the man at the far end of it, made himself almost ooze informality.

'Now come on, Vanek-*an*,' he said, slipping from the higher phase of language and using the lesser honorific as between friends – or at least, not-enemies – 'we don't really need to go through everything again, do we?'

The tension in the room hung on like persistent smoke for perhaps a minute before Clan-Lord ar'Kelayr let his pretence collapse for good. He nodded, and almost smiled; an expression that looked uncomfortable on a face whose muscles were not designed for it – or were at least long out of practice. His method of smiling before now had always been that thin-lipped grimace men use when they deign to notice a joke they really don't care for. An honest grin on that face would have looked like a rictus of terminal agony.

At least now, thought Bayrd with a quiet inner smile of his own, it merely looked like the straining of mild constipation.

And that was an improvement he had never hoped to see.

'My lord ar'Kelayr,' said Eskra, taking advantage of the moment, 'I have a question needing answer. If you would. When did you last see your son?' She paused for the sake of kindness, then finished, 'Alive, that is.'

Vanek shifted his gaze from Bayrd to the woman he had refused to acknowledge from the instant he came into the room, and there was a long moment's uncomfortable pause.

'More than half a year,' said ar'Kelayr at last. 'No. Longer. It would have been the autumn, just after *an Kynyaf Halan*.'

'The equinoctial holyday,' muttered Eskra, half to herself. 'That makes too much sense.'

It was a thought spoken aloud, no more than that, and not for general consumption, but Bayrd caught it and rapped the table for attention.

'Why so?' he asked. Eskra sent him a quick glance of warning that he was treading dangerously close to matters an Alban should not know and a clan-lord should not *want* to know, but enough had been going on that Bayrd was past such concerns. He might regret his course of action later; but later was not now. 'What is so significant about the equinox?'

Eskra sighed audibly, stared at her own hands for a moment, then made a gesture with them that would have been a shrug had it gone further up her arms. 'If you really need to know . . .'

'I do.' He nodded towards Vanek. 'It concerns a dead son, and false accusations, and perhaps treachery in high places.' Ar'Kelayr looked shocked at that, but said nothing. 'We *all* need to know.'

'Very well.' Eskra sounded reluctant, but resigned. 'Your principal Alban holydays represent more than most of you care to realise. Five of them in the year, yes?' The three Albans at the table nodded in a staccato chorus. 'The equinoxes – ' Eskra marked off two fingers, ' – the solstices – ' two more fingers, ' – and year-turning. The first day of the first month of spring.' She tapped her thumb. 'Calendar points. Festivals. Nothing more.' All the fingers folded up into a fist and thumped down against the table.

'Not so. There is magic here. In the Land. In Alba. And this is what magic is . . .'

'No,' she corrected herself. 'This is what *true* magic is: the turning seasons, death and life, growth and decay, and the knowledge of how to channel it. Not just old men with old books. Not just circles chalked on floors. Not just scraps of herbs and muttered words so ancient that their meaning is forgotten. All magic uses words to change the world. And certain times of the year make it easy.'

Eskra stared at the three men along the table. Two were more or less aware of what she meant, the third had no desire to know. She grinned, quickly so that any real humour hiding at the back of the expression would be lost in its brief severity, and saw Bayrd at least grin just as quickly back.

'These times? These days? Why are they different from all other days? Why are they remembered, my lord ar'Kelayr?'

Vanek twitched in his chair and refused to speak.

'*An Gwaynten Pasek*, the Greening, falls in springtime. The festival at Midsummer is *an Haf Golowan*, the Fire. In autumn you celebrate the Golden Time, *an Kynyaf Halan*. Especially if the harvest has been good, yes? But at midwinter nobody likes to think of *an Gwaf Degoleth-ys*, because that is Darkness. So tell me – why have they their own special names?'

No one answered, and only Bayrd met her eyes. He no longer showed any inclination towards grinning.

'Because names are important. Name the thing, call the thing. Four seasons and four names. Only two of them to do with seedtime and harvest. Why? Because *none* of them have to do with the seasons at all.' Again that sharp look; and this time even Bayrd preferred not to meet it. Eskra nodded, as if this was no more than she had expected.

59

'These are the times when the locks and bars are loosened. The times when day and night are one length, or when the balance leans one way or the other. The shortest night . . . and the longest. Then the doors between this world and all the others swing loose on their hinges.'

She sat back in her chair with a grunt of disgust she didn't trouble to conceal. 'And your people have so carefully forgotten it all.'

She looked at them again, and now there was a glitter in her blue eyes that might have been a glint of scorn or equally a twinkle of amusement, a sweeping stare that took in Bayrd just as much as the other two. He didn't know whether that was for his own protective colouration, or because in the past few years all her attempts to improve his understanding of sorcery had only served to reveal how inept he was at using the Talent.

Marc ar'Dru seemed more amused than anything else at being included, but Vanek ar'Kelayr looked uncomfortable at being a party to this discussion at all. He had the air of a man who would far rather be somewhere else, the air of someone whose deepest suspicions have been well-founded. Bayrd knew what those suspicions might be; he had heard them often enough since he married Eskra.

She drummed her fingers briskly on the table. 'Old Magic,' she said. 'High Magic. The Art. Sorcery. Call it what you will, so long as you recognise that it exists. Because that way you can come to terms with it. Deal with it. Or against it. But instead you Albans ignore it.'

'The late Overlord Albanak called for your assistance, lady,' ar'Kelayr pointed out with a touch of that old pose, as of a man scoring a point. '*He* did not ignore . . . it.'

'As I recall events, my lord, he had little choice in the matter.' Bayrd took care not to smile at Vanek's too-selective memory; a smile would have put too sharp an edge on the reproof.

'You Albans ignore the Art,' said Eskra. 'You despise those who have mastered it. That *I* know well enough. Worse, you spurn any of your own with the Talent to begin to understand it.'

Bayrd diplomatically studied the table-top, or the wine in his cup, or his fingernails. Anything to keep expression from his face.

'But my son would not have—' Vanek began to protest.

'We suspect, my lord,' said Bayrd gently, 'that since you last saw him, he was keeping strange company.'

'Not . . . Not magic. Dyrek would never . . .' The man's voice trailed away at some image, some memory, that had begun to give the lie to his defence.

'Vanek-*arluth*,' said Marc ar'Dru, speaking openly for the first time, 'when fear of a forbidden thing has gone, it can exert a strange attraction.'

'The Art Magic has a charm all its own,' said Eskra. Ar'Kelayr gave her a sharp look, but she was not making a joke. 'Because you cannot – or will not – see that it exists, you hope that it might go away. A curious contradiction, that. You must think again, my lord ar'Kelayr. The Art Magic will *not* go away just because it unsettles you, any more than the sun might fall from the sky because it dazzles you. Now listen to me. And listen well . . .'

Bayrd had never seen Eskra in such a passion about anything. Some of them already knew some of what she was talking about, but none of them knew all of it – or, he corrected himself, would admit that knowledge openly. They knew the calendar information well enough, but as for the rest . . .

Alban holydays fell on the last full moon night of each season, as near to the appropriate solstice or equinox as possible, and continued into the day immediately following. Though by comparison with some the Albans were not an especially religious people – someone had long ago decided that there was little point in making supplication to gods who so obviously didn't pay any attention, though courtesy to the Father of Fires and the Light of Heaven was advisable just in case – the seasonal festivals had been observed and celebrated for hundreds of years.

The feast-night was for thanks concerning ventures completed in the preceding three months, and for those members of one's Clan or House or Family who had remained in good health and prosperity. Sunrise of the next day was a time for . . . well, for aching heads from the previous night, mostly, but also for making plans and resolutions for the next season.

Since the full moon did not usually oblige by falling precisely on the equinox or solstice, it was no more than a convenient mark on which to hang the holyday and the festival that accompanied it. But on those occasions when the two *did* coincide, both sorcerers and the wizards who practised the Art Magic were of the common opinion – a unanimity unusual enough in itself – that the conjunction could be used as a focus of great power.

61

An dé Nadelik, the day of year-turning, was an extra day-name on which the year number was formally changed in calendars and chronicles. It fell at the end of winter, taking priority over the Feast of Darkness, and like the others would occasionally match the night of the full moon; more rarely with the solstice. But if it should chance to coincide with all three, then it was considered most unlucky, and no work, task, promise or sorcery was ever begun or concluded on that day.

But if the conjunction of the full moon fell on the Feast of Fire, then that was a day for beginnings and for hopes. Or for conquests. The word slithered like a serpent through Bayrd Talvalin's mind. A Red Serpent.

'Last autumn's festival was on the night of the equinox,' said Eskra. 'And—'

'And this year's Fire falls on the summer solstice?' Bayrd asked, though it wasn't really a question; he knew the answer already. She nodded. 'Then whatever Dyrek was—'

'Now listen to me, ar'Talvlyn—' Vanek burst in, but Bayrd silenced him – successfully and rather to his own surprise – with a single upraised finger.

'Vanek-*arluth* ar'Kelayr,' he said, 'this discussion started badly, but has improved beyond all measure. We'll continue it tomorrow, and it might continue to improve after a night's rest. And I might choose to hear you better if you would call me by my right name . . .'

Then his teeth closed with a click on whatever else he might have been about to say, because realisation that had eluded him all afternoon suddenly came home to roost. From the quickly-hidden shift of expression on Eskra's face, she had seen it too.

Ar'Talvlyn was the old style, the pure Alban version of his clan and family name; Talvalin was the new pronunciation which he had adopted, setting him at one remove from the old ways and making him – perhaps – a little more acceptable to the Elthaneks of Dunrath's domain. So far he had heard no complaints, except from his own people.

But if one were to perform the same excercise on Vanek's name, then the Elthan inflection would change ar'Kelayr, that old Alban name, so that it would become . . .

. . . Kalarr.

4
Mirrors

THERE WAS A great deal more that Bayrd had wanted to ask
Vanek ar'Kelayr about. He had many more questions: about
Gerin ar'Diskan for one thing, and about who Clan ar'Kelayr and
its allies supported in the rivalry for Overlord for another. He had
hoped for many more answers, and perhaps even a leavening of
undiluted truth. But the man was a guest of equal rank, not a
prisoner, and this – now that the earlier unpleasantness had been
set aside – had become a lengthy conversation rather than an
interrogation. Courtesy had to be observed.

In this instance, the courtesy involved seeing ar'Kelayr safely to
one of the all-too-recently completed guesting-chambers in the
north tower, ensuring that his retinue were also provided with
somewhere to sleep, and that all of them were fed. That was the
most difficult part.

For all Bayrd's apparent wealth, few people outside the family
and immediate circle of friends knew that most of that wealth was
being poured, like the mortar holding them together, into the walls
of Dunrath-hold. Plenty of time to accumulate riches, was Bayrd's
view, when where you intend to keep them is strong enough to
make *sure* you keep them.

So it was oven-pudding with gravy again, and a roasted chicken.
Elaborately cooked, elegantly presented, expensively powdered
with spices, but quite definitely chicken. The poor man's meat.

If Vanek-*arluth* looked slightly askance at the pudding because
he knew it was an Elthanek dish, at least he was far too noble to
realise the significance of why it was served up and eaten before
even the meat appeared. It was a trick Dunrath's cooks had
borrowed from the local people, a means to blunt a diner's appetite

before the expensive part of the meal, without being obvious about it. Hence the generous size of the pudding, and the tastiness of its gravy.

But he might have noticed the number of poultry scuffling and scratching around the fortress, and then added that observation to what he and his men – and even the Clan-Lord Talvalin himself – were eating. It might have helped him to draw unfortunately accurate conclusions about that clan-lord's parlous financial state.

Except that Bayrd wasn't eating.

Eskra and Marc each worked at their respective plates with spoon and eating-knife and two-tined fork, and after every few mouthfuls one or the other glanced at Bayrd, or at each other, or muttered some observation about how good dinner was tonight and why didn't he try some?

Bayrd never failed to nod acknowledgement of their attempts, but his appetite, sharp-set less than half an hour ago, had been severely blunted by his half-accidental venture into the world of comparative linguistics.

'An-Kehlahr, Kalarr, ar'Kelayr,' he said aloud, pronouncing the word in Prytenek, in the burr of the Elthanek borders and finally in Old Alban. He seemed to gain more nourishment and flavour from those two syllables than from the several dishes sitting untouched in front of him. They smelt savoury enough – so whichever cook had prepared them was hardly at fault – but if the Talvalins, and the ar'Talvlyns before them, had one failing above all the others, it was the ability to brood about problems to the exclusion of all else.

Except perhaps, went the self-mocking joke, for an unlimited quantity of good-quality wine and a harper to play mournful music when their gloom needed inspiration. Even though there were no musicians in the council room, Bayrd was already halfway down his third bottle of strong white Hauverne, and there was still no sign that the alcohol was affecting him at all.

'Him again?' said Marc ar'Dru, as if he had ever expected it to be anything else. 'It's a coincidence, nothing more. Eat your supper or pass it down here – *ukh!*'

The grunt was a result of Eskra's elbow hitting him a solid jab just under the ribs. Bayrd caught his wife glowering at his best friend, and felt a glum smile tug at the corners of his mouth. They would gather like a solid wall of support behind him or each other when the need arose, but for the rest of the time they teased, they sniped, they insulted each other – and Mevn too, when she and her family came calling.

Married for only six years, but she had presented her husband with three sons and two daughters, the ar'Menez succession secured without a doubt, and she not an inch or a pound or a smile different for all of it . . .

'If it's a coincidence, then it's too much of a coincidence to be a coincidence.' He felt vaguely surprised – and more than a little pleased – to have spoken the convoluted sentence without his tongue tripping on the words or the sense. Assuming there was a sense in it in the first place.

'I, uh . . . Yes, of course,' Marc said, staring, then shook his head and returned his attention to the chicken and a replenished cup of Seurandec red. It was a clan-lord's privilege to drink himself legless on the most expensive vintage in his cellars – and it was his head in the morning, too – but a Companion and Bannerman knew his place, and often enough that was to keep watch over his lord and friend during a drinking-bout. Marc's chosen place in this instance was close to the Seurandec.

'Takes its time, that wine,' he muttered through a mouthful of chicken, 'but it works eventually.'

Eskra glowered briefly at him, but didn't dismiss her husband's words so easily as mere drunken rambling. She had seen him drunk before, for one reason or another, and this, though it lacked form a little, was not like drunkenness. The perception of truth often took strange shapes, and never more so than in those possessed of the Talent.

'What people dismiss as coincidence,' she said, not talking to any one person in particular but addressing the table in general, 'happens a great deal more frequently in life than in the storymakers' tales. *They* at least have a chance to reshape events. To make more sense. Or so they say.'

Marc swallowed the meat half-chewed and laughed dutifully, not entirely sure where all this was leading. 'But we have to put up with things as they happen?' he wondered, smiling. 'The way they write it in the Archive?'

Eskra echoed the smile, but her version of it rang a little false.

'Look at *Ylver Vlethanek an-Dunrath* for six years ago,' she said. 'Find something you know, some event you were involved with. Read it carefully. Then tell me how truthful the Book of Years can be . . .'

'Ah.' Marc rolled his eyes theatrically, trying to lighten the heavy mood in the room a little. 'That bad?'

'Worse,' said Bayrd gloomily. 'They're rewriting history.'

'Historians do that all the time,' Marc pointed out, waving a chicken-leg for emphasis. Perhaps because of the influence of the Seurandec he waved rather too vigorously, because part of the drumstick meat fell off, bounced once on his plate, bounced twice on the floor – and then disappeared doorwards between the teeth of one of the fortress cats. He watched the small black animal accelerate until it reached a comfortable distance out of range, then abruptly sit down, devour its trophy and start to wash. 'Odd, that.'

'What?' Bayrd looked up from his contemplation of the straw-gold depth of his own wine.

'Cats. No matter how many you think there are, it always seems like more.' He looked at the empty bone still gripped between finger and thumb. 'And it never bounces more than twice. It's as if they know. The cats, I mean.'

'The cats?'

'About the food. Bouncing.'

'I thought you said the cats were . . . Never mind. You're drunk.'

'*I'm* sober.'

'Drunk or sober, you two are sometimes worse than children,' said Eskra, eyeing them severely and knowing she was probably wasting her time. 'Even,' and she made the little sign to avert ill-wishing, 'even our two. And Harel isn't four years old yet.'

'I think,' said Bayrd blearily, 'that we've just been insulted.'

'And *I* think that I may have just insulted both my daughters.'

'Not that pair,' said Bayrd with a sudden grin that seemed to clear the wine-fumes from his head. 'Not for a few years yet. But the Archivists, now . . .'

'I wondered when you would get back to that. What are they doing?'

'Rewriting. No.' Bayrd shook his head, and since he had the

wine in one hand Eskra wasn't sure whether the sloshing sound she heard came from the bottle or inside her husband's skull. She took the charitable view.

'Put that down before you spill it. Now. What is history doing to annoy you?'

'Changing. The Keepers of Years are destroying all the oldest Archives and writing new ones.'

Marc ar'Dru whistled through his teeth. 'That bad indeed,' he said, but Eskra merely arched one curious eyebrow.

'And why would they do this?'

'Lies,' said Bayrd. 'Giving us a new past.' He stared thoughtfully at Eskra. 'Your past. Gelert's past. Even Kalarr's past. When the work is done, we'll always have been here. For a thousand, two thousand years. *Your* years. And our own past . . .'

He flickered his fingers in the air. 'Just dust on the wind. It might not be a good past, not all of it. Cowardice and treachery and murder. We were a fierce people then. But we had courage and honour too, more than many can claim. We had family. Ancestors. For a thousand, two thousand years. And now . . . Ashes and dust.'

Eskra stood up and walked quietly around to Bayrd's chair, then put her arms around his neck. 'Is that what's troubling you? We are a conquered people, loved. The conquerors can do as they please. And in a hundred years we and they will all be dust, and the people who live after us will not care one way or the other.'

'That's foolish optimism. Both your people and mine have long memories for history, and for the wrongs done centuries past. Trying to change it or forget it or destroy it will only make it worse.'

'Right now it doesn't concern me. I thought you were talking about Kalarr.'

'I was. Am. If they can change what happened in my lifetime, so that what I remember isn't what my children read, then what's certain any more? What will they say about Kalarr cu Ruruc twenty years from now? Fifty years? Five hundred . . . ?' Bayrd swivelled in his seat to look up at her. 'What will they say about *me* . . . ?'

'That you built a fortress and married a wizard,' she said. 'And were a credit to your name and your fame.' Eskra's arms tightened suggestively around Bayrd's throat and she smiled down at him with most of her teeth on show. 'I would strongly advise you not to question any of that right now. Just give me some of that Hauverne you've been hoarding. And have something to eat. We aren't done with my lord ar'Kelayr just yet.'

Eskra was right, but not in the sense she had intended.

She and Bayrd were roused first by the shouts of dismay from the courtyard below their chamber window, and then by a tentative tapping at the bedroom door. That paused almost at once, but only for the duration of a few seconds' muttered conversation, before resuming as a full-blooded hammering of fists. Even though Bayrd merely stirred muzzily and muttered something obscene into his pillow, Eskra went from sleep to consciousness like the striking of a spark and pulled the nearest quilt up to her chin.

It was just as well, for the door opened immediately afterwards and Marc ar'Dru's head came round the edge, his hair still sleep-tousled but his eyes shocked wide awake. There were no apologies for the intrusion at so early an hour, after what had been so late a night, just a blunt announcement of trouble.

'Ar'Kelayr is dead!'

For a moment Bayrd didn't move. Then he rolled over and opened his eyes to the brightness of the day, flinched and squeezed them shut again, and realised that the queasiness he could feel starting to churn in his stomach had nothing to do with his hangover. Despite the way it was pounding, the headache like two steel bolts in his temples was going to be the least of his problems this morning.

'Five minutes,' he heard Eskra snap, and then the click of the latch dropping back into place, as Marc beat a retreat in face of the tone of voice Lady Talvalin used only when questions and delay had ceased to be an option.

'Wake up.'

'I am awake,' said Bayrd, with all the haste of a man determined to avoid the vigorous shoulder-shaking which normally followed that command. The way he felt right now, any such shaking might very well dislodge the top of his skull.

'Then get up. You heard what happened?'

'I heard it. I just don't want to believe it.' The range of possible repercussions was appalling. For a guest to have died under his roof was one thing – such tragedies did take place, after all – but that it should be the man who had ridden to Dunrath with accusations of the death of his son was quite another, and that there had been no witnesses to their reconciliation . . .

And how had it happened? Sickness? That was hardly possible – ar'Kelayr had been in perfect health when he left the council room. Accidental poisoning? Unlikely, since he had eaten exactly the same as everyone else, and Heaven bear witness that the meat was fresh enough – those same chickens had been a part of the flock running out from under their horses' hoofs when Vanek and his people rode up to Dunrath's gates.

Deliberate poisoning . . . ?

'Not in my fortress, not without my permission, and not for the sake of my honour,' growled Bayrd. He flung back the covers of the bed with only a small groan at what the exertion did to his head, and reached for his clothes.

Vanek, Clan-Lord ar'Kelayr, lay on his back on the floor of the guest-quarters in Dunrath's north tower, his body as composed as though he had merely lain down to sleep on the floor rather than the bed. His eyes were closed and his face was calm. But for all that peaceful appearance his mouth hung slackly open, his skin was cold and pallid and his muscles were already stiff with rigor.

His Bannerman and as many others of his personal retainers as could force their way into the room were crammed against the walls. Their faces ran the gamut of emotions that might have been expected in such a situation: shock, grief, horror, anger against whatever had caused their lord's death, but for the most part no suspicion yet.

Except in the case of the Bannerman Reth ar'Gyart, whose eyes, narrowed and glittering with active and all too focused rage, followed Bayrd from the moment he entered the room.

Ar'Gyart was too old, too wise and, Bayrd was willing to believe, too courteous to make any accusations concerning one *arluth*'s involvement in the secret murder of another. Most men of any rank and honour would have followed Dyrek ar'Kelayr's example and fallen on their own daggers rather than be involved in such a deed.

If two enemies could not live under the light of the same sun, then there were duels, or feuds, or even clan-wars by which they could do something about it. Such attempts at killing had at least had the virtue, if killing could be said to have any, of being open and honest. The reasons for it were known to all, even if those reasons were poor ones; defiance was offered, challenges given and accepted, and when all was over the victor's honour would not permit him to glory over the survivors of the vanquished.

That, at least, in a perfect world of men of perfect honour and respect. Even in an imperfect world, it did not permit the hidden dagger in the dark, or the subtle poison dropped covertly into food or drink.

But this was just such an imperfect world, and there was always a first time. Unless Vanek had spoken to him last night – and from the look on the Bannerman's face no such words had been exchanged – all ar'Gyart knew was that Bayrd Talvalin had killed, or at least engineered the death of, his lord's son.

So why not the lord as well?

As Bayrd watched the *kailin* glowering down at him – there was a full head of difference in their height – he knew his innocence was something of which ar'Gyart had to be convinced. And he knew the task would not be easy.

'Get all these people out of here,' Eskra told the big man. Bayrd glanced hurriedly at his wife, then at the Bannerman, and to his astonishment saw Reth ar'Gyart's expression of unwavering anger and distrust flicker like a windblown candle-flame at the sound of the command. She was a woman, she was a wizard, she was the wife of an enemy and she was an Elthanek – and yet there was something about the way in which she gave the order that indicated she never even dreamed that he would disobey. But he hesitated all the same, and Eskra shot him a look that was halfway between severity and sympathy.

'Go on,' she said, making shooing motions as if to chickens, cats or children. 'Go *on*. I'm sorry. Truly. But there's nothing you can do.'

'They will go,' ar'Gyart muttered, dismissing the others with a jerk of his thumb towards the doorway. 'I will stay.'

'I . . .' Bayrd could hear Eskra weighing up the likelihood of successfully insisting, and saw her one-shouldered shrug as she threw the notion out. 'As you wish.'

'What are you going to do?' That was Marc ar'Dru from the doorway, and there was already a slightly nauseated twist to his mouth. He was a capable warrior, but even after all these years he was still squeamish about coldly-spilled blood, whether it was by violence or the activities of a surgeon.

'Nothing unpleasant,' said Eskra over her shoulder. 'Nothing that . . . have you sent for Master ar'Uwin yet?'

'On his way, my lady.'

'Good. He can do whatever else is necessary. With your permission, Reth-*eir*,' she said to the Bannerman, bending over the corpse and beginning all the small, compassionate, useless actions done by someone unwilling to believe the dead are dead until they have proved it for themselves. The pressure of finger at neck and wrist, searching for a long-stilled pulse. The hand held lightly at mouth or nose, in the hope of a faint trace of breath clouding the jewelled surface of a ring. The raising of an eyelid, in case there might be the merest flicker of life. And it was then that Bayrd saw her catch her breath.

'Ar'Uwin is . . . ?' asked ar'Gyart. Bayrd stepped in quickly, giving Eskra time to recover and conceal any further reaction to whatever she had seen.

'Dunrath's physician,' he said, 'and a good one.' The glower immediately came back to Reth ar'Gyart's face, dropping into place like the war-mask on a battle helm and looking just as impenetrable.

'Do not mock me,' he growled. 'What use is a physician now?'

'I would like to know how your lord died,' asked Eskra quietly, though Bayrd was beginning to suspect she already knew. 'That way we can make a start on learning who killed him.'

Then she raised a finger under the Bannerman's nose as he drew breath for a reply. 'And as for you, right now you will say *nothing*. You might have fewer apologies to make that way. Now. Lift him up, please.'

'Don't you already know?' asked Marc, knowing it would sound better coming from him than from Reth ar'Gyart. 'How he died, that is?'

Eskra flared up slightly, the only sign of strain that had so far ruffled her composure. 'Dammit, Marc,' she snapped, 'I'm a wizard, not a doctor! That's why I sent for ar'Uwin. Now if you can't talk sense, be quiet.'

They all watched as ar'Gyart raised Vanek's corpse from the floor as though it weighed no more than a child. No, not a child, thought Bayrd. A doll. A wooden doll. No child had skin so pale, limbs so inflexible.

'Stop,' said Eskra abruptly. 'Wait.' She bent forward and brushed a lock of Vanek's hair away from the nape of his neck. It hung loose, untied from its warrior's braid, so the man had been preparing for bed when . . .

Whatever it was had happened.

Then Bayrd heard Marc swallow hard, because what Eskra had revealed made a ghastly contrast with the tallow-coloured pallor of the face above it. It was a great blotch of black and purple bruise, mottled greenish where it met the paler skin. The discolouration began within the dead man's hairline, extended across the back of his neck and finally ran down out of sight beneath the collar of his shirt and tunic.

Bayrd cringed inwardly at the weight of whatever blow had been necessary to leave a mark like that, and at the same time wondered how anyone could have achieved it without being heard. Even during the frantic activity of getting here, he had noticed – with a little surge of respect for the man's old-fashioned ideals – that despite being given a room of his own in the guesting-suite, there was a heap of blankets by the door. While his lord had been under an enemy's roof, ar'Gyart had been his guard and slept across his threshold.

'So. Thank you, Reth-*eir*. If you would just lay him on the bed . . .' There was no change in Eskra's voice, no trace of shock that she had just seen where a man's spine had been smashed, and finally Bayrd could bear it no longer.

'Who could have hit him so hard?' he said.

'Hit him?'

'There.' He pointed, not with just one finger but with the whole hand. 'There, on the neck. Where the bruise is, dammit!'

'Nobody.'

'But . . .'

'Hush,' said Eskra, leaning over the body and attempting very gently to move the dead man's jaw. 'Perhaps,' she murmured to herself, taking a pillow and trying to press it up under Vanek's chin. Then she shook her head.

'I can't close his mouth yet,' she told ar'Gyart. 'Not without hurting—' She caught the useless word half spoken and smiled a wincing little smile. 'It always takes time to remember. But the rigor will ease. Then give him his dignity back.'

'The bruise, 'Skra-*ain*,' said Bayrd. 'What about the bruise?'

'That,' she said, straightening, 'is a stain, not a bruise. The blood stopped in his veins when he died. And without life to move it, it sank. Drained downward. Quite normal.'

'Normal . . .' Marc ar'Dru's was a tremulous whisper, and Eskra gave him, then Bayrd and finally ar'Gyart, the same sweeping, scornful stare.

'When you gentlemen kill, you should wait a while. A few days. See what happens to the dead meat you leave behind. It might make you less ready to do it again.' Wearily she scrubbed the knuckles of both fists into her eyesockets, perhaps in the hope that she would feel more awake, but from the look of her face when she finished, it didn't work. 'At least it tells me that he died where we found him.'

'But *when* did he die?'

Eskra straightened up. 'Cold. Stiff. Livid.' Her lips moved in silent calculation, and then she nodded. 'Yes. I'm quite certain. Lord Vanek ar'Kelayr died at some time between when we last saw him and when someone discovered his body.'

'And that's all?'

'What am I? Some sort of magician?'

'Certainly not a comedian. Eskra, there's a time and place for everything, even bad jokes. But not here, and not now.'

'Why not? This comes to all of us, sooner or later. And Vanek was laughing last night when he left us. For the first time in a long while, I think. I'd like to remember that. And anyway,' she met ar'Gyart's dubious gaze and held it with her own, 'I know we didn't kill this man. You know it. Marc knows it. Perhaps even Reth-*eir* knows it. So who did?'

'And how . . . ?'

Eskra Talvalin glanced at Bayrd. 'That much is obvious. You

73

saw me. I knew straight away that. . . I think I must have known all the time. Even before I saw. I've been trying to pretend that I was wrong. But—' once more she eased the dead man's eyelid open with her fingertips, 'how else? Except by the Art?'

Bayrd stared, and felt his headache and his queasy stomach fade amidst the shiver of reaction at what he saw. There was no white to Vanek's eye, and no pupil. Only a smooth, featureless surface that reflected like a mirror; but a mirror that was cracked from side to side by a ragged star-shaped fracture. It was as if someone had silvered an eggshell, and polished it – and then for some reason rammed a thumb straight through the centre. A score of Bayrd Talvalins looked back at him out of the splintered surface, impossible small, impossibly helpless, impossibly far away.

And then he heard the voice. It was inside his ears, inside his skull, as much a part of him as life and blood and breath, and it began to whisper, as enticing – and as deadly – as a vat of molten gold.

All the world is fractured, it said, a suave, sympathetic purr straight into his mind, *and all the light is running out of it. What you see is the reality of today and all of your tomorrows. This is all that life now is, and all that life will ever be. Without me. Without me . . .*

Without whatever power that lurked like a coiled serpent behind that persuasive voice, all the hopes and dreams of human existence would be reduced to nothing more significant than these shocked, minuscule faces. Bayrd and everything he knew and loved would become nothing but reflections in a shattered mirror . . .

Bayrd felt sick. He had watched only three men killed by magic before, and Eskra herself had slain two of them, both quite literally with her bare hand. Gerin ar'Diskan's uncle had collapsed when his life was eaten by a green flare of sorcery that only Bayrd ever admitted having seen. Eskra had killed on the first occasion to save herself from an armoured Prytenek warrior, smashing a palm-sized hole through his chest with no more effort than swatting a fly, and then again in mercy, this time to save a mortally crippled man from the pain she had no other power to ease.

But none of these deaths had ever looked like this, or made Bayrd feel like this. They might have been more destructive, more gruesome to look at, but they had not carried the same cold grey weight of bleak despair. Only the voice promised an alternative. Only the voice, fading now as if into a great distance, had any alternatives to set against the desolation, and even though they were unspoken, Bayrd knew they had to be better than . . .

His hackles rose.

It was a phrase he had often heard in storymakers' tales to describe the onset of sudden terror, and it was something he had thought to have experienced more than once himself: that shiver of apprehension starting at his neck and running like cold water all along his spine. He was wrong.

What he felt now was no shiver, but the clear and distinct feeling of every hair of his body standing on end like the fur of an enraged cat. It was a sensation like no other, shocking in its suddenness, in the crawling sensation that spread over his skin beneath his clothing, in the sudden onset of tremors in the pit of his stomach and a clammy chill on hands and face that he had felt only before a battle. He felt as though he was about to fight something for his life – or equally, run from it in terror.

And just as suddenly, as abruptly as a snapped thread once the voice at last fell silent, the feeling was gone again, and he was able to look at Vanek's body – and even the solitary gaze of that appalling eye – with nothing more intense than regret.

Other eyes were looking at him. Reth ar'Gyart was as scared as any man might be after encountering all the strangeness about Clan Talvalin that he had long suspected, and finding it all too real. Marc ar'Dru looked startled, as though Bayrd had done something possible but unlikely – at which Bayrd looked almost by instinct for the betraying blue sparks of sorcery drizzling like sapphire raindrops from his clenched fists, and saw none.

Eskra merely looked concerned. 'It is an outrage to any lord of this Land, whether his clan be high or low or House or Family, that any man who was once an enemy and who might have been a friend should be slain secretly while a guest beneath his roof,' she said to no one in particular, and just the mode and manner of her statement was enough to make her the new focus of attention.

For seven years, more or less, Eskra Talvalin *an-purkanyath*, the wizard, the lady spellsinger whose craft placed so much value on the weight and meaning of words, had spoken in staccato sentences as though those words were jewels of great price, not to be strewn broadcast without reason. Her brief, brittle phrases had become as distinctive as her pretty red-haired kestrel's face, as the blue and white of her husband's Colours, as the silver spread-winged eagle of his crest.

And that she should adopt such an orotund and prolix delivery – that she had breath to finish the sentence without gasping was a wonder in itself – had the same effect even on ar'Gyart as though she had found herself a table and then thumped her fist on it for emphasis. Bayrd and Marc, far more familiar with her normal mode of speech, were astonished. If she had ripped off a string of the foulest oaths it would have surprised them less, since the Lady Eskra with her finger shut in a door – as had happened in the past – was just as likely to give vent to her feelings as anyone else. Though probably in more languages . . .

'Reth-*an*,' she said, attaching that token of tentative friendship to his name for the first time, 'of your courtesy, go find Master ar'Uwin. We no longer need him.'

'And my lord . . . ?'

'Is safe,' said Bayrd quietly, looking at the dead man again. The spirit was flown and only the husk remained. Nothing that might be done to it could hurt Vanek ar'Kelayr any more. 'Reth ar'Gyart, trust us – trust *me* – this far at least. Your lord came here as an enemy because of the death of his son. He left us last night convinced that what had happened was not the fault of Clan Talvalin. Had he lived longer he might have become a friend.' Bayrd shrugged, dismissing the maybe that would never happen now. 'Who knows: even an ally. And that was why he was killed.'

The big Bannerman stood where he was for several seconds, beside the bed that bore his lord, staring at Bayrd. Not glowering now; just staring, balancing the lies and the truths and the ambiguous statements against what he thought himself. Then his right arm came up and slammed through the movements of a perfect high salute. That was all. He said nothing to Bayrd, nothing to Marc, and merely bowed his head respectfully to Eskra before stalking out of the room.

She nodded acknowledgement and watched him go, and only when the door had closed behind him did she draw in a long breath and release it in a slow, whistling exhalation through her teeth. 'A good warrior, that one,' she said, 'and a faithful retainer. But he frightens me like few men I have ever met.'

Once it had been said aloud, the others could agree, even though rank and dignity would not have allowed either of them to admit that Reth had left them feeling the same way. The older Bannermen, of whom he was one, were not creatures of reason, to be swayed by explanations. Those were merely words, and what were words but breath so often wasted on the air? Their sole currency was honour, and Alban honour could often be very blind to truth. Seeing Reth ar'Gyart salute and take his leave was like innocent prisoners, confined in a cell, watching the block and the axe picked up and put away unused, knowing all the time that if the axe fell wrongly, it would be unfortunate – but not something that could be put right.

In this life, at least.

Yes. In this life. Even if there was no possibility now that Vanek ar'Kelayr could be an ally, there was a chance where his Bannerman was concerned. If the big man's distrust had been disarmed – and since the more subtle of his emotions were as easy to read as those of a block of wood, Bayrd wasn't all sure about that – then he might well help Clan-Lord Talvalin take revenge on whoever had attempted to foul his name with the stain of murder.

Or he might not. There weren't enough people to blame, even though Bayrd's mind kept swinging with the inevitability of a compass needle back towards Gerin ar'Diskan. Gerin was Vanek's rival for land and power; he was Bayrd's enemy for . . . For more reasons than seemed sensible, and sheer spite not the least of them. But was he willing to give his support to someone like Kalarr cu Ruruc? A year ago Bayrd would have said not. And now . . . ?

Now he could not be so sure of anything any more.

'I don't know if it's Kalarr, or if it's Gerin, or if it's both of them,' said Bayrd Talvalin, moving pens and inkwells and sandcasters over the surface of the table, for all the world like an old general reconstructing a long-ago campaign. The remnants of the midday meal lay on its plates and dishes, the clean-picked bones of the slain; more chicken, the leftovers from last night cooked up in different ways, and a great deal of wine.

Since the realities of holding a domain in the Debatable Marches became plain to him, Bayrd was a great believer in the old analogy that nothing bad could be made worse by viewing it through the bottom of a wine-cup. And besides, the still-complaining echoes of last night's hangover needed some sort of palliative before today's took its place.

He thought of that as a joke, and tried it for size once or twice in the privacy of his own head. The joke fell flat. It wasn't as if he needed wine to help him wake up, or wine to help him sleep at night. It just looked that way, to those who came visiting to Dunrath and saw his hospitality. Even so, Bayrd had a feeling that the Ship-Clans held their own opinions, and spread them to any willing to pay the asking-price. They had become rich on trade, the Ship-Clans, and people listened to them.

It was hard to believe that in five years they had risen from being the Houses and Families – there were no real clans among them, either low or high – who were scornfully-titled *an-tlakhnin*, the Undeclared. The people who at the Time of Landing would neither burn their ships to prove willingness to stay, nor turn their ships and return the way they came.

And now, if the mood moved them, they had Alba by the throat. Bayrd scowled at the bottle of wine, three-quarters empty now, and considered all the other things that freighted in the Ship-Clans' vessels. Everything. The country had been at war almost since the keels struck shore, so that now, if it was not grown here, or mined here, or made here, it came across the sea. And if they became puppets dancing to another's fingers on the strings, then the Land would starve.

For someone like Gerin or Kalarr, who in their separate ways had both seen the land they thought was theirs stolen away from them, that would be a fine revenge indeed . . .

It was raining again. There were times when the so-called summer weather of this damned country seemed incapable of producing anything except rain, or drizzle, or mist. Always wet, always grey, always cold. A cold that could seep into a man's bones until not even the wine would keep it at bay. With a grimace that accepted his mood for what it was, Bayrd poured the last of the wine into his cup and thumped the bottle back on to the table. Better drunk than depressed, he thought; better drowsy from the wine than burning inwardly with frustration at the ease with which someone – cu Ruruc, or ar'Diskan, or perhaps even some other enemy yet undiscovered – had reached within Dunrath's walls and snuffed the life out of Vanek ar'Kelayr.

Except that for all the effect it was having, he might as well have been drinking the rainwater that sluiced audibly from the fortress gutters.

'No more wine,' said Eskra quietly, lifting the empty bottle and examining it.

'Why not?' Bayrd was ready to be truculent, given any reason whether good, bad or indifferent. 'It's not as if the stuff is making me drunk.'

'Exactly.' Eskra studied him with the same casual interest she had given the bottle. 'You're not even enjoying the taste. Just wasting it. Let be.'

All of that was true, and none of it amounted to even half a reason for a quarrel. Bayrd carefully shaped his mouth into an expression that might pass for a smile, and pushed the brimming cup away. 'Later, then,' he said. 'Where's Marc? Lost his appetite?'

'More than likely,' Eskra shrugged. 'He didn't seem in a good humour when I saw him last.'

'None of us did. But he knows well enough that a Bannerman Companion is supposed to attend his lord at table. He could at least have made his excuses.' Bayrd eyed the wine, watching the distorted reflection of the room sway and waver in its dark surface. *Like a mirror of blood*, he thought, and wondered uneasily where such a nasty concept had come from. There had been enough ugly reflections already, reflections both mental and visible.

'No matter.' He shook his head, as if the uncomfortable image was no more than a cobweb that had touched his face in the dark. 'I can't blame Marc for feeling the way he does. It's been a foul day. And I saw how much he was upset by what happened to ar'Kelayr. He's always—'

'Been queasy about killing?' suggested Eskra brutally, stalking to the window and gazing out at the gloomy weather. 'Not really. At least his reputation says otherwise.'

'Being able to fight well in the heat of combat isn't the same as looking calmly at what happened this morning,' said Bayrd.

'Very laudable. A clan-lord should always rise to the defence of his retainers. But let it pass. Besides, I know where he is.'

'Where?'

'There.' Eskra gestured at the heavily, leaded window, at its small, rain-streaked panes, and by implication at the sodden world outside. Bayrd got to his feet, noticing with a small, hastily-concealed sway that the wine *had* been taking effect after all, and followed the direction of Eskra's pointing finger. Then the corners of his mouth tugged down in an expression that could have been anything from annoyance to distaste. But whatever else it might have been, it was not a smile.

Though the two *kailinin* were barely recognisable through the thick, bubbled glass, Bayrd could see Marc ar'Dru and Reth ar'Gyart standing together near a sullenly-burning pyre. The rest of Vanek ar'Kelayr's retainers were drawn up in a double rank on the other side. A thick column of greasy smoke was wavering up towards the lowering sky, and he was momentarily grateful that the wind was blowing it away from the fortress. He had smelt enough burnt corpses for one year.

It was only right and proper that Lord Vanek's funeral should take place now. For one thing, he and his followers had arrived at Dunrath on horseback, and going home strapped across his saddle like a dead stag was scarcely the most dignified way to transport their clan-lord's corpse.

Bayrd had regretfully pointed out that no wagons, coaches or carriages were available to carry the body back. The reason was simple enough: he *had* no coaches or carriages in Dunrath's stable-yard, the Elthanek countryside being unsuited to any but the crudest wheeled vehicles.

And any wagons in the vicinity were now needed all the more to help carry material for the fortress walls and food for its siege-cellars. Whatever might happen, whatever might be ultimately believed about ar'Kelayr's death, he preferred to greet the eventuality from behind completed fortifications.

The news from Cerdor was just as bad, if somewhat more expected. Yraine and Erhal ar'Albanak were demanding that their respective supporters stand up and be counted. It meant that Bayrd's time was running out. For months now he had been balancing one side delicately against the other, while avoiding making a declaration for either. But from the sound of this latest report, failure to do something concrete would alienate him from both. Once the power struggle was over, and no matter who won, he and all of Clan Talvalin would have lost.

And now this.

Marc's presence at the funeral pyre was more than just a token gesture of respect towards a dead clan-lord. Here in Dunrath, the fortress and seat of his own lord, nothing like that could be seen as merely the action of a private person. Like it or not, he was Companion and Bannerman to Bayrd Talvalin, and for him to be where he was, and Bayrd not, said a great deal too much about the erosion of their friendship.

There had been his objections to Bayrd's legal and justified treatment of the reavers, and his comments both spoken and silent about Bayrd's failure to control the occasional flare of sorcerous anger. But all of that was reasonable enough, given the way the man's mind worked. It could not have become suspicion that Bayrd was somehow dissembling about his involvement in Vanek's death.

Or could it . . . ?

It could. And that night, in the Great Hall of Dunrath-hold and before far too many witnesses, it was made public knowledge.

Bayrd had always considered that what little remained of Clan Talvalin's gold would have been better spent on stronger walls, or a deeper moat, or almost anything except a feasting-hall and the elaborate ceremonial that such a splendid place encouraged. Time enough for ceremony and ritual when the land was at peace and there was time for such play-acting and dressing-up.

It struck him then and afterwards as ironic that it should have been Marc ar'Dru who was most insistent that the Hall be built at all. As new lord of a new clan, Marc had said when the plans for the fortress were still no more than lines on parchment, Bayrd should set some sort of example to his older peers. Something arrogant and flamboyant, otherwise they would show him no respect.

So it was built, as arrogantly and flamboyantly as Talvalin gold allowed. The flooring was coloured tiling arranged in elegant patterns, brought to Alba by the Ship-Clans and bought from them at no small price. The pillars were carved stone in the likeness of trees with strange small faces peering unexpectedly from their branches. The roof-beams were wood shaped like more branches, this time with birds and beasts among them. Only the walls were plain. After the discovery that naked stone in such a huge, vaulted space breathed a cold that struck to the bone, they were faced with panels of unadorned wood; but that austerity was concealed by costly draperies. When it was done, and Bayrd was morosely contemplating the depletion of his treasury, Marc ar'Dru stood in the centre of the Hall and pronounced himself satisfied. The example had been made.

That was ironic indeed, when one considered how much Marc had been against Bayrd's making a very definite example of the reavers . . . and most ironic of all that it should be Marc rather than Reth ar'Gyart who stood up once again in the centre of the Hall. This time he was fully and formally clad in the crest-coat of Clan Talvalin's Bannerman and chief retainer over the *elyu-dlas* Colour-Robe of House ar'Dru, and he rose to take his lord to task for murder.

It stilled the murmur of conversation instantly, and none of the guests – retainers, lord's-men, a traveller granted hospitality and shelter from the foul night outside only to find it fouler still indoors – none of them even deigned to make pretence of deafness. For one thing, there was no point in it. Marc spoke loud and clear, more so than truly necessary, and even though there was more regret than anything else in his voice, it was still something that no clan-lord cared to hear from the mouth of any man. Least of all from his Bannerman, and Companion, and good friend of many years.

'My lord,' said Marc, 'be assured that it is with sorrow that I say what I must.'

He paused, and it was a deliberate, theatrical hesitation that lit a small, hot spark of anger behind Bayrd's eyes. 'So say it, Marc-*an* ar'Dru,' he prompted into the silence, hating the need to do so and well aware that this was exactly the reason for the pause. 'And be assured that I accept your sorrow.'

This was not the man he knew. For all that their friendship had never been disrupted by a real quarrel, it had been edged with mockery and sarcasm often enough, especially when Bayrd and

Marc's sister Mevn had become lovers that first time. But it had never been like this. When Marc was angry, the anger exploded in all directions like brandy spilled on a brazier of hot coals, and was as quickly gone again. Bayrd had witnessed that, but had never experienced it. Not did he have to endure its brief flare now. Instead there was a calculated undercurrent of insult in Marc's voice, in every gesture, that was subtly but definitely wrong.

Marc sounded like an enemy; more, he sounded like Vanek ar'Kelayr had done yesterday, sour and querulous. When he moved and when he spoke, it was like a puppet from a clumsily presented play. An unsympathetic hand was manipulating the strings, and someone else's voice was mouthing unfamiliar lines.

Could it be Kalarr cu Ruruc's hand? His voice – or at least his words? Was such a thing within the sorcerer's ability?

Bayrd blinked and glanced at Eskra, no longer certain what was and was not possible any more. As usual when talking about the Art Magic, she had given him too much general information and not enough specific detail. Years of wasting her breath had ingrained the habit, because trying to explain the finer points of sorcery to Bayrd had become like teaching a tune to someone with no concept of music. And now that he needed to know . . .

He needed to know only that it was someone else. Because if his longtime friend truly thought all of this, it would be too much to be borne.

'. . . Undeserved butchery of children . . .' Marc was saying. '. . . Not content with a token punishment . . . arbitrary and high-handed . . . dishonourable familiarity with a dishonourable art . . . murder of a guest . . . though unprovable by law . . . to my own satisfaction and deep regret . . .'

There was more like that, much more. So much indeed that even Reth ar'Gyart, with his lord's gathered ashes in a wooden box on the table before him, seemed taken aback by his new ally's vehemence. For all Marc's frequent regrets and sorrows, some of what he was saying veered dangerously close to the sort of unfounded defamation that a clan-lord could answer only with his sword.

And had he been anyone else, Bayrd would have reached long ago for Isileth Widowmaker and let her grim grey blade speak for him. But this was Marc: his Companion, his Bannerman . . .

Much more than that; the *kailin* whom he and Eskra had chosen above any other to stand witness with them before the Light of Heaven when they married. The man whose House and Family had taken the place of any other relatives when their children were born. The man who had fought at his side, who had saved his life in battle – and in the dark days after Mahaut died, when the only ease for the empty hurt in his heart was the steel key to oblivion that every *kailin* carried at his belt.

And until this evening, he had been the same man. Now he stood here, in Bayrd's Hall and Bayrd's fortress and with Bayrd's colours on his back, and made such accusations before witnesses as he would have scorned to even think before.

'I cannot remain beneath this roof another day, another night, another hour,' said Marc, after another of those pauses that filled the Hall with a silence as darkly choking as black velvet. 'I was your Banner-bearer and your Companion and your conscience, but by the rumour of your deeds you have forfeited all my homage and service. Such doubts are cast upon your honour, and such shadows left in the minds of men, that for the sake of my own honour I instantly leave your service. Therefore, my lord Bayrd-eir, *ilauan-arluth* ar'Talvlyn, I defy you, and renounce my faith and fealty, freely given and freely taken.'

He put one hand down to draw the *tsepan* from his belt, and that was an action so freighted with grisly memory that it brought Bayrd to his feet. But the blade was not put to the use that he most feared.

Instead, Marc reached up behind his head and sheared off first the long warrior's braid at the nape of his neck and then the two smaller plaits of high-clan rank that hung beside his ears. 'I renounce my duty,' he said as the blade passed easily through each length of hair, 'to Heaven, if it guard thee and thee guilty; to any lord whose laws protect thee, and thee guilty; and to my honour, lest it make me fear to do . . .' His voice stumbled then, just once, and then recovered as strongly as ever. 'To do what must be done, to leave this past behind.'

Though Marc spoke clearly enough, his voice was quieter now, as though the enormity of this visible rejection affected him more than all the words had done. But it was only when he stripped off the Talvalin crest-coat, slashed the *tsepan*'s blade across the eagles embroidered in silver wire at its shoulders and then dropped the garment to formally tread it underfoot that an audible gasp of shock trickled through the Hall.

He said nothing else, and the click as the dirk returned to its scabbard was like the lock closing shut on the days that had been. Bayrd remained on his feet as his one-time friend turned his back and strode from the Hall. He felt strangely indifferent when he saw that all this had taken Reth ar'Gyart and the other ar'Kelayr retainers so much by surprise that they had to scramble to their feet and hurry in Marc's wake. Even then, the big Bannerman at least remembered himself in time to turn and give Bayrd the hasty Second Obeisance he was due. Marc had not done so. Marc had not even nodded. He had just taken his leave, and taken most of Bayrd Talvalin's reputation with him.

Reth had defied nobody, renounced nothing, and even amid the confused developments of the past few minutes, his manners had remained. The contrast stung. Then the big double doors thumped behind him, and he was gone.

Bayrd slumped back into his seat and stared at nothing. He wanted to be gone as well. Somewhere; anywhere; just so long as it was away from the gawking, speculative eyes of the people who wanted him to leave for no better reason than that they couldn't start to gossip until then. He could see no compassion, no concern, not even from Eskra, whose expression had gone as still and cold as one of the carved stone faces on the pillars.

No. That was not completely true. There was only one sympathetic face among them all – though it stung Bayrd to the core to realise that it belonged not to one of his household, but merely the traveller who was guesting here tonight. That pity surely came not from any honest source, but just from a lack of understanding. Yet any sympathy was better than none at all.

He reached his decision at once. He would leave Eskra to whatever was troubling her, because if she had not already confided in him then it was certain she had no intention of doing so just yet. He would leave all the others to their muttering. And he would offer this stranger a better welcome to Dunrath than he had been expecting, or had received so far.

In his heart he knew that it was just a feeble excuse to open another few bottles of wine, but Bayrd felt certain that he could stand on his head in a barrel of the stuff tonight, and it would never make him drunk enough to forget what he had just seen and heard. Of all the things he would have sworn were impossible, Marc ar'Dru breaking his allegiance had to be so near the top of the list as to make no difference.

The torn crest-coat with the dusty footprints on it still lay where it had been flung down, beside the three braids of fair hair that were unravelling a little now. Bayrd suspected that they might be still there tomorrow. Unless he gave an order that they be picked up, nobody except maybe Eskra would go near them. Such things were unlucky, and carried ill-luck with them as burnt wood carried soot. But he couldn't shape the words, not now. It would be like . . .

Like accepting what had happened.

And perhaps if he didn't accept it, and drank enough tonight, then when he woke up in the morning this would all have been a dream. Marc's coat would be intact, and his hair not self-cropped by that ugly shearing, and they would still be friends.

And no stain would have been put upon his honour by the one man whose blood he could never spill to wash it clean again.

'You there,' he said, standing up and beckoning the man forward, bleakly gratified to hear his voice completely steady. There was a moment of almost-comical confusion at this un-expected attention, the stranger looking from side to side and then behind him before pointing at his own chest and raising his eyebrows quizzically.

'Yes, you. Come with me. We'll drink wine together' – he was conscious of Eskra's head snapping around and her eyes burning into him – 'and you'll tell me travellers' tales. I'll have music played. A fair exchange, eh?'

Only his laugh rang hollow, but since he was already walking leisurely to the broad stairway that led up into the fortress donjon and towards the lord's private chambers, there wasn't time for it to matter.

Bayrd studied the traveller more closely as the man threaded his way from the back of the Hall towards the stairs. He was tall and lean, and though he seemed old enough for both his hair and his neatly-trimmed beard to be pure white, he bore himself as straight as a lance and moved with the quick assurance of someone many years younger. And hair could always be bleached, or tinted, or . . .

Bayrd closed his teeth with a click only he could hear. This sort of suspicion chased its tail like an excited puppy, round and round without going anywhere. The man had no weapons about his person, not even a belt-knife, so why worry? Though he carried a long black walking-stave decorated with a metallic inlay in the shape of a dragon or some other legendary creature, Bayrd suspected it was more for show than use.

At least, he corrected, eyeing the crystalline spike at one end and the long steel point at the other with new respect, for use as an aid to walking. He frowned inwardly, and made a mental note to have words with the gate-guards regarding concealed weapons allowed into the citadel.

What pleased him more was to see that Eskra had risen from her own seat and was coming to join them. Her features had relaxed from their frozen immobility and now shaped a tentative smile instead. Bayrd presumed that either she had come to some conclusion about Marc ar'Dru, or simply set the problem aside and decided to be pleasant as a welcome change in mood from the ugliness of the earlier part of the evening.

Of course, he considered cynically, *she might also be wanting to keep an eye on how much I drink tonight . . .*

With an inward shrug of the shoulders he dismissed the idea as unworthy – until an instant later when their eyes met, and unaccountably Eskra blushed. Bayrd felt his ears go warm, and once again he had the strange impression that there were times – and this was one of them – when his wife was able to read his thoughts as though they had been written in ink across his forehead. Other men said the same thing, in just the same rueful tone of voice; but Eskra was a wizard, which made it all seem rather more likely than not . . .

It was just a pity she hadn't performed the same conjuring trick on Marc.

He saw her shoot a cool glare along the length of the Hall, and her lips compressed slightly at the low buzz of conversation that had already sprung up, even before the clan-lord was properly gone from the room. 'They might have waited until you left,' she observed. 'Or have you forfeited so much respect already?'

'Perhaps. At least they didn't start while I was still in my seat.'

As he turned, Bayrd caught that same look of disapproval in the traveller's eyes – green eyes, the same clear, deep green as emeralds – and briefly wondered why he should have been concerned by the behaviour of another man's retainers. It was as if he had once been in some position of rank or power, accustomed to the respect of his subordinates, and was still displeased to see a lack of it in others. It was hardly a surprise; there could be few men of this age in Alba who had not held some level of command in Kalitz. 'Sir,' he said, 'I regret that you come to Dunrath at such a strange time.'

'Strange perhaps, lord,' said the white-haired man, 'but informative. There are such significant occurrences all over Alba; history is being made around us.'

If not quite written down, thought Bayrd, remembering how the Archivists of each clan were 'correcting' their Book of Years. 'Does history concern you so much?'

'All knowledge concerns me. For those with the wisdom to see it, learning can be an end in itself. Especially since I am . . .' He hunted for the word he wanted and failed to find it. '*An-erhan* is closest. Both a scholar and a traveller, neither exclusively one nor wholly the other.'

Bayrd hid a frown. The man spoke clearly enough, but strangely; part of it was his accent, but much more lay in his inflection and delivery. Both were oddly slipshod, slurred, almost careless, as different in their way from Alban as he spoke it now, as his accidental – and sometimes deliberate – Elthanek mannerisms would have sounded to his own grandfather.

And that word . . . 'Travelling scholar' indeed. It was Alban enough, though *arhan* would be the more proper pronunciation – except that Bayrd had never heard it before. Though that didn't mean as much as it might; each of the Three Provinces had their own words for things the others had no need of, and sometimes the only occasion they crossed borders was in the mouths of journeyers trying to show off. He guessed rightly, for Eskra smiled thinly and nodded.

'A Cernuan title,' she said. 'Indeed, you *have* come a long way to be here. And tonight of all nights. How fortunate for you.'

'Lady,' the traveller said, 'that is the art and science of the *erhan*.

To be where something may be learned at the best time it may be learned.'

'Just so. And a host should learn the rank and style and title of his guest.' Eskra let the words drift back over her shoulder as she walked past the white-haired stranger and on up the stairs. She paused and glanced back at Bayrd, not disapproving of the slip in protocol so much as surprised he needed reminding of it. 'Or is it your intention that he sit nameless at our table?'

Bayrd raised one eyebrow at her. It wasn't as if he had had the time to ask him anything so far; but she was right, as usual. 'No, indeed,' he said, ushering that guest to follow Eskra up the stairs. 'But you forget, my lady, that I have been given other matters to consider.'

'I do not forget,' said Eskra. 'Nor will I.'

'While I,' said the traveller, 'forget my manners.' He pressed one hand lightly to his chest as he bowed his head to her and to Bayrd together, then touched that same hand to his forehead as he straightened. 'My house-name is ar'Ekren. Call me Gemmel.'

5
Spellsinger

THE CLAN-LORD TALVALIN's private apartments took up two floors of the south tower, high in the central citadel of Dunrath-hold. That location made them a last redoubt which could hold off an army if the fortress fell. It also meant they were a place of retreat from the cares and concerns of the world, where they could be shut away beyond the massive doors of eight-inch crossed-ply oak.

Part of that space was taken up with the sleeping and dressing rooms for Bayrd and Eskra, and part was a personal office. An untidy office at that, strewn, at least on Bayrd's side, with a litter of smudged palimpsest parchment waiting to be scraped clean and used again, charred stub-ends of sealing-wax, and all the various other ink, brush, pen and sandcaster impedimenta involved in the everyday work of running a lord's domain.

That was something else he had learned about being Clan-Lord; for every time the swords ran red with the blood of the enemy, there were a thousand times when the pens ran black with the ink of the clerk. Though somehow that didn't have the same heroic spark . . .

Eskra's side of the office was a great deal tidier. It had to be; none of the fortress servants had yet been brave enough to rearrange, or dust – or even touch – the books of sorcery and the Art Magic that she kept on her shelves.

And then there was the retiring-room, as different from those other places of intimacy or work as it was different from the cold, echoing formality of the Great Hall. It was snug, luxurious in the small, human way of overstuffed chairs and scuffed footstools, the floor covered with those comfortable sorts of rug that would not be damaged – though they might possibly be improved – if a spark from the fireplace charred them.

It was a room where those whose days were hedged around by the requirements of dignity and duty and respect could finally kick off their boots, and sprawl like the citadel cats before a bed of glowing coals, and take their ease at last.

At least, if the events of that day allowed them to unwind enough to do so. Gemmel was certainly lounging in long-legged elegance, feet crossed at the ankles as he stretched back and sipped at his wine. Bayrd, however, was still sitting far too upright in his chair, working on the contents of his own cup with more determination than enjoyment. And Eskra . . .

Eskra had actually gone so far as to pick up an embroidery tambour – a pastime Bayrd knew she loathed – so that she looked the very picture of aristocratic domesticity. She had tucked herself on to one of the long couches that were set along the wall to either side of the big hearth, and from this vantage-point in the shadows was watching both men with the same quiet interest as the mottled beige-brown cat curled up in her lap.

There was music being played in the background as Bayrd had promised, for all that it was in a minor key, music to be gloomy by. The prolonged, melancholy chords of a rebec drifted between the ebb and flow of a softly spoken conversation, one that touched on every subject beneath the Light of Heaven that educated people might choose to talk about.

Or at least, almost everything. The subject of the past hour in the Great Hall was being studiously avoided for the time being, although Bayrd was more than willing to discuss the matter with this neutral witness, once Gemmel was ready to discuss it with him. The man was unlikely – and too obvious both in presence and appearance – to be a spy, and even if he was, he could learn as much by talking to any of the people in the Hall. Here at least he would have the advantage of learning the truth.

And perhaps pass on some truth as well.

'You must excuse my frankness, Gemmel-*erhan*,' said Bayrd, 'but for all your desire to be where history is in the making, you don't seem to have taken the proper precautions for travelling at such a time.'

'In what way, lord?'

'I mean, sir, that I would have expected you to come better prepared for . . . for trouble. In any one of a variety of forms. Your, er, significant events can't fail to be coloured by where they take place, and Alba is a violent country, ruled by violent men.'

Bayrd gestured at Gemmel's belt; it was an article of clothing, of adornment perhaps, with its handsomely engraved metal plates riveted to the leather. But it was innocent of the rings and buckles where a man might hang a sword and dagger. 'That's no weapon-belt. I'm surprised to see you travelling unarmed.'

Gemmel shrugged. 'I *am* armed, lord,' he said, 'and with enough weapons for safety, I assure you. Even though I don't carry them quite so blatantly as a *kailin* might. But,' he grinned briefly, 'your guards refused to let me carry them into the fortress at all. They still have them under lock and key at the Great Gate.'

He sounded more amused than anything else, and Bayrd, glancing at the black dragon-carved staff laid on one of the sword-racks set into the wall, suspected he knew where the humour came from. This man probably carried weapons so well disguised that even the best of his guards wouldn't recognise them for what they were. The *talathen* of Drosul, those Shadowthief masters of deception and secret slaying, had taught many things to those whose honour was less of a concern than their survival.

'It was,' Gemmel went on, 'a common enough request where strangers are concerned, of course. No cause for complaint, if the request is politely made – which it was,' he said in response to Bayrd's unspoken question. 'So, no more than a custom of the country, I thought. Especially in a time of troubles.'

If that phrase had been meant innocently, then he would not have grasped the significance of the hard look Bayrd shot at him. And if it was less than innocent, then the man was not only an *erhan* scholar but a consummate actor, for he met the glare eye to eye without so much as a flicker.

'And I continued to think it, right up to the moment when I heard that gentleman downstairs say what was on his mind.'

There it was again, all of a piece with the way he had made himself at home from the first moment of stepping into the room. A cool, assured confidence, rather than the slight apprehension which usually accompanied most people into the presence of an unfamiliar high-clan lord nowadays. Gemmel ar'Ekren seemed as much as ease in these surroundings as did Bayrd himself.

At the same time, Bayrd himself felt more at ease talking to this stranger – and as an equal, rather than just a guest whom he was indulging on an errant whim – than he would have done with any of his own retainers. The retainers, the lord's-men, the musicians and even the silent servants who drifted about the place pouring wine and lighting candles, would all have their own private opinions regarding what had happened here this past two days.

Some of them would believe in him, as they had always done; others would feel that all of their uncertainties after his marriage to an Elthanek wizard had been strengthened; and there would be a few for whom Marc ar'Dru's outburst and departure confirmed what they had always thought. There would be fewer supporters in Dunrath-hold come the morning and, of those who remained, some would still be supporters in no more than name.

But Gemmel, even if he knew enough about both sides to form an opinion, would not care one way or the other.

'I'm sorry,' Bayrd said, with the abrupt realisation that someone had asked a question and was still waiting for a reply. 'Again, if you would?'

'Which is correct, lord? Talvalin or ar'Talvlyn?'

'Talvalin, sir. Always Talvalin. The name of an honourable high clan, whatever else you may have heard.'

'And the other?'

'Is in the nature of an insult,' said Eskra, with all the indifference of one long grown used to insults.

'How so?'

Bayrd felt the corner of his mouth quirk downwards, just a little. *Persistent, aren't you?* he thought. *I would have imagined a seeker after knowledge to be more subtle.* Eskra might have been unconcerned by the question, but he at least was still smarting that the last person to use that particular gibe had been Marc ar'Dru. And then he realised that the man's enquiry had been innocently meant, that he really didn't know.

'One is the name of my blood-clan now. The other was that of my line-family as I used to be. To call me by one and not the other—'

'Makes a derogatory comparison. I see. Of your courtesy, lord, I regret—'

'The question was not asked.' Bayrd was in a mind to be magnanimous. 'The subject was never raised.'

'Except that it was.' Eskra looked first at one and then the other. 'Master Gemmel. My husband's Honour-Codes do not permit him to ask this; they presume that all other men are just as honourable as he. But he is Alban. I am not. So I ask – of *your* courtesy – that you remember the insult. And avoid it even when you leave us.'

'A gracious request, lady,' said Gemmel. 'And graciously asked, for which I thank you.' Once more he made that elegant gesture of touching breast and forehead, and nodded his head forward in lieu of a proper bow. 'And if I could give you some advice as fair exchange?'

Eskra raised her eyebrows at him in silent query.

'You would,' he said, 'make a more colourful and lasting embroidery if you had troubled to put a thread into that needle.'

Bayrd had not thought he would laugh out loud for a long day and more; and maybe awareness of that doleful lack was a reason for his response to what was, after all, a fair but ultimately fairly feeble joke. The sudden snort of mirth hit him coming up just as a mouthful of wine was going down. Its resultant explosion was uncontrollable, messy, and the cause of still more spluttering laughter. Before it was done, his cup refilled, and he and his surroundings mopped down by solicitous servants, Gemmel was chuckling as well.

Even Eskra – her cheeks and ears bright pink with embarrassment – deigned to give him a rather tight smile. But that was all. There was more anger in her eyes than Bayrd liked to see, and it had nothing to do with him being drunk – which he was not, and they both knew it. The cause was something else: Gemmel perhaps, and his unfortunately sharp powers of observation. Or something else entirely.

Bayrd sighed. Whatever it was, he would hear all about it later tonight. But he was glad that the ice had been so irrevocably broken. He was still hurt and angry over Marc's public accusation and betrayal – because that was what it had been: a Bannerman Companion was supposed to stand by his lord no matter what that lord might do – but he was no longer capable of brooding on it to the same degree. That was a relief of sorts.

The music changed. It was still in the minor, but no longer the slow iron moaning of the rebec. These were the chilly measures of a spinet, as austere and beautiful as intricate cobwebs spun by a steel spider, and the words were scored for the high purity of a counter-tenor.

> *At last the glittering Queen of Night*
> *With black caress kills off the day . . .*

Bayrd listened for a few moments, half-turned in his seat so that he could see how, beyond the heavy windows, evening slid from rose to purple and died in the indigo of night. Somewhere out in the darkness a fox yapped. Stars glittered in the black vault of heaven – and for some reason a slow shiver ran through him. He knew the song – it was from a play he liked – and he had heard it many times before. But he had never felt this reaction until now. So it could not be the song. Or could it . . . ?

But it was as if the fire was throwing less heat than it had done until now, and the cold of the great cut stones was leaching out of the fortress walls and into the room.

He glanced at the others to see if they had felt it, or noticed anything amiss, and saw nothing. Eskra and Gemmel, their brief flash of difference forgotten or at least set aside, were in the middle of some convoluted anecdote about a man and a weighted barrel:

". . . then," said he, "since I had forgotten to let go of the rope, I went up again. And halfway up I met the barrel coming down . . ."

For all that it was no more than a funny story, Bayrd had a nasty feeling that when all the layers of the story were peeled away, the man at the end of the rope – and the butt of the joke – would be himself.

Gemmel ar'Ekren had long since gone to his bed in the guest-quarters of the north tower, and the musicians and other servants had been dismissed; but Bayrd and Eskra still sat in the shadowy warmth of the retiring-room, together and yet alone with what-ever thoughts might fill their minds.

For all his determination to get thoroughly drunk, Bayrd had fallen far short of the goal. It was difficult to drink constantly when what he wanted to do was talk, and where Gemmel was concerned talking was the thing to do.

The man was an elegant and entertaining storyteller, with a fund of anecdotes involving family, friends, rivals, enemies and even family pets, and it was obvious within the first half-hour that he was deliberately using that talent. To repay the Lord Talvalin's hospitality, perhaps, as he might have sung for his supper. But it seemed much more likely that he was covering the unpleasantness which he had witnessed with a veneer of amusing memories. It was just a veneer, nothing more; but it had been enough, tonight at least, to blunt the sharpness of the hurt.

And yet it was the sheer unreason of it all that made the edges so very keen. For a friend . . . Bayrd stared at the crumbling embers in the fireplace and realised that it was the wrong approach to take. Thinking with the heart, not with the head. Just remember that it's always the head they cut off.

Very well then, set aside the friendship. Be cool, be political, be the clan-lord who has successfully balanced the two most powerful factions in Alba for the past six months, and so far as both sides are concerned is still perfumed with the scent of roses.

So then: why so sudden? Why no warning? Why no intimation that one's right hand was considering rebellion?

Because that was the true purpose of a Bannerman and a Companion: to be the right hand of his clan-lord. The man who was his lord's conscience, and the guardian of his honour. And the *kailin* who, for the sake of that lord's honour, would set aside his own honour and do those deeds that the lord could not.

Except that Marc had refused, in a back-handed sort of way, to do any such thing.

There had been the merest, briefest suggestion that Kalarr cu Ruruc's death would be a benefit to all, and with that, the unstated implication that Marc should cause it. He had not said 'yes', and he had not said 'no'; but he had said, 'only if it will not affect my honour', knowing full well that because it would, Bayrd would not give him the order.

Honour. That was always the stumbling-block.

It was the same with Gerin ar'Diskan. Bayrd had fought his father in a formal duel, for some reason he could no longer remember, but to fight the son as well would smack too much of bounty-hunting. The only acceptable alternative, to declare clan-war, would merely be a suicide more protracted than the use of a

96

tsepan, since Clan ar'Diskan's warriors outmatched those of Clan Talvalin by a factor of four to one – and that was even before their respective allies were taken into consideration. Even so, Bayrd was growing cynical enough to believe that this might be another attempt to manipulate his actions, as had happened with the reavers. But he was not going to be drawn again.

Otherwise this would have been the perfect time to declare a small war. The land was without the strong hand of an Overlord, and the two candidates for the position seemed more concerned with destroying one another than with the ultimate responsibility of bringing peace through a stable rule. Even without Gemmel's accidental – if it had *been* accidental – slip of the tongue, these days were becoming uncomfortably close to the old Time of Troubles, the Age of the Country at War. Especially since there were other enmities among the Albans, far older than the infant hatred between Talvalin and ar'Diskan.

There were Clans and Houses and Families whose hatreds were so ancient that they would think nothing of defeat, if only they could be assured of dragging their enemies down with them. Obliteration was a sweet thing to embrace on the way into the darkness, if only it included one's dearest enemies.

It was small wonder that the Cernueks and the Pryteneks and the Elthaneks looked on in amusement as their erstwhile conquerors faced each other down like duellists. *They* had all fought enough for decency, and then just as decently laid down their arms. For a people not carrying the leaden weight of the Alban Honour-Codes, life in respected defeat was far sweeter than any amount of honourable death . . .

And still none of it explained what bug of madness might have bitten Marc ar'Dru.

But the more that heavy satin silence of near midnight hung about them, the more he began to suspect that Eskra knew. Or could guess, from the depths of her wisdom in the Art. Cu Ruruc and ar'Diskan might both have gained from what Marc ar'Dru had said tonight, but Bayrd had not forgotten – and might never forget – the strange compulsion that had spoken so persuasively in his head as he stared at the shattered lens of Vanek ar'Kelayr's eye.

What was it the players said? 'The world is fracted and corroborate': shattered all apart and then renewed. But those

97

broken pieces may not necessarily have been put together in the same shape. Just *a* shape, which is not the same thing at all.

Bayrd had long learned that there were many pleasures about marriage besides the obvious; and one of those was that a husband and a wife could, after some years, almost hear one another think. With Eskra it probably came easily enough, what with the Art Magic and the sorcery and all the rest. But for Bayrd, when it happened it was something worth attending to. And it was happening now.

She was ashamed of something.

Not the children; it was only the circumstances of the past two weeks that had kept Harel and her little sister Marla so much in the background. Not the wine; that was more a long-running joke between them than any real criticism.

But the more Bayrd tried to think of something innocuous, the more his mind kept veering back to what he was certain that it really was. Something that gave the lie to all his nurtured theories, made his enemies innocent – at least of one offence – and reminded him of what Eskra had been before they married. What she still was. What she could do and whom she could influence, far more easily than Kalarr.

Marc.

And he did not know how to be sure if he was right or wrong in his suspicions – except to ask directly, and risk a loss of peace far worse than any war.

Bayrd spent a long time sitting hunched beside an iron rack of hot rocks in the citadel's bath-house, as if some of what was troubling him might melt away in the steamy heat. It didn't. Afterwards he lay sleepless and swathed in towels far into the short summer night, wondering how a man could ask his wife if she had somehow engineered the betrayal of a dear friend's trust; and if the response was 'yes', then *why* . . . ?

In the end, it always came down to why.

He could guess that Eskra was awake as well. She was beside him, but as far from his side as their great bed allowed, and the barrier of mistrust lying between them was like the naked sword of the old story. She knew something was wrong. And perhaps she knew exactly what was wrong.

That didn't make matters any easier.

This was a stupid situation for them to be in; a situation where the right word might be the first step towards sorting matters out. And yet to say any word at all, and discover it to be the wrong one, might also be the first step towards escalating this already-awkward issue into the first major – and probably worst ever – quarrel of their married life.

Bayrd Talvalin smiled grimly to himself in the silver and black of the moonshot darkness. Alba, the Land on which his people had set their claim for less than ten years, was already simmering on the edge of civil war, and he was worrying about a domestic dispute. Granted, it was somewhat different from the norm, but even so . . . His smile grew wider, if no more humorous.

Then it froze on his face as he abruptly and completely became wide awake.

Eskra had not moved, and from the rhythm of her breathing she had drifted at last into an uneasy slumber. But asleep or awake, she was certainly not the cause of the small metallic sound he had just heard.

It was one of those noises which needs to be heard in the wrong place or at the wrong time, and when they are, they act as an immediate focus for all the senses. The rasp of a sword unsheathing right behind you; a twig snapping underfoot somewhere in the undergrowth; the protracted creak of a floorboard in a supposedly-empty house.

And the tiny scrape in the silence of three hours past midnight as someone softly and stealthily tries the latch of your bedroom door.

The servants knocked and waited for permission. The children did neither, but were noisy about it. But thieves – or assassins – would be very far from noisy. They would sound just like this. And in the present climate Bayrd knew which of the two was more likely. He rolled sideways out of bed and reached for a robe, found nothing, and wrapped one of the scattered towels tightly around his waist instead.

It wasn't such a foolish gesture of modesty as it seemed. There was something frightening beyond all proportion to the threat about meeting a possible armed assailant in nothing but bare skin. It went beyond mere nakedness and into a horrible sense of vulnerability. But it was also a feeling that was easy to neutralise; that length of cloth around the hips helped a little.

And the cool weight of a sword in each hand helped a lot.

Unlike his robe, the *taiken* and *taipan* had been in their proper place, secured by their respective belts to the weapon-rack by the head of the bed. For all that the shortsword's locking collar had a tendency to stick in the throat of the scabbard, tonight its curve of blade came out smoothly, with only that momentary catch-and-scrape that no amount of oiling or polishing had ever managed to cure.

And Isileth . . .

Isileth Widowmaker slipped from her black battle scabbard with a sound like a steely intake of breath and an ease that was almost eager.

There was just enough moonlight for Bayrd to catch the shift of shadows as the door's latch lifted again. That second attempt had no more success than the first, because – wanting to keep a prospective squabble between their lord and his wife at least one door's thickness from the servants – he had dropped the inner bar.

Of all the bolts and locks meant to keep intruders out, that one was the least significant. It was no more than another latch, though one without a handle connecting to the outside. It rattled as the door was tested, a tiny noise, but one which brought Bayrd's eyebrows together in a frown at the strength needed to shift one of his citadel's ponderous oak doors in its frame.

Then he saw a blade, or at least the moonlight reflecting from its surface. A thin, flexible strip of steel had been forced between the edge of the door and its jamb, and was questing up and down for the obstruction. It would never move a horizontally sliding bolt, but if it came up beneath the inner latch . . .

As Bayrd realised what was happening, and cursed himself for not making the move far earlier, he discarded stealth for speed and threw himself into a shoulder-rolling dive across the corner of the bed in an attempt to slam one of the three main bolts into place.

And even then he wasn't quick enough.

Both latches snapped up together and the door burst open, spilling armed men into the room. How many, he didn't know for sure. They were hard to count and even hard to see, because all of them were dressed and hooded in the same charcoal grey, the very colour of shadows in moonlight. Quick as moths they flitted out of the frame of the open doorway and into the shadows where they belonged.

Talathen, said a voice in Bayrd's mind. Shadowthieves. From Drosul. But how? By whose command? And why?

It wasn't assassination, or he'd be dead by now. A *kailin* on the bloody business of feud might have met him honourably, sword to sword, but where these mercenaries were concerned, the Honour-Codes only got in the way of completing whatever task they had been hired for. They'd have opened the door all right, but the only thing to come through it would have been arrows or poison-tipped darts. Then if they didn't want his life, what *did* they want?

Events had already happened so fast that Eskra was still no more than drowsily aware of them. But she was shocked out of sleep by grey-gloved hands dragging her across the bed, and her scream answered Bayrd's silent question plainly enough. They wanted hostages. And that meant there would be others.

After his children.

Somebody, somewhere, was playing the Great Game, and had stepped it up by several levels of intensity. The surge of anger that came boiling up inside his eyes turned the moonlight scarlet and the shadows to a flaring incandescent purple. Images moved against the eerie blaze of unlight. Five of them were grey; one was pale and struggling against the rest.

Whether it was rage, or outrage – or even sorcery – that had come to his aid, Bayrd Talvalin didn't know or care. But he was no longer blind in the darkness, and that was the only thing that mattered.

He dropped his shortsword with a clatter against the floor and put both hands to Widowmaker's hilt, and when he moved, it was almost as if the *taiken* was dragging his hands and arms along, rather than being propelled by them. But in either case the final result was the same.

The cut was *tarann'ach*, the striking thunderbolt. It was a full-force focused strike downward into the angle of collarbone and neck, meant to defeat the great shoulderplates of Alban battle harness. But despite his sinister grey mask and clothing, the shadowy figure under the long straight blade was not wearing any armour at all.

And for Isileth Widowmaker, mere flesh had never been an obstacle.

The longsword's point rang against the wall and a fluttering spray of sparks marked where the metal gouged the stone. There was no such trace to show where it had also sheared through meat and bones. For a moment there was no apparent change in the grey silhouettes clustering around the bed. Then one of them sagged, slithering forward and sideways both at once in a way that should have been impossible.

The man fell apart.

The Shadowthief's torso had been severed diagonally from shoulder to opposite hip, through ribs and spine and breastbone and all of the soft inner organs they contained. He hit the floor in two separate pieces, and spilled out a ghastly mess that glistened in the moonlight.

Then Eskra managed to wrench one hand free of her captors, and a second later Bayrd heard an appalling bang. It was a sound sharp as the clapping of hands, but magnified a thousand-fold so that the windows rattled and his ears rang from the concussion, and another of the *talathen* staggered away from the bed.

At least his body did.

For an instant there had been a nimbus of emerald-green fire surrounding the man's head, and in that light Bayrd had seen – and wished he had not – the grey hood distend explosively as something atrocious happened to the skull it covered. Now it dangled down between his shoulderblades, a limp sack with nothing solid left inside it.

Bayrd was grateful that the corpse fell to lie on its back with the sagging horror underneath. For all its speed, that had been an ugly way to die. He was grimly accustomed to the destruction wrought by edged weapons, but this was different. It was a shocking enough sight that his red rage began to cool. His eyes began to darken again, and the night crept back across the glare that had filled the room and allowed him to see the *talathen*.

Until Eskra snapped a word of power and there was a sharp crackling noise. All of the oil-lamps in the room ignited at once, and there were no longer any shadows for the Shadowthieves to hide in.

Bayrd could hear a short, vicious rattle of words from one of the three surviving *talathen*. He had guessed right: the language was Droselan. None of them had drawn any weapon so far, and the snarled command was a reminder not to do so even now. It made him more and more certain that their purpose here was the taking of captives rather than lives. Definitely a move in the Game, though not an honourable nor especially acceptable one. But had their employer forgotten to warn them about the consequences of breaking into any *kailin*'s room after dark, never mind that of a clan-lord?

Or had the omission been deliberate? That, too, might be perceived as an acceptable move.

'Halt!' he shouted in the parade-ground bellow he hadn't needed to use for a long time. '*Teyy'aj hah! Kagh telej-hu, taii'ura!*' The Droselan words came back with surprising ease, but then it was a language where orders and the imperative mode seemed more common than the softer forms of speech. 'Drop all your weapons! Drop them now!'

'We will not, ar'Talvlyn,' said the one who had spoken before, who seemed to be some sort of leader. His Alban was precise and without accent. 'But we will leave here now. You will let us go, unharmed and without hindrance.'

Bayrd shifted Isileth in his hands, flexing his fingers on the long hilt, for the next cut. 'Give me a reason why,' he said.

'*Né, né. St'teyyn ess'kai djuh, tulath,*' said Eskra, the Droselan Bayrd never knew she spoke slurred, venomous and perfect. 'Give *me* a reason.' She spoke in a voice that Bayrd had never heard her use before, and would be happy not to hear again. If there were ever words in the sound that Isileth's edges made as her blade left the scabbard, they would sound like this. 'Tell me why I shouldn't blow your backbone through the wall of this fortress.'

Her right arm was levelled at the *talathen* like a weapon, hand open and palm towards them, and green sparks writhed over its skin and spat across the spaces between her fingertips.

'Just one reason,' she said again, pulling the bed-sheets up around her naked shoulders with one hand. The other hand didn't waver. 'One. But make it good.'

The chief *tulath* hesitated, looked at the still-open door as though measuring his distance to it, glanced back at that ominous crawl of sparks, and then thought better of any such attempt to get away.

'We have your children,' he said simply. 'How would you prefer that they die?'

'How would *you* prefer to die?' countered Bayrd. 'And how slowly?' Blood and other fluids streaked the grey gleam of the blade in his hands, and the stench of opened entrails was heavy in the air. It was the Game. It was, it was. But how to counter such a move . . . ? 'There's nowhere for you to go.'

The hard, calculating eyes behind the slits of the grey mask looked him up and down, and twinkled briefly as though a chilly smile had crossed their owner's face.

'Ah, but yet there is, ar'Talvlyn,' he said, and now that smile was very audible. There was none of the desperation that Bayrd had hoped to hear, no attempt to make a deal with the man carrying the sword. Just an unpleasant assurance that the scales were weighted in his favour.

'We can go out of this fortress, and by a more direct route than we came in. You have no guards left alive on this level of the citadel. Understand me. If we do not walk from this room, then Clan Talvalin dies with you. Because your witch-wife is merely an additional baggage. We took the children first.'

'Bluff,' said Eskra, but even Bayrd could hear the uncertainty in her voice.

'Can you be sure, witch?' said the *tulath*. 'Really sure? How sure can you really be? Consider which of us was fast asleep until a few minutes ago. Consider what I lose if you're right.' The man leaned casually back against the wall, folded his arms and looked at them both. 'Now consider what you lose if you're wrong. Then say "bluff" again. If you dare.'

Slowly the sparks died from Eskra's hand, and slowly she lowered it as though returning a weapon to its sheath. Bayrd watched her resolve crumble like a sandbank in a high tide. Though they would be better bargaining-counters alive, there was no doubt that Harel and Marla would be killed if it became necessary. *Talathen* had not earned their reputation through idle threats and unkept promises.

And this one had chosen his argument cunningly.

It was a secret concealed from all but the closest of their confidants – but then one of the well-paid talents of the Shadow-thieves was to learn about such things. They were master players in the Game, where the death of an opponent might well be an admission of defeat, while the use of him, the bending of his will . . . By something like this. After Marla's long, difficult birth, Master ar'Uwin the physician warned Eskra not to hope for others. Harel and Marla Talvalin were the only children she and Bayrd had, or would ever have.

But whether this *tulath* knew it for certain, or was just hazarding his and his comrades' lives on a common guess, Eskra would never take the risk. She wouldn't let Bayrd take it either.

And the masked man knew it. He was a bold one, a skilled player. Perhaps even a Master. There were some, still. But part of their Mastery was in keeping their skill concealed. As this one's skill had been hidden, until it was needed to save his neck.

He bowed low, secure enough in his safety that he could offer the back of that neck to Bayrd's blade. 'Thank you, lady,' he said, all greasy insincerity now. A thought seemed to strike him as he straightened up, and he chuckled behind his mask. 'Our patron thanks you too. That look on your face has confirmed what was no more than a rumour.'

So he had been guessing after all. Bayrd's teeth clenched; the weapon of his children in an enemy's hands was sharp enough already, but this bastard had just put an extra edge on it.

Truly ruthless men, like the Albans of three or four generations past, would not have let the holding of hostages stand in their way. Children were a renewable resource. But Talvalin children of the blood-clan were not renewable.

Now the Shadowthieves knew it. Soon everyone would know it. The *tulath* could strike his own deals with as many 'patrons' as he chose, and sell the merchandise of information to the highest bidder. And still neither Bayrd nor Eskra dared do anything about it.

'Your choice, ar'Talvlyn.' The man spread his hands expressively. 'Do I and my companions leave? Or are you the sort of man who likes to gamble for high stakes?'

'Go,' said Bayrd, his voice little more than a whisper. 'Go far, and go fast. Just remember. Soon or late, I will find you. Whoever you are, wherever you go, I will find you. And then we'll have a reckoning. Just the four of us. You, and I, and the ladies.'

Bayrd could see the glitter of the man's eyes as he glanced at

Eskra. And then, realising what was meant, they went wide and stared at Widowmaker. The longsword was still poised in striking stance above Bayrd's hands, like an unhooded hawk waiting for the last mistake the *tulath* would ever make. The Shadowthief knew it and began, perhaps, to suspect what Bayrd Talvalin had known all too clearly this past few minutes.

He was not just holding the sword. He was holding it back.

Whatever little parting witticism the *tulath* might have ventured died on his masked lips in that instant. For all the strength of their position, he and his henchmen had been lucky. So far. And luck can be stretched only so far. Without another word, without even a derisive salute of farewell, all three of them made for the door.

A slow, sullen rumble passed through the room. Once again the windows rattled, and even the heavy door swung a few inches on its iron hinges. It was a sound like the sonorous reverberation of distant thunder, a herald of the summer storms that could sweep in from the Blue Mountains and be gone within an hour. But that made no sense.

Bayrd chanced a sideways glance at the window. The moon, low to the horizon now, hung in a cloudless sky. There was no sign of impending rain, much less a storm of the magnitude that rumbling had implied. Even the air lacked the sticky heaviness he had come to know all too well.

Instead it seemed charged with the tingling of discharged energies that usually *followed* such a storm, and especially after some vast thunderbolt had bridged the distance between Heaven and Earth, and left a glowing clangour like the echoes of light imprinted on the eyes of everyone who saw it. Then Bayrd saw the bedroom door move again.

The first slight movement had been strange enough, though explicable as some freakish effect of the thunder – or maybe an overspill of the leashed magics that still seethed within the room. But the second time was ominous.

Every door in Dunrath-hold was at least eight inches thick, a triple ply of oak braced and studded with iron, each layer of beams set at right angles to the next so they could not be split straight along their grain. When the clan's finances allowed, Bayrd intended to sheathe them all in iron; something that even Marc ar'Dru, that notorious spender of other people's money, had thought both excessive and unnecessary. The doors, he had said, were strong enough as they stood. Certainly they were weighty enough, a weight that sometimes made them difficult to open and shut.

Even more certainly, they did not swing to and fro with every passing breeze.

Bayrd watched the trio of *talathen* as they walked towards it. Towards an open door. Towards their freedom. And all he could think was that he would not have gone near that door right now, not for all the gold of the Three Provinces.

But he watched events develop with interest. It was the cold, malicious interest of a man whose home had been invaded, whose family had been threatened, whose servants had been killed, and who now had a chance to witness the perpetrators of those acts find their own way to hell. And he was not disappointed.

The door swung back from under the nearest *tulath*'s hand just as the man reached for its handle. It was almost closed now, and it had moved as smoothly – to Bayrd's mind – as if the corridor beyond it had just drawn in a long, deep breath.

The Shadowthief spoke aloud for the first time when he swore at them, snarling something in gutter Droselan that might, under the obscenities, have been a warning for them to stop their funny business. He took a step closer, gripping the iron ring of the handle to wrench the door open again. There was no need. Before the man could throw himself aside it flew open of its own accord.

And it was moving as hard and fast as a poised hand slapping an unwary fly.

As two hundred pounds of iron and timber smashed ponderously against the wall, a single half-formed shriek of terror was swallowed up by the massive boom of impact. After that, only liquid sounds remained.

The hinges of the doors of Dunrath-hold were so designed that when they were fully opened, each door lay almost flush to the wall. The space behind them was usually no wider than a finger's thickness. And this door was no exception.

Bayrd had seen plays in which part of the comedy business involved one character or other being caught by an opening door. He wondered now how he could ever have laughed at such a thing. Some of the lamps had been snuffed by the gust of wind as the door slammed open, but those that remained were more than enough. Their light reflected from a great blotch of oozing wetness splattered over the stones of the wall, and Bayrd had no desire to see any more than that. The pictures created by his imagination were already bad enough.

Only two *talathen* remained. One of them still said nothing, even after what had just happened – Bayrd commended the man's discipline, if nothing else – but the leader made up in volubility for his companion's silence.

'You're insane, ar'Talvlyn!' he screeched. 'You think you're so clever! You think because you've killed one of us you can start to make terms? Is that it? Is it? You're wrong, man! You don't know how wrong you are! Because you've just killed your own children!'

It might have been shock or fury that put such a trembling shrillness in the man's babbling voice, but Bayrd recognised fear when he heard it. The *tulath* was terrified. After the Father of Fires alone knew how many of these brutal missions of kidnapping and murder, he realised that he was confronted at last by a man and a woman who cared nothing for his threats.

A woman, anyway. What had moved the door was sorcery or Art Magic, and knowing the *talathen* as he did, Bayrd would never have dared. He wondered where Eskra had finally found the courage to call their bluff, and glanced encouragement at her.

Then a queasy chill slid through him like a dagger as he saw the look on her face. What had happened was not her doing. But it had happened all the same. And the consequences would be the same.

Harel and Marla might be dead already . . .

That too was where the Shadowthief's terror lay. He wasn't so much afraid of sudden, immediate extinction in the heat of rage, but of what might follow being taken alive. There was enough human wreckage in this room to show some of the ways in which he might have died already, but those had at least been quick. Without the clan-lord's infant daughters as a surety, there was nothing to stop the full weight of justice from descending on him. And it would descend slowly, through punishment as prolonged and inventive as hatred could devise.

But Bayrd still didn't know who could have laid power on the door so that it killed a man . . .

Until Gemmel ar'Ekren stepped into the room.

His dragon-patterned black staff was held like a spear in both hands, braced at port-arms across his chest, and there was a blue-white flame fluttering like a pennon from the tapering crystal at its point. The scholar inclined his head in a curt bow, deep enough for courtesy, but not so deep that his cold green eyes ever left the masked faces of the two *talathen*.

'Your daughters are safe, lord,' he said.

Eskra caught her breath in a little gasp that was almost a sob. 'And the men sent to take them . . . ?'

Gemmel's gaze flicked sideways to the door and the crushed and flattened corpse behind it, then back to the surviving Shadow-thieves. The black staff swung down and around to level at them. 'Also safe,' he said. 'They need not concern you.'

Bayrd Talvalin had never fainted in his life before, but it was a close-run thing this time. The feeling that swirled up inside him like a cloud of warm, sweet smoke was so intense that for a few seconds, for the duration of four shuddering breaths, the room swam around him. He didn't sway, didn't stagger, didn't even close his eyes; but he wanted to laugh, to sing and caper like a fool, to kiss his wife, to run to his daughters and hug them, to embrace this stranger who had saved his children . . .

To go off somewhere alone, and cry for sheer relief.

There was a click, and then another gasp, but this time it wasn't made by Eskra. One of the *talathen*, the subordinate who had never spoken through all that he had seen, stared at nothing with bulging eyes, then sagged forward on to his knees. Blood darkened the grey mask over his mouth as he exhaled blood, and another blotch spread on his chest around the small, bright metal point that bulged from his tunic. Then he collapsed on to his face and didn't move again.

The weapon that had killed him was still in his leader's hand. Bayrd recognised it, though he had never expected to see one capable of use. Even before the Albans left, Kalitzak armourers had been trying for years to perfect what they called a *telek*, supposedly a weapon that could shoot darts without the need of a bowstave to provide its power. But they had never been able to make a spring – of steel, bronze, horn, sinew or whatever – that was both small and still strong enough.

Not until now.

'Damn,' said the last *tulath* dispassionately. 'I had hoped it might go clean through and take one of you as well.' Then he shrugged. 'But I couldn't decide who to aim for anyway.' His hand opened, letting the *telek* drop with a thud on to the corpse's back. It was the only movement he could possibly have made that wouldn't have seen him dead an instant later.

Nobody said a word. Of all the killings tonight, that had been the most callous, the most in keeping with what was said of Shadowthieves. The man stared at them in turn, his eyes bright in the lamplight. Bayrd knew what he could see: his own future, what little was left of it. First there would be the questions: who had sent him? why? how much had it cost? All the answers he would refuse to give. Then there would be the rigorous interrogation to squeeze the juice of information from him, like an apple in a cider-press, and finally the useless pulp would be thrown away.

'At least now he won't be talking out of turn. And neither will I.' Bayrd could hear that sound of a smile in the *tulath*'s voice again, even though there was little enough for him to smile about. 'But if the Father of Fires is good, ar'Talvlyn, then one day I'll be back. To kill you.'

The Shadowthief turned, took the two long strides and a leap that was all he needed, and flung himself straight out through the window. Out into the darkness that was his only protection now.

And out into two hundred feet of empty air.

Bayrd Talvalin sprang after him, knowing even as he moved that he was half a second too late. There was no sound from outside, no long, trailing scream – or even the laughter that Bayrd was half-expecting. Just a brittle tinkling as the few fragments of glass not carried out by the *tulath*'s leap fell from the window-frame on to the pinewood floor. It had been as quick as that.

For a few seconds he stood very still, watching, listening, shaking his head, still not certain that it was all over, then slowly lowered Widowmaker's point to the floor and leaned on the pommel, shivering. That was partly from reaction, but mostly because the night air blowing through the shattered window was cold on his naked skin. Bayrd looked about for his robe, and found it at last. He reached for the garment gratefully – then his nostrils filled with the sheared-copper stench of blood and he felt the fabric's warmth and sodden weight. He made the mistake of looking down, and winced. Hastily dropping the robe, he very carefully and thoroughly wiped his fingers on the towel still wrapped around his waist.

'*Talathen* are supposed to be able to do almost anything,' said Gemmel behind him. 'But I don't think they can fly.'

'No.' Glad of anything else to look at, Bayrd tore his eyes from the half-corpse at his feet and glanced at the broken window; hesitated, then stared harder. 'Not fly.'

He wasn't sure whether to laugh, or curse, or even applaud the *tulath*'s audacity, because there, sunk into the wood, was a grapnel hook of blackened steel with a thin black rope trailing from it, out and down and away. He stepped forward, moving very carefully, mindful of his bare feet and that a glass splinter is like an enemy; it's always the one you don't see that gets you.

There was no weight on the rope. Either the man had somehow fumbled his catch on the way through the window and was lying smashed and dead at the foot of the tower – which Bayrd very much doubted – or he was even now slipping across other roofs, other battlements, other walls, and away to safety.

'Not fly,' he said again. 'But I think they can do anything else short of magic.' Bayrd looked at Gemmel thoughtfully. 'And speaking of the Art . . .'

'Never mind that for the moment, lord,' said Gemmel, reversing his staff and ramming its spiked pommel-cap into the floor as easily as a knife into a loaf of bread. 'Look to your lady.'

Bayrd stared at the black staff and guessed it would sink just as easily into a floor of tile, or stone, or maybe even metal; then the import of Gemmel's words sank in as well, and he turned to stare instead at the pallor of his wife's face and the ribbon of blood trickling from between the fingers clamped around her arm.

'Just a flesh wound.' Eskra produced a feeble grin from somewhere and managed to keep it in place. 'Isn't that what I'm supposed to say? Especially when it's much worse . . .' As Bayrd made for the bed she moved her hand away, looked in disbelief, then shook her head and laughed shakily. 'But what should I say when it *is* just a flesh wound? I've cut myself more badly sharpening a pen.'

That wasn't quite true. Whatever had caused the damage had left a deep, clean cut in her bicep. Not a *telek* dart, then; that would have been an obvious puncture or a ragged gash. They never did find out, either then or later, and put the injury down to something that had happened during that first frantic struggle in the dark. Bayrd was happy to leave it at that, because the alternative was more sinister than he cared to consider.

His own thought was that he had inflicted the wound himself, but the thought remained unvoiced; because to say anything out loud would have forced him inexorably to the darker suspicion underlying it. That Isileth Widowmaker, that hungry blade, had made an attempt to eliminate her only rival for his affections.

And he had long ago stopped laughing at such notions.

One of the oldest of the many traditions surrounding Albans and their great *taiken* longswords was that they should not be drawn under a friendly roof for any reason save display. It held that the curved *taipan* shortsword was the only blade proper for use beneath one's own roof in the defence of home and family. It was something which provoked smiles of tolerant mockery from the younger generation of *kailinin*, all of whom knew well enough that if the need arose, they would use whatever was first at hand, be it axe or mace or sword of any length at all.

But Bayrd had an uneasy feeling that, in common with many of the old customs, the reasoning behind it – however long forgotten – was a sound one. Sorcery and the Art Magic had long been considered beneath the notice of a true Alban warrior, and with that lack of notice went other knowledge. Knowledge that he, and maybe others, had long preferred to ignore even when it was blatantly obvious to all but the most deliberately blind.

When the wielder's blood was up, even the lesser, nameless *taikenin* could be frighteningly indiscriminate in their hunger. There had been evidence enough of that before the Albans left Kalitzim, and much more of it in the past few years when longsword met longsword in the small feuds over land. Even then, in their proper place on the field of battle, that hunger was not quite so dangerous as in the confines of indoors.

But the named-blades, weapons whose history and lineage was often older than that of the men who carried them, were another matter. They could be dreadful things, all too easily awakened, and reluctant to sleep again even when their work was done. The stories said that they were live blades: and in more than just the casual sense of being sharp – rather than blunted – steel.

Weapons, so the saying went, were neither good nor evil; only the deeds done with them by men. That was a trite platitude, and never more so when used of a named-blade *taiken*. There was supposed to be something of the soul of the smith in every blade forged by a master. If that soul was dark, given to violence or impatience, then so too was the sword.

It might make the blade especially dangerous to the members of a given clan, or unlucky and given to missing the stroke, or turning in the hand at a vital moment. That was why knowing the provenance of a given *taiken* was so important. It could be a matter of life and death.

No one knew for certain who had hammered Isileth all those years ago from the billet of braided star-steel that gave the blade her formal title. But her new name was just as appropriate. In the Alban language, *widow* was like *wizard* and *warrior*: it had no gender of its own, and so could be applied equally to both.

Bayrd looked once more at the cut in Eskra's arm, and shivered again. And this time, he was sure that cold was not the cause.

Widowmaker was back in her scabbard and the scabbard safely restored to its rack on the wall; the fire in the retiring-room had been lit again, to provide somewhere they could be while the vile mess in the bedroom was being cleaned up; and the children were with them.

Marla was sound asleep in Eskra's lap with all the unconcern of a two-year-old who had never really woken up, while Harel, not quite four, filled with excitement at being up so late and determined to make the most of it, was fighting a losing battle with her own heavy eyelids. Neither of them looked frightened; Bayrd guessed that they had never even seen their potential kidnappers, much less whatever sudden savagery Gemmel ar'Ekren had visited on the Shadowthieves' heads.

A strange one, that. *An-erhan*: a traveller, a scholar, almost certainly a soldier or worse at some time in his past, if the way he had snapped orders at the guards was an example. If the way he was stalking the corridors of the citadel even now was any indication. And all the time, a sorcerer.

'No, lord,' the old man had corrected, 'not a sorcerer. That's too much a user of the Talent. I'm just a bookman and an enchanter. A spellsinger. *An-purkanyath*, you would call me.'

Calling him a rescuer would be more appropriate; and yet no more appropriate than discovering their guest was a wizard. Looking at the matter objectively, it was strange how little surprised either he or Eskra had been. As if they had known his secret all along – if it was a secret at all, and not something Gemmel had kept back simply because no one had asked him about it.

Now there was a fine sort of question to ask strangers, thought Bayrd, smiling to himself. *Are you a wizard, sorcerer, enchanter or in any other way involved with the use of the Art Magic?* He played briefly with how any other clan-lord would react, and felt his smile go sour.

Why bother?

They were all reacting badly enough already. Especially the one who had sent the *talathen*. Who had it been? What had they hoped to gain by a kidnapping, that they could not achieve by the simple assassination that would probably have succeeded? And what would he do when he found out at last . . . ?

So many questions, so few answers. Bayrd closed his eyes briefly and stared at the red darkness inside their lids, but he could read nothing useful written there.

There was a bandage around Eskra's arm, and a simple charm of binding underneath it. That was nothing complex, no spell of woven words to promote unnaturally rapid healing, just the sorcerous equivalent of the dozen or so stitches that would otherwise have been needed to hold such a wound closed. She was capable of nothing more, and – even assuming he had the ability to control his Talent better – nor was he. Gemmel, perhaps expecting their refusal, had never even offered before he went out on his rounds to inspect the sentries one more time.

So now they were both drained, exhausted, beyond the level of weariness that cries out for sleep and into the dull, aching fatigue beyond, where even sleep is too much effort and just sitting still is as much as anyone can do.

And now would be the perfect time for a second group of *talathen* to enter the fortress and try to complete what the first squad had begun. Though the corridors of the citadel were more heavily guarded than before, those lords'-men and retainers had reached their peak of vigilance an hour ago, when the attempted kidnapping and murder was still a hot outrage in their minds. He knew from personal experience that such a peak could never be maintained, that it would start eventually to consume itself like a sheet of paper flung into a fire. Within a matter of an hour or so, in the slack twilight time between the end of the night and the beginning of morning, Dunrath-hold would be no better protected than it had been before all this began.

He shook the notion from his head. No. His weariness, and a delayed reaction to the bloody business upstairs, was making him depressed, as it so often did. Nobody could get into Dunrath unnoticed, much less get out again alive. As soon kick a beehive, and then hope to steal the honey without being stung. They were safe now, until the next time. With the thought and as if on cue, Harel's head drooped sideways at last, and she slept.

Bayrd gazed across the room, watching Eskra. She was no more than an outstretched hand away, staring at the hearth, half-dozing, neither awake nor asleep but lost in a waking dream as her imagination wandered through the intricate tunnels between the glowing coals. There was no thought of the quarrel any more; it was forgotten now, washed away in the blood from Eskra's arm, in the blood of the dead *talathen*, in the brutal reminder that many worse things could happen than the loss of a friend.

''Skra-*ain*?' he said, softly so as not to wake the children. She blinked and came back from wherever she had been, looked at him and smiled slightly in the fire-warmed stillness.

'Mmm?'

'About Marc ar'Dru.' Bayrd was watching closely, but her drowsy expression didn't change. 'Tell me what happened to him. What made him say what he did? What made him different?'

'His own wishes.'

'Oh . . .'

Bayrd had been expecting hesitation; a marshalling of thought; an oblique response that only gradually spiralled in towards the truth. Certainly nothing so direct and blunt, and any answer at all besides this one.

'But . . . But he was my friend.'

'And still is. He just doesn't know it. And won't until I release him.'

'You?'

'Listen more closely, loved. Remember what I told Vanek ar'Kelayr?' Eskra's blue eyes narrowed, all drowsiness gone so that Bayrd wondered if it had ever really been there at all. The sapphire stare bored into him like twin needles. 'No. Evidently you don't.'

Her shoulders moved in the suggestion of a shrug, just enough to make her meaning plain, not enough to waken Marla. 'No matter. With one thing and another we've had more to think about this past couple of days than a half-hearted lecture on the Art that wasn't being heeded anyway. I was talking about *an-pesoek'n*. The small charms that sometimes have more effect than High Magic,' Eskra grinned briefly, 'because nobody expects an adept to use them.'

A word wandered up from Bayrd's memory and through his mind. 'You said that cu Ruruc might have used a . . . a glamour, wasn't it?'

'Well done.' Eskra patted her hands together in a silent, sardonic imitation of applause, even though a brief smile blunted the edge of any sarcasm. 'You would be a capable enough pupil, loved, if all the other burdens of lordship didn't keep getting in the way. Yes. A glamour.'

'Why?'

'You really don't understand, do you? Even now.' Marla shifted on her mother's lap, yawned, snuggled down again and returned to sleep without ever having been properly awake. Eskra stroked her daughter's dark hair and said nothing for a while.

'Marc ar'Dru has been your friend for years,' she said at last. 'You've known it: I've known it. But because of that simple knowledge, you've never seen that he's also the best and most faithful retainer you've ever had. Or will have.'

She toyed with the long ringlets of Marla's hair again, winding them around her fingers and then letting them coil free once more.

'Bayrd-*ain*,' Eskra's voice was so soft now that she might have been speaking to the sleeping child, 'he's gone to act as your spy in the enemy camp. And he would have done it whether I helped him or not. Because he was willing to set aside his own honour so that yours would remain spotless. But at least this way he has a chance of getting out alive. All thanks to a small spell that changed the way he perceives his loyalties.'

'You did that to him? Made him change? Made him say what he did?'

'Yes. Rather than see him put his neck on the chopping-block. Yes. I did. Is that so wrong?'

Bayrd shook his head; not a denial, just an attempt to understand. The convolutions of politics were one thing, but this deliberate deception and induced betrayal were – or had been – beyond his experience.

'Marc would have gone anyway. Because someone had to. His words; not mine. I had no reason to doubt his sincerity then. I still don't. But now there won't be a week, or a month, or a year of silence before we learn how he died. If we ever learned. He won't die. Because he won't be discovered. Not by accident, not by the most subtle questioning, not even by sorcery.' She met Bayrd's dubious glance without wavering. 'But in the meantime I will see what he sees. I will hear what he hears. I already know what he thinks . . . and what he knows.'

There was something about that last, a thread of quietly salacious amusement too thin to surface as a smile, that made Bayrd's cheeks burn with embarrassment. 'So what does he know?' he said, sidestepping the unspoken question with a spoken one of his own. 'What does my one-time Companion think?'

'That he despises you for what happened to ar'Kelayr. That he's an Alban *kailin*, an honourable man, and by the suspicious death of an enemy who was also your guest, you've proven that you most certainly are not.'

Bayrd gazed at her without expression, but there was a hurt flicker in his eyes as though every word made him wince like a slap across the face. Eskra's touch as she reached out towards him was far more gentle than that.

'His defence, my loved. And your defence too. No matter how close he comes to Kalarr cu Ruruc or Gerin ar'Diskan, he won't attempt a murder. The least wizard worth his hire would know it. And cu Ruruc will be certain. No matter what spell I laid on Marc, he would never do that. Not unless I wrenched his brain so far asunder that it would not have been Marc ar'Dru any more. But after that, when all of them are sure of him, he'll be able to come far closer, hear and see and know far more, than the best actor.'

'Because he isn't acting.'

'No. Marc could never act that part well enough.' She reached out to touch his hand again. 'But it's only the spell, loved. Nothing but the spell. And when the time comes, he'll be able to lay that spell aside more easily and willingly than he ever did your faith and fealty. Trust me. Will you trust me . . . ?'

'Have I a choice?'

'You do,' said Gemmel's voice from behind them both. 'You can accept the lady's word, or you can stand up and walk out now.'

''*Lath Jowl!* How long have you been there?' Even though Marla whimpered in her sleep and Harel stirred a little, Bayrd managed to modulate the snarl in his voice just in time. He didn't manage to stop his right hand from closing on the hilt of his *taipan*. The left hand was busy trying to prevent his chair from toppling backwards to the floor as he surged up and out of it, and by the time he was fully on his feet the curved blade of the shortsword was already clear of its scabbard and glittering wickedly in the firelight.

Gemmel studied man, and sword, and wife, and children, then gave them all that sweeping gesture of the hand and the little bow over it, less than ashamed about intruding on a clan-lord's private apartment, never mind what even the least observant of men might have heard was a clan-lord's private argument.

'Long enough,' he said. His look at the two feet of steel in Bayrd's hand was that of a man dismissing something that was no threat. There was something about the old wizard's superb, assured arrogance that dampened even Bayrd Talvalin's anger, perhaps because it was meant to impress no one.

'And what gives you the right to pass judgement on any choice of mine?'

'Professional courtesy, as one wizard to another,' Gemmel said mildly. 'Or should that be, one wizard among his peers?'

Bayrd opened his mouth, reconsidered in the same instant and felt his teeth click shut on half a dozen possible responses. He returned the *taipan* to its sheath with a long, deliberate rasp of steel, and stared at Gemmel all the time he did so.

'Never mind that.'

It was Gemmel's own verbal sidestep to the same question, and on Bayrd's lips it might have sounded clumsy. But it was as adroit as any evasion he had executed on the fencing-floor, because it acknowledged and ignored all in one. Even while all his attention was focused on the wizard, he sensed a quick smile of approval from Eskra – although there was no disapproval of a man who had obviously never heard of knocking on a closed door before coming through it.

Professional courtesy, thought Bayrd. *It works both ways. Or maybe all three . . .*

'Professional courtesy indeed,' said Gemmel. There was no indication if it was a continuation of what he had said before, or a blatant reading of Bayrd's mind. 'But courtesy or not, it doesn't make the lady's decision, or that of your Companion,' – and he even managed to give the Alban title its proper honorific inflection – 'any more or less the only thing that could have been done in such a circumstance.'

'And what would you know about it?' That was deliberately rude, there was no oblique interpretation to take the sting out of it. And yet Gemmel did no more than raise one eyebrow in another acceptance and dismissal that immediately put Bayrd delicately in the wrong.

'You can do better than that, lord,' he said. 'I've seen and heard it. So I can assume that what you said wasn't from the heart. For which I thank you.' Again there was the bow and the hand-sweep, this time with such a smile that Bayrd would have been a churl even to attempt recovery of his fading advantage. Wisely, he didn't waste the effort.

'*Kha'dagh!* Enough of this. Master Gemmel, I owe you more than attempts at sarcasm. For the lives of my children, my wife – and mine too, when the end came. And I owe you for my honour, which the *talathen* were trying to steal. So how can Clan Talvalin repay you? Gold? Silver? Rank . . . ?'

'With respect, lord, you have little enough gold or silver that you should spare none for passing strangers.'

There was a silence after that. It stretched like a noosed neck, long enough and tight enough to become far more than just uncomfortable. 'Is it that well known?' said Bayrd at last.

'Well enough that I heard it on my way here.' Gemmel gazed carefully at the fire; it was probably less hot than the humiliation burning in Bayrd Talvalin's face. 'You're luckier than I think you know, Bayrd-*arluth*. What I heard a dozen times had more than a dozen excuses to explain it away. And that was from peasants, yeomen farmers, people with nothing to gain or lose by telling what they thought was truth. Instead they defended you. Protected you. Lied for you . . . It's as good as silver.'

'Almost as good. You can't buy anything with loyalty, no matter what the stories say. And I still owe you.'

'Land, then. I've a mind to settle in Alba for a while.'

Bayrd grinned, a brief, cold baring of teeth that was gone before any humour it might have carried could catch up with the expression. 'To watch the Albans cut each other to ribbons in a war, then write about it for the sake of scholarship?'

'Perhaps,' Gemmel hesitated, then shrugged slightly, 'not.'

'Your excuse; your choice. Land I have in plenty, at least. Clan Talvalin can make claim to hold everything from Redmer to the Blue Mountains. It ought to be enough for you to make another choice. So: do you want a farm, a manor, a river valley, or what?'

'Some of my . . . studies might prove disturbing to any near neighbours. So . . . Somewhere desolate. Without any people living there at all. A piece of mountain slope would be more than adequate, I thank you.'

This time Bayrd laughed out loud, enough that both children stirred in their sleep and Eskra gave him an angry look. 'A mountain? Man, I'm offering you pasture, meadow, forest – and you want a mountain! What in the name of the Father of Fires would you produce there?'

Gemmel glanced at Eskra; his raised eyebrow was much more of a despairing shrug towards someone who might understand than any amount of lifted shoulders. He looked back at Bayrd, still amused at such foolishness, and shook his head.

'Something to outlast a war,' he said quietly, and watched the amusement fade. 'Scholarship, perhaps . . .'

6

Games

MARC AR'DRU'S SHOULDERS were hunched under the weight of a silence that had grown more oppressive with every mile he travelled and every hour that passed.

It was not as if he had no one to talk to. Ten lord's-men had ridden with Vanek ar'Kelayr to Dunrath, and now they accompanied his ashes home again. Those men were more than eager for any conversation that would ease the funereal atmosphere, even though everything they said was tinged with a slight confusion over why Marc had acted as he did. He had been a Bannerman, a clan-lord's Companion, a *kailin-eir* of high rank, a position these retainers could only ever dream of, and he had thrown it all away on a point of principle.

But the one man whose voice he wanted to hear, *needed* to hear, for the approval it would carry and the absolution it would grant, remained obstinately silent. That man was Reth ar'Gyart, who had been Lord Vanek's Bannerman. He rode now at the head of the column with the dead man's longsword Katen slung across his back, and said not a word more than was absolutely necessary.

Despite his doubts, Marc was still convinced that he had done the right thing, and had maintained his own honour and respect, by defying the suspicious actions of his lord. He had seen both Bayrd and Eskra use sorcery and the Art too many times to be convinced that, just this once, they might have used it wrongly in the hope that they would not be found out. But at the same time, he could not shake off a feeling of having been manipulated into that decision by some force, some persuasion beyond his control.

No matter what the reason – or was it just an excuse? – might be, the set of ar'Gyart's back was radiating censure of all that he had done. That stung. The Bannerman had obviously approved of the stand that Marc had taken, otherwise he would have refused his company on the ride back to Hold ar'Kelayr. But he approved of nothing else.

Marc was still angry at Bayrd, an anger made deeper and more intense because it was mingled with regret. What Bayrd Talvalin had done was so pointless; he had been such an honourable man, and to have placed himself in such a dishonourable position that the only option open to his chief retainer was formal defiance seemed – to that retainer – an act very close to stupidity. The Talvalin Clan-Lord had never been stupid before, and Marc couldn't understand why he had picked the present troubled times to start.

It was plain to everyone that Bayrd Talvalin stood to gain something from Vanek ar'Kelayr's murder, if only a respite from the older lord's accusations about his son. His protestations of outrage and innocence had been most persuasive, but for all that, Bayrd had failed to convince any right-thinking *kailin* that he had neither complied with nor approved of ar'Kelayr's death. That was enough for him to forfeit all rights to fealty – even though Marc was the only one to actually take leave of his service.

And yet, because of that same lack of proof one way or the other, Reth ar'Gyart's old-fashioned mind plainly thought it far more honourable if Marc had set his reputation beside that of his lord and remained in Bayrd's service through thick and thin. Or at least, until the suspected wrong-doing had been proven beyond all doubt.

Marc felt like the bear in the story, with his paw in a cleft tree. Opening that paw would let him go free, though he would lose the honey he had found; but keeping the paw shut to keep the honey would also keep him trapped. It was one of those paradoxes tutors delighted in throwing at their students, where either decision could be seen as the wrong one and neither decision was completely right.

Marc ar'Dru did not yet know for certain which one he had made, much less which of them was the worst mistake . . .

He and ar'Gyart's party had ridden together across the moors for almost three days now, and in all that time he and the Bannerman had exchanged no more than a few words; brief, necessary communications, far removed from the amiable gossip of travelling with Bayrd and Eskra Talvalin. They, though Clan-Lord and Lady in their own domain, always had a friendly word for anyone who rode with them, or indeed for anyone they met along the way. The encounter could be with high-clan, or low, House or Family, farmer or peasant labourer, but there would always be a greeting or a salutation exchanged.

That was one of the many things that set them apart from the other Alban lords of the old high-clan bloodlines, one of the many petty reasons – apart from the great Causes of enmity and rivalry – why people such as Vanek ar'Kelayr and others like him disliked them so. They had no sense of their own rank and position. While ar'Kelayr, on the other hand . . .

Marc stared for a moment at the wooden box strapped with such care behind the cantle of ar'Gyart's saddle. That was his position now. But while he lived, there had been a man of set opinions, one whose view of the turning world and his own place in it had been as fixed as the stars against the vault of Heaven. At least, as fixed as the stars had been . . .

Until last night.

The banked campfire had been between them as always. Reth ar'Gyart saw it built like that every night, just as he and his men slept on the far side of it every night, even when that might mean sleeping far out in the open instead of in whatever shelter they had found. He always allowed Marc the shelter, with the scornful suggestion – never voiced – that the younger man was soft enough to need it. Marc had watched him lay the *taiken* Katen and the casket of ashes on the ground at his head before he rolled up in his blanket, so that even in death he slept at his lord's feet. But on that first night out of Dunrath, ar'Gyart had also laid his own longsword at his side in readiness, and Marc had been more hurt and insulted by such a gesture of distrust than by any intimation of his weakness.

Company on the road ar'Gyart may have been, but that was all, and it would end when they reached Hold ar'Kelayr at Erdanor. Their relationship had never been between *kailinin*, not even the formal, distant association between men of equal rank. The fire and the steel said as much. They were a wall, built to separate the true retainer from the faithless lord's-man, the righteous from the opportunist – and always there was the memory of that other fire, the one which had created the box of ashes ar'Gyart guarded with such care.

Ar'Dru had been a Bannerman Companion to a high-clan lord, and had thrown that rank and title back as though it was a currency which had lost its value. But even though his own lord was dead, it was plain that Reth ar'Gyart saw himself as a Bannerman Companion still.

Marc had been lying awake in his bedroll as he had done on all the other nights since leaving Dunrath, smelling the scent of the heather and staring into the velvet glitter of the summer sky, wishing for a gloom to match the tenor of his thoughts. On this night, as on the others, Heaven failed to oblige. There had been a heavy overcast and a sullen rain on the day he denied his fealty to Clan Talvalin, and since then, as if in approval – or in mockery – of what he had done, the days had been bright and the nights clear.

This one was no different. It was cloudless, the moon more than halfway to full, its light silvery and cool after the heat of the day. All the rest was star-flecked dark, except for the soft, heavy skein that hung across the centre of the sky like a weft of smoke all strewn with diamond splinters, the great constellation called the Lady's Scarf. But for all the darkness that lay to either side of the Scarf, it was still far too cheerful for Marc's mood.

Every once in a while there would be a scratch of brilliance to mark the passage of *an golwan-sùl*, a sunspark struck from the Forge of the Father of Fires. It was common enough on clear nights, and more often in summer when the Forge burned hottest. Only the most ignorant and superstitious peasants ever called such things 'falling stars'.

Stars didn't fall.

Anyone could see that much, if they took the trouble and could count to a large enough total. No matter how many *golwanin* left their brief, bright tracks across the night, no matter how many must have fallen since the world was beaten out on that same Forge, there were never fewer stars at dawn than there had been at dusk. They changed their position, of course, as the Lady shifted the hang of her Scarf to match the changing seasons; but they moved together, in relation to each other, not one at a time.

But last night he had seen one that did none of these things, because last night he had seen a star appear where no star had been before. And then he had seen it slip from its place.

And fall.

It was as inconceivable as though a jewel had torn free from the Lady's Scarf and tumbled down from Heaven to the floor of the world.

Had such an event been described to him, Marc knew he would have smiled tolerantly and nodded agreement, or laughed out loud and dismissed the incident as nonsense – his reaction depending entirely on the rank and status of the speaker. But he had seen it for himself, and Marc ar'Dru was old enough and cynical enough to have grown out of the common habit of disbelieving the evidence of his own eyes. Once a man started to doubt his own five senses, then whose senses was he expected to trust?

Even in the face of the patently impossible.

His folded arms had been behind his head, an uncomfortable pillow propping him up to stare out towards the eastern horizon at an area of the sky that lay between the constellations of the Two Hunters, the Hawk and the Hound. That part of the sky was star-dark, a blackness barely tinted with the suggestion of deep blue that came with moonlight. Marc would have sworn on any oath both then and later that there had been no star in it. That there had never been a star in it. Not even those faintest of glitters that could only be seen by the strongest eyes, and then only on the deepest, coldest, clearest nights of winter. But suddenly there was.

Anywhere else, anywhere more spectacular, and it might have been lost amid the glory of the Lady's Scarf. But in the darkness between the Two Hunters, in that one place of all the sky, it was unmistakable.

And acting as it did, it was unmissable.

The point of light winked into existence as though someone impossibly far away had unshuttered a lantern. In the moment of its birth, and for a time afterwards that seemed no longer than the blinking of an eye yet was just long enough to be perceived, the new star surrounded itself with a corona of all the splendours of a rainbow. It was a momentary splendour, one that should have been heralded by a fanfare of trumpets, or greeted by a thunder-clap of noble noise.

Yet there was nothing. Only the ringing silence of Heaven, and the small sounds made by birds and insects in the Alban summer night.

Marc had seen that same crystalline flash of colour only once before, when light from a low sun had struck through a perfect raindrop hanging like a jewel from a leaf. An instant later his horse's shoulder had brushed against the branch, and the drop had fallen, and the moment had gone beyond recall.

But he had never seen it in the night sky. And he had never, ever seen the light that birthed it *moving* . . .

The tiny brilliance faded as it had done when the raindrop fell, leaving the new star behind. And that star was indeed moving; slowly, but not so slowly that it could not be followed past the Hunters, up the vault of Heaven and through the Lady's Scarf like the point of a bright needle.

Marc had known then that this was a dream, and soon or late, all dreams end in waking. It was certain that what he was watching was no *golwan-sùl* struck from the great Forge, for it moved too slowly. Nor was it a star, or it would not have moved at all.

So it was something from his own mind, brought to life and light by his troubled thoughts, and once he awoke – or managed to reach a deeper and more comfortable sleep – the light would fade away. Contented by his own reasoning, of that swift clarity found so often in dreams and so seldom in the waking world, he continued to watch without fear or concern.

It brightened even as he watched, like a blown fire; but this was a colder brightness than any ember. It was like a fragment of the moon, or a mirror carried from a distance, whose reflection might grow even while it showed only light, not heat. Even at its largest, it was still no bigger than the brightest of the true stars, and as it passed beyond the silvered half of the moon and out towards its darkened face, it began to fade. The light dimmed more slowly than it had grown, and that too was not the sign of a sunspark. *Golwanin* moved fast and died abruptly, true sparks from the Forge. This one's death, though quick enough, had been gradual by comparison.

Marc's eyes followed the thing's track beyond where its light went out. If this was a dream, then it was the proper thing to do. If it was nodding wakefulness, then those eyes would roll back beneath the cover of their lids and he would sleep at last.

And anyway, he was an Alban *kailin-eir*, a trained warrior, and most especially an archer. Such eyes, trained for a lifetime to follow the flight of arrows from friend and foe alike, habitually followed any moving thing they watched for a little longer than was truly necessary. It was sometimes how that lifetime was prolonged.

That was why he saw the thing in the instant when it flared into new brilliance. No longer the chilly, remote glitter he had seen before, this time it was a glare of heat, blazing down from a point of intolerable yellow-white, through brilliant orange and the red of a dying cinder, visibly slowing as it descended towards the west. At last it dwindled to no more than a faint trail that ran as much across the inside of his eyes as across the sky, and the darkness of his dream returned again.

But the flash far off on the western horizon had been real enough, a flicker like summer lightning, the harbinger of a storm on the edge of the world. It was harsh enough to throw the Blue Mountains into stark silhouette, and bright enough for the after-image to be no faint, half-imagined track within Marc's eyes, but a jagged blotch of glowing purple in the shape of the sky above the distant peaks.

And still there was no sound. Then he realised what he was truly hearing. No sound; *no* sound at all. The night noises were gone, as if every living thing in the world was holding its collective breath.

Marc ar'Dru remembered that silence with utter clarity, just as he remembered what came after. It had not been huge, not shocking him with great force – but in its implication it had been as terrifying as only a whisper can be. Under him, under his back where he lay in his bedroll on the unmoving earth . . .

It moved.

The movement was no violent shock, nothing more than a slight trembling. But it felt eerily familiar, a shudder as though he was not out here under the stars, landless and lordless, but in his own bed – and someone had lain down beside him.

That was when the men on the far side of the fire woke up at last. Marc heard Reth ar'Gyart come awake, he and his sword together, all in a rush. He had slept through the lights and movement in the heavens, but that faint tremor in the earth jolted him awake as suddenly and surely as a kick in the ribs. There was a mutter of dubious voices from the lesser retainers, but Marc heard the rustle of a blanket kicked aside, and the crunch of a mattress made of heather and bracken, as ar'Gyart sat upright in his makeshift bed. With those sounds he heard a quick scrape of steel, and knew the man's *taiken* had cleared its scabbard in the same instant. Ar'Gyart expected treachery, and expected it from him.

'What was that?'

Reth's voice was always a low, carrying growl, and since his lord's death in Dunrath it was edged with suspicion as a knife is with steel. Whether the man was as truly wary of him as all his other actions had suggested, or just distrustful of the world in general, Marc had neither known nor cared. He still didn't care.

'Must have been thunder,' he had replied, pitching his voice in the drowsy tone of someone no more than vaguely awake. 'I don't care. So long as I don't get wet . . .' Then he had rolled himself tighter into his blanket and pretended to go back to sleep with ar'Gyart's derisive snort as a short-lived lullaby.

It had not been a good time for explanations of lights in the sky, *golwanin* or falling stars – and even less for why Marc had not been honestly asleep. He had doubted then, and felt quite certain now, that there would never be such a time. Ar'Gyart was not the man to hear about anything that could be associated, however improbably, with sorcery or the Art Magic. Not after how Lord Vanek ar'Kelayr had died.

Sleep came and went after that, and even when he slept, strange lights and sounds had continued to trouble his dreams until the morning. All in all, it had not been a restful night, and Marc was glad to see the dawn.

Until that morning came, and then he was not so sure. Typically, there was no trace that anything untoward had ever happened.

No visible trace, at least. But it was there in Reth ar'Gyart's attitude towards Marc, more sullenly suspicious than ever, and in the way that attitude had begun at last to spill over into the behaviour of the other lord's-men. There were fewer of them willing to talk to Marc than ever before. Of the few who dared ar'Gyart's displeasure, what had once passed for conversation had degenerated so far into pointless chatter that it was no longer worth any of Marc's attention.

So what? he thought to himself. *They all know me by now. Or think they do. It won't influence . . .*

Influence what? Influence who? The next lord who might be willing to accept his service? That was a question he couldn't answer, even if there was another such lord within reach. And because of what he was, what he had become, Marc doubted it very much. Not when even the lesser retainers had begun to treat him as an outcast. As he turned his head and felt again the movement of roughly-cropped hair against his neck and ears, he began – hating it – to accept matters at last.

That cropping marked him far more than anything he might think or believe or say. An Alban *kailin*'s hair was worn long; loose only when bathing or preparing for bed, but at all other times plaited into the tight braid that marked a warrior. At the very least – though fashions changed in this as in everything else – it was worn in a single horsetail caught by a crested clip.

Only *eijin* wore it short, so that people of honour could more easily see and avoid them. And whatever he might do, or say, or even think in the privacy of his own mind, Marc ar'Dru had become an *eijo*.

With that single dramatic gesture of repudiation when he cut off his own braid, Marc had made himself into an Outlier, a landless, masterless warrior whose status was next to nothing in the Alban hierarchy. *Eijin* weren't popular at the best of times. Their treatment depended so much on what had brought them to such a lowly state, and the more Marc brooded on it, the more he realised that his case was among the worst of all.

Some warriors left the service of clan or House or Family on the death of the lord who had received their fealty, holding that allegiance to have been a personal thing between *kailinin* rather than a matter to concern the dead man's line. Whether or not that view was shared by the line in question, and by the other lords to whom they might later offer service, depended very much on circumstances. Leaving full-grown heirs who would already have their own circle of friends and relatives, and perhaps little time for their dead parent's henchmen, was far less reprehensible and lacking in honour than abandoning an immature child.

Sometimes, too, a man might take exception to a lord's behaviour or policies, and give him or her a defiance as an admonishment and a hint to mend their ways. That was what Marc had done – or assumed that he had done. But without positive proof of ill-doing, that reprimand should have been made privately rather than in full public view . . .

Otherwise such retainers could be seen as taking this opportunity to cause a loss of respect and confidence that any enemy might be proud of. And if their lord had enough opponents, there was always the unspoken question: whose instructions had they been following? That of their conscience – or of the adversary who had paid them?

Because of that, they weren't trusted; as ar'Gyart had already demonstrated so eloquently, in a reaction Marc suspected had been more instinctive than at a conscious level. And the oldest, most traditionally-minded high-clan lords wouldn't even tolerate such an *eijo* in their presence or under their roof.

It was as bad as that.

Marc ar'Dru had thrown away much more than a comfortable and respected position with Clan Talvalin. He had become unreliable. If his high-minded attitude could turn him against the lord who had been his friend, and who had elevated him to a rank beyond that attained by most members of a mere low-clan House, then it could turn him against any other lord whose fealty he might claim.

Unless he was given no chance to do so, and the easiest way to make sure of that was to have nothing to do with him.

Not even the old stories had anything good to say about *eijin*, except for those driven by the needs of vengeance, or with wrongs to put right. It was well known that fireside tales favoured the more romantically downtrodden characters; lovers separated by the feuding of their families, a youngest child who stood to inherit nothing but was the only truly honourable among several children, a warrior whose nobility was not appreciated until tragedy struck.

All good, uplifting, ethical stuff, at least for the most part. Even villains – though this was often condemned by the more moral –

might be presented as darkly glamorous heroes if their villainy could be shown in a sufficiently dramatic light.

But not such an *eijo* as Marc had become.

There were some who would not even permit them to be spoken of in Hall, as if the very word was tainted. *Eijin* were unhappy creatures at best. At worst they were as short-lived as mayflies. When no one would raise a voice in their defence, much less a weapon, then old grudges could be easily settled . . .

The more that Marc brooded on what had happened, the more he blamed Bayrd for what had happened. If he had been in error, Bayrd would have said so. If there hadn't been guilt, Bayrd would never have stood in silence and let him say what he had said. If he had been innocent, Bayrd would have protested it in front of all the ears who had heard Marc's accusation. And if he had been guilty, and a man of any honour, Bayrd should have confessed it so that there would have been no doubts cast on the honour of his Bannerman Companion. Instead of which he had stood mute and let things happen as they had.

Marc broke his fast, trying to relieve his feelings by grinding his teeth far more than really necessary on flat biscuits of waybread and a few strips of jerked meat. One had all the taste and texture of dry wood, the other was like leather, and it was all washed down with herb-steeped hot water passed to him grudgingly from the cooking-fire. As he ate and drank – or at least chewed, and tried to swallow, then chewed some more – he remembered the fragrant tang of Hauverne and Seurandec wines, the crisp, savoury scent of a roasted chicken simply served, the laughter and the warmth of friendship around the table that was better than any sauce . . .

And he began to hate the very thought of the Clan-Lord Bayrd Talva—

No. He had been no more than ar'Talvlyn, not so very long ago. Let him be ar'Talvlyn again.

Again there was the ride in silence, sombre despite the sunlit brilliance of a summer day on the burnt bronze and dark green bracken, on the white and purple heather. This time the silence was more profound than it had been on any of the previous days. Nobody spoke to Marc at all. He wondered if that was their own decision, or whether Reth ar'Gyart had finally issued orders to that effect. He cared neither one way nor the other. *Eijo* or not, with the land in its present state, teetering on the edge of self-created turmoil, any man might make his own way in the world.

Ar'Talvlyn had done it.

Once the tinted lenses of friendship had been finally thrown away, it was all too obvious that his one-time comrade was no more than an adventurer, a freebooter, a reaver like the young men whose heads had been set on spears as a warning to others who might imitate them. But Bayrd had differed from them in one important respect: with an eye for a larger prize than just the next man's cattle. He was a player in what the Albans in Drosul and Kalitz had long called *an Moy'Aleth*. It was the Great Game, whose first and only written rule was that 'what can be seen is not truly seen at all'.

To the blind, or the ignorant, or the trusting, it was nothing more than spying in disguise, gathering intelligence about a potential enemy – and in the purest forms of the Game, *everyone* was a potential enemy – to such an extent that the knowledge became a weapon of such power that no other weapons needed to be used.

Marc should have realised that a long time ago, except that his misplaced loyalty had blinded him to the truth. In the Great Game, *potential* prefaced every player, every possibility: gain, loss, victory, defeat, ally, opponent. Everyone else might be a friend, or might equally be an enemy. Every move might be a trap, and should be treated so. Advantage and disadvantage swung from one side to the other like a weight hung on a cord. It was a fact of life that should always be remembered.

Bayrd ar'Talvlyn had never forgotten it, that was plain, though he had concealed the awareness with a consummate skill that was the mark of a master player. Gerin ar'Diskan had forgotten it, made himself vulnerable by such carelessness, and had lost the land he coveted; Vanek ar'Kelayr had forgotten it, put himself into the enemy's hands, and lost his life; Marc ar'Dru had forgotten it, placed too much trust in someone else's honour, and lost his status, rank, position and respect.

He would not forget again. And now that he knew the Game was being played in Alba as it had been played in Kalitzim, he was like a man who had rediscovered the use of weapons after being unarmed for far too long.

There would be a war. That much was certain. Ar'Talvlyn was hardly the only lord in Alba to be a player, and Marc was hardly the only *kailin* to have realised what he now knew. When war came, and with it battle, conquest and the seizing of land, then he, Marc ar'Dru, would be on the winning side.

No. He would play the Game properly. No matter what moves had to be made to achieve such a result, whichever side *he* was on would be the winning side. That was how the Game was played, with rules known only to the players themselves and subject to change from one moment to the next. That was how Bayrd had made his moves, and so subtly that until now his honour had remained untarnished. For all Marc knew, it still *was* untarnished, and he and his honour were the pieces which had been sacrificed to prove it . . .

Marc blinked as he emerged from a daydream of complex plotting and manoeuvre, and discovered that he had been left behind. His horse had taken the chance to slow from a walk to a disinterested amble, and ar'Gyart's party were no more than a cluster of distant specks. Maybe they had taken the opportunity to ride on when he had offered it, maybe it had been nothing so deliberate, but whatever the reason, they were already the best part of a mile ahead of him.

He grinned sourly; this was more evidence, in a small way, that some game or other was being played. The lessening of an opponent's esteem in the sight of his companions was as un-equivocal a move as any other. It was near enough midday that they might soon stop for the noon-meal, or even, if he was right in the lie of the landscape at long last, that they might reach Erdanor and Hold ar'Kelayr before that. Either way, it would be less than seemly if he came straggling in behind the rest. Marc shook the reins and jabbed with his heels, urging his horse and the pack-pony in tow into something approaching a canter.

And just at that moment, all hell broke loose.

For all the distance between where he sat and ar'Gyart's people, Marc's eyes were good enough to make sense of what he saw. What made it worst of all was that he was close enough to see it all, but still far enough away that nothing he might do could be of any help if help was needed. In the drowsy, disconnected moment between his daydream and the sharper lines and colours of reality, the dozen distant figures of ar'Gyart and his followers were suddenly ringed by another score of men who had risen from concealment in the bracken.

He could make out no other details from such a distance: neither who the newcomers were, nor whether they were armed, nor if they were, what weapons they were carrying. Without knowing that, he couldn't even guess at why they were here, what they wanted, what they might do next . . .

But when the first rider spilled from his saddle, and an attenuated shriek hung on the air like the sound of a rabbit taken by an eagle, Marc was abruptly quite certain that whatever else the group of men might be, they were no welcoming committee.

He threw the pack-pony's leading-rein loose from his saddle, tugged his bow free from its case and nocked an arrow to the string.

What was he *doing*? He was without helmet, without harness, without even a coat of plates hidden under fabric such as the cautious wore in doubtful company. And he owed these men nothing, ar'Gyart least of all. Three-quarters of a mile of open country separated him from the action, and beyond all doubt he had already been spotted. How many other men might be crouching in the bracken for him to ride within range . . . ?

There was a second scream, and now Marc could see an occasional staccato flicker between one side and the other, a horizontal sleet as polished shafts of arrows caught the light. Another man sagged over his horse's neck and slithered to the ground, but now at least two of the archers on foot were now dead or wounded, sprawled back into the heather.

All Marc had to do was wait. There was no need to put himself at risk, no need even to beat a retreat. He was a mounted man, the enemy were all on foot. If any of them started moving in his direction, he could be out of sight before they came within bowshot.

And doing any of these things stuck in his throat like a chunk of unchewed bread.

What if they had been less than well-disposed to him? What if they had put him firmly in his place? What if Reth ar'Gyart had tried to behave in a manner as severely righteous as his own dead lord? At least they had accepted him, if only after a fashion, and if they had put him in his place, that place was more than most *eijin* might expect to be given at all. And as for Reth – well, there were worse ways to behave. The men being killed out there were the closest he had to comrades in the Debatable Lands, and without them, he was alone. Vulnerable. Helpless . . .

Marc would never have thought it possible that he would be a victim. But then, until four days ago, he would never have thought that he could be so utterly alone as this.

He listened to a third scream, a horrible mingling of disbelief and anguish he had heard – and caused – too many times before, the sound of a man ripped by steel and trying to deny the mangling of his own flesh. It etched into his hearing like a mordant acid into copper, a sound and a reason that might not have happened had Marc ar'Dru thought less about what he might or might not do, and simply done it.

He slammed heels to his horse's flanks, and charged.

The bow thumped once, twice, three times as he thundered closer, before he spun the weapon back into its case and reached for sword and axe. Marc's *taiken* was a nameless blade, without any lineage, but that had never detracted from its edge. There were yells of dismay, then a sharper yell of pain and a thud as his horse stumbled over someone who didn't get out of the way in time. Marc cut to either side, missed both times, and then he was inside the ring of footsoldiers.

No. Not footsoldiers. They weren't soldiers at all, and no more armoured than he was himself. The hard-suppressed terror of a blade ploughing into his unprotected body faded at once. It didn't go away completely – that was arrant folly – but at least it diluted enough for Marc to flip a cheerful, cheeky salute towards Reth ar'Gyart before he flung himself out again at the nearest opponent.

What they were, he still didn't know. Why they were here, he still didn't know. But what they were doing here he knew only too well. They were trying to kill everyone riding a horse. And that included him.

The native Elthanek and Prytenek people had been calling their Alban conquerors *mergh-arlethen*, Horse Lords, almost from the moment the keels hit the beach on the Day of Landing. Their own rulers, High Lords like Gelert, rode only as a token of rank and fought, when they had to, on foot. The Albans, however, had been mounted warriors for more generations than were recorded in even the oldest Books of Years, had won first recognition and then fame as mercenary cavalry – and for too long a time, the more hidebound among them had tried to rule their new domains in just the same way.

'You can conquer a country from the saddle,' some wit had said a few years back – no one was willing to accept responsibility for the observation – 'but if you want to rule it, and rule it well, then you'd better get down on to your own two feet just like everyone else. That lack of height changes the perspective quite remark-ably . . .'

Very few had done so, and those who had faced ridicule. Bayrd ar'Talvlyn was one of them. At least, he was ridiculed by his own people, the Albans. But he was supported, and praised, and even lied for, by his other people, the Elthaneks. Except that he called *them* Albans as well.

If he had not been so soured against anything Bayrd had done, and so busy fighting, Marc might have paused to wonder about the incongruity of his own thoughts. Instead he lashed out with the axe in his left hand at a half-seen movement, and heard and felt the ringing chime as steel sheared wood and the thrusting spear became nothing more dangerous than a long stick.

The attackers broke and ran, even their wounded scrambling up from the ground and hobbling away. They left no corpses. Marc stood in his stirrups and yelled a warshout after them, incoherent triumph more than any formal challenge or defiance. But with the relief, the delight, the sudden restored sense of his own worth that came surging up inside him, he had to do something. That, or burst.

It was impossible that the arrival of one more man, one more sword, had tipped the scales and spoiled their confidence so much, but there was the evidence: discarded weapons and running men. He watched them go, poised and ready in case this was some clever stratagem to deceive, reluctant to believe that this retreat was just because of him. But then, he had to believe it: it was happening.

Marc looked down at the severed spearhead, not really seeing it for a moment. Then everything seemed to click into focus, and he saw it indeed. Not a spear, but a pike. To the uneducated there was little difference: both were metal blades attached to the end of a long pole, meant to thrust and pierce. But to a *kailin*, and especially a *kailin* who had seen service against the rebels in Durforen north of Kalitz, the difference was separated by an unbridgeable gulf.

Spears were made by armourers. They might be tanged or socketed depending on how they were forged, and some of them could be of as fine make as the more common swords. But a pike was usually made in secret, and by no more than a common blacksmith. It was a simple weapon: a lozenge of metal for the blade, and below that two flat wings hammered around the staff for a socket, then secured with rivets. A spear was for a warrior. A pike was for a rebel . . .

And what lay at his feet was definitely a pike.

Less than ten years ago in Drosul, men had been executed for making them, villages had been razed when two or three had been found hidden in the thatch of just one cottage. Now they were in Alba. Rebellion followed the appearance of these crude pikes as morning followed sunrise. But not here, surely. Alba's troubles were among its lords, not among its people. Marc stared at the ugly, angular chunk of wood and metal and wondered what else it might mean – besides the all too obvious that his mind was trying to avoid.

'You're a better man than I believed,' said Reth ar'Gyart's rough voice behind him. Forgetting what his eyes were telling him in the wonder of what his ears had just heard, Marc kneed his horse around to look at the older *kailin-eir*. Ar'Gyart wasn't smiling; his face was not one of those where a smile looked comfortable. But he had pitched his words loudly enough for everyone nearby to hear them plainly.

'You have the look of an *eijo*, Marc ar'Dru, and we have treated you so. But you are *kailin*, and honourable. And I salute you for it.'

Reth might not have managed a smile, but there was a warmth in his face that Marc had never seen before. He eyed the Bannerman for a moment, suspicious even now that this might be just some sort of ugly joke, some other move in the Game. But there was no trace of mockery, just the unease of a man who had found himself mistaken in his judgement and was courageous enough to admit it in the hearing of lesser retainers.

'I will speak well of you when we come to Erdanor, and this error will be set right . . .'

As Reth spoke, making a sort of clumsy formal speech out of his apology, Marc looked at the lord's-men, the ones who had spoken to him cheerfully enough yesterday and not at all today. They also looked embarrassed, and relieved that matters were sorting themselves out to their leader's satisfaction. These were just ordinary men, far removed from the politics of feud and clan-war. They served their lord for duty's sake, as much as for honour; for the roof above their heads and the food they ate in Hall, and the respect that a worthy clan-lord's service brought them. Nothing else. Marc guessed that they would rather have talked as not, and were glad this was all over.

'In the meanwhile, since we are not far from the gates of Hold ar'Kelayr, you shall ride beside me as a token of respect . . .'

As for the fighting, and the wounding, and the dying: that was what they were for. It concerned them far less than the intangibles of forced enmity against a one-time friend. And this time at least, no one had died. There had been some ugly wounds inflicted by those pikes: it was coarse metal, unable to hold a properly sharp edge, and ripped rather than cut, tore rather than pierced. But for that same reason, the damage was much less than it might have been.

Even the arrows had not killed . . .

There was a sound in the air like a pigeon's wings, and whatever triviality ar'Gyart had been saying stopped abruptly with a loud, fleshy smack.

When Marc's gaze snapped back towards the sound, Reth's eyes were slightly crossed as if still trying to focus on what had happened, even though they were already glazing. There was a double trickle of blood running from his nostrils, but little other indication of the destruction done inside his head by the last arrow of all. Its grey-feathered flights rested between his dark eyebrows as though they had been placed there by a careful hand, the rest of the shaft protruding from the nape of his neck like a second warrior's braid. More blood was dribbling from its point.

Ar'Gyart was dead already; it was only the action of his shocked nerves that was making him twitch and shudder so, as he keeled rigidly out of his saddle and sideways to the ground. At least, Marc hoped so.

If not, the man took a hellish time to die.

And that was all. There was no attempt to resume the attack, no other arrows except that single fatal shot, and not even a trace of the man who had loosed it – although no great attempt was made to find him. Wandering off across the landscape looking for a hidden archer who could shoot as well as that was just another elaborate form of suicide.

At least they heard what he said to me, Marc thought grimly as he watched three of the other retainers strap ar'Gyart's body across his saddle beside the ashes of his dead lord. *All of them heard it. Let them deny it if they dare.*

There was no real likelihood of that. He was treated as the little column's saviour, as some sort of paladin, as everything Marc knew that he was not. They even gave him the signal honour of carrying Lord ar'Kelayr's sword Katen, a blade he wouldn't have been permitted to so much as touch no more than an hour ago. For all his determined resistance – and given how he had been treated over the past few days – Marc would have been more than human had he not basked in the acclaim just a little, as though it was sunshine after a week of rain. That didn't mean he had to believe what they were saying. But he did stop correcting it.

And anyway, he reassured himself, they were only lord's-men. Such gushing praise would hardly convince whichever *kailin-eir* was now in command at Erdanor that everything they said was true. But he might accept enough of it to offset any unsavoury rumours about this new hero, and that would be reward enough.

To perfectly satisfy the requirements of irony, a scarred and grizzled Bannerman like ar'Gyart should have died in his bed. Even without that, his death was ironic enough. To be killed after the fight was over; to be killed by a chance arrow; to be killed by a peasant rebel who had paused for no more than a moment in his headlong flight . . .

And the greatest irony of all was that it should have happened so close to home and safety. Marc had been right when he recognised the country through which they had been travelling: Hold ar'Kelayr and the fortress of Erdanor had been no more than five miles from the spot where Reth ar'Gyart died. They reached it in less than an hour. An hour too long for Reth.

Below them as they crested the last rolling sweep of moorland lay the fortress, built on an island in the swift-flowing River Erden from which it took its name. The place was a natural fortification, and there had been an Elthanek castle on the site when Clan ar'Kelayr took seizen of the domain around it, some five years ago.

Part of the old castle's fortifications had still been plainly visible the last time Marc had ridden here, on official business between the Clans Talvalin and ar'Kelayr. Since their domains adjoined each other – if the Debatable Lands lying between them were ignored, that is – there had been a moderate amount of communication between the two clan-lords. Only moderate, however; ar'Kelayr had never been able to forget that he, too, had been cheated of the Dunrath holdings by Bayrd's victory. Their relationship had been polite and stiffly formal, nothing else, and the two had avoided meeting face to face whenever possible. Only retainers and Bannermen shuttled to and fro with messages.

That last time it had been something innocuous; permissions asked and granted for logging and charcoal-burning in the northern part of the forest of Baylen, or some such. It could equally have been to do with hunting rights. Marc couldn't – or didn't care to – remember. But whatever his reason then for being away from Dunrath, it hadn't been like now. The times had changed.

And so had Erdanor. But hardly so much, not in just three years . . .

Marc ar'Dru shook his head. Having seen how much trouble Bayrd Talvalin – *no* he thought, *keep it ar'Talvlyn, that makes separating the* before *and the* now *so much easier* – had gone through during the construction of Dunrath, Marc wouldn't have thought such extensive building was possible in so short a time.

But then, he was neither an architect nor a master mason – and anyway, there it was. After lights in the sky, and fights on the ground, and going from being a clan-lord's Companion to being an outcast to being a hero, all in the course of four days, worrying about what had or had not been done to a fortress since he last saw it was very low on Marc's list of concerns.

Perhaps because of the heat, the Erden was throwing up some

sort of mist. Certainly he could clearly see the outlines of the old fortress, the ones with which he was familiar. The rest, nearer the river, were vague, shifting images like trees seen through rain, changing their shape depending on whether he was looking straight at them or merely catching them from the corner of one eye. Those walls and towers looked more like something that had grown out of the ground than anything built with stone and mortar, and skill and sweat and muscle. The outer walls were smooth and shiny, a slick gloss that seemed to come from more than moisture in the air.

Marc wondered if ar'Kelayr had started a return to the old Droselan style of building, where they used not raw stone faced with painted plaster but bricks fired with a coloured glaze. Azure blue was the most popular, recalling a summer sky even in the depths of winter; or bright chrome yellow, to give the grimness of a fortress wall a more cheerful look – and also, for the piously-minded, to make a token gesture of patronage towards the Light of Heaven and the Father of Fires. This wall was neither. It was red. And not just any red, at that.

It was vermeil.

That colour was deep scarlet or rich crimson, less bright than vermilion and less sombre than cinnabar. The colours, patterns and crests of Alban banners and standards all had their own individual meanings, attributes for good or ill. It might have been considered best to avoid any unfortunate colours – certain shades of red, three of the five tones of black, various others – except that tradition held clan colours of exclusively fortunate aspect to be overly proud, and an invitation to misfortune . . .

But vermeil was blood-red, redolent with violence without glory, the most unlucky tincture of them all. Marc had never before seen it used alone, without some other colour to blunt its harmful influence. The only suggestion he could read from it was that Clan ar'Kelayr had a great deal more confidence in its own power and prestige than anyone else believed.

They were an old high-clan line, that couldn't be denied even by their enemies; they had never been truly important, as such things were normally measured. At least, not outside their own minds. But the times were strange, alliances were being forged and broken like the work of an apprentice swordsmith, and there was no knowing what treaty might have been secretly concluded.

Marc ar'Dru managed to keep a smile from his face only from respect for the presence of the dead. A man willing to be a ruthless player of the Game could indeed make his own way in a troubled world. But he could make it so much more quickly in association with a clan whose star was rising.

This time, respect or not, he *did* smile. A star had fallen last night. A star was rising today. The balance was moving to restore equilibrium; and he intended to move with it when it started to swing upward at last.

As they rode closer he could see the banners above the walls, floating in the warm, moist air or snapping when an errant breeze caught them. Like the walls and towers of the fortress, they were red for the most part – though unlike the walls, they at least were banded with other colours. Some of them Marc expected: the blue and red of Clan ar'Kelayr was everywhere, as was only, right above the Clan-Hold.

But he hadn't been anticipating the white and red of Clan ar'Diskan. Gerin ar'Diskan and Vanek ar'Kelayr had been the original rivals for the lands and domain that Bayrd ar'Talvlyn now held, and nothing that he had heard this past ten years had done anything to suggest they had grown any more fond of each other. Yet the ar'Diskan banners were there, and could not be denied.

And there was one in particular, a black and red he didn't recognise.

Then Marc shook his head. No, he had been mistaken. The Clan-Lord's long pennon flying above the citadel wasn't black, just a deeper shade of blue striped with undulant dark shadows. Some odd trick of a mind still confused by the past few hours' events, or maybe of the wind and the mist and the light, had turned those shadows where they lay across its patterning of red into the shape of a crimson serpent.

Then the wind shifted, and the light changed, and it was what it had always been, a blue banner striped with scarlet.

They entered through the Father's Gate, that in any other hold would have been the Great Gate; but here, in a fortress built on an island where there was only one causeway, one bridge and one gate, it could be called whatever the Hold-lord pleased. And it had pleased ar'Kelayr to call this one the Father's Gate. There seemed to be a jest hidden somewhere, but if so, then it was so

142

subtle that Marc didn't know where to even start looking for the laughter. Until he began to ride towards it.

The stone causeway extended only a part of the way out across the river, its span supported on no more than two stone buttresses, sunk into the river-bed and sharply angled to better cut through the force of its current. All the rest of the bridge, right to the gate itself, was wood; and Marc did not need an especially sensitive nose to smell the oil-filled troughs beneath its surface. No trouble here about axing through supports in the face of enemy arrows, *and especially arrows shot as accurately as that last one today*. One touch from a torch and the whole structure would go up in flames, taking any assault with it. This was the Father's Gate indeed. The Father of Fires. . .

The iron-faced liftbridge and its counterweight dropgate seemed almost excessive after that. Marc eyed the place in the manner he had been taught so very long ago, before Landing, before Alba, when he was just a Captain-of-Ten in the Kalitzak cavalry. 'How would you command the taking of this fortress?'

How indeed? Short of damming the River Erden far upstream and waiting for the water to subside – 'and what, Captain ar'Dru, will you do with the water while you wait?' came the instructor's voice again, far more sarcastic this time – and then sending in a full-scale assault all around the perimeter, this would be a devilish hard nut to crack by any other means.

The knowledge was curiously comforting.

Then Marc's eyes narrowed a little. There were people standing beneath the arch of the gate, on the fortress side of the threshold, and it was very plain that they were waiting for him. More: they were waiting for him to cross the threshold into their domain, without invitation and by his own will. It was an entry in the old way, without risk that anyone might be accused of coercion.

If that was how they wanted it, then that was the way they would have it. Marc gave his horse a little touch of the bit and a matching pressure from his heels so that the animal arched its neck and paced haughtily across the last span of bridge. Even though his mount was just a nameless nag – he had refused any of the fine horses that had been his by right as Bannerman to Bayrd – he concealed a quick grin of satisfaction at the way the beast had behaved. None of its fine-bred stable-mates could have done any better.

Still in the saddle, he studied the men who came to greet him, recognising a few: Ivern ar'Diskan, Gerin's second son, and some of his personal retainers – that explained the banners, though Marc was looking forward to hearing what had brought *him* here, into the fortress of a clan who, if they weren't his father's enemies, were certainly less than friends.

At least the ar'Diskan'r were looking more pleased to see him than they had done on the last three occasions Marc had met them. There wasn't a comment about his status, or even a dubious glance at his cropped hair. It was as if they knew what he had done, why it had been done, and appreciated the stand he had taken.

There was one other man, standing a little further back in the shadows of the gate, who seemed a stranger at first. Tall, dark-haired, lean; what little Marc could see of his face suggested he had the sort of angular good looks that went with a carving adzed from oak and left unsmoothed. But when he stepped into the full sunlight, ar'Dru realised he was as wrong about that as he had been about the colour and crest of the citadel's pennon.

This man wasn't dark. Far from it: his hair, done up in the three braids of a clan-lord, was as fair as Marc's own . . . had been. All right, still was, even if there was less of it.

He was handsome almost to beauty, his eyes blue, his skin clear, his stride confident, and his mouth curving in a smile of welcome that was as honest and open as a child's. He was everything an Alban *kailin-eir* should be, everything that should be striven for and everything that, thanks to human nature, was so seldom achieved; for besides an appearance that would make any man envious and any woman sigh, he was courteous and honourable, honest and worthy of respect.

How Marc knew all those things about him only at first sight and when the man hadn't even spoken yet, he couldn't have said; but he knew it all the same, and felt his own face breaking almost without volition into a matching smile.

'Welcome, welcome, welcome,' the man said, an outburst that would have sounded effusive from almost anyone else. But from that face, and warmed by that smile, it was uttermost sincerity.

'I am Kurek ar'Kelayr,' the man said. 'My later father's eldest son, and now Clan-Lord ar'Kelayr.' Marc looked at him blankly. His memory was insisting that Vanek ar'Kelayr had had only one son, Dyrek, the young reaver who had killed himself in Bayrd ar'Talvlyn's despite. The memory hovered for a moment, like a butterfly; then like a butterfly it fluttered away.

'You haven't seen me before, of course,' Kurek continued. 'Given your past service, our two clans have scarcely been close these past years. And then, you've guested in Erdanor no more than . . . How many times was it? Four? Five . . . ?'

'Five times, *arluth*,' Marc responded automatically. 'But why?' Blond eyebrows, fine as spun gold, lifted in polite enquiry. 'Why haven't I seen you, in any of those five visits?'

'Because I was in Cerdor, Marc-*eir*. In Cerdor. Speaking with the Overlord Albanak, and later with his children. Someone had to. I regret that my father had difficulty forgiving Albanak-*arluth* for that business over the Dunrath domains, and as for my poor brother,' Kurek's broad shoulders lifted in a shrug more dismissive than regretful, 'you saw for yourself how his mind worked. He was a hothead. That was why it sat so loosely on his shoulders.'

'Of course . . .' That sound of uncertainty shouldn't have been in his voice, or at least it should have been far better hidden. A high-clan lord was speaking to him as an equal, and it wasn't just lacking in respect, it was downright insulting, for a *kailin* with hopes of soon being in that lord's service to doubt what he had been told. But the doubt was there, all the same. 'You were in Cerdor?' he repeated.

Kurek's brows shifted again, this time they drew together in the merest suggestion of a frown, and for an instant Marc felt that the young lord's concentration was focusing solely on him. 'I was about my father's business,' Kurek said, his voice flat and toneless.

And for all that Kurek ar'Kelayr had not yet uttered a single word of sorrow about his father's death, his explanation seemed to make a sort of perfect sense.

7
Tactics

THE GHOST OF a savoury scent still haunted the air when Bayrd
Talvalin turned from the window and resumed his seat at the
table. He sniffed, and smiled in fond recollection of meals past,
and this last one in particular.

The previous week, he had swallowed his pride at last – along
with a last platter of chicken, the taste of which meat was
beginning to stick in his throat – and had ridden with Dunrath's
steward to Redmer village to spend an educational afternoon with
Youenn Kloatr, the headman there. Behaving like a lord rather
than a warlord had served, at least for those few hours, to take his
mind off other matters. It had even managed to turn the clock
back, to a time when the acquisition of a given quantity of food
and drink and fodder was a concern not complicated by the
feigned treachery of friends and the feigned friendship of enemies.

Bayrd had seen no action during his military service in Drosul,
at least nothing involving the flashing of heroic swords in the
sunlight. There had only been the small, scuffling combats of pen
and parchment and requisition, as a *kailin tleir'ek*, a Captain-of-
One Hundred – himself – tried to get any one of a number of
Quartermasters to part with the supplies that from their behaviour
they had paid for out of their own pockets.

Pigs had been his thought then.

Oddly enough, pigs had been part of Youenn's answer as well, and
pigs it had been. There had been rabbits mentioned, and pigeons, but
mostly pigs. Bayrd had left his steward to deal with the logistics of the
business – he was a clan-lord and a *kailin-eir*, not a farmer – and had
celebrated his own cleverness with roast pork. Or it might have been
ham, or bacon. Some part of a pig, anyway.

There was a dish of small pieces of tender piggy on the table right now, toasted crisp for eating with the fingers, after dipping each one in a dull-red sauce whose innocent oily surface hid a fragrant pungence hot enought to bring tears to the eyes of a genuine dragon. Beside it was a glazed pottery jug of ale, drawn from the cellars in the deep caverns far below Dunrath, and still so cold that moisture was beading attractively on its glazed surface.

And next to that was the dart which a man had used to kill his companion.

Bayrd picked up the lead-shod *telek* dart and rested it on the tip of his index finger, watching thoughtfully as the wicked little missile pivoted on its point of balance. It tipped off eventually, falling on to the table heavily enough for its sharpened point to be embedded in the wood.

'Nasty,' said Eskra, looking up at the sound of impact. She reached out and rocked the dart free, weighing it thoughtfully in the palm of her hand. 'Very nasty.'

'But effective,' Bayrd corrected. 'A useful weapon. We should adopt them.'

Eskra made a face at him. 'You would say that. It could have killed you.'

'A lot of things could have done that. Including you. But none of them did.'

'Not for want of trying.'

'The *talathen* didn't want to kill me. They didn't want to kill anybody. What they wanted—'

'Is something I know well enough. Drop the subject.'

Bayrd did as he was told. That had been a grim, frightening night, and its events were still too recent for Eskra Talvalin's peace of mind. When she was feeling out of sorts or ill at ease about something, she had few scruples about spreading her discomfort in all directions, on the offchance that dilution might relieve the bad taste such feelings left in her mouth. 'All right,' he said. 'Dropped.'

There had been news from Cerdor two days ago, and that news had answered some of the questions which had been lurking at the back of Bayrd's mind since the night of the Shadowthieves. One of them gave only a crooked sort of comfort: the blame for the raid could not be laid at Gerin ar'Diskan's door. Clan Talvalin had not been the only ones paid a visit by the *talathen*. There had been others, and they had been less fortunate.

Lord ar'Lerutz's youngest daughter had been taken, and the lord's own sister; two of Lord ar'Dakkur's sons, and a daughter; all but one of Lord ar'Sanen's children, and his wife as well. Children, wives, brothers and sisters of half a dozen other clans and Families; more than thirty in all. And that number did not begin to include the retainers and servants, guards and lord's-men and faithful *kailinin*, who had been killed or wounded during the abductions.

All of the victims were being held somewhere in Cerdor. But nothing more than that: somewhere. No one yet knew exactly where, or why, or by whose orders. That the Overlord's clan were involved was certain – otherwise, why Cerdor at all? – but not which one of the two rivals had decided to put pressure on their wavering supporters.

Or on the other's supporters . . .

That was the problem. The parents and other relatives of some of the hostages had not yet made their positions clear on the matter of the Overlord's succession. Bayrd had been one of them. As for the others, they were evenly enough divided in their support for either Yraine or Erhal ar'Albanak that nothing could be deduced from the evidence at hand.

It wasn't beyond the bounds of possibility that whoever had done this was acting in a back-handed manner, capturing the children of their own allies so as to alienate their rival by assumption of dishonourable behaviour. Such pressure to change a political stance was not uncommon in Drosul; but it wasn't approved of even there, and it was actively despised by the Albans, who had long considered themselves above such dishonourable machinations.

Until now.

And there was always a chance that the pressure was intended to force one side or the other *not* to change. It was typical of such a situation, to answer one question and create a dozen more. Once the first demands were made, matters would become clearer. At least it would be obvious who was behind all this.

But in the meanwhile there was the growing threat in the north, where Kalarr cu Ruruc exercised his own brand of persuasion on sons who had been stolen in a manner as complete as, but far more subtle than, the hostages in Cerdor. Their henchmen were joining them already, some willingly by the demands of honour, others at the command of their own lords. The end result was the same.

And there was an irregular but steady trickle of *eijin*, dismissed retainers, passed-over lord's-men and other such unsavoury people making their way northward. All of them bore arms, and all of them were trained in the use of what they bore. Erdanor was becoming a barracks for the largest private army in Alba; and sooner or later, in the manner of such armies, it would be put to use.

Bayrd retrieved the dart and laid it on the table, spinning it and watching the rotation slow and waver to a halt with the point aimed at him, the butt towards Eskra. He spun it again. This time it stopped in the other direction – at least until Eskra reached out one long finger and delicately directed it away from her.

'Avert,' she said, though what her stare said was *don't do that again*. Bayrd lifted the dart, turned it over in his fingers and then very deliberately stuck it back into the table-top, pointing at nobody now, and harmless. *Better*, said Eskra's eyes, hooding behind their lids a little.

'And Reth ar'Gyart?' asked Bayrd. 'What about him?'

'He died. I saw him die.'

'Through Marc's eyes.'

'Don't think that made it any easier. It didn't.'

'But it can't have been that much of a surprise. You said it might happen; you were *expecting* it to happen. And you still haven't told me why.'

Either Eskra was a better actress, playing a better part, than at any other time Bayrd had encountered during all the years of their marriage – or her expression of surprise was entirely genuine. 'I thought you knew,' she said. 'I was sure of it . . .'

'With Gemmel ar'Ekren turning out to be a good deal more than he seemed, and stars falling out of the sky and terrifying people—'

'It was just one star.'

'That's still one too many. And call it foolish if you like, but I can't shift from my mind the thought that Gemmel had something to do with it. The thing happened just after he left; it fell towards Meneth Taran in the Blue Mountains, where he told us he was heading; and then there was—'

'You're right, loved,' said Eskra, smiling slightly. 'I *do* call it foolish.'

'Then no matter. But with that on top of all else, and somebody in Cerdor playing their own version of the Great Game with my children—'

'*Our* children!'

'. . . as unscheduled pieces on the board, I'm surprised that I can still remember to eat when I'm hungry.' He selected another piece of meat, dunked it in sauce, chewed – then coughed as the spices bit his throat, and put the fire out with a hasty swallow of ale. 'You see?' Eskra smiled, as he had hoped she might; but the matter still remained unresolved. 'As for Reth, no. I don't know. So tell me . . .'

Eskra did, and it made unsettling listening. Kalarr cu Ruruc was behind both killings, they both knew that much already, but where Vanek ar'Kelayr's death by sorcery was meant to clear the way for Kalarr to become the new ar'Kelayr Clan-Lord – and conveniently discredit Bayrd at the same time – Reth ar'Gyart's death was a straightforward hired murder. Not an accident, not an act of war, not even an act of rebellion by a peasant against the only representative of his lord that he could reach. Just a murder, committed to order and probably for money.

'Another *tulath*?' Bayrd said softly, not so much a question as simply speculating aloud. Eskra broke off and glanced at him, then shrugged.

'You know more about the Shadowthieves than I. But perhaps. One man's gold is as good as another. For all we know, Kalarr's is better than most. And we are already aware that there are *talathen* in Alba.'

No matter who had carried it out, the attack had been intended for a single purpose: to kill Bannerman ar'Gyart before he could return to Hold ar'Kelayr at Erdanor and see what had been happening. And it had succeeded.

'Why ar'Gyart especially?'

'You saw him. The man had an aversion to magic stronger than any I've ever seen before. He wasn't as susceptible as other people.' Bayrd still looked blank, and Eskra groaned inwardly. 'You know how some people can never learn to read, no matter how hard they try? As if the letters and the words just don't make sense?' This time Bayrd nodded, frowning slightly, wondering where all this was leading. 'That's like Reth ar'Gyart. He and the Art would have been like oil and water.' Eskra considered her own words for a second, then allowed herself a small, satisfied smile. 'Oil and water. Yes. It's a better image than I thought. They'll mix, but never completely, and once you stop mixing they separate again.'

'But what's it a better image *for*?'

'I told you. Ar'Gyart and magic. And since what cu Ruruc has done to his own appearance and to Erdanor involves so much of the Art, it was better for him that ar'Gyart not live to see it.'

'But the glamour . . . ?'

'Wouldn't work on Reth ar'Gyart. I told you: oil and water. It might work, but it would need to be renewed. Constantly, from minute to minute, maybe even from second to second. And it wouldn't start to work even then, without cu Ruruc shifting the entire focus of the spell – and all of his concentration – on to that one man. And as soon as he did *that*, he'd lose his control over the rest.'

Bayrd whistled thinly. That made a sort of sense. 'A nice balancing-act; it's not one I'd like to try. Murder is so much simpler. But what made ar'Gyart so different from the others? His inability with magic: this oil and water business you're so proud of?'

'Partly. But also desire.' Bayrd's eyebrows shot up. 'Or more correctly the lack of it.'

'That's a peculiar choice of words where Reth's concerned.' They both knew what he meant. 'Desire' might have been an odd word to use in such a context at all, but it was odder still with reference to ar'Gyart, who lived for the observation of his Honour and for very little else. The man had never married, and even to a people who loved salacious gossip it was common knowledge that this wasn't for lack of a suitable match or even because his interests didn't tend that way.

Reth ar'Gyart simply had no inclination to change the habits of a lifetime. He could be faithful to his lord, or to his lady – but not to both. And because it involved that Honour of his, the lord came first. It was an attitude which had made him a figure of fun among the younger Albans, but it was a mockery which at the same time was tinged with reluctant respect.

'All the others in Erdanor,' said Eskra, 'low-clan, high-clan, all of them, and Ivern ar'Diskan just as much as all the rest, want to believe in this Kurek ar'Kelayr.' She snorted derisively. 'Though he might have taken the trouble to adopt a less obvious name. Whatever. He offers them a chance of more than they have. More than faith. More than fealty. More than the restrictions laid down by your Alban Code of Honour. You heard him.'

'I heard you.'

'All right. Marc heard him. I heard Marc. You heard me. Happy now?' There was a good-humoured stubbornness in the way Eskra said that which made Bayrd quite sure she was ready to continue until he gave in. So to save time, he gave in at once.

'He was making noises that I've heard before,' he said. 'In Kalitz. It's a human enough failing: everyone would like to believe they're more important than they are. Or think so, at least. And be told so. That's what he's doing.'

'And they're believing him. That's what makes it so dangerous. How long is it going to be before they start trying to prove it?'

'He'd be a poor sort of orator otherwise,' said Bayrd, and laughed. It faltered when Eskra failed to join in. 'Oh, come on. If they didn't believe what he said at least some of the time, and that something good for them might come of it, then they'd be elsewhere. Back in their homes, maybe. Or back in Kalitz, hoping for employment as mercenaries. Most of the so-noble high clans started that way, generations back. The wheel turns, eh?'

'It's who gets crushed in the turning that concerns me. You're ignoring him, Bayrd-*ain*. Ar'Sanen, ar'Dakkur, ar'Lerutz, they're all ignoring him, because thanks to someone in Cerdor they all have other things to think about. Do you know, I doubt if they even know enough of what's happening here to ignore it properly!'

Eskra drew little spirals and circles on the table-top, gazing at them as though they were convoluted symbols that held some meaning only she could read. 'If enough people ignore him for enough time,' she said, 'then there'll come a time when he can't be ignored. But he'll be powerful enough to ignore *you*. All of you. Except the ones who might be of some use to him. And I don't know which would be the unlucky ones.'

Bayrd didn't reply, but when he leaned forward and threw another few logs on the fire, that small gesture said more than words. Summer it might be, sunny it might be, warm it certainly was; but there had been something about the quiet assurance of Eskra's words that had turned the whole room cold and dark.

'Come on,' he said at last. 'That council meeting, remember? Iskar and the other *kailinin* are waiting for us.'

'I'd rather stay here.'

'You're expected. Needed.'

'Bayrd-*ain*, I've got a feeling that something's happening in Erdanor. Something to do with Marc. I should—'

'You should live your own life for a while.' Bayrd smiled and took both her hands in both of his. 'You can't spend every hour of the day inside Marc's head. You can always eavesdrop later.'

'Later may be too late.'

'Loved, if you're going to start thinking like that, then why bother getting out of bed in the morning?' He hesitated, considering. 'You couldn't activate the spell during—'

'During the council meeting? Hardly. If I'm expected, if they're going to be asking me the sort of questions that only I can answer, about Kalarr, and the Art,' she watched Bayrd nod uncomfortably, 'then I'll need all my wits about me. And nobody else's getting in the way.'

'Then let it be, just for an hour. Please. For me? So that I can have *your* company: you alone, not some half-and-half fusion of my wife and my best friend.' He grinned quickly. 'Though it's sometimes more like a *con*fusion.'

Eskra sighed. There was no arguing with Bayrd in one of these moods, at least not in any good-humoured way. He could be incredibly stubborn sometimes; not often, but from the sound of it this was one of those times. She nodded, and let him help her from her seat.

Probably nothing would happen in Erdanor except another of those interminable bigoted sermons that Kalarr – she couldn't think of him by any other name – was so fond of delivering. The man was a typical wizard, in love with words, and especially when they were delivered by that even more beloved instrument, his own voice. If she could be certain that Kalarr would do nothing else but talk, Eskra knew she would sleep more easily at night.

Except for worrying about the *talathen* and when they might come back, and about what Gerin ar'Diskan might be planning independently of everything that had already happened, and all the other threats and problems of which Kalarr cu Ruruc was only one . . .

'How many of your fathers shed their blood to win this land?' asked Kurek ar'Kelayr. 'And what have you gained from it?'

It was one of his familiar tricks of speech, to address the table in general but nobody in particular. If there was no immediate answer, he would continue his monologue until something sparked a response, and in the meanwhile . . . well, the man was evidently fond of the sound of his own voice.

Glass and metal clinked as several flagons of wine circulated among the men seated around the large table. Some of them still picked sporadically at the wreckage of the meal; others just picked their teeth.

'A younger son may not inherit,' said one of them, in the tone of one stating the obvious. 'You know it; we all know it. We've,' a wave around the table, 'always known it. The law and the tradition—'

'Is an old law and an old tradition, from an old country. This,' Kurek's wave of the hand was a far more expansive gesture, one that took in all of the fortress of Erdanor, and by implication the domain surrounding it and the lands beyond it, all the way from here to the sea, 'this is new. We need new traditions, new laws, new customs for this new Land. And we have them,' he added quickly before anyone else could correct him. 'Just . . . not all of them are good.'

The wine was good, thought Marc ar'Dru. And the fire was good, and the food had been more than good. He had eaten better in Erdanor on this ordinary night than on several guesting-feasts he could remember in Dunrath. He felt full, and comfortable, and more than a little drowsy. Kurek ar'Kelayr and his gaggle of immediate cronies were off again on one of their never-ending spirals of discussion about how Alba and all of the rest of the world could be put right, if only *they* were given the opportunity to do it. Marc stifled a yawn. He had heard it all before, since he came here. A dozen times. A score of times . . .

And yet it wasn't boring him. No one was expected to

contribute an opinion, Kurek was capable enough of filling the air with words all by himself, but on the few occasions when Marc had felt moved to speak, his words had earned the kind of courteous attention that had made him ashamed of their stumbling delivery. They had not sounded like Kurek.

Now *his* words stayed in the memory, sensible, reasoned, a compliment to the wit and wisdom of those privileged to hear them. Those words were curiously lacking in some respects: he had only twice spoken of his father, his brother, of the Bannerman Reth ar'Gyart and the presumed rebels who had killed them. After that the entire subject had been dropped, as if it was no importance.

In a way, Marc knew he was right. The dead were dead and gone; better by far to live with the living. And there were more people living in Hold ar'Kelayr right now than he had seen in all the weeks since his arrival. During the day, and the constant round of military exercises, the babble of voices was a constant confusion. They all spoke Alban, more or less, but some of them spoke with foreign accents, Yuvannek and Droselan, that spoke of mercenaries who had crossed the sea with an eye to war for profit. That was only to be expected: pay and plunder attracted hired soldiers like rotten fruit drew wasps.

Marc had grinned crookedly to himself at that. It had certainly attracted the Alban horsemen down from the high steppes, all those years ago. And now look at them. One-time mercenaries buying mercenaries in their turn. Which land would *these* men conquer when their time came? he mused. What would they call it? And where would the mercenaries come from when *they* went hiring swords and men to use them? It was a circle – an eccentric one, to be sure, that didn't spin true – but it was the kind of thing that Eskra ar'Talvlyn used to delight in. He wondered incuriously what she was doing now. Trying to shelve up her husband's slipping reputation, probably. A wizard and a murderer . . . they made a fine pair.

But there were other accents that made Marc think much harder about Kurek ar'Kelayr's influence: provincial dialects that suggested he was somehow gaining support from some very unlikely parts of Alba. It sometimes seemed to Marc that only he was aware of how incongruous that was. Kurek was a *kailin-eir* and high-clan lord who openly despised the Elthan and Prytenek people, calling them enemies and far worse; yet there were some of those same people in his service.

Though not at the table: this meal was for high-clan Albans only, and Marc guessed that he was here more by association than in his own right. No matter; it hadn't affected the taste of the food. But he had raised that matter of privilege and position only five minutes before, no more than mildly interested in a reply.

'If they want to die on our behalf,' someone had said callously in response to his question, 'then why worry?'

'It's more than that, and you should have the wit to know it.' That had been Kurek's voice: unmistakable, smooth and unctuous, bland as cream, but able to cut like a whip when he heard stupid statements being made without authority. 'An ally can always earn respect. Even honour. It's when they expect it as a right and a privilege, just because some slut of a sister has made an advantageous marriage with one of us . . . But yes,' he had added as an afterthought, 'they'll be in the front rank of any battle.'

'To see them dead?' asked Marc.

'To see them earn the respect they so earnestly desire. Anyone can stand well out of harm's way and shout encouragement.'

'But it takes guts to stand at the front? That we'll have to see.'

'Yes, indeed,' Kurek had said. 'What a very appropriate choice of words.' His grin turned wolfish, a thin, twisted smirk that made him look entirely different from the smiling, affable lord of the fortress who spoke so well and kept such an excellent table.

Marc had seen it happen several times since their first encounter by the fortress gate. He might be gazing, absorbed by some thought of his own, in Kurek's direction, and for an instant, especially if the Clan-Lord was talking to another of the guesting *kailinin*, he would seem to see someone else. It was a sensation as peculiar as looking into a mirror and not seeing yourself. No. It was more subtle than that. Like looking at yourself in the mirror, and discovering that the reflection hadn't reversed . . .

And then Kurek would notice, and return the stare with a smile, or perhaps just the hint of a frown – and the oddness would be gone again, taking any curiosity with it.

Like the few minutes that had just passed. Kurek had slipped just once, that time, like a snake startled into striking. Normally his venom was much more understated, more reasoned, more . . .

More acceptable, thought Marc, listening to the man now.

'. . . This much advantage at least,' Kurek was saying. 'I'm not a younger son. I can – I have – inherited Erdanor, Hold ar'Kelayr, all its lands. Most of you aren't so fortunate.'

There was a growl of assent from the younger men. Normally they would have sat in silence, or merely nodded their approval, but in the course of the meal they had all drunk enough wine or ale, and drowned enough of their inhibitions, for their responses to become more vocal.

'The Overlord Albanak took possession of this Land in the old way,' said Kurek. 'Taken by the sword, held by the sword, defended by the sword. But what are those swords doing now? They're turning in our hands, turning against us all. And who stands to gain from all of this? Not our fathers, not our elder brothers, certainly not ourselves.'

He paused, to moisten his lips with the merest sip from his cup and listen to the rumbling groundswell of favourable opinion. 'Those who benefit, those who are being shown the most favour, are those who least deserve it. We conquered the people of the Three Provinces; we beat them in fair fight, man to man and sword to sword. And now, in less than a generation – no, far less than that, less even than ten years! – we treat with them as equals! Equals . . . ? *Eirin*, gentlemen, these are a conquered people. When in all of history did defeat bring such rights?'

Ivern ar'Diskan muttered something into his wine-cup that neither Kurek, nor even Marc sitting almost beside him, could hear; but his tone made the meaning plain enough.

'And the grounds for such behaviour, for such benevolence towards it? To more speedily bring peace to the Land, they tell us. "Peace" and "prosperity". Here? Now?' Someone laughed harshly, and Kurek allowed himself a brief, bleak smile. 'We're living in a country that is teetering on the brink of war, and people who should know better still bandy such words about as though the words themselves had weight. If this is the sort of peace that comes of even-handed dealing with the vanquished, then I want no part of it!'

Marc knew the sound of good sense when he heard it, and so did the rest. Some of them cheered aloud, others merely banged their wine-cups against the table as applause.

'Worse still,' said Kurek, 'we're all of us far too well aware of what else those fathers are doing. And not just fathers; brothers who will become lords and fathers in their own time; and high-clan lords who should have more respect for their lines, their clans, and for the purity of their blood. *Our* blood . . .'

The applause faltered into an uneasy pause, doubt and wariness holding further reaction in check until they could be certain what might be appropriate.

'They are taking this mad policy still further.' Kurek's voice had dropped almost to a whisper, but in the silence of the room each word was clear enough. 'They are taking mistresses, taking consorts . . . Father of Fires, those who can are *marrying* this conquered people, and making their bastards legitimate and equal to those born of a pure Alban line.'

He put his hands flat on the table and stared down at them. 'And again, they call this equality. Equality.' Kurek laid one hand over the other, covering it, holding it down, and looked up at all the hot, resentful eyes around the table to make sure that his message was quite clear. '*This* is equality, once a fallen enemy is given precedence over those rightfully entitled. Equality.' Kurek gazed at them all, one by one, and each man knew that the words were directed at him alone, taking him into his leader's confidence, appealing to his intelligence.

'It's no more or less than a usurpation of the rights of blood, bought and paid for with blood. A usurpation just as certain as though they had drawn blade and taken back what we have claimed and conquered. But if they had taken with the sword what we have taken with the sword, then we could call them honour-able, open, worthy adversaries. They have not. Because they fear us! So instead they deprive us of what should rightfully come down to us and to our children, not by courage but by cunning. They steal it, like thieves from the shadows.'

Kurek shrugged. 'We are the true sons of our fathers, born of Alban mothers. But because we are the *younger* sons, we are forbidden to inherit land or rank or style or title. All because an old law from an old land, made and observed and enforced by old men, tells us that we can't! So this new land might as well be handed back to the Elthans and the Pryteneks and all the others right now' – there was a mutter of angry criticism at the mere proposal, but Kurek just smiled – 'since in a few generations it's going to be back with them anyway. And it will be as if the pure Alban clans, the bold ones who took this land with the strong arm, had never existed . . .'

A hot outrage had been building up inside Marc ar'Dru as Kurek spoke, and it sat like lead in his chest so that he felt almost breathless with the weight of it. He was willing to allow that some of what Clan-Lord Kurek had said was nothing but common sense; but too much of the rest was beginning like an insult directed specifically at Bayrd ar'Talvlyn and his wife. Marc had his own views about Bayrd, and about what he had and had not done – he would not have been sitting here otherwise – but there had to be a limit somewhere. For the sake of honour, he couldn't sit still any longer. Something had to be said.

In the instant that he moved, Kurek's head snapped around. Marc found himself at the focus of an extraordinary blue-eyed stare, cold as ice, hot as fire, burning into his mind as if knowing not merely what he was about to say but the very thoughts which had prompted the words. Kurek ar'Kelayr was still smiling, but the smile had thinned and chilled until it was no more than a slight stretching of his lips.

'You were about to speak?' he said, soft as the warning hiss of a snake in the grass.

Marc blinked, swallowed, and knew exactly what he had intended to say. For just a moment, the clauses had been a little confused, the phrasing a little slipshod; if nothing else, one's powers of rhetoric were exercised by the discourses carried on in Erdanor. That spasm of outrage had teetered for a few seconds on the edge of outright and undignified anger, enough to make his speech sound foolish, but though it still burned behind his breastbone he had it under control.

'Bayrd ar'Talvlyn,' he said, 'has gone one better than that. He's married an Elthanek woman—'

'I already know that,' said Kurek, with the air of immediate disinterest from a man half-hoping to hear something new, but cheated of the revelation by common gossip.

'She's a wizard.'

'I already know that, too.' Kurek began to turn away, a gesture so dismissive as to be downright rude, except that Marc didn't see it that way. There was only the justified annoyance of an intelligent man whose time was being wasted.

'They won't have any more children than their two daughters,' he added, desperate for some sign of approval. 'So Dunrath's physician told me.'

Kurek ar'Kelayr paused, glanced back at him, raised his eyebrows, and started to smile again. 'Well, now, this is rather more interes—'

'And Bayrd has the sorcerer's Talent.'

The clank and rumble as Kurek's wine-cup fell from his fingers and rolled across the surface of the table was loud enough, even over the murmur of conversation, to turn heads all over the room. He looked down at it, and at the spreading pool of wine which a servant hurried to mop up, and he didn't seem in the least annoyed by the mess. Rather the reverse. He was grinning broadly when he returned his attention to Marc ar'Dru, so broadly that Marc could do nothing else but match the grin even though he wasn't quite aware yet of what it was he had done.

'You,' said Kurek softly, 'have just sung as well for your supper as I've ever heard.' Marc still didn't know exactly what the Clan-Lord ar'Kelayr meant, but he was filled with a warm glow of pleasure at having done . . . Well, whatever it was, he had done it right.

The least commendation from Kurek ar'Kelayr had that effect. It always sounded far more sincere, and thus more gratifying, than far more solid rewards and higher praise from anyone else. Though Kurek was a high-clan lord, thought Marc with satisfaction, he always treated even the least of his retainers – and indeed people like himself, who were no more than guests in Hall – not just as his equals, but as his friends.

But there was little friendliness in the peremptory way he appropriated Ivern ar'Diskan's chair so that he could sit beside Marc. The short, sharp command of 'Ar'Diskan, move yourself!' sounded more like a master addressing his servant than the genial voice which he had been using until now.

Ivern was plainly not accustomed to such treatment. He had long been the most important of ar'Kelayr's friends and supporters, not so much because of any abilities he might have demonstrated as because of who he was: the second son of a high-clan lord, and not just any lord but Gerin ar'Diskan, ruler of the strongest domain in the whole of the Province of Elthan. But Marc had something new, something that was suddenly much more influential than family: he had information about an enemy.

Ivern hesitated, his face darkening with anger as he glared first at Marc and then at Kurek. But then his expression changed, the high colour drained to a pallor almost of fright and he got up more quickly than might have been expected. Marc, still basking in the warmth of approval, was unconcerned both by the anger and the fear. He merely wondered idly what had been said or done in the past to provoke such a reaction; then put the thought aside as Kurek ar'Kelayr sat down beside him, all brisk business.

Kurek's voice had lowered almost to intimacy, so that even in this crowded room their conversation was almost completely private. Marc was surprised, pleased, even flattered by the attention, and even more so by the affable manner in which it was conducted.

Since he had come to Hold ar'Kelayr at Erdanor, there had been several other occasions when he had been questioned, much more closely than this amiable interrogation over a flagon of wine. That hadn't surprised him, even when one of the questioners had been young ar'Diskan. Bayrd ar'Talvlyn had made few friends in the north, and there was no love lost between Lord Gerin's sons and anyone to do with him. No matter how much a lord's retainer might profess to have dropped that allegiance, one could never be too careful.

On all of those other times, if the questions slanted towards sorcery or the Art Magic, and its employment by Clan ar'Talvlyn, Marc had managed to evade the issue. He couldn't remember exactly how he had sidestepped giving any answers, or even why he would need to do so. Except, maybe, for the disgrace any decent *kailin* would feel when admitting familiarity with such a subject, while talking to one man whose father had been cheated by sorcery, and living in the fortress of another whose father had been *killed* by it.

But now it was as if that barrier of shame had been removed, or at least not set in place by whatever had prompted it before. Kurek showed no animosity as Marc told him how he had learned of Bayrd ar'Talvlyn's ability with the Talent; indeed, he seemed more than pleased, especially when Marc elaborated.

'It's not so much an ability as an inability,' he said. 'He can't control it – at least, not well. The woman Eskra seems to be the only one who can—'

'Are you sure?'

'Well, I've never seen him do anything as if he really meant to. It always seems to be more hope than intention, if you understand me.'

'I do indeed. But was it always so? Even with that notorious business when he cut off his own hand?'

'I believe so, yes. He told me that he hoped Eskra might be able to heal him, if he couldn't do it himself.'

'But he went ahead and cut?'

'Gerin-*arluth* ar'Diskan did the cutting—'

'Of course. I was forgetting. But go on . . .'

'And Bayrd said that he would have done it anyway. An honourable sacrifice, he called it. Something any Bannerman Companion should be willing to do for his lord, and a long way short of laying down his life.' Marc grinned and held up his own left hand, wiggling his fingers. 'I call it a fair exchange. He wasn't risking his sword-hand; and he got the domain of Dunrath out of it, no matter what happened.'

'And could Eskra have cured such an injury?'

'Maybe. Maybe not. I don't know. I've never seen her do it.'

'But she's still a better sorcerer than Bayrd? You're sure of that?'

'Kurek-*eir*, I'd rather not talk too much about such things, if you don't mind.'

'Why?' said Kurek, his voice briefly sharp and suspicious. 'Are you afraid of giving away too many secrets? Don't forget that they're the secrets of a lord who wasn't too concerned about giving away your honour . . .'

Marc blushed; it was the first time that anyone in Erdanor had reminded him of that, but perhaps because of their courteous restraint, it still smarted. 'No!' he snapped. 'No . . . It's just that, well, magic isn't . . . isn't *nice*.'

It was a clumsy choice of words when there were so many others, but it described almost exactly how he felt: hot and embarrassed, as though he had been caught talking about something sleazy.

Kurek patted him on the arm. 'I know exactly what you mean,' he murmured sympathetically, getting to his feet and shoving the replenished wine-flagon towards Marc. 'It makes you want to go and wash your hands, doesn't it?'

As he strode quickly from the room, looking very pleased about something and not waiting for a reply, Marc nodded agreement, even though he knew what Kurek had said wasn't completely right. He poured himself a brimming cup of wine and gulped down half of it, swirling the chilly sourness of it around his teeth and tongue as though to rinse away another, foul taste. Talking about magic didn't make him just want to wash his hands, or even his mouth. It made him want to go and wash his *mind*.

'Cerdor and the southern lords know little enough about what's going on here,' said Askelin ar'Goel, the castellan of Dunrath, 'and they care still less. They have their own concerns, and anyway, has anyone even *told* them?'

'Who would you tell?' Eskra asked no one in particular. She glanced at the questioning faces up and down the table. 'There isn't an overlord, there isn't a High Council—'

'But lady, there *is*!' Iskar ar'Joren insisted. Eskra shot him a glare at the interruption.

'. . . that anyone will trust,' she finished. 'The lords of the Council would normally advise the Overlord. In the absence of an Overlord,' she shrugged, dismissing the High Council and all its works, 'each one of them has his own agenda, to benefit himself and his own faction. No one else. And certainly no one up here in the wild north, where nothing of significance every happens. So . . .'

She seemed to be daring Iskar, or Askelin, or anyone else – including Bayrd – to take exception to the way she had all but usurped control of the meeting. For his part, Bayrd sat quietly off to one side, arms folded, listening carefully to what was being said, but far more interested in the way expressions on faces shifted as the discussion swung to and fro.

'So we deal with this ourselves,' said one of the others, 'and answer to Cerdor afterwards. If at all.'

'Alone?' said Iskar.

'There are alliances enough, of one sort or another,' said Eskra. 'Between this clan and its supporters. There are a number of Houses and Families who have gained benefits from Clan Talvalin. Use them. It's time to – what is it you Albans say? – call in your markers. So do it.'

That was the problem. After the incident with Vanek ar'Kelayr, and then the denunciation by Marc ar'Dru directly afterwards,

Clan Talvalin were not as well thought-of, or as well supported, as they had been no more than five weeks before. Bayrd knew the accusations well enough; how it was all his fault, at least to a certain extent; how he had gone too much on his dignity, distanced himself too much from the whole ugly business – and uttered not a word to formally deny even the ugly rumours that followed his Bannerman's departure.

And then there were the hostages. After that sudden spate of kidnapping, nobody was willing to trust anyone, anywhere, any more. Trust had become equated with vulnerability. Vulnerability meant weakness. And weakness meant defeat . . .

That was Kalarr's intention: to divide and to conquer, in the best traditions of strategy. The division was already happening, clear enough even to the untrained eye. As for the conquest, that would happen when he was ready. Today. Or tomorrow. In a month. Or not for half a year . . .

Eskra had her suspicions already, and after rapping with her knuckles on the table loudly enough to become the focus of everyone's attention, she began to outline them. It would happen, she said, within a month, or within a half-year. At the summer solstice or the winter, Fire or Darkness, on one of the cusps of the year when Kalarr could rely on more than just the power of swords and spears and arrows.

And still Bayrd sat quietly and studied the faces of his chief retainers, gaining more information from an occasionally un-guarded frown or grimace than from a hundred words.

The other *kailinin* were starting to look uneasy at all the talk of sorcery and the Art Magic. It was a shifty, furtive look that he had come to recognise all too well, a poorly-disguised wish to be somewhere else while such subjects were being discussed. Eskra's mouth quirked in a contemptuous sneer, and Bayrd caught the expression just in time, because he knew what would follow: another of her notorious 'you're trying to pretend that what you don't like doesn't exist' lectures.

'Like it or not, *eirin*, gentlemen,' he said, 'these are matters which have to be accepted. And dealt with. Now, unless you have constructive comments, please sit quiet and pay attention.'

'Lord, I am a man of honour!' Kian ar'Terel – it would have to be Kian, of course – was neither quiet nor sitting. He surged up out of his seat; and then he froze halfway to upright as he met Bayrd's cold glare and realised what his next words might have been: *And you are not* . . . 'I, er, I don't have to listen to this,' he finished lamely.

'That's exactly why you have to listen,' said Bayrd. 'Or do you want to renounce your fealty as well . . . ?'

There was no threat in his voice, no intimidation. Just a calm acceptance that made it sound far worse. The *kailin* hadn't been given any reason to take refuge behind anger or pride, which was just as well. Bayrd knew his man, knew the way his mind worked, and knew that would have been the last push over the edge, not just for Kian ar'Terel but for the several others whose vacillation wasn't quite so obvious. Yet.

Lose one, lose them all. Keep one . . . and who knows?

Ar'Terel was a good man, in the sense that Reth ar'Gyart had been good: decent, honest, honourable – if a little inclined to harp on the subject – but not overly endowed with the crookedness of mind that had become so necessary nowadays. He saw things in stark black and white, with no blend of grey at the borders. That was what had made him such a loyal retainer for so long: an inability to see that anything his lord might do would be wrong.

It was also why his view could swing to the other side so radically; there would be no pause while he tried to understand why that same lord should suddenly prove himself devious and lacking in honour. But the others respected him; that was why Bayrd spoke softly, instead of grabbing Kian by the front of the tunic and shaking some sense into him. It would be a waste of time. Men like that never saw sense.

The moment stretched taut as a bowstring, the tension in the air almost audible. Then it relaxed as Kian straightened his clothing with an unnecessarily violent tug and settled back, almost ashamed of himself and determined not to show it. Bayrd thought he could hear the release of held breath – and then was certain that he heard a breath being drawn in a good deal closer.

It was Eskra, and the expression on her face told him everything that she was about to say. He promptly kicked her, hard, and that breath came out not in accusing words but in a single sharp yelp of pain. All apologies for his clumsiness, he reached out for her hand, squeezing it. But for all the tenderness of the gesture, his grip was anything but gentle.

Not now, said the look in his eyes. It was that cold stare again, a reminder that he wasn't playing any game now – except perhaps the Great Game – and that he would hurt her if he had to. Eskra was breathing hard, surprise mixed with anger, but he knew she had more practical common sense than any three of the honour-besotted *kailnin* sitting at the table. Even then, it was several seconds before she subsided, rubbing hurt ankle with hurt hand and glowering at him.

The little by-play hadn't gone unnoticed, and they both knew it. For a few seconds Eskra had been on the verge of changing from being their lady, their lord's wife, and an acceptable advisor on the unacceptable, to an Elthanek wizard no more deserving of respect than any other potential enemy. Once that respect was lost it would have been almost impossible to regain, and with it would have gone any hope Bayrd might have had of explaining Kalarr cu Ruruc as a far more dangerous threat than just one more man with more troops under his command than seemed reasonable. With the country in its present state of unrest, all those soldiers seemed very reasonable indeed.

They were also still reasonable in another way, at least for the present. Though there were almost three thousand of them – neither Bayrd nor Eskra revealed how they could be so certain about the numbers – that was still few enough to deal with, if the dealing was done quickly. Not by Clan Talvalin, at least not alone.

But there was one lord in the Province of Elthan who had enough household troops under arms to do it, only one. And that was the problem. Bayrd could have wished that it was somebody else, anybody else at all. Because that lord was Gerin ar'Diskan. They all knew it, even though nobody mentioned the name aloud. There was no need.

'Are you suggesting that I go cap in hand to Gerin ar'Diskan – Gerin, of all people! – and ask for his help in this matter?'

This time Bayrd didn't have to watch for unguarded changes of expressions. The way none of his lord's-men would meet his gaze told him more than enough about how they felt. A swirl of conflicting emotions came seething up inside him, each so different that he didn't know whether to let the laughter or the anger out first. But they combined, more or less, each moderating the other, and showed at last as a bitter sort of smile and a glint in his eye that was very far from a twinkle of amusement.

'I am,' said Eskra simply. 'Even if these other gentlemen don't dare,' she glanced at them, 'whether from good manners or for some other reason . . . But I'd rather you went up to Hold ar'Diskan of your own free will, with your cap in your hand – and when did you last wear a cap of any sort? You'll have to buy one specially – than have your head carried there on the point of someone's spear.'

There was a soft murmur of discontent from the other *kailinin* of the council; all, Bayrd noticed, except for Iskar ar'Joren. The one-handed man was sitting very still, in the stiff, immobile posture that usually covered a nod of approval. Bayrd hushed the rest of them to silence with a gesture of one hand. 'Do you think that so very likely?' he asked.

This time it was Eskra who nodded. 'Likely enough,' she said. 'That's why affairs like this are conducted through envoys. Not face to face. And especially not with a man who has let all the North know that he can't stand the sight of you.'

'Quite . . .' said Bayrd, not at all sure how to take that.

'Cu Ruruc outnumbers us already, lord,' said Iskar. 'Three thousand men, you said. We have less than five hundred.'

'And the walls of the fortress,' Askelin ar'Goel pointed out.

'And the walls,' echoed Bayrd. 'Yes. I had forgotten.' He could see Iskar shaking his head, dismissing the proposal.

'You're the castellan of this fortress, Askelin-*eir*,' Iskar said. 'The Captain of the Walls. But walls can be a trap to catch you in, if you don't have enough men to keep the enemy outside them.'

'Five hundred against three thousand,' said Bayrd. 'Is it enough?'

'No, lord.' Iskar's human hand and iron hook moved together on the table-top, describing an encircling manoeuvre. 'That many men could attack even Dunrath at more points along the fortifications than we could defend. They would come over in four, five different places at once, catch us between themselves, the walls and the others outside.' His hand became a fist. 'Finish. There'd be no need for a siege. It would all be over in a day.'

'And you say this . . .' Eskra began, and Iskar straightened his back.

'. . . as Dunrath's Captain of Artillery, lady. We haven't enough engines to keep an enemy back from the walls, nor enough men to keep that enemy from coming over. But Gerin ar'Diskan has both . . .'

'But no inclination to listen,' said Kian. 'Certainly not to you, lord.'

'What makes you so sure of that?' If Bayrd sounded a little sharp, it was hardly surprising. No lord cared to hear his own men make such judgements in that disparaging tone, even if everyone present knew them for the truth.

'Well, lord, for this long time you and he are . . . Rather, you once were . . . That is, I mean—'

'You don't know what you mean, Kian-*eir* ar'Terel,' said Bayrd in a voice like the beginnings of severity. Then he laughed, a short, sharp bark, but real mirth for all that. 'No. You know what you mean all too well, but you can't say it without insult to your lord and thus to your own honour, and so like the gentleman you are, you can't say it at all. Let it be. I'll say it for you.'

He looked at the *kailinin* sitting at the table, hard men one and all, and none of them harder than his own lady wife, whose icily practical mind sometimes chilled even him. 'We all know this: Gerin ar'Diskan has no cause to love me and mine, for any number of reasons, and he's as likely to give me my head in my hands as any help against Kalarr. Or that cap I have to buy. If Gerin won't hear me, then we'll be in no worse case than we are now. But if he does listen, even just a little . . .'

'Joking aside, lord,' said Iskar anxiously, 'if you went anywhere near Lord ar'Diskan, he might indeed try to kill you.'

'He might. But I doubt it. He made threats like that six, no, nearly seven years ago. And for all the times that I've suspected him, nothing came of it. When I was his Bannerman, he was an honourable lord . . .' Bayrd's voice trailed off and he drummed his fingers on the table. He had never liked being wrong, and liked admitting it even less. 'And he may still be. If that's so, then I've been doing the man an injustice all these years. There's only one way to find out.'

'Lord?'

'As the Lady Eskra reminded us all, the custom in such situations is to send an envoy. And if the matter involves rival clan-lords, then that envoy should hold the rank at least of Bannerman.' Bayrd smiled grimly. 'Well, I don't have a Bannerman any more. So . . . If someone can find me a cap to hold in my hands, I'll go myself.'

8

Players

FOR ALL THE wealth so blatantly displayed in Hold ar'Kelayr at Erdanor, there were some passageways and corridors within the walls of the fortress that were dark and crowded with shadows, as if no one cared to waste the price of a lamp, or even a candle, to light them. Marc ar'Dru always used one of them to get from the citadel to his chambers. It was a quicker route than the usual one of descending three flights of stairs, crossing the inner and then the outer courtyard, and finally climbing yet another flight of stairs. He had stumbled once or twice in the early days, before his feet had learned the uneven lie of the rough-paved floor and his eyes were no longer deceived by the gloom.

But no amount of practice was any protection against a man hiding in those shadows with a club.

He heard the scuff of footsteps behind him and started to turn, but he moved far too late to do anything – including duck or dodge. His hand was no more than halfway to the hilt of his *taipan* shortsword when the club hit him.

The blow was precisely aimed, by someone who knew his business – and who also knew that his victim was right-handed – because it landed square on the nerve cluster of Marc's elbow. The impact didn't cause pain so much as a tingling chill, but immediately the entire arm went numb. Even if he had managed to get the *taipan* from its scabbard, his limp and useless fingers wouldn't have closed around the hilt.

An irrational part of Marc's mind tried to identify the weapon rather than the man: it had to be something like leather stuffed with sand, solid enough to stun nerve and muscle but not so much that it would break the bone beneath if it was wielded properly.

The realisation was more frightening than facing a spiked mace, because it meant that whoever had sent the man with the club wanted him intact and as undamaged as could be managed. The obvious reason for *that* was so that he could answer questions.

Marc had seen enough during his service in Kalitzim to know some of the ways he might be persuaded to answer them. That was most frightening of all.

He took three frantic backward steps away from his attacker, still unable to see him as anything but one more shadow among so many others, and somehow managed to draw the shortsword with his left hand. His only reward was a blurring second strike on the other elbow, and another icy shock running down through the marrow of his bones to his very fingertips. The *taipan* dropped with a clang to the floor and was immediately kicked down the passage and out of reach.

From beginning to end, from armed to helpless, the action had taken less than ten seconds.

There wasn't even a pause before a third blow, delivered with nicely-judged force just above the ear, filled Marc's vision with more stars than he had ever seen in the night sky and sent him after his sword to the ground. The stars flared more brilliantly still, then winked out one by one as they drowned in the shadows . . .

'Wake up. Wake up!'

Marc heard the voice as if through a thickness of wool stuffed into his ears. It was sharp and insistent, but nothing like so sharp as the slaps across the face which punctuated each command, back and forth, rolling his head loosely on his neck with each blow. But they didn't succeed in waking him up, and his only signs of life were the reddening hand-prints on each cheek and the slow ooze of blood from one nostril.

'You fool! You hit him too hard with that thing!' said the sharp voice.

'No, lord.' This was a different voice, deeper and wearily patient. 'Watch.' A finger and thumb groped at the lobe of Marc's ear, taking hold with the nails, and then those nails pinched, hard. It sent a stab of excruciating pain through even the grey woollen fog in his mind, and his eyelids fluttered at last.

'Again, lord?'

'Again.'

The pain was even worse this time, because the grey fog was thinning fast. A foul sensation of nausea was taking its place, and Marc had to fight down the need to throw up. He managed, if only just. That deep voice had been right; he hadn't been hit too hard. Otherwise – he knew from unpleasant experience – he would have had no option in the matter: consciousness and vomiting would have followed one another like dawn and day. Instead, and leaving only a sour taste of bile at the back of his throat, the nausea backed down to a roiling queasiness in his stomach.

Marc risked a deep breath, then another, and finally opened his eyes.

His long, lean face was carved into angles by the fall of light and shadow from two lanterns. Ivern ar'Diskan stared down at him, and the expression on the man's face was far more familiar than the genial smiles of the past few weeks. Now it was a typical ar'Diskan scowl, suspicion mixed in equal parts with hatred. Familiarity didn't make it any more welcome, especially when Marc realised that Ivern, a shorter man than himself, was only looking *down* at him because he had been tied wrist and ankle to a heavy chair.

The inadequate lighting showed Marc only that they were in some cellar or store-room, cluttered with the vague shapes of old furniture and presumably far away from where anyone might hear what was going on inside. His stomach heaved again, and he tried and failed to suppress a retch and a sour acid belch.

Ivern sidestepped, sneering at him. 'Go ahead,' he said. 'Foul yourself. In a few hours from now it won't matter.'

'What . . . ?'

'Don't play the innocent with me.'

Marc had gone to enough theatrical melodramas in Drosul that he almost laughed at the cliché; except that it wasn't especially funny from where he was sitting. With the stink of the lamps and the tang of dust and sweat, the place even smelt like a theatre; but these lamps were not the guttering, metal-shaded footlights that lined the stage, and the sweat was his own, and smelt less of heat and crowding than of fear. He shook his head, trying to get some sense through the confusion and the aching, but Ivern grabbed a handful of his hair and tugged it savagely back until they were eye to eye.

'I know why you're in Erdanor,' ar'Diskan said. 'I know who sent you. I know what you're doing.'

Marc gazed blearily at the other man, and blinked. Either Ivern ar'Diskan was talking nonsense, or he was just hearing noise. Given the way he felt, one was as likely as the other.

'Then why in the name of the Father of Fires won't you tell me too?' he mumbled. 'Because I'd like to know as well.'

Ivern studied him in silence for a few seconds, then simply said, 'Hit him.'

'Yes, lord.' Now that Marc's senses were in better order, he could tell that the deep voice came from behind him. He still hadn't seen the speaker yet, but whoever it was had an Alban riding-quirt this time instead of his loaded club.

Marc ar'Dru had been comforted by the awareness that Ivern wouldn't dare to kill him out of hand, or even do something that would leave physical evidence needing explanation to Kurek. Either case would prove he had been usurping a lord's authority under his own roof, and that was an activity not only dishonourable but dangerous, even when the lord was far less . . . volatile than Kurek ar'Kelayr seemed to be.

But the cut of the whip shattered the illusion, and made him realise that just for the moment, Ivern didn't care what Kurek might think.

There was no hiss of it being drawn back, just a deafening crack as it hit him. The thin lash, ten inches of plaited leather thongs, slashed across Marc's face from the corner of one eye down to the point of the jaw. The weal it left behind burned like the track of a hot iron, and in a few seconds he could feel a thin warm trickle running down to his chin and dripping off it. But if they wanted to hear him cry out, they were using the wrong instrument; the sheer shock of the quirt's impact had a stunning effect, and though it throbbed damnably now, the real pain wouldn't make itself felt until later.

Marc ground his teeth on a savage grin that managed to conceal the terror fluttering in his belly, and decided that he wouldn't bother mentioning this mistake. Whether through youth, or lack of the more brutal forms of experience that had been available in Drosul, or just plain anger, Ivern hadn't yet thought of using proper methods of rigorous interrogation.

Foremost in Marc's mind was an intention to *keep* him from thinking of them. If that meant he would have to suffer an ordinary beating, then he would.

And he would be grateful for nothing worse.

There had been an abortive rising against King Daykin of Kalitz, three years before the Landing in Alba. Marc had been only a cavalry Captain-of-Ten, and had seen no action to speak of; but he had commanded part of the guard detachment during the execution of the rebellion's ringleaders. It hadn't been anything excessively complicated or cruel – half-hanging followed by decapitation for the most part, and then the heads and bodies burned on a great fire – since there were so many victims that anything more elaborate would have taken the greater part of the day.

But what had stuck in his mind had been the sight of the men and women who had undergone extreme questioning before they died.

Not all had been tortured: some had confessed on capture and their confessions proven correct enough that no further encouragement was needed. Others had been taken late enough in the business for nothing they knew to be of any use, and they were simply used as numbers to complete the example King Daykin intended to make.

For all his crooked cunning and political machinations, he was a strangely non-vindictive man, that little King: he had said that a certain number of the rebels would die, and a certain number it had been. A large number, certainly, but no more than that. Further reprisals had been strictly forbidden, Daykin's intention and hope being that the sooner all this was forgotten, the sooner there would be peace again. It might have been optimism then; it was still working now.

But it had done nothing for those who had suffered the full rigours of a Droselan interrogation . . .

Marc had sat in his saddle at parade-rest, now and again needing to quiet his restless horse, and watched them pass by in the wooden carts. He had heard the thin noises drifting up over the rumble of the wheels, and he had known that the waiting noose and cleaver no longer held any terrors for these people. Rope and edge would be a blessing and a mercy for each one.

Blank faces whose features had become open wounds: without eyes, without noses, without ears, they retained only their all-important tongues. Hands and feet that lacked fingers and toes, cut away or wrenched from the sockets; limbs that had been dislocated by weights and pulleys; skin welted by far heavier whips than was being used on him, or seamed and crisped by fire and heated oil and molten metal. These were no longer people on their way to execution; they were just carcasses heading for the final stage of a butchery that had begun a week before.

Some of them might have been reluctant to betray comrades or friends or family, but others had truly been ignorant. The end result had been the same.

And no matter what questions Ivern might think of asking, Marc was in that position now. He had no answers with which to save himself. And the end result, unless he was very lucky indeed, would still be the same.

'Again, lord?' said the deep voice. There were footsteps, and Marc craned around far enough to see that the bulky shape standing beside him was one Etek ar'Gellan, a low-clan *kailin* who fulfilled the function of Ivern's chief henchman – as near in rank to a Bannerman Companion as a younger son could aspire to – as well as his bodyguard and, apparently, torturer.

'No.' Ivern smiled nastily and held out one hand for the quirt, then stood in silence for a few seconds while he ran the thin lash through his fingers in the approved manner of someone who could use melodramatic clichés with a straight face. 'Not yet. Wait.'

'Why wait?' Marc spat out something – skin, blood, a flake of leather – and stared malevolently at ar'Diskan. The other man looked surprised.

'Bold words,' he said.

'Practical words. You can beat me all day and night and I'll never tell you a thing.'

Ivern whistled thinly between his teeth. 'Bold words indeed, ar'Dru. Do you think that you're so strong?'

'No . . . I just don't bloody know what you're talking about!'

Ivern sighed, the sound of someone wearied by the constant foolishness of his fellow men, and returned the quirt to ar'Gellan. He made a small gesture of dismissal with one hand. 'Hit him again.'

A few shrill, pain-filled seconds later, and Marc ar'Dru had no doubt about what he was spitting this time. It was definitely blood. Lines of searing heat criss-crossed his face and shoulders, his lips were split and one eye was swelling shut. And yet, underneath the hurt, Marc felt grimly pleased with himself.

He had never thought of himself before as being particularly brave, but if bravery meant the ability to defy and mock an enemy when that enemy held the upper hand, then he supposed he was being brave after all. Especially when the difference between courage and cowardice was also the difference between leaving this cellar with all his limbs and organs in their proper place, or . . .

Or not.

The consequences of that wisecrack hadn't been so stupid as it might have sounded, because it meant he had read Ivern ar'Diskan perfectly. Though it wasn't going to get him out of this unscathed, it might keep the damage to an acceptable level.

Ivern wasn't much of a sadist, or if he was he was hiding his enjoyment well. But he was much more a character out of those Droselan melodramas he seemed so fond of, though the little bastard didn't even know it. He plainly thought that his theatrical words and gestures were the height of sophistication, and Marc prayed he had never been to the Iron Theatre of Durforen, with its productions based around bloody revenge and elaborate cruelty. From Marc's point of view Ivern was playing the villain's part: that much was painfully obvious.

But seen from Ivern's side, he was a hero who had trapped a spy and a potential traitor who had inveigled himself into the Clan-Lord ar'Kelayr's good graces – and in so doing, pushed Ivern ar'Diskan out. That reasoning was at least preferable to accepting he might no longer be as useful as he had been.

And there lay the difference between them. After what had happened at Dunrath and on the way here, Marc was still grateful for any appreciation at all that a lord might show him. Ivern, on the other hand, had grown addicted to it.

'You're going to have some explaining to do when Kurek sees my face,' Marc said. As the words left his mouth he thought for the first time about why he had been hit so consistently about what had been a fairly handsome face. His guts clenched momentarily into a cold, hard knot as he realised there might, just might, be a reason behind Ivern's fury that he had never ever considered. Not wounded pride, not concern for loss of status.

Just simply jealousy.

And that was the most dangerous of all, because it was far less inclined to listen to reason.

Ivern had recovered the quirt again – he seemed to think it gave a worthwhile emphasis to the difference in their positions, even though using it himself was beneath him – and was tapping it lightly against his palm. 'If he ever does,' he said.

'Bold words, as you might say yourself. Then I'll be interested to hear how you'll account for my disappearance. You've given some thought to it, I presume?'

The look that flicked across Ivern's face told Marc that he hadn't given it any thought at all. He was *right*, and that had been sufficient – until now, when the little worm of doubt began to bore into the apple of certainty. He had seen fear of Kurek on Ivern's face before, and then with no more apparent reason than now.

Marc ar'Dru wondered what hold Kurek had over his supporters to produce such an effect as this; for all his quick flashes of anger, all the starker for appearing out of the midst of a smile, he had never shown himself cruel.

And not just *needlessly* cruel. In a race of hard and often ruthless people, ruled by lords who of necessity sometimes had to be just as hard and ruthless, Kurek had been one of the most benevolent clan-lords Marc had ever seen. Almost unnaturally so. He wondered what the other side of the coin might look like, and guessed that Ivern had seen it at least once. That was a string a wise man might play on to his own advantage.

'Before you do some permanent harm that we'll both regret,' he said carefully, 'me right now, and you when Kurek finds out about it, why not listen to me? It's willing information, not something to stop your,' he glanced sidelong at Etek, reluctant to grant the big lout any sort of formal title, 'your friend from hitting me.'

Ivern coiled the quirt's lash around its stock and used it to chuck Marc under the chin. 'Why should I?' he asked.

'Why not? It's not going to hurt *you*.' Marc tried a quick, grim smile and winced as it split his lip still further. 'Or me, just for a change.'

'I'm listening.'

'Then what am I supposed to be doing? Who sent me? Why? What for?' The whipstock nudged his jaw, not roughly, just a warning, but he flinched as its braided surface rasped against broken skin.

'I'll ask the questions, ar'Dru.'

Marc closed his eyes and groaned. He should have expected that response. Damn it to the nine hot Hells, he should have expected those very words. Straight from the script of a third-rate play. What he needed most of all was not some indication of what was going on, but a copy of the script for whatever production Ivern ar'Diskan thought he was performing. And the first thing he would do would be to look at the last page and find out if he survived that long. At least there was one person he could blame, and be sure of getting it right.

'This is all Bayrd ar'Talvlyn's fault,' he said viciously.

'Now we're getting somewhere.' Ivern's voice was approving, and Marc stared at him. Realisation dawned like the sun coming out from behind the cloud.

'Is *that* what you think . . . ?' he said. 'That I was sent by him?' Ivern nodded silently. 'To spy for him?' Another nod. Marc licked his lips, tasted the blood, felt the sting of raw flesh. 'To get myself hurt, or maimed, or maybe even killed . . . For *him*?'

'You are Bannerman to Clan Talvalin,' said Ivern. 'Bayrd's best friend. Your honour would . . .'

Despite the pain that was beginning to grow in his face, he almost laughed out loud. But a boiling hatred of his once-friend was also fighting for precedence. Finally Marc could do nothing but glare in disbelief, for the few seconds that was all it needed for the anger to be re-channelled against the man who stood in front of him.

'I am . . . I *was*, you imbecile,' he snarled at last, lurching forward in the chair as if trying to sink his teeth in Ivern's arm. 'Was, was, was! Can't you understand that? Past! Done with! Gone! You blind, deaf, stupid, bloody-minded idiot! And you have the gall to harp about my honour? What honour has ar'Talvlyn left me? Eh? Eh? Answer me that if you can!'

Ivern blinked at such an outburst from a man tied prisoner, and his confidence wavered. 'I thought—' he started to say.

'You thought? No! You didn't think at all! Didn't you hear

what I told Kurek when I first came to Erdanor? Can't you see my hair? Would a *kailin-eir* Bannerman throw over all I had, throw aside my honour and my respect, turn *eijo* and lay myself open to murder by old enemies once I was out of the protection of a high-clan lord, and all on a pretence?'

Ivern ar'Diskan stared at him as the outburst died away, and Marc could almost hear the abacus-like ticking as fact and surmise and supposition each slotted into their proper place. Or maybe it was just the patter of blood dripping off his chin.

The man couldn't be so stupid as to miss something so obvious, could he? But then, Marc suspected there was a horrible correctness when he had called him someone who didn't think at all. Ivern was young – young enough, indeed, that if truth were told he probably wasn't yet entitled to the warrior's braid he wore – but for all that youth he had the single-minded, or more likely mindless, stubbornness of the oldest Alban lords. The sort of men who, if they could once be convinced that black was white or wet was dry, would defend that view to the last drop of their and all their retainers' blood.

'A pretty speech, and well-delivered,' Ivern said at last, and he looked almost regretful. Marc swore inwardly, feeling a renewed tingle of fear through his ebbing anger. 'But it's almost exactly the thing a spy *would* say . . . if he were well primed, and expecting an interrogation such as this.'

'If he was all of that,' said Marc, 'then wouldn't the speech be something else? Something you wouldn't expect?' The anger flashed again, useless now, but as hot and bright as oil spilled on hot coals. 'Or do you just think everyone's as stupid as you . . . ?'

It went past ar'Diskan as though he hadn't heard it. He was too busy securing the quirt, lash to stock to wrist-strap, and that looked sinister. It implied that he was done with such inconsequential methods of persuasion. 'You were right about your face,' he said with a brief glance over his shoulder. 'Explaining it would be difficult. Unless I have proof one way or the other.'

'One way or . . .' Marc couldn't finish. His skin was clammy with sweat, his stomach was churning, and the time for bravado and luck was long gone now. Because he knew what Ivern meant.

It was a fundamental part of Droselan justice: if guilt or innocence could be proven in no other way, then a certain level of compulsion became necessary and was acceptable before the law. Even free confession wasn't exempt. If it couldn't be proven true by any other means, it had to be confirmed under duress by the application of sufficient pain that no elaborate lies could be concocted. So that only the truth remained.

Etek ar'Gellan bent over him, checking the thick ropes at wrist and ankle with fingers that were equally thick, equally strong, equally unfeeling. Then steel rasped, and Etek drew a short, curved skinning knife from its scabbard at his belt.

'Start with the left hand,' said Ivern ar'Diskan, his voice sounding as though it came from far away, down an iron passageway clanging with iron echoes. There was a thundering like drums in Marc's ears, surely too fast for a heartbeat, as he braced himself to bear a pain that was always worse in cold blood on the surgeon's table rather than shed hot in battle.

'One finger at a time. Given how his lord cheated my father, it's no more than appropriate . . .'

'What are you doing?'

Kurek ar'Kelayr's voice didn't sound angry. It sounded as it always did, quiet and calm and unruffled. But there was something beneath the calmness, a chilly strength which cut like the edge of the curved knife poised just above Marc's first knuckle.

A thread of scarlet ran from under that edge, where the skin had parted beneath no more than the weight of the blade. Marc ar'Dru was staring at it still, as if by seeing the nail and the finger's-end in place, he could imagine them back into place even when the steel had done its work. There were no crawling blue sparks of the Talent to tell him that the joint might be replaced once it had been severed, only the stinging icy heat of the thin cut telling him that no matter what might happen, it would hurt.

For all his hatred of Bayrd ar'Talvlyn, he realised at last, after almost seven years, what a gesture it had been for Bayrd to offer his own wrist to the sword's edge in place of Gerin ar'Diskan's. Whatever had come after, whatever hidden motives there might have been behind the sacrifice, it had been noble; because win or lose, praise or blame, he had given his pain willingly in the service of his lord.

Marc tore his eyes from the skinning-knife only when it lifted away from his finger, not daring, as if it was a distant archer still without bowshot range, to ignore it until the danger was past. That carelessness had killed Reth ar'Gyart; it had killed a dozen other men of Marc's acquaintance, on the field of battle or worse, during a hunt, when people were too often inclined to shoot at sound rather than at sight of a target.

'I said, what's going on?'

There was a babble of words from Ivern, a torrent of explanation that Marc barely heard. A few expected words drifted to the surface of the stream – 'traitor' and 'spy', 'suspicion' and 'proof' – but the rest were nothing more than background noise. He was soaked with sweat from the skin to the surface, through shirt and tunic and jerkin over all; there was a haze of moisture on the nap of the jerkin's fabric as though he had gone walking out of doors on a foggy morning. But he had not discarded his honour, neither cried out for mercy nor been sick nor stained his breeches in the terror of imminent mutilation.

If that was bravery, then he supposed he had been brave.

There were more footsteps approaching him, not Etek's heavy, deliberate tread but the quick, precise footfalls of a man both lighter in body and lighter on his feet.

Kurek.

'If you suspect anyone of anything in this Hold, Ivern-*eir*,' he was saying, 'you bring those suspicions to me. You do not take things into your own hands, no matter how certain you might be. Erdanor is Hold ar'Kelayr, not Hold ar'Diskan. My fortress. Not yours.'

'But, lord,' and that was the first time Marc could remember Ivern using the title, 'lord, this was in the way of being a private affair between Clan ar'Diskan and this man. He was, let me remind you, a long-time henchman of Bayrd ar'Talvlyn.'

Ivern was standing at Kurek's back, badly placed to see the expression which flicked across the face of the man he called lord when he spoke those words. Marc saw it; and he was glad he hadn't provoked it. The only chilling part for him was that orders had not been given at once for him to be set free. If Kurek could be convinced, even slightly, that Ivern was right to act as he had done, then matters would continue from where they had left off. And that bastard Etek still had his knife . . .

'You may remind me,' said Kurek, not turning, his voice as controlled as before, 'but in future you should be a deal less insolent about it. We are not equals, you and I. Not in this fortress, not outside it. I am the Clan-Lord here. Let me remind you of that.'

He put one hand under Marc's chin, heedless of the blood that immediately began to stain his cuff, and with the other began gently investigating the welts and lacerations left by the riding-quirt.

Marc shuddered slightly at the contact. For one thing, any contact with the raw pinkness where skin had been flicked off smarted like boiling water. And for another, it felt unpleasant in a way not connected with pain. Kurek's fingers had a lighter touch than most physicians Marc had encountered, but it didn't feel like a surgeon's examination. It was more tender than that.

But nor did it feel like a potential lover's concern, despite what he had begun to think might be the real reason for Ivern's fury. He was familiar enough with how that felt as well, both rough and gentle; one of his past mistresses had been Vitya ar'Diskan, a lady almost as dangerous in bed with her nails as was her cousin Ivern in a locked cellar with a whip and a knife and a henchman to use them at command.

And the door had *been locked*, he thought irrationally. *So how did Kurek get in . . . ?*

The fingers touched again, pressing against a cheekbone to check if the bruised and broken skin above meant perhaps a shattered bone beneath. The pressure was light, but for all that, if there had been broken bone beneath then ropes or no ropes the pain would have made Marc try to leap out of the chair. No. That indifference proved it. There was no human compassion here at all.

If felt more like the cool solicitude of a man for a useful piece of delicate machinery that might have been broken before it had fulfilled its function. Marc had seen it before, in Dunrath: Iskar ar'Joren caressing one of his damned catapults as if it was an injured horse when the thing's throwing-arm snapped during a practice shoot. There had been no foolish transfer of affection to an inanimate object, just an anxiety that the accident might have caused more needless damage than he could see.

'No permanent harm,' Kurek announced at last, and though it

made Marc feel better, it wasn't being said for his benefit. 'Fortunately for you.'

'What do you mean, fortunately?' Despite his earlier nervousness and flood of apologetic explanation, Ivern bristled at the hint of threat.

'I mean just what I say. Now cut him loose.'

'Not until I'm sure—'

'*I'm* sure. That should be sufficient.'

'How can you know?'

Kurek looked at the blood on his fingertips where he had probed the wounds – and perhaps deeper than the wounds. 'I know. Cut him loose.' His gaze shifted from his stained hands to Etek ar'Gellan's face.

Etek didn't move. Kurek ar'Kelayr might be a high-clan lord and outrank everyone else present, but like a good henchman he was waiting for the word from his own lord, and that word hadn't yet been given. Kurek stared at him, and Marc, but not Ivern, could see the surprise and annoyance at this silent disobedience change to a small, tight smile. 'I won't tell you again.'

And still Etek didn't move.

Not until Kurek put out one hand, index finger extended, as if to touch the big man in the middle of the chest. He didn't even make contact, but there was a sharp crack, like the breaking of a twig, and a tiny incandescent spark jumped between fingertip and body. Both sound and spark were far too small for what they did.

Etek ar'Gellan was flung into the shadows as though shot from one of Iskar ar'Joren's catapults, fifteen or twenty feet backwards with his own feet clear of the ground, until his flight stopped short with a thud against a wall somewhere in the darkness.

'Blast you to the Black Pit!' rasped Ivern, fear of Kurek and fear too of a blatant use of the Art Magic all forgotten in an insensate spasm of arrogant rage. 'Who do you think you are, to manhandle *my* servant?'

Kurek turned slowly to look at him, cradling his right hand in his left. The top joint of the index finger was purpling with a bruise and the nail was already black. 'I have already told you once,' he said, his voice deceptively gentle. 'I am the lord of this place. And in this place I can do as I please. So guard your tongue.'

There was more menace in that single soft-spoken warning than in any amount of the shouting that Ivern's father indulged in, and the younger ar'Diskan flinched as though threatened with his own whip. Marc watched, and flinched too, but inwardly. He had placed their relationship now, and guessed that variations of it might be the same for all the other lords' sons in Erdanor.

It wasn't that Ivern and Kurek had ever been lovers, or that Ivern might have a trusted retainer's respect for his lord. He was just a dog with a cruel master, kicks one moment and caresses the next, without any rhyme or reason, always off balance. And he stayed in Erdanor and continued to endure it because it had the cruel comfort of familiarity. With Gerin ar'Diskan for his father, that was the only treatment he had ever known.

And still he had what passed for pride, scarred and dented though it was. Marc could hear it in his voice, covering the tremor of fear, as he drew himself up and tried without success to stare Kurek down. He could see it in the fingernails dug into palms to keep his hands from shaking.

'So you are lord in Erdanor, and Clan-Lord ar'Kelayr. I know it. I accept it. I have always accepted it. But it does not give you the right to address me like a vassal. Have you forgotten, *lord*, who my father is, and what he is, and what he owns and holds and rules . . . ?'

'You forget so quickly, ar'Diskan. Once you passed the threshold of this fortress, *I* became everything that deserves love and fealty and respect and honour. Not your father, not your brother, not any lover you might have left behind. And I know just who and what your father is. Gerin ar'Diskan is so haughty and inflexible, so unwilling to listen to reason, that Erhal the Overlord is leading an army north from Cerdor to destroy him.'

'Lies!'

'Truth.'

'How can you know this?'

'I know.'

'How can you be sure?'

'I can.'

'Erhal can't be the Overlord. His sister Yraine and her faction would never permit it. He's no more than a child.'

'Seventeen. Old enough.'

'Three years off *eskorrethen*. Young enough.'

Then Ivern's face took on a crafty look. 'This is some sort of test, isn't it?' he said. Kurek's face didn't change. 'You're trying to trick me. Because nobody can be Overlord of the Albans under their own name. So why hasn't he taken the title of Albanak, Landmaster, like his father and all the others before him? Eh? Answer me that . . . ?'

'New customs for a new land? His sister would be Albanak if she assumed the title. It might be that Erhal wants to be a little more distinctive than that. Perhaps he wants to give over the style and title of Overlord completely. Perhaps he wants to be called King . . .'

Ivern's lips curled at such a ridiculous suggestion. 'Nobody would stand for that,' he sneered. 'Not the lords, not the people, not even his most faithful retainers. And they wouldn't even declare him Overlord, never mind *King*, unless . . .'

Ivern's voice trailed off. Faithful retainers would not. But faithless retainers, those with everything to gain as supporters who controlled the lord they supported – those would be just the people to acclaim an under-age youth as lord, or prince, or king, or any other title that they chose. Because the rank and the title would be meaningless. He would be a figurehead, a puppet who would dance as they pulled on the strings. They would act in his name and by his mandate, as they would have done had they dared lay claim to the rank of Overlord and Landmaster themselves.

Usurpation not to power but for the manipulation of power was a daring, and classic, move of the Great Game.

And though they had been enemies for almost as long as the Albans had been in Alba, his father and Bayrd Talvalin had one thing in common. They had so far managed to walk the tightrope between one faction and the other, without incurring the enmity of either. Until now.

'What can he . . . What can *we* do?'

'Better,' said Kurek, warmth flowing back into his voice and washing away all memory of anger, of accusation, of any cause for fear. Ivern relaxed, and smiled. 'Much better. More like the Ivern I thought I knew. So then. We'll march my forces out from Erdanor towards Segelin and Hold ar'Diskan, wait until Erhal and your father are done with hacking at each other, then move in and make an end. You'll make a wiser Lord ar'Diskan than your father or even Arren . . .'

184

Ivern nodded acceptance that he should replace his father and elder brother, almost as though something had blocked out his understanding of just how that replacement was to be achieved. Then someone groaned. It was a hoarse, anguished noise, and though it was still bobbing in that imbecilic puppet's nod, his head snapped around towards the source of the sound. In that instant, as his mouth opened in silent shock at what his eyes could see, the closing meshes of Kurek's glamour shattered like a delicate net of spun glass kicked by a spiteful boot.

Etek ar'Gellan came lurching out of the darkness where he had been thrown. His face was smashed and bloody, and the noises that pain and effort were forcing through his slack lips were unrecognisable as speech. One leg was bent at an angle through the knee-joint, and he dragged the useless meat and bone behind him, more a prop than a limb. But something kept him moving.

And the heavy skinning-knife was still clutched in his right hand.

'Fool,' said Kurek very softly, and favoured him with an appraising glance, very plainly deciding whether or not he was still dangerous. 'My compliments on the quality of your retainers,' he said idly to Ivern. 'A pity this one doesn't have as much wisdom as he has strength. Or he'd have known when he was well off. As it is . . .'

He made a quick, dismissive gesture with one hand.

There was a protracted rushing, roaring sound, a noise somewhere between that of wind in tall trees and the crash of surf on shingle. Then there was a glare of harsh light that slapped all the shadows in the cellar flat against the walls, and a shrill squealing, the noise damp wood makes on a fire.

It came from ar'Gellan.

A blazing globe of flame surrounded him, and the big man writhed briefly at its core, blackened and twisted, the wick of a monstrous candle. Then he dwindled, and crumbled, and died. The flame winked out and a faint drift of grey ash sifted down through the last eddies of heat. The knife he had been holding dropped out of the empty air and hit the stone floor with a clank; except that it was a knife no longer, but just a charred, fused lump of metal.

And that was all.

As the spell drained power from him, other spells maintained by that same power wavered and began to fail. Kurek's face darkened, his hair darkened, he even grew taller, and though his old-appearance still shimmered through the new as if it was a reflection seen through a half-silvered mirror, he was Kurek ar'Kelayr no longer.

Ivern stared at the stranger beside him, at the ash strewn on the floor, at the melted knife in the midst of it, and this time there was no anger to conceal his shock, nor any charm of glamour to warp what he saw or how his mind responded. 'You always condemned the use of magic,' he said helplessly. 'You always said—'

'Never mind what was said, That's past. This is necessity.'

'Necessity? To do that to a man? To burn him like—'

'To do it quickly. If I remember aright, my "brother" Dyrek ar'Kelayr preferred the slower method of firing an occupied house.'

'That was war!' The stranger who had been Kurek regarded him sceptically, with a glitter of what might have been amusement in his dark eyes. 'At least . . . at least it was a raid. But it wasn't magic! Kurek, what's happening here?'

'Kurek? No. Not Kurek any longer. That play is over. My name is Kalarr cu Ruruc. And you must do as I say.'

Ivern gaped at him blankly. It might have been courage, or it might have been deliberate insolence, or – as Marc thought – it might have been that Ivern's brain had simply stopped accepting what was happening around him.

Kalarr waited. And waited some more. And then his temper flared as suddenly as the flame which had eaten ar'Gellan, and he uttered a huge, wordless cry of rage and swung his open hand at Ivern's face.

There was no other power this time than his own muscles, but there was far more of that than seemed reasonable. Ivern ar'Diskan spun half around under the impetus of a slap that had carried more force than many punches, and fell down.

When he came up again his *taipan* was out of its scabbard and levelled in a trembling hand. Kalarr stared at it, then at Ivern, and smiled a slow, wide smile that showed too many teeth for humour. Those teeth grated audibly together, the sound of a man exerting effort, and in the time it took for three of Ivern's panting breaths,

Kalarr's face changed three times. It became Kurek again, and then Ivern himself, and finally returned to what had to be its true shape.

'You aren't as useful as you believe,' he said brutally. 'In fact, you never were. But now you've become a nuisance. A small, whining annoyance, like a mosquito. Do you know what happens to mosquitos, Ivern ar'Diskan?'

This time there was no rush of light and heat. Only chill and darkness flooded the cellar now, flowing from the chasm that had opened, not just in the floor under Ivern's feet, nor even in the wall behind him.

It yawned all around him, a gateway torn through the very structure of the world, sucking the air of the cellar through it in long streamers of icy fog. Beyond it lay a vast black drop into nowhere. There were stars at the bottom, but these stars were not the friendly twinkling sparks of the night sky.

They burned steady, with never a twinkle. They burned cold.

Ivern's shriek trailed away into impossibly distant gulfs and silence, but long before it faded beyond hearing, the black starshot abyss slammed shut like the jaws of an iron trap.

Marc ar'Dru stared at where the void had been, and never moved. He was only too aware that he was the last and only remaining witness to what had been said and done here, and of the best way to keep such a witness from talking.

But Kalarr dragged one of the other chairs over in front of him and sat in it, backwards, his arms folded and cradled across the back. Then he just gazed at nothing, breathing hard, a man trying to regain control of his breath, or his temper . . .

. . . Or his appearance.

Because that still flickered like the two faces of a spinning coin, one minute bright and the next dark, polished and dull, day and night: fair, handsome Kurek giving way to black-haired, elegant Kalarr. And slowly, the face of Kalarr was gaining prominence. Or no longer being hidden, as if the need for concealment was past.

Neither face was ugly, but of the two Kalarr's was by far the most forbidding. By the set of features it was a young face, but there were deeper lines in the skin than there should have been, and a shadow deep within the eyes, that made him look older than his years.

They were blue eyes, like and yet unlike Kurek's; his were bright and clear, like sapphires, like Marc's own. Alban eyes. These, like everything else about Kalarr, were darker, a deep cyan like the poisonous salts of iron. A sinister glamour hung about him, that both attracted and repelled.

The word *glamour* struck a small, spluttering spark in Marc's mind, but no fire, and as Kalarr cu Ruruc's gaze focused on him, any meaning the word might have had was lost in the shadows of that sombre regard.

The combination of black hair and dark blue eyes was something Marc had seen before, a long time before. Not among his own people: blue eyes went with fair hair more often than not, so that Albans with dark hair tended more to have grey eyes, or brown. And then he remembered, an image seven years old rising up through the pain and the confusion and the simple shock of the past half-hour. There had been men of that colouring with Gelert, the day after the Landing, when the High Lord of Prytenon came face to face with Albanak the Overlord of the Albans for that one and only time.

Gelert's hair had been red, not black, but then red hair could be either common enough to be a stamp of the family line – like House ar'Lerutz – or so unusual that it would appear only once in a generation. The thought went round and around until it wore itself out with the effort of trying to make sense when so plainly there was none.

'There was a time, not long ago, when I might have listened to ar'Diskan's suspicions,' said Kalarr cu Ruruc. He had always been Kalarr; Kurek ar'Kelayr was gone, as though he had never existed. 'I might have given credence to them, even. Because I was suspicious myself. I watched you, when you came here. Followed you, overheard you, took note of where you went and who you saw and what you said.'

'I saw nobody.'

'There was nobody else. Only me. And if I wish it,' Kalarr smiled, made a small movement with that bruised and blackened index finger, and the ropes knotted around Marc's wrists and ankles fell away, 'I can oversee the running of the fortress without the need even to leave my chair. I wondered about you Marc ar'Dru. To defy your lord is one thing, but to turn *eijo* for emphasis . . . It was too much emphasis, I thought. Or thought then. But now, now you are more than halfway mine. And soon you will be mine completely. Even without coercion.'

'Coercion? I was never forced to anything.'

'Just so. Or it would have snapped your mind, and what use would have that been to me? No. The reed that bends easily is always the most receptive to gentle pressure.'

At first that sounded like some sort of delicate insult, but for the life of him Marc couldn't see where the gibe lay. As he looked into the blue eyes that were so dark with secret wisdom, he knew that even in jest this man would never insult a companion or a loyal retainer.

After what he had seen, there was still a small, faint doubt lingering back in the furthest recesses of his mind. It was almost as if the voice of someone infinitely far away was shouting warnings. Marc dismissed the voice, dismissed the doubts, dismissed the warnings.

If Kalarr cu Ruruc chose to regard him as his friend and lord's-man, then he would repay that trust, and be both.

9
Allies

EVEN THOUGH IT wasn't raining, in Bayrd Talvalin's opinion it was another typical Elthanek summer's morning. That meant there was no sun visible, even though it had been above the horizon for more than three hours now. Instead there was mist, and chill, and no colour to the day. There was nothing but shades of grey.

The mist that hung low to the ground was dove-grey; it swirled behind the horses so that they left a wake like that of a ship in still water. The low moorland hills were leaden-grey, rolling off into the mist as though they were dissolving into it and the world ended just beyond the limits of sight. Even the sky was pearl-grey, an overcast like a grey pillow pressed over the face of the world and smothering the life out of it.

But there was a world beyond the mist, and it was intruding in a way that couldn't be ignored. Bayrd had seen them more than once, a flicker of movement that was gone as soon as seen.

Horsemen.

It was a small column, though it still outnumbered the twenty men who rode with him. These riders had been shadowing his on the western skyline for more than an hour, arrogantly careless of being seen – when the mist permitted – and confident of their advantages. They had all of them: the advantage of height, of familiarity with the ground, and above all of surprise.

Because it didn't really matter that he or anyone else had seen them. With every swirl of the mist they were gone again, and had to be refound: and each time they were in a different place. It was as if they were playing a game, and not the usual Great one. This was simpler, more childish, but just as deadly.

It was 'See me, Don't See me, Die.'

'You've seen them too?' he said to Eskra, watching her stare at the distant ridge. His voice was no more than a murmur. It was a pointless precaution, since the other riders were well beyond earshot and his own retainers, aware of the tension that hung in the air as thickly as the fog, had pulled back a decent distance to give their lord and his lady privacy in which to argue. Even if it wasn't really an argument, more a sort of worrying aloud.

They might be out of earshot, he thought, but probably not out of bowshot. There was something about the way they moved that made it plain they were manoeuvring to maintain that advantage above all.

'I've seen them.' She glanced at him, then back at the hillside, but in those few seconds the mist had rolled over its crest and once again there was nothing to be seen. 'Gerin's men?'

Bayrd shrugged, but the movement of his shoulders was lost inside the heavy travelling-coat he wore to keep out the damp cold of the mist. 'I hope so,' he said. 'I really hope so. Otherwise Kalarr cu Ruruc has been moving a deal too fast for my liking.'

'No. I would have known.'

'Would you . . . ?' Bayrd reined Yarak to a standstill – there was a clatter behind him as the rest of the column followed suit to maintain their distance – and looked at Eskra thoughtfully. There wasn't accusation in the look, just concern. 'You let Marc go in harm's way, and now there's no good way to get him out again. You told me that you could spy on Kalarr in safety through his eyes, and now you tell me that those eyes are clouded. You told me—'

He thumped his clenched fist against the pommel of the saddle hard enough to startle Yarak and make the grey mare skitter sideways until he leaned forward and gentled her again. ''Skra-*ain*, it doesn't matter what you told me any more. If it was true then' – she opened her mouth to protest, but closed it again as he hushed her with a quick gesture of his hand – 'it isn't true now. All of it changed with what you told me last night. That my friend was pretending to be my enemy, but the pretence has gone too well. That Kalarr knows about you—'

'Everyone knows about me.'

'Yes. But he knows about me, too. And what I don't know is

what sort of weapon that knowledge could be. How much support could I lose? How many men? How much respect?'

'Respect is—'

'What buys and keeps *kailinin*. Not silver, not land, not promises. Respect. Honour. Things you can't hold in your hands or carry in a purse. The thing I'll need most of all if Gerin ar'Diskan is even going to give me the time of day.'

They had been on the road to Hold ar'Diskan this past three days. The normal journey required five; a man alone and in a hurry could do it in two. For an armed column equipped well enough to be an adequate honour-guard between one high-clan lord and another, three days was better than good. But Bayrd was still afraid it might not be good enough.

For all Eskra's promises, her plans had gone savagely awry after Ivern ar'Diskan's death – although that, like what Kalarr had found out, could be a sharp weapon one way or the other if it was used properly. And as for the rest . . .

It was as if Marc ar'Dru had somehow managed to pull down the shutters on the window through which she had been peering.

Ivern was dead; Etek ar'Gellan was dead; something was happening in Cerdor, if Kalarr was to be believed; and he himself had finally laid aside his pretence of being a son of Clan ar'Kelayr. But what had happened after that was still a mystery.

Marc was still alive, Bayrd was sure of that much. Eskra had told him – gently, as bad news was always broken, but clearly enough that even he could understand the implications behind the complex phrases of the Art Magic – that she would have known if he too had been killed. And he had not. But he was no longer encharmed, no longer protected by her spell-borne pretence of his hatred for Bayrd. And he was still alive. That, she had told him quietly, could mean only one thing.

The feigned hatred had become real.

The mist began to thin out and, having begun, cleared so swiftly that Eskra stared distrustfully at the last vanishing wisps. When the weather was right, conjuring a mist for concealment and controlling it so that it stayed in one place was one of the easier enchantments. Even though she knew that at this time of year mists and fogs were common enough on the moors, this too-convenient disappearance made her uneasy.

She was the only one who felt so. All the others, Bayrd included, were glad enough to see where they were going, where they had been – and most important of all, who else was out there. Kian ar'Terel had seen a banner, or so he claimed. Red and white, with black blotches that might, looked on with an optimistic eye, have been a black bear. If that was so, then the men on the ridge were ar'Diskan's. That was a sort of comfort.

At least they weren't cu Ruruc's. Or ar'Kelayr's; or far too many other people who would be more than happy to find the Clan-Lord Talvalin almost alone on the Elthanek moors.

But that raised more worries for Bayrd. If he set his pride aside and faced the truth, then there was no denying that Gerin ar'Diskan was the most powerful lord in the northland. That meant – or should have meant – that he had no need for such boundary-riders as these. Unless . . .

Unless he was suspicious of something, of raids, of surprise attacks. Or maybe of assassins from Cerdor. The answers to all those questions were inside the walls of the fortress of Segelin. Assuming Bayrd and his party ever got that far.

'He knows,' muttered Eskra. 'I don't know how he found it out, but he knows—'

'What?' Bayrd's voice cut through the sound of her fretting, and she straightened up to stare at him.

'What do you think? You want to ask him when we get there? He knows who's coming calling, Bayrd. That's enough. And he wants to see you dead.'

'He's an honourable man,' said Bayrd, aware that he sounded like someone trying to convince himself. What had seemed entirely reasonable in the council chamber of Dunrath lacked credibility out here in the wilderness. From the look on Eskra's face, she heard that tone of voice as well. 'At least he's a practical man. He may want me dead, but he wants Dunrath as well. Murder won't help him get it, or keep it anyway. He'll need consent from . . . from Erhal, or Yraine, or whoever is finally approved as Overlord after all this is over. Otherwise what's the point?'

'You, dead.' Her voice was flat, the statement simple. Bayrd forced a grin on to lips that didn't feel inclined to carry one, and managed to keep it there.

'You do harp on one string sometimes, loved. He's had plenty of chances to try that over the years, and he hasn't yet.'

'As you say. Yet.'

'So why would he do it now?'

'Because of the confusion. Kalarr in Erdanor, you out on the moors in a mist—'

'It's gone.'

'And who's to tell, if you, and I, and all these others, aren't alive to say so?' She shot another glare up the hill, to where the other troop of horsemen should have been but weren't. 'These are troubled times, and they thought we might have been a raiding-party. We weren't identified until too late. How sad. Accidents happen, Bayrd, even in clear air; remember Reth ar'Gyart? But most of all, there's no Overlord to prevent someone from taking the law into their own hands.'

Bayrd drew breath to correct her, and Eskra wiggled her hand in the air, a 'maybe, maybe' gesture that he knew all too well. 'All right,' he conceded. 'No *proper* Overlord. And Kalarr might have been lying for his own benefit.'

'Small benefit to Ivern, though.'

'Ivern was ar'Diskan'r.' Bayrd flashed another quick grin; it was smaller this time, but more sincere. 'He was like his father. Stubborn. Stupidly so. He wouldn't bend in the breeze, and he couldn't stand up to the storm.'

'Will you tell Gerin that?'

'About his son being stupid? He probably knows.'

'About his son being *dead*.'

'I might. But without proof . . .'

Eskra smiled grimly. 'As you're so fond of saying yourself, what's the point?'

And then the horsemen crested the ridge and came thundering down from the hill, and the most immediate points were those of their spears.

It looked so like the long-anticipated ambush that Bayrd was within a breath of ordering a counter-attack; but an instant later he had thrown both arms out wide as a signal for his men to remain as they were. There was more than steel on the points of those spears. Wreaths of green leaves had been wrapped around them as a sign of peace, and Bayrd breathed a small sigh of relief.

The young *kailin-eir* commanding the newcomers reined his horse to a flashy, skidding halt on the turf, and even before the animal had properly recovered itself he had risen in his stirrups to give Bayrd and Eskra the deep, elegant bow from the waist that did duty on horseback as Second Obeisance.

'Lord, lady,' he spoke the titles as though he meant them both, 'I am Aymar ar'Haleth, Bannerman to Lord Gerin ar'Diskan, and your guide to Segelin.'

'I thank you, Aymar-*an*,' said Bayrd, acknowledging the bow with the curt nod that was all a Clan-Lord required – especially one whose insides were still fluttering with shock. This man was what he had once been, and he gave his replacement a wry look. 'But I know well enough where Hold ar'Diskan lies. We need no guide.'

'My lord,' said Aymar, 'I must insist.' There was no need for any crudely threatening gestures like waving at the spears behind him, which green branches or not were still weapons. He was too good a Bannerman for that. But there was enough steel in his voice to suggest that argument was not an option.

'Then I thank you.' Bayrd nodded again, dismissal this time. 'Lead on.'

Not a guide, he thought. *Just an escort. Gerin* must *be worried about something. I wonder if it's the same thing that—*

And then he realised that the escort was a guide after all, and for a very good reason: Segelin was set for a siege.

Banners flapped sluggishly from its towers, and the clan-lord's long standard drifted from the topmost turret of the citadel, the only touches of colour in that whole grey mass of stone. Despite what he had told the young *kailin*, Bayrd had never seen it before; and looking at it now, he knew he was in no great hurry to see it again.

The architecture of Hold ar'Diskan was severe to the point of brutality. It had been built very much to impress on any who saw it – the Elthanek vassals of the domain, for the most part, and any visitors with an eye that understood – that this was the residence of the ruler of the land, a ruler who had taken that land by force, and if need be would keep it by force.

For all that the fortress of Segelin had towers as tall as any in the Land, they didn't seem to loft towards the sky. Instead the whole structure seemed to squat ponderously on the earth, like a huge beast crouched over the body of its prey. Bayrd studied it for a few moments more, then shook his head and dismissed the image; it wasn't deliberate enough.

Hold ar'Diskan's shape and posture said much more than that. It was a wood and stone and metal boot placed across the throat of the entire domain. And its lowering presence had never been more obvious than now.

For a long bowshot all around the walls, any vegetation that might have softened the grim outline of the fortress had been scoured away, uprooted or scythed or burned, clear down to the bare earth. Now that earth was white, coated with chalk from the hills or the fine white limestone sand from the shores of one of the nearby lakes.

Where it had come from was of small account; why it was there was obvious. On even the darkest night, anyone trying to cross that great pale expanse and approach the fortress walls would have no shadows to hide them. They would be the shadows, and a good enough target to shoot at.

But there was more, and an even better reason for Bayrd and his people to pay close attention to their guides. Someone had been planting lilies.

That wryly humorous name described not the deep-belled flowers with long stamens at their centre, but the interlocking array of conical pits that had been dug into the ground, with a sharp spike at the bottom of each one. They were everywhere; most were covered, but others had been deliberately left exposed, as a warning to anyone on horse or foot who might attempt to rush across the exposed ground. There was a route through the lily-field – that was what the guides were for – but anyone trying to find that route without help would do so under a storm of arrows from the fortress walls.

And more than arrows . . .

Tree-trunks had been sunk into the ground at intervals around the perimeter of the cleared area. They formed three or four concentric circles with the fortress squatting at the centre, and each ring of posts had been painted a different colour to act as fall-of-shot markers for the engines on the walls. Those would shoot darts, or rocks, or even nets of smaller stones that would spread out in flight to cover a wider area. And they would shoot them far too accurately for comfort.

'The artillery's been ranged in, lord,' said Iskar ar'Joren quietly. Bayrd could see that. There were craters bashed into the white ground that had nothing to do with the digging of lilies, and long straight gouges left by the heavy artillery-darts. He wondered for an instant why the marks hadn't been covered up again, then guessed that, like the presence of the uncovered lilies, such proof of Hold ar'Diskan's readiness and long reach would do nothing for the courage of any attacking troops.

'All this because of me?' he said dubiously, not really meaning it. Eskra shot him a glance and a crooked smile.

'Don't flatter yourself,' she said.

'I wouldn't dream of it.'

'Gerin's domain is further north than yours. He's closer to—'

'To something he knows nothing about.'

'To something he's bloody suspicious about, loved, or he wouldn't have gone to all this trouble. And now we have to convince him that where Kalarr cu Ruruc is concerned, it might have been a waste of time . . .'

'Greetings to you, *arl'th-eir*, my lord,' said Lord Gerin ar'Diskan. And that was all. It was courtesy as cold as he could manage, and still fall short of actual insult. He didn't rise from his seat, didn't make any gesture of salutation, didn't do anything at all but sit slumped in his chair at the far end of his Great Hall and glower at the people standing in the doorway. Gerin always glowered well; he had plenty of practice.

Bayrd hadn't really expected to hear the word 'welcome' on this man's lips, but as he walked easily up the length of the Hall, it still shocked him slightly to see how much Gerin had changed from the man he once knew, and not for the better. The ar'Diskan'r were known for being hot-tempered and passionate, great eaters, drinkers and roarers of florid invective. They were – and few knew it better than he – the sort of good friends that made bad enemies. But they had never been bitter, never brooded over their real or imagined wrongs. They had never been like this.

The changes were in more than just his attitude. Now there were strands of silver in the shaggy mane of hair and the moustache that lay across the swarthy features like a black bar. That was age, it came to everyone, but the other changes Gerin had wrought upon himself. He had always been stocky, but now his waist was thicker and his hatchet features had coarsened. His nose and cheeks were patterned with a network of tiny cracked veins, testimony to the innumerable bottles of wine he had consumed over the years in an attempt to blunt his frustration over Dunrath and several other such matters, and there was a watery, protuberant look to his brown eyes, eyes that had once been hot and bright as those of a falcon.

Bayrd felt strangely saddened by it all, and sadder still that nothing he might say would be accepted as anything but an affront.

'I trust you, my lord,' he said, ducking his head to give Gerin the quick bow due to an equal.

Ar'Diskan snorted, managing to imply with that one sound that he expected a greater level of respect, and that whatever Bayrd might choose to believe, they were not and would never be equal in rank. 'Trust what?' he said. 'That I'm well, that I'm sick, that I'm dying . . . ?'

'I trust you,' Bayrd repeated, trying not to let this nettling have any effect. It was strangely easier than it had been with Vanek ar'Kelayr; Gerin had never learned the knack of getting under a person's skin to the same extent . . . not unless he used a blade. 'As an honourable man.'

'Ah. I see. You trust me not to kill you out of hand, is that it?'

'Something like that. After all, I came here myself, of my own free will.'

Gerin grinned unpleasantly. 'If free will means because you had no other choice, then I'll accept it. From what I've been hearing, ar'Talvlyn, you're having to do a great deal for yourself nowadays. Just can't get the help, eh . . . ?'

It was true enough, even though Gerin's sneering voice made it sound much worse. Trust and sincerity aside, this was the sort of duty that was assigned to Bannermen, especially in dealings between lords who might reach for a *taiken* at first sight of each other. But in the absence of such a high-ranking retainer, and when sending anyone of less status would be not just an insult but the death of the unfortunate messenger, there was indeed no other choice.

Bayrd's response was just a bitter smile. He had hoped that Gerin might be more impressed. Small chance of that. One thing about Lord Gerin ar'Diskan had not changed at all, and that was his stubborn streak.

'Set aside why I came myself, then. Will you hear what I have to say?'

Gerin shrugged. 'It hardly matters. Nothing you might have to say to me matters any more.'

'Do you know the whereabouts of your children?'

'What kind of a question is that? And what concern is it of yours in any case?'

'Curiosity.'

'Hah!'

'All right then. Call it the concern that one lord might have regarding the affairs of another, when those affairs might overlap his own.'

'Light of Heaven, but we *have* learned a fine and proper way to talk in the past few years, haven't we? Where? Cerdor?'

'Now there's a place I try to avoid.' Bayrd waved Eskra, Kian and Iskar to seats, then shifted Widowmaker where she hung in peace posture across his back for the first time in months, and perched comfortably in one himself.

'I didn't grant you permission to sit down,' growled ar'Diskan.

'I didn't ask,' said Bayrd pleasantly. 'You'd get too much satisfaction from refusing.'

After almost six years, he was remembering how to deal with the members of Clan ar'Diskan, and the most successful way had always been a nicely-measured, always humorous impertinence. Not insolence; straying too far in that direction was dangerous where a high-clan lord was concerned, even with those more even-tempered than Gerin. But the carefully-judged level of cheek was something that had always worked when he had been Bannerman and Companion to the man in front of him. For all his own roaring, Gerin had seemed to equate it with conviction in the rightness of an opinion, even though that opinion might differ from his own. And even though the speaker was an enemy.

He rumbled something low in his chest, but didn't press the

point. Bayrd could see that despite everything else, he too was growing curious about such bold behaviour. It was a relief. Despite all the reasons he had given Eskra about why Gerin wouldn't kill them all out of hand, Gerin himself had reasons enough to do exactly that, and probably enough justification that he would get away with it. But the blow had been withheld so far, and Bayrd suspected it would continue to be so. For all his many faults, no one had ever accused Gerin ar'Diskan of being stupid.

'Your children, my lord,' he said again. 'Do you know where they are?' Gerin stared at him, twisting the tips of his moustache between finger and thumb, trying to understand the reason for the question before he answered it. Bayrd kept his face as unreadable as he was able.

'Cerdor,' Gerin said at last. 'Arren is, at least.'

'But doing more than merely learning how to express himself correctly, I think. Yes?' Gerin said nothing. 'Gerin-*eir*, let's stop pretending. We both know each other's policies in the matter of the Overlordship. Neither candidate meets with our approval, for – ' he waved his arms shoulder-high in an extravagant shrug, '– for several good and proper reasons. But neither of us can come straight out and say so. Instead, we balance between the two. Yes?'

'. . . Yes.'

'So. And Arren is trying to ensure that whichever faction comes out on top – once the High Council finally makes up what passes for its collective mind – will be the faction that you, his wise and far-seeing father, have been secretly backing all along. He'd better work fast. I have news of Erhal ar'Albanak: he's declared himself Overlord.'

Gerin grunted, but didn't look overly surprised. 'Old news,' he said. 'Last week it was the woman. A month ago, it was Gyras ar'Dakkur, acting on behalf of the Council.'

'I mean it,' Bayrd insisted. Without proof, that was all he could do, and the time was not right to explain how he knew the difference between new fact and old rumour.

'They all do. And it's all a great secret – except that everyone knows it already.'

'All right,' said Bayrd, abandoning his attempt to convince Gerin, at least for the present. 'But now let me tell *you* a secret.' The Clan-Lord ar'Diskan's expression didn't change – he was working as hard as Bayrd to keep his thoughts concealed – but had he been a dog Bayrd was convinced his ears would have pricked up at that one word. 'I am on the point of declaring for Yraine ar'Albanak.'

Gerin stared at him, blinked twice and then roared with laughter. It had an unpleasant edge to it, and Bayrd listened to the sound with a sour smile on his face. Gerin's support, he recalled, would of course be for Erhal, once he was finally pushed into making a decision.

And that was ironic, since it was supposedly Erhal who was leading a force northward to destroy Clan ar'Diskan for not giving such support earlier.

'Declare for a woman,' spluttered Gerin, wiping his eyes and regaining control with difficulty – if he had ever lost it in the first place. There had been something very forced about the last few hearty guffaws. 'A woman Overlord . . . ? In this country and at this time! By Heaven, ar'Talvlyn, you missed your calling. That was as good a joke as I've heard in weeks.'

'Which one? The woman, or the support for her?'

'Both, man, both. How many of the other lords would stand for it?'

'As many as were commanded to, Gerin-*eir*. Especially if there was a sword in their back – or in the back of someone dear to them.'

'So that's it, eh?'

'*It*, my lord? Which *it* do you mean?'

'Persuasion. Or at least attempted persuasion.' Gerin heaved his bulk from the embrace of the chair and strode to the side door of the Hall. 'Come here,' he said, beckoning. Bayrd followed him, and looked up in the direction indicated by Gerin's pointing arm.

Six heads leered back at him from their spikes atop the citadel's inner wall. The birds, the insects and the hot weather had all been at them over the past while, but Bayrd could still put a guess at how long they had been there. About as long as a similar number of corpses had been mouldering in unmarked graves beyond the outer walls of Dunrath.

'Attempted persuasion,' said Gerin again. 'They came looking for hostages, and they found nothing but a pain in the neck . . .' He was smiling with a dour satisfaction, and the smile broadened when he saw Bayrd's face. 'You too, eh?'

'Equally attempted,' said Bayrd. It was grotesque – but somehow appropriate – that it should need such macabre relics to bring them even this little distance closer together, but for the first time in six years he and Gerin ar'Diskan had a trace of common ground.

'The funniest part of all,' he heard the older man say, 'is that there was nobody here for them to kidnap. Arren in Cerdor, the wife with her family at Hold ar'Lerutz in Datherga—'

'They raided Datherga, my lord,' said Bayrd, 'and took Lord Keo's sister and his youngest daughter.'

'Yes, I know. But they didn't know my wife was there. Careless of them, don't you think?'

'Very. And your son Ivern, my lord . . . ?'

'Wasn't here.' The shortness of the reply was plainly meant to deter further questioning. It didn't.

'Was he not, my lord?' Neither of them had heard Eskra come up behind them, and Bayrd had the small but definite pleasure of seeing Gerin start at the sound of her voice. 'Then where was he? In Cerdor, with his brother? Or somewhere else?'

Gerin ar'Diskan swung around and his black brows drew together as he scowled down at her, breathing hard but saying nothing. The contrast was an interesting one, thought Bayrd. Gerin was head and shoulders taller than Eskra, and maybe twice her weight; but there was no doubt at least in his mind about which of them was the stronger person. It had nothing to do with physical strength: Gerin could have snapped Eskra in two pieces like a twig – if she let him live so long. But there was more than mere brawn under consideration here, and all three of them knew it. Lord ar'Diskan had the look of a man who wanted more than just a *taipan* shortsword at his belt, but equally, he had the look of one who wouldn't dare try drawing even that.

Granted, he was biased, Bayrd conceded to himself. But equally granted, he knew what he was seeing.

The big clan-lord was furious that she had made him jump, and seen him jump; he hated her because for all these years he had believed that it was her sorcery that had played a part in his loss of the Dunrath domains, since it had given Bayrd the courage to put his hand at hazard. And he didn't care for women who – what was it he had said once? – 'put themselves forward'. Who 'didn't know their place'. Eskra was a sorcerer, and even though he had been married to her for the past six years, Bayrd still didn't know what her proper place might be.

Except beside him.

'Dyrek ar'Kelayr was keeping some strange company before he died,' Bayrd said into the awkward silence. For a few seconds he thought that Gerin hadn't heard him.

Then the dark eyes shifted and registered his presence again, and when they blinked it was as though Gerin was a man coming awake after a deep, uneasy sleep. 'Before Dyrek died?' he said. He glanced at Eskra again, but his gaze slid away without meeting hers and touched briefly instead on the black steel of the sword-hilt at Bayrd's left shoulder. 'You mean, before you killed him.'

Bayrd would have groaned with impatience, had there been any point in it. 'Do you still believe that?' he said.

'What else is there to believe?'

'Try the truth.'

'Your truth, or my truth? They aren't the same thing.'

'The choice is entirely yours, my lord. But Dyrek killed himself. I watched him do it. And not for fear of worse,' he said to forestall the accusation gathering in ar'Diskan's face. 'Because I *would* have killed him, have no doubt about that. You would have killed him yourself, for what he did.'

Bayrd looked at ar'Diskan's face and reconsidered. 'Well, you might, anyway. After all, the people he roasted were nothing but Elthanek peasants – and don't bother to protest, my lord, I've heard it all before. But there's the difference. He burned my vassals in their own house, and listened to them scream until the roof came in. Out of consideration for his rank – and for nothing else, he didn't deserve any more – I would have taken his head off, quick and clean. And he knew. So he killed himself to spite me.'

'Spite . . . ?'

'To prove something.'

'Father of Fires, man, what could he prove on the point of his own knife—'

Bayrd's head jerked round and he favoured Gerin with a sardonic smile. 'So you *did* hear the whole story after all. And because it was me, you refused to believe it. Ah, well. But what could he prove indeed? That he was braver than I was, because he wasn't afraid of dying? Ramming a *tsepan* through your own skull doesn't prove that to me. It might prove that you were stupid, or impatient, or . . . Never mind.'

Bayrd looked out of the door again, back up at the six heads with what remained of their lips stretched in permanent, ragged grins. 'But it might also prove that you were more afraid of someone else than of the man who was going to kill you. Dyrek threatened me with reprisals, you know. On the edge of oblivion, and he threatened me . . . with the Red Serpent.'

Gerin concealed the involuntary twitch of his mouth very well, but not well enough. Bayrd saw it; Eskra saw it; and both of them let it pass. For the present.

'He is Kalarr cu Ruruc,' said Eskra. 'High Lord Gelert's son. Late of Prytenon. And no lover of the Albans who took his land away. You know what that feels like.'

Bayrd was expecting the rage those words ignited in ar'Diskan's eyes, but even so its intensity still took him aback. 'Through no fault of mine, my lord,' he said. 'I told you then, and I'll continue to tell you. It was not my intention to cheat you. The Overlord Albanak—'

'Is dead and out of my reach.' The low growl of Gerin's voice was far more menacing than any shout of fury could be. 'You're not. Remember that, both of you. And don't try my patience again.'

'I meant no insult, my lord,' said Eskra, so smoothly and sincerely that she almost convinced even Bayrd. 'But I had to focus your mind on what this Kalarr feels, and why. Hatred such as you cannot encompass. For all of us. You; my husband; my children; every Alban in this land, down to the child born today. And those he would call traitors. People who live with his enemies. People who were conquered and have dared to be still alive. People like me. Do you understand?'

Gerin stared at her, and the fire in his eyes cooled and went out. 'I think so,' he said. 'I hope so.' Then he shook his head. 'But as for you,' the heat returned just a little as he swung on Bayrd again, 'I'm still not persuaded about the ar'Kelaryr'n. The death of the son and the death of the father followed too close together. They were too . . . too convenient.'

'For whom? Me? I lost my Bannerman—'

'I know the feeling.'

'My respect, several of my own lord's-men and two allied Houses. I gained nothing. If that's convenient, my lord, I want no part of it.'

'I've heard three versions of the same tale,' Gerin persisted stubbornly. 'And the one I find most convincing involves that damned sword, and black sorcery.'

'Not black,' Eskra corrected. 'Sorcery isn't black. Shades of grey, perhaps,' she said, remembering the morning. 'But wizardry and the Art Magic . . . Now that's another matter.'

Gerin shot her a look of disgust, as a man might when a normally dignified lady appears for the first time dirty, drunken and foul-mouthed. 'I have no desire to know any of this,' he said coldly.

'Not even for your own safety's sake? Then you'd better forget that knives are sharp, and falling off tall buildings is bad for your health. Because it's all the same thing in the long run . . .'

'Peace, 'Skra-*ain*. There'll be time for it later.'

'If we have a later.'

'Hush. My Lord ar'Diskan, isn't the fact that I came here to try and convince you of, all right, of my truth instead of yours, at least a demonstration of good faith?'

'Of arrogance, maybe. And a poor view of my intelligence.'

'Or maybe a truth that isn't just yours or mine.'

'So we're back to the truth again, are we?'

'Where else is there to go?' The hectoring tone was gone from Eskra's voice, and she spoke quietly. 'Either you believe what we're trying to tell you, my lord, and something useful comes from all this wrangling – or you don't, and Kalarr cu Ruruc devours us piecemeal in his own good time.' She eyed him thoughtfully, because there had been that same suppressed twitch as before at the mention of the sorcerer's name. 'Now. What about your son?'

'Ivern is dead.'

This time it was Eskra's turn to jump, as sharply as if she had touched a hot coal. 'What . . . ?' That her voice could be so steady was a credit to whatever training sorcery and the Art required of its students, but Bayrd could see how white her face had gone. His own face couldn't be much better, even though he had only heard Ivern's death described. Eskra had seen it through Marc ar'Dru's eyes, as closely as seeing it through her own. 'What did you say?' she tried again.

'I have no younger son,' said ar'Diskan sombrely. 'I asked him as his father, and he ignored me; I commanded him as his lord, and he defied me. I no longer have a son of that name.'

Bayrd Talvalin could feel the blood thudding in his ears, and he was certain that there was a tremor in his hands. Coincidence, so the scholars said, happened more frequently in life than in any of the talemakers' stories, because life, they said, was never so tidily plotted. Bayrd could well believe it. But how much this bleak repudiation – which seemed to have worked both ways – might serve to soften the blow of Ivern's real death, he didn't know.

He had no proof that might serve to convince Gerin ar'Diskan. Bayrd closed his eyes, clenched his fists, gritted his teeth, and felt no better. There was never any proof – not of plotting, not of murder, not of usurpation in Cerdor. There was just his word; and that was worth little enough elsewhere, and nothing at all in Segelin.

But there was one other thing the scholars had said, when they weren't busily squabbling over whose theory was to be the most favoured on any particular week. Every once in a while, to prove something they weren't entirely sure of except the existence of irony, one of those coincidences made sense.

And though he didn't know it when the alarm trumpets started to scream from the walls of the fortress, it was happening to Bayrd right now.

The man brought into the citadel by Aymar ar'Haleth looked less like the saviour of sense than he resembled something one of Gerin's hunting-dogs might bury under a tree. For several seconds neither Bayrd, Eskra nor the two retainers could understand why Aymar treated this dusty, muddy, tattered ragamuffin with such concern, or why Gerin ar'Diskan threw his arms around the man and all but wept on his shoulder as he helped him to a chair.

It was only when the first coating of mire – mixed, as they could see, with spatters of dried, caked blood – had been sponged away that they realised he was Gerin's son Arren . . .

A man who by all intents should have been in Cerdor.

He was injured in several places besides the long gash on the forehead that had made him so hard to recognise. None of them were serious, though that was only through good luck. Bayrd knew arrow-wounds when he saw them, and right now he was looking at four or five.

'Get the surgeon in here!' bellowed Gerin, raging about in an ecstasy of concern and getting in the way far more than he helped. It was strange for Bayrd to see how a man he knew was a cool, controlled warrior could act like a headless chicken where his own son was concerned. At least, when that was his obedient eldest son. 'Fetch fresh clothing! Bring food and wine!'

'Enough for all,' added Eskra as the gaggle of servants hurried past her, and if Gerin heard he didn't countermand the request.

Arren ar'Diskan was hungry, thirsty, aching from hours in the saddle, and most of all he was exhausted; but like his father and his late brother, the family stubbornness was able to put everything else behind his need to explain what had brought him here. Bayrd and the others suspected that they already knew, and once Arren began to speak they were sure of it. It was the same warning as before, but this time from a source that even Gerin would find impeccable.

'Erhal ar'Albanak', he began, speaking carefully through a hoarse, dust-abraded throat that no amount of wine or water had yet rinsed clean, 'has declared himself Overlord by a majority mandate of the High Council.'

For Bayrd at least, it was worth all the time and trouble and insults to see the expression on Gerin's face when he heard those words, and he resisted an overwhelming temptation to say *What did I tell you?* But only because Lord Gerin's own mind was saying it for him.

'How did he achieve the majority?' Bayrd asked. 'And why wasn't it unanimous?'

Arren blinked at Bayrd as though realising for the first time he was there. His eyes took in the blue and white Talvalin crest-coat, the silver spread-eagles at the shoulders, and above all the black hilt of the *taiken* Widowmaker rearing like a striking snake beside Bayrd's head. He passed a dry tongue over dry lips, blinked again, then glanced sidelong at his father as though asking permission to answer the question.

'Hostages,' he said at last. Bayrd heard Eskra swear under her breath. 'He holds hostages from most of the clans and Families and Houses, as surety for the good behaviour of their lords. If he had hostages from them all, then surely the mandate *would* have been unanimous.'

'And this good behaviour is of course whatever action he commands, or that his faction approves?'

'No faction, my lord.' Water, wine and food had arrived as he was speaking, and Arren paused to rinse the dust from his mouth. Then he looked at the circle of apprehensive faces. 'He's acting independently.'

'But he's only seventeen!' Gerin burst out. 'How would any lord on the Council—'

Arren thumped his fist on the arm of the chair, even though from the way he winced, the effort hurt him. 'Didn't you hear me, Father?' he demanded. 'He has hostages! When he was last in the Great Tower, he all but emptied old Albanak's treasury to hire *talathen* assassins from Drosul . . .'

'So now we know who was behind it,' said Bayrd in an undertone.

'Another precocious brat,' muttered Eskra. 'Just the way cu Ruruc started.'

'. . . and took prisoners from everyone he might need to control. Not just the obvious ones: his opponents and the Undeclared. He sent them after his own supporters as well. To guarantee their loyalty. After that, nobody could oppose him . . .'

'Except for a couple of clans in the north,' said Bayrd savagely, 'because his *talathen* failed to take any hostages from them. But they didn't oppose him because they were too busy opposing each other. Isn't that right, my lord Gerin? We've been playing dog in the manger here for far too long. You haven't trusted me because you think I tricked you out of a fairly-won domain, and so you routinely disbelieve anything I might say – as we heard not half an hour ago when I told you exactly this. And I haven't trusted you, because years ago you made threats against me. Threats that you've been too honourable to carry out!'

'Now wait just a minute,' Gerin began.

'That was a compliment, man,' snapped Eskra. 'Accept it and shut up.'

'So while we've been playing our own small, private version of the Game, we've been overlooking the Grand Moves made by everybody else. Gerin-*eir* ar'Diskan, do you need any more proof that we should forget past differences?'

'This isn't exactly the reason you were giving me "not half an hour ago",' said Gerin, stubborn and pedantic to the last.

'Fires of Heaven, man!' Bayrd's fist came down on the arm of his own chair, and since he was not only unhurt but was holding a brimming goblet of wine, the result was much more impressive than Arren's effort. 'If this isn't enough, then what in the Nine Hot Hells do you want for proof? A siege-train outside both our Holds, and each time flying the same banner? Do you want to see the roof cave in before you're convinced your house is on fire?'

'He's right, Father,' said Arren.

'You keep out of this,' Gerin snapped automatically; then blushed bright red at the enormity of what he had done. It was one thing for a man to keep treating his sons as children, but quite another when one of those sons had made a most un-childlike headlong ride from Cerdor to Segelin with enemy warriors in pursuit for at least part of the way.

'I will not keep out of it,' said Arren, and for the first time Bayrd could hear old ar'Diskan's voice coming out of his son's mouth. It was as hard and inflexible as Gerin had ever sounded and, perhaps wisely, Gerin heard it too and paid it heed.

'What, then?' he said, his façade of indifference crumbling under the weight of necessity. Arren stared at his father, then at Bayrd.

'An alliance,' he said simply. 'Otherwise, just kill everyone, burn the fortress, and save yourself a great deal of time and trouble.'

'Don't talk rubbish—'

'Have you seen Erhal's army, Father? No? Well, I have. Two thousand horse, three thousand foot. I'm talking sense.'

'And then there's Kalarr,' said Eskra sweetly. 'Did you forget him? Another three thousand men. No; probably more by now. And he owes you, my lord ar'Diskan. He owes you much more than—'

'Not now. You're not being very encouraging, loved,' said Bayrd. The endearment had teeth in it.

'You want encouragement?' said Eskra, though she steered away from the other and far more sensitive subject. 'All right. Here's encouragement for you. Individually, you're both dead. Damn it, individually, we're all dead. Never mind Kalarr cu Ruruc for the moment, just consider Erhal. My children; your children. Dead.'

Her eyes flickered towards Bayrd's; he met and held them for no more than a second, but in that second he gave her a nod that was approval for preparing the way, but also a warning not to go any further down that road. Without proof, which not even Arren could supply, the news about Ivern would be a pointless hurt, and one that could even destroy the pact that they were trying to build.

'How long will Arren survive you, my lord ar'Diskan? When you're buried under the rubble of this citadel and these lands are under the Overlord's hand, who's going to make him give them up? Because no matter what he's done to make himself secure, no matter how many hostages he holds, from however many clans and Families and Houses, you aren't dealing with Erhal alone. This seventeen-year-old boy has the whole of the High Council behind him. They're still using him, even if it isn't just as a figurehead to disguise the workings of their own white hands.'

Eskra picked up a cup of wine and drank it down in two gulps. Bayrd watched her warily. He had seen his wife in a passion of annoyance before, overflowing with impatience at the sheer stupidity of people who seemed to be maliciously blind to what was happening around them, but he had never seen her teetering so close to the edge of real anger. When Eskra Talvalin got angry, she got quiet; and she was very quiet and controlled right now.

'The Council daren't back down from any decisions he might make, any orders he might give – remember the hostages? But they can "advise" him on those decisions. They can "make recommendations", and hostages or no hostages, they'll have that boy dancing to their piping all the more eagerly because he'll still be convinced that he's doing it of his own free will!'

'I weep for him,' Gerin snarled.

'You should.' Eskra's shoulders drooped, and suddenly she looked as weary as though she, too, had just ridden all the way from Cerdor. 'Nobody else will. And somebody must, because what's being done in his name will blacken it—'

'Then let it be blackened!' It was the usual ar'Diskan blaze of temper, but it looked to Bayrd like the last flare of resistance.

'Are we to be allies, then?' he wondered aloud, not asking a direct question just yet.

'Allies, ar'Talvlyn. Not friends.' Gerin had the harried look of a man not quite sure of how he had been manipulated into agreeing to this situation, and still less idea of how he was going to get out of it again. 'I'm setting aside our differences. Don't think for one minutes that I'm forgetting them.'

For all that, there was general relief, and even Kian ar'Terel cracked one of his wintry smiles. 'You're a stubborn man, ar'Diskan,' said Bayrd, bowing acknowledgement more willingly than he had bowed greeting earlier on.

'Practical, ar'Talv—' Gerin hesitated, then shrugged. 'All right. Let it be Talvalin, then. But yes. I'm just practical. I don't trust you any more than you trust me, and if you do, then you're a fool.'

'Then call me a fool.'

'You're a fool.' There was a short, uneasy silence, broken at last by Eskra's soft laughter at all the posturing she was being forced to witness. This was the second time in less than a month that Bayrd had invited someone to call him a fool, and let them get away with it. Bayrd looked at her, then at Gerin. Gerin looked at her, then at Bayrd. Slowly, they both smiled. 'Yes,' said Gerin ar'Diskan. 'You're a fool indeed. But an honourable one for all that.'

10

Endgame

'WE'LL MEET THEM in open battle,' said Gerin, unrolling a great sheet of parchment across the dining-table in his private chambers and securing its corners with weights. The various ar'Diskan'r officers and *kailinin* who were present paid it no great heed, but Bayrd, Eskra and their two retainers Kian and Iskar studied it with an interest they did their unsuccessful best to conceal.

It was when Bayrd saw Arren ar'Diskan smiling behind his hand that he gave up on the pretence, twitched his lips into an even thinner smile that he didn't bother to hide, and let his head tilt slowly to one side as his eyes followed the courses of rivers, the edges of forests and mountain ranges, even the seashore that marked the limit of the Land.

Most of all, his gaze tracked along the red-inked boundaries of clan domains, noting that the parchment had been scraped and redrawn on several occasions to keep those boundaries current as they shifted with marriage, alliance and inheritance. That wasn't too surprising: the features of a country didn't change, the political borders did. But this, after all, was Gerin ar'Diskan.

That he might be one of the many Alban lords trying to make documentary sense of their new possessions wasn't so unusual. Bayrd had such charts himself, more or less completed, and some of them drawn in even finer detail than this in an attempt to keep track of which family owned which patch of grazing-land at any given time of year. But because of that very reason, they were small, each one covering only a couple of meadows at a time. To see a map of an entire province – in fact, more even than that: it showed the whole of Elthan and part of Prytenon as well – as drawn in such detail *was* unusual, and disturbing.

Gerin commanded between three and four thousand ar'Diskan *kailinin*, even before any calculations started to include the allied clans and Houses, and various smaller families who owed him an obligation of armed duty in his Household forces in exchange for their lands. When a clan-lord of Gerin's known pugnacious temperament had so many soldiers under his banner, then neighbouring lords with fewer troops on call were well advised to look to their defences. When that same aggressive lord had a chart such as this in his possession, he couldn't help but worry.

And it was only one map. Bayrd wondered what the others might show him, if he dared to open the wooden locker and rummage through its contents. But there was an honour-guard of six men in the room, as a courtesy to the higher-ranked people such as himself and Gerin, and one of those six was standing nonchalantly right beside the chart-locker with its two keys on his belt. It was unlikely that any attempt to open it without permission would be well-received.

Finding out would have to wait.

Bayrd turned his attention back to the map on the table, but he made a small mental note to himself. It was obvious that the *talathen* Shadowthieves had no scruples about working in Alba as well as in Drosul, and if one could afford their services then they were more than just kidnappers and assassins. High though it would be, that cost might prove a worthwhile investment sometime in the next few months or so – always assuming he survived the next few weeks. And, he told himself, fighting the rising tide of reservations, it was less dishonourable to employ them as spies if the ultimate intention of that spying was to keep the peace.

Once something like peace had been restored, of course . . .

He watched Gerin setting up stacks of carved and inlaid counters along the decorated edges of the map. They were wooden, stained in several colours to show various allied and opposing sides, each one with a horseman or foot-soldier carved into the top and small metal numerals let into its edge to show how many it represented. The big man moved with all the speed and assurance of someone who had gone through this same routine many times before.

Who had been the enemy last time? wondered Bayrd, because

the friendly side was very obvious. Those were the red counters, each inlaid with a black bear mounted on a plaque of polished ivory. He lifted one of them to examine it more closely. Just a small disc of wood, coloured and carved and inscribed. A playing-piece for a war game, or even for the Great Game, but little more than a toy for all that. And yet it had the same unsettling feeling in his hand as any one of Eskra's sorcerous grimoires. *Yes*, he thought, putting the piece back where he had found it. *Who* was *that last enemy, Gerin? The one who prompted you to set your siege-lines, or someone else entirely? And who might it be again? Me . . . ?*

'So then,' said Gerin, consulting a sheaf of scribbled notes and arranging green counters accordingly. 'Erhal has . . . two thousand horse . . . about here –' *click* went the counters, 'and three thousand foot with them.' *Click* again. They all studied the map some more while he started to organise the disposition of his own troops, muttering under his breath.

'Clan ar'Diskan can match them for horse,' he said, placing the appropriate counters, 'but we've only half that number of foot until Gyras ar'Dakkur gets off his fat backside.' Bayrd and Eskra exchanged glances but said nothing, though that sort of comment was fairly rich, coming as it did from a man whose own rump looked as though he carried a pair of cushions down his breeches.

'If he ever does, Father,' said Arren ar'Diskan. 'Hostages: you always forget about the hostages. Both of Lord ar'Dakkur's youngest sons, and one of his daughters, are sitting in the Great Tower at Cerdor even as we speak. And their health depends entirely on how he behaves.'

'Ah. Yes.' Gerin balanced those extra counters on the palm of his hand and stared at them, considering before he reluctantly put them to one side. 'Using women and children as weapons. That's not an honourable way to make war.'

'But it's effective,' said Eskra. 'I thought that was the whole reason behind using one weapon rather than another. Effectiveness.'

Gerin looked at her, then sniffed. 'It's quite clear, lady, that you don't understand.'

'I'm a woman. I might have been a hostage, and a weapon to use against my own husband. So try me.'

'All right. There's no glory in threatening a man's family—'

'Ah. Glory. I was wondering when you'd mention that.'

'And forcing him to break his word of honour.'

'About acting as an ally, you mean? Oh, my lord, I understand all that perfectly.' She reached over and picked up the counters that would have represented Lord ar'Dakkur's men, then put them down near Erhal's troops, red counters and green side by side.

'They may not be fighting for the Overlord, but they're certainly not fighting for you – and who knows what other demands Erhal or his advisors might make? Once a man's been forced not to support his own honourable allies, it can't be much of a mental jump before someone starts to think that the same threats could force him to fight *against* them.'

She slid the two stacks of counters together, and whether by accident or for deliberate effect they clicked as they met, then rattled quietly as the separate stacks ran together. The heap they made was ominously large, and the red ar'Diskan allies were on top. 'That's what I'd do.'

Gerin gave her a long, cold stare that she met without blinking. 'It's an infamous suggestion,' he said.

'Why? You claim to be a practical man, my lord. The first step's already been taken. The second's only going to be a matter of time.'

'The other lords would never—'

'Listen to your son, Gerin-*eir*. The other lords have very little choice in this, as in so much else. Otherwise Erhal couldn't have mustered such a force in so short a time. I doubt that many of them owe their fealty to him, except at one remove, through fear. How many of these other lords and Heads of House are in the same situation as Gyras ar'Dakkur? All of them. Except you, and Bayrd, and,' she paused delicately, 'whoever is now lord of Clan ar'Kelayr.'

'Which clan,' cut in Bayrd before Eskra could start another lecture, 'since it's now no more than a vassal House under the heel of Kalarr cu Ruruc, doesn't count for much any more. Except in the little matter of three thousand household troops. I don't see those troops on your map, Gerin-*eir*. Hadn't you better . . . ?'

For all that he clearly didn't much care for the way that the suggestion was made, Gerin was just as clearly relieved to be talking about something other than Eskra Talvalin's ruthless approach to warfare. He drummed his fingers briefly against the map, but stopped abruptly as its stiff parchment transmitted enough vibration to make the sinister pile of counters at its centre shift over one another, a soft rustling sound like the scales of a snake in grass. Red mingled with green as the snake slithered.

Red scales, for a Red Serpent.

'Three . . .' Gerin ar'Diskan's voice cracked on the word, and almost squeaked. Nobody smiled. He cleared his throat with unnecessary vigour, picked up a clattering handful of black wooden discs, and tried again. 'Three thousand men, you say?' Bayrd nodded. 'In what proportion?' Bayrd glanced at Eskra, who shrugged. He shrugged too.

'Call it one thousand and two, horse and foot.' He watched as the numbers were counted out and arranged in the vicinity of Hold ar'Kelayr. 'That's just a guess. The disposition, anyway. But the numbers are right.'

'Were right,' said Eskra. 'They might have gone up, but hardly down. Not with that one.' For just a moment she looked sombrely at Bayrd. 'What Kalarr has, he keeps, unless taken from him by force.'

Perhaps fortunately, Bayrd missed the look. But he heard Gerin catch his breath, and saw an expression cross the other lord's face, wondering all too plainly why Bayrd Talvalin didn't see fit to keep some sort of curb on his wife's opinions. Why couldn't he make the blasted woman say something optimistic for once . . . ?

As Gerin stumped off to refill his wine-cup, Bayrd almost smiled at the thought of trying such an impossible task. And besides, from what he had seen and heard since entering Hold ar'Diskan, what Eskra was saying was very likely the first unvarnished truth that Gerin had been made to listen to in a very long time. If he didn't like the sound of it, then that was just too bad.

'Three thousand with cu Ruruc, and five thousand with Erhal, and . . . damn it all, lord,' Iskar ar'Joren shook his head, grimly amused, 'there are more armed men shown on this map than there were at the Landing!'

Bayrd looked, counted, and gave him a lopsided grin. 'We could have done with them then, right enough. There might not be this trouble now.'

'But if you landed with so few,' said Eskra, 'then where have they all come from?'

'Besides the lords'-men?' Bayrd eyed the map, slid a couple of counters across the blue-inked sea to where the coast of Yuvan would have been, then shifted them back. 'Renegades, mercenaries, late-comers of all kinds. You name them, they'll be there. Adventurers for the most part, if you want to give them a kinder name. Not because it's Kalarr or any of these others leading them – so far as that's concerned, they might still be looking at the face of Kurek ar'Kelayr, even if . . .' He hesitated, staring at the map but not seeing it. 'Even if Marc isn't. But there's a chance for profit: employment, plunder, whatever. Or land. That always draws them.' He laughed shortly. 'It drew *us*.'

'But these are the sort of courageous bravos who always wait until it's safe,' said Iskar, sneering. 'They'll never risk a gamble like the Landing.'

Bayrd moved one of the counters idly, then restored it with finicky neatness to its proper place and glanced at Iskar. 'Maybe. Some of them might also be the sort who didn't know. They'd have been wading up through the surf beside us, if they'd had a chance to find out what old Albanak really had in that crooked mind of his.'

'Um.' Iskar drew complicated patterns on the map with his steel-hooked hand. 'I suppose so, lord,' he conceded at last. 'But if they'd known, then Daykin of Kalitz might have known as well. And there'd have been no Landing at all.'

'What a shame,' said Eskra sardonically. As the only Elthanek present, and thus the only representative of the people whose conquest they had been discussing so idly, she was entitled, even expected, to make such remarks in just such a tone of voice. But there was still a warmth in the way she spoke that suggested some good might have followed the Landing after all.

'At least you outnumber Kalarr,' Bayrd pointed out as Gerin returned, continuing the conversation as though the other man had never moved. 'You won't even have to rely on your levies.' He gestured to the counters on the map in case Gerin hadn't noticed.

He had; but there was another problem than just a matter of numbers. 'Yes,' he said. 'But cu Ruruc's a wizard.'

Eskra bowed slightly and smiled. 'Well, so am I. And so—' Bayrd almost kicked her there and then, but she caught her tongue just in time, leaving him wondering what was making her so careless – and, with a crooked sort of amusement, what Gerin would have said had the truth slipped out. 'So is many another good friend of ours.'

'Yes. You would have such friends, I suppose,' growled Gerin.

'Of course, my lord. Just as hunters keep company with other hunters and horsemen with other riders, so wizards have friends who—'

'Thank you, lady.' Gerin ar'Diskan looked and sounded thoroughly flustered by the turn any conversation with Eskra could take. 'If I don't need to know about such matters, then I'd be grateful if you didn't enlighten me.'

'As you please. But it might broaden your view of the world . . .'

''Skra-*ain*, enough,' said Bayrd. In common with so many other faintly scandalous secrets, it was mildly entertaining to watch the squirming of someone not privy to them. But the diversion too often gave way to uneasy embarrassment, and that was happening now. 'What you might do, loved, is give us some idea of what we might do about Kalarr.'

She thought for a few moments, studying the map and the faces of the other *kailinin* with equal care. 'If you can stomach the taste,' she said finally, 'I could give you one stone for two birds.' They looked at each other, then at her, and carefully turned their attention back to the map.

'And that is?' asked Gerin ar'Diskan, when the silence had dragged on long enough that it was beginning to irritate him. 'Well, lady? We're waiting.'

'Kill Erhal.'

Held breath came out in a chorus of sighs of relief that she wasn't going to propose something shocking after all. In fact, there was a murmur of slight surprise that Lady Talvalin's great scheme should have turned out so ordinary. There was going to be a battle between two armies, and Erhal ar'Albanak was – at least nominally – in command of one of them. That made him fair game. And whether he was truly acting on his own, or with the clandestine backing of some members of the Council, he was still the cord that tied his disparate army together. Cut the cord, and . . . Yes, of course they would kill him! Or at least they would try.

Only Bayrd and Iskar and Kian kept watching her, and of the three it was only Bayrd who saw the freezing glitter in her eyes as she listened to the others babble. Kian and Iskar probably suspected they knew what she had really meant – but he alone was certain.

'You mistake me, *eirin*, gentlemen,' she said, and there was a rasp of impatience in her voice that hadn't been there before. 'If I had meant "kill him in battle" I would have said so.'

'Assassination?' The Bannerman Aymar ar'Haleth looked at her as if she had just said something particularly filthy.

'Not assassination. Not if you're thinking of poison in the cup, or a knife from the shadows – although I can't see any difference between that and a *taiken*, except that you wouldn't have to cut anyone else before you could reach him. I meant, kill him in such a way that not only do we get rid of him, but Kalarr cu Ruruc gets the blame. Kill him by the Art Magic.'

Bayrd was the only one of all the men in the room who didn't swear, or flinch, or back away from her and make the 'avert' gesture with one hand that was meant to turn aside the ill-luck of the suggestion. But it was Gerin who stared at her for a long, long time, and it was he who picked up one of the green counters that represented the Overlord's forces, and turned it over in his big, blunt fingers, and voiced aloud what all the rest were surely thinking.

'How could it be done,' he said, 'without *you* getting the blame instead?'

There was another murmur, a ripple of dismay among his *kailinin* that their lord could even consider such a proposal.

'And what,' demanded Aymar ar'Haleth, 'is to stop cu Ruruc using magic against *us*?' He was Gerin's Bannerman and his lord's public conscience, expected to protect that lord's reputation from anything that might sully it. But neither his title nor his position had anything to do with the way he asked his question. His own honour had nothing to do with it either. The man was terrified.

'Nothing.' It was Bayrd rather than Eskra who spoke, and there was the memory of old death in his eyes. 'Remember Gerin's uncle Goel, back in that first winter?' From the looks on their faces, they did. 'I saw green fire eat out his brain. And he wasn't the only one to die. There's nothing to keep Kalarr from trying that again—'

'Trying it, certainly,' said Eskra, sounding cheerful enough that she might really mean it. 'You're being too gloomy, my love.

Remember something else about those killings? They were individual deaths, not some sort of mass slaughter like a plague, or a fire.' She looked at the *kailinin* with slight disapproval. 'Or a glorious battle. Unpleasant, yes, especially if it happened to you. But you might break your neck falling off a horse. How many of you Horse Lords are afraid of horses . . . ? Yes. I thought so.'

She grinned broadly at Aymar, so that for an instant Bayrd thought she might have been on the point of patting his cheek. Perhaps it was just as well that she didn't. But the grin didn't go away either. 'And what happened after those killings? This one was sent to find me – well, someone like me – by Lord Gerin himself, and by the late Overlord Albanak. And since deaths by sorcery stopped directly I came back, and since I'm still here . . . Well, *eirin*, I think I could be an adequate deterrent once again. Bayrd's right. Nothing can stop Kalarr using magic. But *I* can stop it having any effect.'

'But what if we face him in battle?' Arren sounded nervous, having caught something of Aymar's mood. 'Wouldn't he try to blast us and the ranks of our soldiers?'

Eskra shook her head, the grin growing into a quiet, throaty laugh. 'Listen to yourselves,' she chuckled. 'Like children telling nasty stories to keep from being frightened by a thunderstorm. And don't look at me like that, my Lord Gerin, I meant it kindly enough.'

Bayrd wasn't so sure; but kindly meant or not, her cutting comparison was having some sort of effect.

'Because you hate and fear the Art so much, you know nothing about it. And that ignorance gives it credit for being more than it can ever be. Blast you with fire where you stand? Maybe . . .' there was a rustle of unease, '. . . but he'd be more likely to hack at you with axe or sword. That would be just as fatal, but I don't see you fretting about it. Sorcery, gentlemen, is tiring, and not to be relied on when there are simpler ways of doing things.'

'But the soldiers? Surely that would be the simple way to—'

'Bows are simpler. Spears, too. To say nothing of a hole in the ground with a spike at the bottom. Just make sure to meet him on ground of your own choosing, not his – and I've been assured that's one of the first requirements of a battleground, yes?' This time they actually laughed a little. 'Otherwise he'd definitely try to work you mischief.'

The laughter stopped abruptly.

'But he could do it with or without magic. He could just plant lilies, as has been done outside this fortress, and then entice a charge across the prepared ground. Or he could try to charm destruction into the very substance of the ground.' The *kailinin* twitched and twittered like spooked horses. 'But that would do him very little good unless he was certain that someone would be standing on that ground when the power of the spell was loosed. Blast your soldiers? No. If he even dared attempt it, he would tear himself apart . . .'

It was Gerin who laughed this time. 'That would be something to see,' he said. 'And perhaps, when all this is done, I might even see Ivern come back again.'

Bayrd's insides turned over. 'No,' he said quickly, far too quickly. 'You won't.'

'No . . . ?' Gerin stared at him, not understanding. Or maybe not wanting to understand. 'And what might you know of it?'

He could have played the courtier's part and been less blunt, have couched the news in some careful, roundabout phrases, and he knew that Gerin wouldn't have thanked him for the trouble.

He could have played the coward's part and kept quiet, let the older man have his dreams until all was over, and he knew that it would have been the most dishonourable thing he had ever done.

There was nothing to be gained by the news now, and nothing to be lost. No more than two hours past he had been determined, proof or no proof, to use his knowledge of Ivern's death as a lever against cu Ruruc, if Gerin couldn't be swayed by anything else but anger. And then it had become unnecessary. More than that, it had gone in a single instant from being no longer needed, to being far too late to say a thing about it.

But now, when the cue had been spoken and the time was right at last, Bayrd wanted above all else to be able to say something else. Your son betrayed you; but your son was suborned, your son was enchanted, your son is alive. All of it was true.

All but the last part.

'How did it happen?'

Gerin's voice sounded just as it had always done, but his face had the look of a man stabbed to the heart. Whatever hard words had passed between him and his youngest son when they parted would be there for ever now. Whatever hopes of reconciliation he had been concealing behind that swarthy mask and brutal manner had been dashed beyond all hopes of recovery. And though it had come from the lips of the man who was his ally now but his enemy at all other times, yet he was pathetically grateful for the news.

'Kalarr cu Ruruc killed him,' said Eskra. She didn't offer any harrowing details, and was grateful to be asked for none.

'Why?'

Eskra hesitated a moment, and Bayrd could see her considering and discarding half a dozen comfortable lies: that Ivern had defied Kalarr, that they had fought, that Gerin's life had been threatened . . . But in the end, she told only the truth, and Gerin knew it.

'Because he was like his father,' she said. 'Stubborn.'

'Thank you.' Just that, nothing more, and still there was no change in his voice. 'Do what you must to free us from the threat of Erhal's army, *purkan'th-eir*. So that we can turn our attention to . . . to this Red Serpent. There is just one thing.'

He didn't shout, but for all that the words filled the room. 'When we meet his army, the rest are yours. But cu Ruruc is mine and mine alone. He owes me a life. The bastard killed my son . . . !'

'I'd rather not have had to do that,' said Bayrd quietly, when they had a few moments to themselves, 'and I'm glad to be done with it.' He glanced at the little gaggle of ar'Diskan retainers surrounding their Clan-Lord at the other end of the room. 'How long have you had this scheme about Erhal in mind?'

'Long enough,' said Eskra in the same soft voice. 'But I couldn't put it forward myself. Someone had to ask. And not you.'

'Why? Was it one of those sorcerous laws you've been trying to explain this past six years?'

'No. It was plain common sense. I'm the only Elthanek in this whole room. What would all your honourable Albans do to the one of Them who suggested killing a high-clan lord by magic? Even *that* high-clan lord . . . They'd have taken off my head, and yours if you tried to stop them.'

'They'd have tried.'

'No matter. It's their own idea now.'

'And will you do it?'

'Oh, yes. Bayrd-*ain*, understand this. Once all the *talathen* who raided Dunrath-hold were dead, I made a promise: that I would find out who was responsible, and I would kill them myself. Erhal or Yraine, Kalarr or —' she shot a covert sidelong look towards their grieving host, 'or Gerin. Even now would have made no difference. I would have done it anyway, somehow, somewhen; and I'd have made sure that whoever it was knew why they had to die. Not for me. But for the children. For Marla and Harel. Ours – and the ones who didn't get away.'

'Then it's all turned out very convenient, hasn't it?'

' "Convenient?" Now you sound like ar'Diskan in full flight. Don't tell me you disapprove?'

'I wouldn't dare.' It rang a little false, and they both knew it, but Bayrd had long abandoned his own people's notions of the niceties of war. It had earned him the sort of reputation that Dyrek ar'Kelayr had thrown in his teeth all those weeks ago, but it had also brought a certain peace to his domain that few of the other lords enjoyed. 'If one death can prevent a thousand . . .'

'Then you don't think there's anything wrong about an evil action done with good intent?'

'Is it evil, then? Because you've spent long enough in telling me that there's nothing evil about the Art. Just what it's used for.'

'Bayrd, *please* . . .' And it wasn't until then that he realised Eskra was really concerned. Despite all the hard words, all the toughness. But when it came to the push, she needed reassurance after all. This wasn't hot blood or fear, in defence of life or family. No matter how sound the reasons behind it, the deed would be as cold and calculated as the use of a block and an axe.

'Do it,' he said, 'and do it as well as you know how. This Land can well spare Erhal ar'Albanak.'

'More than you can spare Marc ar'Dru.'

Bayrd's eyes widened slightly. Of all the subjects that had been discussed today, he had done his best to keep that one from his mind, and he thought that he had succeeded very well. Until now.

'Yes,' he said. 'Yes . . . What are his chances?'

'No worse than anyone else's. Kalarr never learned how he was being spied on, so,' and she shrugged, 'he's alive. You think you owe him something, don't you?'

'Not just think, and not just something. His life, or at least a fair chance at it. He let us prepare, he let us overhear cu Ruruc's plans – and he would have tried to do it even if you hadn't helped him. Whether it's Kalarr's glamour, or because he really hates me now as much as he pretended to, he was still my friend who put himself in harm's way and tried to help. If I can do something, I will.'

'*Forward . . . !*'

The trumpets blared and the drums rolled until their echoes came slamming back from the walls of Segelin, and the army of Clan ar'Diskan began to march. Their armour glinted for a while, and their crest-coats shone with the rich scarlet and white colours of the clan; but before they had travelled more than a hundred yards from the fortress, the glinting dulled and the colours muted as a drifting cloud of chalk-dust from the scoured perimeter rose and settled in their wake.

They moved forward in a single long column six men wide, the foot-soldiers leading and the mounted *kailinin* bringing up the rear, and Bayrd had been curious to see how unwieldy a mass of men and horses could negotiate the twisting route that would lead them safely through the field of lilies that surrounded Hold ar'Diskan.

In the event, they didn't have to. Thick, circular slabs of timber had been laid across enough of the spiked pits, plugging them, so that the path from the fortress gate was almost a straight line. It had taken twenty men, three hours and four carts to make that road; but with all the wooden plugs connected to each other by hundreds of yards of rope, it would take only minutes for two men and a windlass to let the lilies bloom again.

Bayrd, Eskra and the others sat well off to one side and watched them pass out through the gate. 'Cu Ruruc will be approaching from the north, lord,' said Kian ar'Terel, 'and Erhal's army from the south. How will we know to place our force correctly?'

'Kalarr cu Ruruc is a wizard, Kian-*an*,' said Eskra. 'So am I. Rest assured, we'll all find each other soon enough. And you can tell Lord Gerin so.' The man saluted his acknowledgement and cantered off.

When he was well out of earshot, Bayrd turned to Eskra and

looked at her in silence for a few minutes. 'And then you'll kill Erhal,' he said at last.

She stared back at him, armoured and helmed, unaccustomed to the weight – and also less than happy with where it had come from. Bayrd and the other Talvalin *kailinin* were wearing their own battle armour, packed in case of need before leaving Dunrath, but Eskra was encased in a harness given to her by Gerin, the only *tsalaer* in the armoury that had been small enough to fit her slight frame.

It was inevitable that it should once have been Ivern's.

'I'll do that at the proper time and not before,' she said, shifting uncomfortably with a slight rattle of mail against plate. Whether the discomfort came from the height and the weight of the armour, or from the subject under discussion, it was impossible to tell. 'It'll have to be the most effective time. Remember, we don't just want him dead. The High Council can't be given time to think of anything but the enemy who killed him. And it'll have to be the right enemy, or I'll have done it all for nothing.'

'Then how will you have to . . . do it?'

Eskra drew a deep breath and let it out slowly, then gave him a tight, mirthless grin like those he had seen on the heads spiked above Segelin. 'You don't really want an answer to that, loved,' she said. 'But you've seen a few examples of what a killing sorcery can do. Just think about those – and rest assured, I'll do him justice.'

'There they are,' shouted Kian ar'Terel, standing in his stirrups and pointing. 'There, there!'

Tiny points of light were twinkling merrily far out across the moorland, edging a distant shadow that had nothing to do with the darker shade of Baylen Forest to the west. On this perfect summer day, so perfect that even Bayrd Talvalin could find nothing to complain about, a faint wisp of dust meandered into the blue sky. It looked so insignificant that Kian's response seemed out of all proportion.

'Calm, dammit,' Bayrd snapped. If he couldn't complain about the weather, except that it was already too close to the solstice for comfort, then he could at least vent some of his nervous annoyance on his excited retainer. Anyone else, and the reaction wouldn't have been so out of the ordinary; but Kian was normally such a cold fish.

Eskra was watching him, and smiling a neutral sort of smile. 'I told you there'd be no trouble about finding them,' she said.

'Yes,' said Bayrd. 'But which *them* are these?'

'They're coming up from the south. Erhal's people.'

'Then,' and Bayrd rose in his own stirrups and peered at the visible horizon, 'where's Kalarr?'

Eskra stared thoughtfully at the edge of the forest, three miles away across open, rolling country. It was no great distance to cover in a cavalry charge, and she was remembering cu Ruruc's words, overheard through Marc's encharmed ears. *We'll wait until Erhal and ar'Diskan are done hacking at each other, then move in and make an end . . .*

'You know more about troop movement than I do,' she said. 'Could they be among the trees?'

Bayrd looked, waited, considered, and then nodded. 'Possibly. But Fire Above, that would mean they've been tracking Gerin's army for more than a day, that they've missed a dozen chances to take the entire column in flank, that they didn't even attack the camp last night . . .'

'All right. I understand now. But could they be there?'

'Yes.'

'Then that's where they are. Tell Gerin.'

'What . . . ?'

'Do it!'

This time there was no dignified cantering: once he was given the message, Kian ar'Terel wrenched his horse around, clapped heels in his flanks and took off at a full gallop in a showy spurting of dust. Eskra watched him go, shaking her head. She ran her fingers through her hair, grumbled something about wearing a pot-lid in this heat, then put on her helmet and began very carefully to tighten its chinstraps.

'You really mean it, don't you?'

'I don't make jokes about men carrying steel. At least, not unless I know they'll laugh. I told you before, Bayrd-*ain*. I can recognise him. I can sense his presence. Just as you can close your eyes and still point straight to where the sun is. He's in the forest. Watching and waiting like the scavenger he is.'

'But if he's hidden, then how—'

'Am I going to throw Erhal's army at him? Just wait. Leave that to me. You won't have to wait long.'

Bayrd could see how she was nipping her lower lip between her teeth, and could even see a thread of blood where she'd broken the skin. 'Is it dangerous?' he asked gently, even though he wasn't sure what he could do if she said 'yes'.

'Dangerous? A little. All sorcery is. But I'm healthy, well-fed, well-rested – ' she forced a grin at him, ' – and the spell I have in mind needs no more effort than having a baby.'

'No more effort . . .'

'I know what I mean.'

'Yes. That's the point.'

The two armies had been drawn up in their various ranks for half an hour now, and still nothing had happened. There was no wind to cool them, and that half hour of immobility in the hot sun, the grittiness of the settled dust, and the flies that battened on men and horses alike made their patience a punishment. If Kalarr cu Ruruc was truly watching from beneath the shadowed eaves of Baylen Forest, then there was little for him to see.

'What are they doing?' muttered Eskra, as Gerin and his personal retainers trotted up and down the length of the battle-line for the fifth – or maybe the fiftieth – time. 'What are they waiting for! An engraved invitation on a silver tray?'

'More or less,' said Bayrd. 'A formal exchange of challenge and defiance, anyway. But Gerin's not going to offer that until he's sure he's chosen the best formation against superior numbers.'

'Doesn't he trust me?'

'It doesn't matter if he does or not. Why should he make it obvious that he might have something in mind besides a proper battle? And, well, just in case. Look.' He pointed as a hundred or so horsemen wheeled out of their position and took up another fifty yards to the rear. 'You see. That covers the flank against any—'

'What I see is that Lord Gerin has spent too much time with his map and his little wooden counters. They don't sweat; they don't get thirsty; and they don't need to pee!'

'Ah . . . And you do?'

'Fortunately not. I need all my concentration for the spell, so I – oh, Firefather, now what?'

'Count yourself lucky there aren't any mercenary troops on either side.' Eskra glanced at him from under the rim of her helmet and pursed her lips as if determined not to satisfy him by asking why, so he told her anyway. 'Because the next step would be for the mercenary commanders to meet with each other and the opposing lords, to possibly renegotiate their contracts.'

'You mean to tell me that one of them could buy up the enemy's army?'

'Part of it, anyway.'

'This is a joke.'

'No. A standard tactic.'

'I wasn't laughing, loved. This *is* a joke. For six years I've heard and read how your people won your invasion because the old High Lords of the Provinces – *my* people – made war for sport and didn't treat it seriously. Yes?'

'Well, yes. I suppose.'

'You suppose. So how does treating war as a business make it any more serious?'

'Profit . . .'

Eskra turned her head and stared at him, waiting for the smile, the wink, the grin that never came. 'You mean it. Light of Heaven, you really mean it!'

'No. But Gerin does, and this is his . . . What is it?' Eskra said nothing, but Bayrd closed his teeth on whatever he might have said next because her expression changed, became distant and unfocused, almost as if she had fallen asleep with her eyes wide open.

'Marc's there,' she said, coming back with a blink. 'He's there with cu Ruruc.' Bayrd didn't ask how she knew; there could be a dozen ways, and he might not understand half of them. 'And the glamour is slipping.'

Now that, Bayrd did understand. 'Glamour? Not your charm? Then it was cu Ruruc all the time?'

'So it seems. Good.'

'Why, good?'

'Because Kalarr is using his power for other things. When he killed Ivern and Etek, he was able to focus more fully on Marc.

That swamped my little spell, and made me think that it didn't work – or need to work – any more. But Kalarr cu Ruruc knows I'm here just as much as I'm aware of him. He knows *you're* here, and that makes it even worse.'

Bayrd looked blank, and Eskra patted him on the arm. The rasp of metal against metal sounded anything but romantic. 'He knows you have the Talent, hopes you can't use it, but doesn't dare assume. You're an unknown factor in his planning. So he's taking precautions. A spellshield, by Heaven and the Light of Heaven!'

'So you can't do anything to him,' said Bayrd dourly. 'And we're up against Erhal's unbroken army.'

'No, no! I never intended to do anything to *him*. But he doesn't have the sort of mind that could grasp such a simple difference.' Her impulsive good humour faded to grimness as swiftly as it had arisen, and she swung from her saddle to the ground. 'All right,' she said. 'It's time.'

Bayrd dismounted as well. Not knowing what to expect, he grabbed both horses by the reins up near the bridle and held on tight, only to be somewhat disappointed by what followed.

There was no drawing of circles, no chanting of eerie spells, not even a consultation of the two books of sorcery that he knew Eskra carried in her saddlebags. Instead she simply plucked a handful of grass-blades and began to weave them into a loose braid. She added more and more until the braid became a sphere, talking gently to it – or perhaps only to herself – as she did so.

But as the braid grew longer and curved around on itself to form the first curve of the hollow globe of grass, Bayrd saw sparks begin to crawl along it. A hotter and more vivid green than even the summer grass itself, they moved like tiny spiders, leaving a fine thread of silver webbing in their wake. Before many minutes had passed, the loosely braided stems of common moorland grass had become a thing more like a costly jewel of emeralds and spun glass. It lay on the palm of Eskra's hand and sparkled in the sun, no larger than a child's fist, delicate, harmless and altogether beautiful.

Until she raised her arm with a creak of leather and a scrape of mail that sounded harsh and jarring after the soft murmuring of her voice, and flung it overarm towards the forest. It was too fragile for such treatment, and should have flown apart or drifted to the ground. It did nothing of the sort.

Bayrd's head snapped around in an attempt to follow it, but eyes that could track an arrow in the air could see nothing but a faint, receding twinkle against the blue sky, like a star falling from the Heavens. But he knew when it reached its destination.

As if someone had poured oil into a brazier, a globe of jade-green flame threaded with lines of burning silver erupted from inside the edge of Baylen Forest. For an instant the treetops became stark silhouettes, their shadows reaching out and down from underneath this new green sun. Then that sun rebounded from the forest as though from something solid, like a ball bouncing from a paving-slab, and arched high into the air before tipping over and descending into the midst of Erhal's army.

More than half a mile separated the self-styled Overlord from where Bayrd Talvalin stood, but he still braced himself for the crash and roar of impact as the green fire landed squarely on the great ar'Albanak clan banner and sent it whirling up in flames. But there was no such sound, no such explosion; only a huge gasp like an indrawn breath – or a breath choked out by force – as the green sphere collapsed into itself and the threads of silver drew tight as a noose as they disappeared. And then all was silence.

Until the screaming began.

'What did you do?' he whispered, even though he had neither need nor desire to find out the details of what had happened to Erhal; what he had seen had been as graphic as he wanted, now or later.

'Convinced them. Look.'

A ripple went through the army as though it was a single creature rather than five thousand individuals, spreading outward from where the fire had struck before contracting in again. And then the screaming changed. It was a thin sound over all that distance, but it was clear enough that Bayrd could tell the instant when fear and confusion became shock and rage. Men who might have killed Erhal themselves were pushing forward to see what had happened to him, and then surging back filled not with satisfaction, but with fury, at how their lord, their honour and their strength of arms had all been insulted.

The single creature shook itself as the ranks recovered their positions, and then, in silence, without drum or trumpet, challenge or defiance – and without paying any further heed to Gerin ar'Diskan's small force, even when it marched to join instead of fight them – the army of the Overlord of Alba began to move.

Towards Baylen Forest.

'That was easier than you let on,' said Bayrd. His voice was low; after what he had just seen from the quiet of their vantage-point, shouting seemed somehow disrespectful.

Eskra cuffed at him, though the blow was as feeble as a child's. 'You do what I've just done, then call it easy,' she snapped; but there was no real edge to her voice, nor any strength to put it there. 'I had to convince men who would as soon go back to Cerdor and rescue their families that they'd been personally slighted. After that, it *was* easy. Your people, loved. Know one of them – ' her hand closed on his, ' – know all of them. Most, anyway.'

She leaned her armoured head against his armoured shoulder, then swore wearily and straightened up, tearing impatiently at the straps and laces. 'At least I don't need this damned shell any more, and you—'

'I need it,' said Bayrd abruptly, moving like a man coming from a dream to full wakefulness without the period of pleasant drowsing in between. 'I need it now. And so does Marc ar'Dru. I got him into this mess . . .'

The rest of the shout was lost in a thudding of hooves.

The construction of an Alban war-saddle was such that a man couldn't really vault into it from the ground. Bayrd Talvalin made a creditable attempt to do so, even though he was still halfway between afoot and mounted when the grey mare Yarak shot off like an arrow underneath him.

After what had happened, there was no time to waste. Prisoners would be a luxury that the Albans would ignore, and Gerin ar'Diskan was likely to slaughter anyone in cu Ruruc's presence. From the sound of it, that meant Marc.

An arrow – whose, he neither knew nor cared – scythed past him as he came within range of the forest. By now the bulk of the two armies had forced their way beneath its shadows, and he could hear shouting and the clangour of steel above even the sounds of his own speed. Bodies lay here and there, fewer than he had expected to see and none of them struck down by anything . . .

231

Unusual, he thought, his mind shying from any more specific description.

Yarak slewed to a halt and he flung himself to the ground. If nothing happened to either of them between now and later, the mare would still be waiting when he emerged again. Nobody would – could – steal Yarak, and she would be safer here without an armoured man on her back to draw enemy arrows. He remembered the shaft which had scraped past his helmet on his way across the moor, wondering vaguely who in all this chaos the enemy might be.

And where, in all the chaos that he could hear but not yet see, he might hope to find one man among so many, when they were all trying to slaughter one another. Especially a man who would probably look like Kalarr cu Ruruc's chief lieutenant. Find him; keep him in one piece; and try to do the same thing for himself.

'Luck,' said Bayrd. 'Blind luck. And you.' Isileth Widowmaker hissed as he slid her from the scabbard. 'Especially you.'

Then Bayrd plunged into the gloom.

Finding Kalarr and Marc should have been easier than he dared to hope, and luck had nothing to do with it. All he had to do was follow the bull-bellow that was Gerin ar'Diskan's voice, plain and clear even above the sounds of battle; and even in dead silence he might have tracked the Clan-Lord by the trail of shattered bodies Gerin left behind.

Somebody lunged at him with both hands full, a mace in one and a war-axe in the other, and even though his eyes were growing more used to the distracting dapple of bright sunlight cutting through the deep green shade, Bayrd still had no time either to identify the man's crest-coat or identify himself.

He met the axe with a glissading block that sent the weapon screeching in a shower of sparks, and took the mace alongside the head in another shower of sparks that were entirely inside his own skull. Bayrd staggered sideways, lashing out backhanded at his opponent in an attempt to clear himself the space and time to get his breath and senses back.

It gained him more time than he expected. Yelling triumphantly, the man was already charging forward to finish him off with the axe raised high above his head, and he ran straight into the full-force sweep of Widowmaker's blade. Bayrd felt the crunch of flesh and metal giving way beneath the *taiken*'s edge, and heard whoever it had been crash back into the undergrowth without a sound.

Bayrd paused, panting, his head reeling, listening for Gerin's voice and trying to get his bearings. There had been – his mind hunted for the figure – nearly twelve thousand men crammed into this forest; and except for the dead, this was the only one of them that he had seen.

A skin-crawling thought of what Kalarr might have done with the rest touched briefly on his mind, then went away almost as fast. If Eskra had been right, then he hadn't the power for anything so huge. If he had power for anything right now except headlong flight, while he still had a head to call his own, because he could hear Gerin again, a raging voice demanding combat, satisfaction and cu Ruruc's head in equal measure.

Despite the pounding ache inside his own head, Bayrd laughed harshly and started to run towards the sound.

Then an unseen hand reached out from between the trees and pushed him in the centre of the chest, his feet went out from under him, and he was flung backwards into the bracken. His ears were clanging again, and not from that blow on the helmet; there was heat on his face, and not from the exertion of running in armour on a summer's day; and there was a black and orange-purple glow blotting his vision, that flared into new life with every blink of his eyes.

Bayrd lay there, dazed, aching, but grateful for the immobility and the silence. Because all of a sudden, it had gone very quiet in the Forest of Baylen. No shouts, no screams, no clash of weapons. There wasn't a sound except for those which belonged there: the wind in the branches, the stirring of small creatures – though most of the small creatures had probably been frightened away by the sounds of battle, and what he was hearing was the faint settling of his own armoured body as it crushed down the bracken.

That was strange. He was convinced that somewhere in his memory of the past few seconds was the echo of some colossal noise and light and heat, but as if that memory was wax the heat had smoothed it clean.

He struggled to his feet – not easy when those feet were supported six inches off the ground by a mattress of flattened bracken – and with Widowmaker poised in one hand, walked carefully in search of Gerin. Or Marc ar'Dru. Or even Kalarr cu Ruruc, provided he was already dead.

He was.

The banner that Bayrd had heard described so often was smashed so hard against a tree-trunk that its very weave had started to unravel. The red snake writhing across it was still clear enough, but the black silk of the rest of the flag was charred and still smouldering.

On the ground beneath it lay a corpse. Like the flag, Bayrd had only ever heard descriptions of Kalarr; tall and fair, or tall and dark, depending on who he was attempting to deceive. He was none of those things now, but a little, shrivelled, blackened thing, so seared by whatever had happened here that his burnt body didn't even smell bad. But his head was still on.

'So Gerin didn't find you,' said Bayrd.

He leaned on Widowmaker's pommel and stared down at the charcoal doll, trying to think all the noble thoughts of a *kailin-eir* facing his dead enemy. Instead, whether from weariness or from headache or from simple lack of interest any more, he was thinking absolutely nothing.

'Gerin did,' said a voice behind him.

Bayrd came upright with a jerk, the longsword's blade whirring as he whipped her to a ready position. And then relaxed, feeling the long leashed-in fear seeping out of him like water from a sponge.

Gerin ar'Diskan leaned against a tree and grinned at him with a mouth that lacked at least one of its front teeth. His armour was in tatters; it looked as though it had been ripped off his body by main force and thrown hastily back on, for all that it no longer fitted the body it had been made for. Even Gerin himself looked strange; different somehow . . .

And Bayrd felt a momentary worm of doubt move through his mind. Or was it a snake . . .

'Father of Fires, but you're still jumpy today!' said another voice. Marc's voice. He was standing beside another of the scorched, smoking trees, not leaning on the trunk but simply propping himself up against it, looking as confused as Bayrd was feeling. The reason was obvious enough; there was an oozing

234

purple bruise the size of a fist – *whose fist?* – on his forehead just over the temple.

Bayrd Talvalin looked from one to the other, realising how alone he was in this smoke-stinking clearing. Then Gerin stepped forward, if it was Gerin at all, and Bayrd began to raise Widowmaker in case it wasn't . . .

And then he let the point drop to the moss again, and laughed shakily. Gerin ar'Diskan had gone into battle a black-moustached man with straight black hair. He had come out of it a man whose hair was singed curly and grey, where it hadn't been scorched down to the skin. As for that sweeping moustache, all that remained of it was a crumbling smear of ash under his nose. For an instant he had looked fair-haired and clean-shaven; for an instant he had almost died.

But the instant was over.

And so was the battle. There were rustling sounds amongst the trees, furtive noises, but none of them threatening. They were the sounds made by survivors who were determined to continue that survival by running away, just as quickly and as quietly as they were able. Bayrd listened for a few seconds, than ran Isileth Widowmaker back into her scabbard and hoisted her to the peace position at his back. He looked at the burnt body on the ground, then at Marc and at Gerin.

'What happened?' he said. Gerin poked at the corpse with his toe.

'Your lady wife once said what might happen to cu Ruruc if he over-stretched himself.' Lord ar'Diskan was trying to remember his dignity, trying to remember he had just won a battle, trying to remember that the man in front of him was an enemy of six years' standing. He was failing on all three counts. All that he was remembering was that his son had been murdered, and that the man who had done it lay dead at his feet.

'Yes,' said Bayrd. 'She said that – that he would pull himself asunder.'

Gerin drew back his boot and kicked the body, and it flew apart. He stared at the drift of ash and cinders for a few seconds, then drew a deep breath through his nose that the uncharitable might have called a sniffle. 'She was right.'

'Then it's over.'

'For now.'

Bayrd wanted to find Eskra again, wanted to bring Marc out of this place, wanted to learn what had been happening in Hold ar'Kelayr, and above all wanted to discover what had happened to the flask of wine he had so carefully secured to his saddle. He didn't need enigmatic comments. 'Over is over,' he said flatly, 'and now is now. Let tomorrow take care of itself.'

Gerin ar'Diskan smiled a small smile to himself, and bowed ever so slightly. 'I'm sure it will,' he said. 'In my experience, it always does . . .'